RESONANCE OF STARS

Greenstone Security Book Five

ANNE MALCOM

Editing: Making Manuscripts
Proofreading: All Encompassing Books
Cover Design: Simply Defined Art

1

"How DOES it feel being the most in-demand actress in Hollywood right now? Arguably one of the most talked about and famous women in show business?"

Horrible. Nauseating. Suffocating.

My smile was as fake as my teeth, tits, and tan. "It's such a blessing. I feel so lucky to be given chances in Hollywood as a woman, cast in movies directed by women. It's been a long time coming, and I know we still have a long way to go, but it feels good."

I made sure to speak softly, to sound unsure almost, humble. If I'd learned one thing, the media was not kind to arrogant women. Even if they had every right to be arrogant. Even if the woman in question had pulled herself from a life of poverty, beatings, dirty sheets, and empty stomachs to superstardom. Even if said woman was paid millions of dollars per movie and owned a mansion in Beverly Hills. Of course, the stomach was still empty because that's how it worked.

I was starving right this moment. Which wasn't outside the

norm, but I hadn't even indulged in my meager excuse for lunch. Every second of this day was spent promoting the shit out of this movie, smiling this fake smile, answering mundane questions, and counting down the seconds until I could leave. Hunger was now mingled with annoyance.

Breakfast was coffee and a cold pressed juice. My head was pounding from lack of sleep and the fucking lights glaring at me in this suite at the W Hotel.

This was my last interview. I'd been here for hours, smiling, pretending I was proud of this piece-of-shit movie my agent talked me into.

I usually made a point to be proud of every movie I put my name to, because I'd earned the right to do that. At the beginning, when I was poor and desperate, I took what I could. And I was proud of that, even if the movies were terrible. They'd got me to here.

But now, after all my hard work, I had enough money and fame to be able to pick my own movies. Apart from this movie, the one I was pushed into doing.

I wasn't on a relentless crusade to only portray certain women or even change the way women were viewed, but I also wasn't about to be some fucking housewife in a movie purely there for her pretty face or comedic relief.

I'd dropped the ball on this one.

The director was the darling of the industry. He'd collected many awards throughout the years for his edgy, dark films. I'd known as soon as I'd read the rambling script it was going to be a dud. Over ten years in the industry had given me that insight. I was intelligent in many ways—because if you weren't, this industry, this world, would eat you alive—and had a knack for knowing when a crappy script would turn into an absolute disaster.

A crappy script wasn't always the end of the world. With a

good cast and an excellent director, it could be salvaged. This director was known to be excellent, but I'd never liked a single one of his movies.

Which should've made me more forceful with my agent when she told me to reconsider. She wasn't usually one to try and fight me when I made a decision but there were a lot of high-profile stars in this one. There was a lot of hype. A lot of money to be made.

I didn't relent because of the money—I had plenty of that—though I did have a sickening obsession with always making more. Nor was it about the star-studded cast. I was well past being impressed by movie stars.

The truth was, I was tired, which was not really something I should be at thirty-four. Then again, Hollywood was already preparing to try to put me out to pasture, cast me as the hot mom or bitchy boss.

I was happy to play the bitch, but I was already exhausted thinking of the fights ahead of me. Which was why I relented to the movie.

And why I was sitting here with that pounding headache, empty stomach, and ever-present smidge of self-hatred.

The interviewer was boring, from her mundane questions, right down to the mousy hair and lipstick on her teeth—which I hadn't told her about, despite what girl code said. I'd tried it once and was labelled as a bitch because of it.

All I was thinking about was a giant martini—not because I liked them but they were the most sensible, calorie wise—two olives, and a treat for dinner. Maybe some soft cheeses. Or I'd go wild and have prosciutto as well. No bread. I hadn't eaten bread in years.

I'd just wrapped on this movie. I'd worked fourteen-hour days, barely slept, had pretended to like all the assholes on set, and I'd be jumping straight into my next project at six tomorrow morning. I deserved *one* treat.

Just one, though, because Cannes was in two days and my dress was custom. If I even drank too much water, it wouldn't fit right, and unflattering lighting and devious photographers would find an uncomplimentary photo to splash over the tabloids. I shouldn't care about that, being a modern woman and a feminist. But having the entire world debate over whether you were pregnant or had just gotten "chubby" over a picture taken at a wrong angle would do some damage.

I could've done some serious interior work on my trauma, on my demons, found ways to be healthier in the way I viewed myself. Could've figured out a way to get my validation from inside me, not from what the industry wanted me to be. What the world wanted me to be.

But in the end, it was easier to starve myself.

My mind was in a thousand different places, which was why I didn't notice the reporter go from mousy to feline.

"What do you say to the rumors that you engaged in a relationship with your co-star, Jeffery Anderson, and that you are responsible for his divorce?" She asked it in the same tone as before, but it hit its mark, maybe even went a little deeper than normal, because she'd seemed so unassuming.

She had timed this well, since my publicist, Andre, who would normally step in right now, had just left on a call. He wasn't one to normally do such a thing, since his job centered around diving into interviews when questions such as this were asked and be the rabid dog I loved him for. He had obviously gotten the same mousy vibe from the reporter, which was saying something since he had a razor-sharp eye for such things.

I gritted my teeth.

Jesus Christ.

I *had* engaged in a relationship with that asshole. Big mistake. Good thing the relationship consisted of groping, bad kissing, and sex that lasted less than a minute. All those men that housewives had as their 'Hall Pass'—with their eight-pack, perfect hair and giant biceps—they usually had small dicks and no manners. Sexually or otherwise.

I did *not* break up his marriage. It was already broken up. For years. The best-kept secret in Hollywood. His wife, Angela Steele, was a well-known TV actress that hadn't been able to break into film. They'd gotten together as a publicity stunt, married for the same reason. There was definitely no love between them at the beginning of the relationship, but whatever like or tolerance they had for one another was long gone, especially since Angela's career had skyrocketed while Jeffery's only got a minor bump. I knew for a fact he only got the lead role in this movie because he'd threatened he'd do a tell-all about his relationship with Angela if she didn't pull strings to get him the job.

They fucking hated each other and only got together for photo shoots, events, or social media shots. They lived on separate coasts and whenever Angela was in town, she was sleeping at a well-known rapper's house. They'd been together for almost as long as she'd been married.

Jeffery fucked everything that moved and that was a poorly kept secret. I'd been aware of what a whore he was, but I just hadn't cared. You wouldn't find an honorable man in the business, and if you did they were either taken, gay, or rightly thought I was a total bitch.

There was one man I'd been trying to get out of my bed the night I'd decided to sleep with Jeffery. We'd been on location in the middle of nowhere in Scotland, I'd had one too many whiskies and decided to swap out my vibrator for a real man.

Not that he was one.

But that didn't matter. The truth didn't matter. What mattered was that me being a home-wrecking slut would sell a lot more magazines. Even though newspapers were dying a slow death, tabloids were thriving.

Oh what a world.

"You know better than I do that female and male leads in most movies with a romantic element have to face these predictable rumors," I said, still softly, but there was an edge to my voice. One I knew she'd recognize. A warning. My eyes narrowed. "Usually, it's the female lead being asked, of course. The man is usually given time to speak about the movie itself, his career achievements, not belittled about achievements or his personal life. But as a woman, I'm sure you understand the reasons for that." I smiled tightly. I wanted to rip her skinny fucking neck off.

She tilted her head. She'd got the warning. But she wasn't as faint-hearted as she seemed. There was no blush of embarrassment in her cheek, not even fear in her eyes. "You've been linked to a number of men you've filmed with. Most notably, Kieran Love, whom you were engaged to. Have you been looking for the same love since? Or have you been looking to ruin prominent relationships in Hollywood as polished revenge?"

Because I was practiced at this game, I didn't give any inclination that the mere mention of that name forced bile up my throat. I kept that placid, superior smile firmly in place and regarded this woman a little more closely.

Not mousy at all.

Someone was looking to make their career. Make a reputation for herself. She'd certainly done her research. All of the barbed comments snuck through my barriers and drew blood.

I smiled at her, more genuine now. Impressed. Women had a

unique talent to injure other women by poking at wounds men had created.

"Revenge?" I repeated with a chuckle. "No, I do not waste time or energy on revenge." I paused, not moving my eyes. "On men, at least. It's in their nature to betray. Not that I accept that, but at least it's not to be expected. Women who betray women on the other hand, I would consider worthy of revenge. Even in the town where half the female population have scars from the heels of their sisters using them as footstools to further themselves." I purposefully crossed my legs, showing off the sharp point of my Louboutin's. "I'd be sure to remember that, if I were you."

She blinked at me. Once. Twice. The feline disappeared. The mouse returned. Once again, I'd made an enemy. One I'd hopefully scared enough to put off trying to cross me. Because I did not do idle threats.

* * *

I did not get my cheese or my multiple martinis that night.

No.

I did get to witness a murder though, and that caused me to forget about everything but the way the blood spattered from the man's head when the back of it was blown off.

I'd been casually dating him, which I guessed made witnessing his murder that much worse.

Salvador Esposito. He was a rich Italian who was as shady as they came but he was nice-looking and gave great head. He also didn't give a fuck about who I was or how rich I was. He didn't really give a fuck about me at all, which was great because the feeling was mutual.

Since the broken engagement and heartbreak fiasco, I'd made a vow not to become that cliché woman again. You know, the heartbroken, pathetic woman that latched on to the boring, safe accountant just so she'd have someone to sleep next to.

No, I hated sleeping in the same bed with anyone. I chose to have sex like a man. No connections, no sleepovers, no cuddling. I'd been doing extremely well at this, and Salvador had seemed to revel in the fact he'd found a woman he didn't have to woo. We'd only been screwing for a couple months, and I could honestly say I knew nothing about the man that did not pertain to the size of his dick or the way he used it.

Still, I didn't want to see him get his head blown off.

I'd played in a lot of scenes where someone was murdered.

Died in plenty more at the beginning of my career when I was the hot girl destined to be murdered in the first ten minutes.

None of that was like the real thing.

Obviously.

Death had a smell, a feeling, a silence.

It was ugly, rancid and terrifying.

Terrifying, because I witnessed it and the man holding the gun doing the murdering was vaguely familiar. I'd seen his photo in many newspaper headlines—I still bought the dying medium—and he was well known in Hollywood. Shit, I think I'd been introduced to him at a save the animals, or save the oceans charity benefit.

His name escaped me, which I didn't think would be the social faux pas it normally would considering he'd likely murder me too if he saw I was there. Tucked behind a bookshelf that was sparse thanks to some asshole interior designer obsessed with minimalism. If he looked up and to his right, he'd see me and I'd be dead. Everything inside me that wasn't urging me to throw up—luckily my stomach was empty—was screaming at me to run.

But if I moved, if I breathed too loud, it would call attention to me. He was in front of me, in front of my only means to escape.

So I had to somehow leave it up to fate if he would see me and kill me.

It wasn't fate that got me here, it was my anger. That little bitch reporter had gotten far deeper under my skin than she should've. It was common knowledge in Hollywood that mentioning Kieran in an interview was a sure-fire way to get fired. Our relationship had been public, all-encompassing and for a time, we'd been the darlings of Hollywood and the world. People had been obsessed with our fairy-tale romance. Our careers skyrocketed. There wasn't a day that went by that we weren't headlines. But it was not the reason for our engagement— not for me at least.

I'd loved him.

My first love.

And, what I decided would be my only love.

He was intoxicating. Older. Classically handsome and rugged in a way not many Hollywood men were. He was a method actor, which meant when he got a role about a man who got lost in the woods and lived off the land for years, he'd trained to be authentic. Not for years, of course. But two months. No cameras. No handlers. When he was cast in an overdone Shakespearean epic, he would only speak in Elizabethan English for the entire period of filming. Which would've had his female counterpart labeled as a deranged bitch, but he'd been considered a genius.

So yeah, he'd impressed me. He gave me a kind of attention I'd never known. And that was saying something considering I'd just become accustomed to having the entire world paying attention to me. Of course, as a foster child starved of love, I'd sucked it all up. Sucked *him* up. The man who was so sure of himself. So distinguished. So talented. He was a presence. One of the true movie stars—which were rare in Hollywood, no matter what it seemed.

I should've known better. Life had jaded me, so I didn't have naiveté as an excuse. Worse than that, I *let* myself love. Trust. And then my heart was split open for the entire world to see.

The email he'd used to break up with me leaked. Yeah, he broke off an engagement in an email. And I suspected he was the one who'd leaked the email. Not because I'd cheated on him or betrayed him in any way. Because that's what Kieran did. He liked to play with people. Liked to see how they would react to tragedy. Heartbreak. Life was a movie to him. He was the director.

I wasn't about to let that happen again. Hence me choosing men who were rich—so they weren't after my money. Who weren't in the business—for obvious reasons. And who were as cold-hearted as I was.

Salvador was cold-hearted. Figuratively.

Now literally.

Well, he'd only just been shot in the last few minutes, so I was guessing his heart was still warm.

I'd let myself in with the key he'd given me for nothing other than convenience. I made sure that he never came to my place, never entered my space. And I arrived late at night, whenever I felt like I needed to be fucked. Salvador lived in a gated community in Calabasas, one of the most expensive and security-heavy communities around LA.

I should've known something was up when his gate guard wasn't there, and the golden gates opened on their own. Then there were the two security guards that were usually strolling somewhere around the plush grass of his estate. Armed. Heavily.

I'd known from the start he was sketchy. Not many people who were as rich as he was were squeaky clean. If you wanted to be rich, you had to be prepared to stain your soul. I'd also suspected he had ties to some kind of crime syndicate, which hadn't really bothered me either. I wasn't the police, moral or otherwise.

But even knowing those things about him, I hadn't trusted my gut feeling that something wasn't right with the absence of guards. Didn't look to the worst-case scenario. I'd been too pissed off for such things, too stuck inside my own head. But I'd known something was wrong the second I walked from the large foyer into the formal living room.

Raised voices. Not something that would usually cause alarm, as Salvador was Italian, after all. But something had crawled up my spine so I'd stopped just short of walking into the living room.

"I did what you asked," Salvador hissed.

"I know," a flat, calm voice replied. "Which is why I'm here. You're no longer of use to me."

I peered around the bookshelf right around the time a muted gunshot rippled through the air. Salvador's body hit the marble floor with a thump and blood immediately spilled out from the hole in his forehead.

I'd thrown my hand over my mouth to stop my gasp and immediately hit the floor. If the shooter had looked up, he would've seen me. I was crouched behind a bookshelf, watching the murderer scroll through his phone with one hand and casually hold a gun in the other hand. I was watching him and thinking about my ex fiancé... *I need to get out of here.*

That was not practical, thinking about anything but the man with the gun. I should've been taking note of details. If I survived this, I needed to be able to describe him to police.

He was wearing a bespoke suit. Had a three-hundred-dollar haircut. A fucking fake tan. He looked like he should be managing a hedge fund and not splattering brains all over a floor.

He was not what I imagined a murderer to look like. He looked like he was doing his fucking taxes in front of a dead body.

He looked far too...normal.

Coleson Kitsch.

I was attending a charity event wearing couture, he'd leaned forward to kiss my cheeks in greeting. I'd pegged him as just another billionaire in a nice suit. Men at those things never had one exact job title. They were "businessmen," which meant they had friends in high places and tax havens all over the world. His lips had been on my fucking skin. He'd made an impact because he'd reminded me of Kieran, in a bad way. His gaze was intense. Probing. There was something slightly off about him. Which of course, attracted me to him. I didn't like the nice guys. The straight edges. Kind eyes. Too weak. Too easy for me to walk all over.

The ones with cruelty in their gaze, those were the ones that intrigued me. Even in our brief interaction, I'd seen that in Coleson.

Good thing I was whisked off by Andre before I could engage in some not so subtle flirting. Andre had muttered something about not mixing myself up with Kitsch and I'd dismissed it as him trying yet again to pair me with someone in the industry.

He glanced up and my stomach jumped into my throat. He was looking right at me. There was no way he could miss me.

And I was frozen.

I didn't get up or try and run, didn't look for a weapon on my own so I could act like the heroine I so often played these days. No, I was completely and utterly predictable. The weak woman, unable to move, awaiting her death.

I saw it all with stark lucidity. Heard it all. His shoes clicking on the marble floor as he approached me. The urine trailing down my leg. Another muted shot and maybe a flash of pain then nothing at all.

Saw all of this in less than a moment and yet I *still didn't fucking move.* Wasn't it meant to be fight or flight? Not cower behind a fucking bookcase, seconds away from releasing your bladder.

But it didn't happen. The releasing of the bladder or the murder. His blue eyes flickered away, he glanced down at the body once more before walking away.

His shoes clicked on the floor.

And then there was nothing but silence.

That terrible, dead silence that would ring on the insides of my skull for the rest of my life.

2

It was not my idea to pull into the underground parking lot of Greenstone Security at midnight.

So not my idea.

It was my publicist's idea.

Because he was the first person I'd called when I was sure that Coleson was not coming back to murder me. I was that useless. My life was so managed, so organized for me, my first instinct was to call the man who took care of most of my problems for me. Not, you know, the police or anything else.

To Andre's credit, his pause after I told him I'd just witnessed a murder was less than a second before he started shouting orders at me.

I'd listened, because I was afraid, uncertain and too fucking weak to do anything else.

The police arrived at the mansion within minutes, only half an hour before Andre himself, which was impressive considering the LA traffic.

He'd been by my side the entire time, or as often as he could be while the police questioned me. First it was the uniforms, but as they recognized who I was—immediately—they made calls and a detective in a bad suit took over questioning.

Luckily, they didn't seem to think I had anything to do with the shooting, since they'd arrived so soon after I'd made the call. They'd swabbed my hands for gunshot residue "to rule me out as a suspect." Briefly, I wondered what would've happened if they'd found it. Or, if no one believed my story and they pinned the murder on me. The trial would be big. A circus. Huge news. The killer movie star. The spectacle of it all.

Likely, my high-paid defense attorneys would get me off. Probation. House arrest. That's just what happened when you had enough money and fame. The right status.

But no, of course they didn't take it further. They took my word for what it was, the truth. Maybe because they couldn't imagine the woman they'd all likely jerked off to doing this, but more likely because my all white outfit didn't have a speck of blood on it.

Things changed drastically when I finally managed to say the name of the man I'd recognized doing the killing. I'd been off to the side with the detective at that point, the scene already buzzing with uniforms. Such a quick and effective response was only reserved for the rich.

The detective had been scribbling my statement in a notebook, until I said the name. Then he stopped, pen midair, frozen for a moment. His eyes met mine. They were no longer cold, jaded from years on the job. No, they were alert now.

"Are you sure? This is very important. Are you sure you saw Coleson Kitsch commit the murder?"

Something inside me told me to lie. I had no reason to, but there was a deep instinct that screamed at me to protect myself. Hide the truth amongst all the other hidden things inside me. Another lie wouldn't mean much, I was good at it.

If I told the truth here, everything would change. It was an odd thing to think without all the information I'd later learn, but a woman's intuition was nothing but somewhat magical.

Of course it would be a federal crime but I wasn't overly concerned with that. Self-preservation was more important for a narcissist like me.

But something caught me. Was it the horrible stillness of death that would follow me around for the rest of my life? Was it a shred of decency inside me?

It didn't quite matter why I uttered, "Yes, I'm sure." All that mattered was that I did.

Things moved very fast after that.

The detective shut his notebook, stepped right into my personal bubble, and informed me not to tell anyone what I'd just told him. Well, apart from Andre, who was within eavesdropping distance.

Then we were taken to the station and men in decidedly more expensive suits took their time interviewing me. They weren't so much concerned with the details of the murder but making sure I was absolutely *sure* it was Coleson whom I saw.

It seemed my intuition was right, this was a big deal. *He* was a big deal. Especially when there were talks of things like witness protection and Andre, of all people, talked the suits out of this because he'd made "other arrangements."

My very expensive lawyer then handled the details so I was relatively ignorant, despite being interviewed for hours. As a competent, intelligent woman, I should've gleaned more details from the situation, if not demanded them. I was not scared to demand things. Not afraid to come across as a bitch.

In fact, it was the norm.

But things were not fucking normal right now. So I let two men—ones I paid handsomely—take care of things for me. Something I'd never done. However fucked up I was, however cold I was, I'd always been in the driver's seat of my own life.

All it took was a gunshot to surrender the wheel.

Andre was cursing into the Bluetooth. The person on the other end of the phone was on speaker, but I couldn't make out a single word anyone said. Everything was a dull roar.

Until we pulled into the parking lot. Until something pinged in my brain and I realized where I was. Who I might face.

I was in enough shock after the police station to actually get in the car with Andre when he ordered, and I didn't even ask him where we were going. He was one of the only people that did that, stood up to me, ordered me around. Everyone else was too scared of me, rightfully so.

"No, she's taking a break from filming indefinitely. She's going to a retreat in fucking Bali to realign her goddamn chi. And if you don't halt this fucking film you're a fucking idiot. You know you'll never get someone as good as Anastasia Edwards in your whole life," Andre snapped. He hung up. Then regarded me.

He did not like what he saw.

Not because of my hair or outfit, or makeup, which considering the circumstances, were all impeccable. He was reading me much like a professor would read a textbook written by a first grader. He knew the fucker was wrong by the first sentence.

"I can see you're all hyped up to argue with me," he said. "Don't. You're in the middle of a fucking crisis right now. Not one that I can handle, I'm the best in the business of handling your scandals, your image. Your sex tape gets leaked? I'm your guy. You have an affair with a married man? I'm also your guy. You need to go to rehab and pretend you're on a fucking yoga retreat, I'm most definitely your guy."

He paused, a meaningful pause because Andre was all about impact, drama. He might've raised his brow if the amount of Botox in his forehead had allowed that. He wasn't much older than me, but his skincare routine was about the same as mine.

His jet-black hair was pulled back into a tight pony, making all the angles of his face that much more pronounced. His caramel skin was smooth of any facial hair since he'd had it lasered off years ago.

That made his square jaw all the more prominent and masculine, as well as the fact he always wore ten thousand-dollar suits, in variations of black. He was in demand with every single person in LA. Men and women. We didn't have the kind of relationship where we talked about our love life—mainly because he had to clean up the huge disaster mine had been—but Andre worked far too much to ever have one. He screwed when he needed to and didn't bother himself with romantic entanglements.

Selfishly, I liked that, because he had more time for me. I'd never needed a man more than I needed Andre.

"Of all the fucked-up things I'm an expert in, I'm not specialized in the area of murder," Andre said. "I'm *not* the best at making sure you stay alive to testify. Now, I will be able to keep your involvement under wraps for the time being, to the media at least. My contacts go all the way to the gutter, just not the underworld." He grinned. There was something else to it, though.

Fear. The man who I'd never seen so much as frazzled was scared.

"I'm not gonna know if they've got word on you," he said, quieter now. He didn't need to tell me who "they" were. I'd figured enough to know that Coleson had contacts all over the city, on all sides of the law. The reaction from the cops showed me that.

"If they *do* have word on you, it won't matter if you're in your mansion with the world's best security. They'll find you. And kill you." He paused. "And then I'll have to find another job, which will be a pain in the fucking ass. So don't give me your trademarked fork tongue. Just get out of the car and march those Choos into the fucking office."

At the start of the speech, I was ready to argue, to get my

trademark way with a trademark hissy fit. But by the end I was tired and scared. Andre's fear was catching. He was the only person in the world I trusted. Mostly. He wouldn't be saying this, we would not be here if he didn't legitimately think I was in danger. So I got out of the car.

My heels clicked on the concrete and the sound was nothing like a gunshot, but it took me right back there. I smelled blood, fear, and human excrement.

People shit themselves when they died.

They sure left that out of the movies.

The parking lot was practically empty, but walking toward the elevators we saw a collection of cars. Trucks, mostly. Macho man trucks. A couple manly sports cars that somehow did not scream "midlife crisis." Macho man sports cars.

I knew the men of Greenstone Security were all macho men, each more attractive than the last. They were so alpha you almost choked on the testosterone radiating out from their pores.

I knew this because I'd worked with them before.

I also knew not a single one of these macho men liked me. At all.

Macho men like that had soft, caring, funny, and selfless wives. Not all of them were married but most were. I'd seen photos of their wives because they were involved with Lexie Descare—and her band, Unquiet Mind—as well as connected to a motorcycle club in Amber, California.

The women were also well known in the LA social circles. For being kind. Selfless. Beautiful in a natural way that didn't require Botox, fillers, or starvation that my beauty did. However, they were also crazy as shit, had almost died at the hands of drug dealers, been kidnapped, and had generally caused havoc.

I was nothing like those women. My job, my image, my past, made it impossible to be warm. Sure, there were plenty of movie stars that were personable, down to earth and likeable. They weren't me.

I wasn't sure I knew *how* to be likeable.

And I did my fucking best to convince myself it didn't matter to me that these attractive men—one man in particular—detested me.

My hand shook as I pressed the elevator button.

* * *

Duke was tired.

He was tired, because he'd been on a job for the past three weeks.

He'd gotten shit for sleep and hadn't had a meal that didn't come from a drive-thru in recorded memory.

The plan was to sleep for twelve hours straight, hit the gym, then find someone to fuck. Unlike the rest of his friends, he hadn't settled down with a woman and that suited him just fine. *That* life was not for him. He was happy to have no-strings arrangements with women who were good in bed and knew the score.

Shitty assignments aside, he had a good job, one that paid more money than he knew what to do with. Had a decent crib with all the nice shit he wanted. Had guys—and Rosie—to drink beer and shoot the shit with.

Yeah, his life was good.

Well, not right now. He'd been on his fucking street, dreaming of *his* shower, *his* beers, and *his* sheets. But he was sitting in the fucking conference room after midnight wearing the grime from the road and serious blue balls. But Keltan had called him in. Said it was important. And if his boss said it was important, it was.

Keltan knew what Duke had been doing. Knew he'd been on

the job for three weeks straight. He wasn't an asshole, and he wouldn't have called on him if it wasn't serious.

He would not have called everyone in the employ of Greenstone Security from their beds, their wives, their kids if it wasn't really fucking serious.

Having Keltan utter the name of the client had each of the men—and Rosie, because where the fuck else would she be?—looking pissed off. Rightfully so.

"Anastasia fucking Edwards?" Duke bit out.

The vision of the woman popped into his head. Red hair. Emerald eyes. Blowjob lips. Perfect tits.

Black fucking heart.

Still, his cock twitched at the thought of her, which must've been due to how long it'd been since he'd had a woman, not the woman herself. Duke might've been about no strings, but even he wasn't stupid enough to go near a cold-hearted bitch like her, no matter how beautiful she was.

And she was a fucking knockout.

Keltan nodded, looking sorry, but not as sorry as he should be. Keltan knew how Duke felt about her. How the whole team felt.

Duke clenched his fists, hating the fact that her red hair would not escape his fucking mind. "Are you fucking kidding me? She's a nightmare."

"A nightmare is the kindest possible word to describe her," Rosie said, something out of character, since the woman was not in the business of shit-talking other women. Even if they were bitches.

Keltan didn't argue this because he knew firsthand. She'd been a client in the past. A bossy, bitchy, snobby client. Sure, they set up shop in LA, so that was expected. But she was something else. She had this *way* about her. It was hard to put your finger on —describe—unless you'd experienced it firsthand. It was an undefinable magic. Rosie had coined her "Voldemort."

"She's in deep shit," Keltan told the table. His expression was grim.

That sobered Duke. Keltan wasn't someone easily rattled or who looked grim. Since his wife had been stabbed on the sidewalk and survived, he had little to be grim about. Especially now that they had kids. As crazy as the bitch was, Duke doubted Lucy would get herself caught up in deadly shit that could take her away from her family.

"How deep?" Duke couldn't imagine one of Hollywood's most well-known actresses in shit beyond running out of cold-pressed juice. He knew she drank it, because she'd asked him to "run out and get her some" like he was her fucking assistant and wasn't happy when he'd refused.

Duke had been spoken down to plenty of times working with celebrities. Not as often as one would expect, since a good majority of them were actually decent. The ones who weren't had stopped bothering him.

Which was why he hated that Anastasia somehow managed to affect him so much. Duke considered himself someone who could keep his shit together. And he had. In many worse situations than some actress talking shit to him.

But it was *her*.

She snuck under his skin, drew blood. He fucking hated it. Hated her by proxy. No one had gotten under his skin since he'd returned stateside. Duke had believed that the war had turned that shit off. Made him incapable of feeling what the rest of his team did.

Anastasia didn't make him feel good. But made him feel something. And that scared the shit out of him.

"She witnessed a hit," Keltan clipped. "Obviously, this isn't public knowledge since she has a damn good lawyer and publicist, and it pains me to say it, a good head on her shoulders."

Everyone at the table was listening intently. No matter how

big of a nightmare she was, she didn't deserve to see someone die. No one did. But they also knew they wouldn't be out of their beds, away from their wives, if this was a run-of-the-mill murder.

"She can put Coleson Kitsch at the scene," Keltan added.

Swift intake of breath around the table. "Fuck," Luke muttered.

Keltan nodded once. "Yeah."

Coleson Kitsch was one of the richest and most crooked men in the city. And saying that about LA meant something. He'd been on Greenstone's radar for a while. Same with about every law enforcement agency there was. Everyone knew the fucker was into drugs, murder for hire, and prostitution. Human trafficking, specializing in young girls. Shit that made them sick. But he had powerful friends. He was smart. Nothing more dangerous than a smart, rich psychopath with friends in high places.

There had been exactly two people that had survived shit, witnessed shit, and tried to pin him. They'd both disappeared. From protection. And this wasn't a semi-retired cop guarding a cheap motel room. These were Feds. DEA. Agencies that should've been able to keep a civilian safe long enough to testify.

They hadn't.

Which meant Kitsch's reach went all the way into the institution—which wouldn't be surprising considering how crooked law enforcement was underneath it all—or he was just that fucking dangerous. Could be a mix of both.

"Someone knows that she's not gonna be safe with uniforms or undercovers," Keltan continued. "No matter what. And that someone knows that we're not gonna leak, we're not connected, and we're the best."

All true.

But if Kitsch knew they were caught up in this shit, then they were up against it. Kitsch would figure out the connection. Eventually. Through the process of elimination more than anything else. He'd go looking for her through friends in law enforcement, he wouldn't find her. Men like him were smart enough to know not many outfits could make actresses disappear, and he'd eventually figure out Greenstone was involved. They were the best. He would use everything he could to get them. To draw blood. To get what he needed. No one was off limits. Women. Children. *Fuck.*

Every man in this room had something precious to lose. Something that they'd already almost lost.

Keltan would not have taken the job if there wasn't more. He wouldn't endanger his wife or his kids. Not for a second. He looked carefully toward Heath. "Wire's found connections to Fernandez. Kitsch had a business relationship before we took him down."

Another swift intake of breath. Heath went still.

Rosie muttered a slew of curse words that would've impressed truckers and sailors alike.

Fernandez was the man responsible for Polly's kidnapping... and more. It had been one of the biggest blows to them all. Polly had somehow stayed human, stayed bright after inconceivably dark shit.

Not dark like midnight. Dark like a fucking abyss leading straight to hell.

Duke still had nightmares about the vision of her being chained in the back of that truck. Walking around for months with no light, no life in her. She'd managed to get herself out of it. Get fucking Heath out of it. Didn't mean those marks weren't still there.

More proof that these women were stronger than all the men in this room put together.

"Goes without saying, we get this fucker behind bars, we get a piece of justice for ourselves in addition to sparing others from his shit," Keltan continued. "She's on her way up now. But I'm not gonna take this job unless each of you is solid on this."

"She's a woman in need," Luke said immediately, glancing to his wife. "She's most likely gonna die an ugly death if we don't take this."

Keltan nodded. "Odds are high."

No one at the table hesitated.

* * *

I was not someone easily intimidated. It had taken training, obviously. But life had given me enough shit that I'd learned that being intimidated was the same as being afraid, and being afraid was weak.

I was both intimidated and afraid sitting at this table.

Of course I wasn't showing it. My expression was carefully crafted into that "I'm better than all of you" expression I'd mastered over the years. It was born out of the need to survive by lying to myself. In truth, I was the worst of the lot. Born into trash and dirt. It hid somewhere underneath expensive body creams, a fake tan, and perfume.

"Ms. Edwards, you understand the gravity of the situation you're in?" Keltan asked me after we'd all sat down. He hadn't introduced me to anyone, something I was used to being as famous as I was. But I didn't think this was about fame. This was about infamy. I'd worked with many of the men at this table. I'd been a total fucking bitch to each of them. I hadn't wanted to. No matter what people thought, I didn't want to be thought of in this way. Not by men who had shown to be nothing but decent. A lot of decent men would've walked out on me, and I wouldn't have blamed them. But the Greenstone men had a reputation for keeping their word.

So they'd worked with me. I'd paid them handsomely. But it wasn't about the money. It was the respect I'd failed to show them because I was utterly fucked up.

I purposefully looked only at Keltan and not the rest of the table. Specifically not the muscled, blond-haired, blue-eyed Nordic god that hated me.

"I think I'm aware that witnessing a murder is somewhat serious," I said dryly.

The man did well to hide his own loathing for me. He clung to the professional mask well, they all did, except the beautiful woman staring at me. To most other men, her look might've been seen as mild. But her eyes were narrowed in a way only women could recognize. In a "I know your game, and I'll rip your hair out if you try and fuck with me" way. She scared the heck out of me. I also loved her leather jacket. I didn't think there would be an opening for me to ask her where she got it from.

My tone was snooty and arrogant. Meant to rub them the wrong way. I'd do anything to not be treated like what I really was. A victim.

"You are aware of the reason you're here?" Keltan continued.

I sucked in a breath. "Not entirely." I glanced beside me at Andre, who was looking serious, which in front of all of these handsome men meant the situation was dire. "I'm aware that I need protection, but I'm not aware why it needs to be at midnight." My tone was clipped. Unimpressed. It was low of me to speak to Andre like that, in front of an audience, no less. Outside of my norm for sure. I had my reputation but I had my limits. Demeaning people in front of anyone—or demeaning them in general—was not part of my repertoire. But holding on to my façade was getting trickier.

Plus, Andre knew me as well as anyone could, and he likely knew the score. His emotional skin was about the same thickness as an elephant's, the reason he'd been able to stomach working with me for as long as he had.

Keltan's eyes narrowed ever so slightly. Obviously not

impressed with the way I spoke to Andre. "Coleson Kitsch is very dangerous."

"I also got that by the fact he blew someone's head off," I said, my voice even. My insides were roiling, vision starting to get blurry since I hadn't eaten a thing since...breakfast?

I made an effort to straighten my spine. Not sway in my seat.

"This isn't just a run-of-the-mill murder, sweetheart," the woman interjected with sweet venom that impressed me.

I turned my gaze to her. She looked good for midnight. Not as good as me. Exceptionally beautiful in a natural way. Messy curls. Kick-ass outfit. Killer gaze. "I wasn't aware that any murder was run-of-the-mill," I replied, matching her tone.

She raised her brow. Opened her mouth. Maybe to say something unkind—which I deserved—but the hot macho man beside her put his hand on hers and leaned in to murmur something in her ear.

"There have been two other witnesses under federal protection, both disappeared," Keltan said. "I assume that's the reason your publicist was smart enough to get you here at this hour, considering he must like you alive."

Andre grinned. "I listen to a lot of podcasts about organized crime."

I almost smiled. Almost. As it was, my lip merely quirked before I managed to regain my mask.

"So you will be able to protect me better than the law enforcement can?" I made sure to make it sound like I didn't believe that. Which I didn't. "All due respect to those witnesses that came before me. They weren't as...well known as me. I think it might be harder to take down someone like me—"

"You can die just as easily as a normal person, no matter how much money you have, no matter how many movies you've starred in, no matter how many people know your name," the women interjected, proving that a man, not even a hot macho one, could silence her.

She didn't like me. She was making that clear. But she wasn't being cruel or rude. I saw that. She was being real.

I held her gaze. She didn't look away. *Wasn't impressed.* I liked that. I made sure to hold the stare for long enough to make a point, then I turned to Keltan. "Okay. But I've got to ask, don't I have some kind of legal obligation as a key witness in what I can only assume is a big case to be in contact with the police and DA? Not to mention the other state and federal officials who seem very interested in this case?"

Keltan nodded. "Usually. But considering the nature of the case and what has happened to previous witnesses, I think they'll be more than happy for us to take over the protection detail. Again, that's what you pay us for. We'll handle that."

"You'll handle the LAPD and, I can only assume, the State Attorney's office?" I clarified.

Keltan nodded once.

I didn't argue with him because, they had their reputation for a reason.

He narrowed his eyes. "We gotta get something straight here. You hire us, you pay our bill, but you do not call the shots. We are the best in the business. We know our shit. So you do not argue with us. You do what we say, you'll stay alive."

I pursed my lips. I was not used to doing what people said. It was something that came from a stubborn soul and not my fame or fortune. I had a reputation in the business for being difficult. Because one director, famously misogynistic wanted me to do full frontal nudity for no other reason than he was a pervert and wanted to appeal to fellow perverts. He also got satisfaction from controlling beautiful women, from fucking them, because they wanted to further their career.

Interestingly, all it took was one powerful man to create a

narrative for me that would follow me through the years. I could've tried to fight it, but instead I leaned into it. If men wanted a bitch, they'd get one.

But the man staring at me did not want things from me. Not sex, because he had a large wedding ring on his finger and not an ounce of desire in his eyes. Not to control me, because something in his eyes also told me he was not so insecure in his manhood he had to exert power over women. None of these men at this table were. Once you'd looked into the eyes of a man like that director, you learned to look for the glint.

They didn't have the glint.

They were good people. Whatever that meant.

"Okay," I repeated, the word yanked from inside me.

Keltan nodded, then turned to the man I'd been avoiding the entire time. "Duke, you good for this?"

I froze.

No. Say no. Everything in your body says no. Follow your hatred for me. Do not do the macho-man, alpha-male thing and say yes just because you want to act honorable.

Duke looked at me for the first time since I sat down.

Not flinching came from years of practice.

"I'm good for this," he said.

Fuck.

3

"I PACKED FOR YOU."

I raised my eyebrow. This was outside Andre's job description. When I'd interviewed him almost a decade ago, he'd made it clear he would not run errands, would not deliver food to me, and definitely would *not* pack for me.

He hired competent assistants and stylists for that.

Obviously, we could not make use of the insane team I paid to do things I should be able to do for myself.

Andre was the only person who knew the truth. What he knew was what only a handful of federal and state officials knew. Greenstone Security would be the only people who knew my location. I'd have no contact with Andre after this.

Duke acted like it was a magnanimous favor, allowing me to return to my house to shower and pack.

I was glad to have Andre as a buffer between us, as I was terrified to be alone with the man that was supposed to be protecting me.

"I could've packed," I said to Andre. Theoretically, I was perfectly *able* to do the things I employed people to do for me. In normal circumstances, I didn't have the time to do them. Now, I had time. Not a lot, but enough. Enough to do things like shower and grab food, although my stomach was too unsettled to eat. I settled for a premade smoothie in the fridge.

The mere concept of packing had been a cause of panic for me. In fact, I'd all but collapsed to the floor of my marble shower just thinking about what underwear I'd need.

I knew enough about basic psychology to understand that I was freaking out about doing such a basic thing, because I was not allowing myself to freak out about the not-so basic thing of seeing the man I used to sleep with getting his brains blown all over his marble floor.

I knew that in my mind on the floor of the shower, but it didn't do much to help me with the panty situation.

So I came out of the shower, smelling of expensive lotions, shampoo and panic. And found Andre, with a large Louis Vuitton suitcase, a matching cosmetics case above it.

No doubt he would've picked the perfect panties, not because he had experience with women's panties, but because he was Andre.

"You *could've* packed," he lied. "But I doubt you would know what to put in for a mystery trip to a safe house, weather unknown, where you're going to hide from a powerful murderer until you testify against him."

I regarded him with a half-smile. "And *you* know how to pack for such a trip?"

"Of course I do." He tilted his chin up. "I have many powers."

My smile left as many things hit me. Like the mystery trip with the hot macho man who despised me. Like the fact I didn't know how long I'd be gone. Like the fact I didn't know what my future held, and it was beyond my control. Like I didn't know when I'd see Andre again.

He was the only person that knew the real me. And, surprisingly didn't hate me. He was my person, my best friend...even though I paid him.

Because he knew me, he clocked the change in my mood. "Don't break down on me now, sweetie. I might have to go back to my faith if the ice queen starts crying to signify the end of the damn world."

My half-smile came back. "What are you going to do?" I asked suddenly, remembering that he was also aware of Kitsch. He might be in danger too. "Why aren't you coming? You need witness protection too."

He laughed. "Ah, I've needed that since my first boyfriend. But don't you worry that pretty little head. The Adonis at Greenstone assured me I'd be covered. And not in the way I'd want to be by any of the men there. Fuck, even the chick would almost turn me straight." He paused. "I'm good, Anastasia. I'm far too egotistical to put myself in any danger for you."

I smiled fully then. He was right. That was why I liked him so much. He was just as egotistical and selfish as I was.

"You'll get through this, girl. You'll come back, better than ever once you survive this part." He narrowed his eyes. "You'll survive this part." He stepped back. "Now do your hair, your makeup, and perfect that armor for the trip. I've got a feeling you're gonna need it."

I thought of Duke downstairs.

Yeah, I was gonna need it.

But Duke struck me as a man who tore right through any kind of armor, couture or iron.

I was going for the former, because that's all I had. And I was going to fight to the teeth to make sure that Duke didn't get under my skin.

I was going to try my best to lie to myself and think he wasn't already under there.

* * *

"There's a hot man downstairs who looks pissed off," Andre declared, walking back into my room after he'd left me to get ready. I'd heard him shouting from his "office" next to my bedroom. He must have been canceling photoshoots, ad campaigns, and whatever else I'd committed to for the next few months. "And I'll say, he wears pissed off *well*."

My stomach dropped. This was real, this was happening.

Of course, it started getting real the second I watched Salvador die.

But there was something final about the neatly packed bags on the ottoman at the end of my bed.

"Okay, I'll be right down," I told Andre, who, without asking, grabbed the bags.

Yet another thing the man was not paid for and had refused to do. He gave me a sad smile and left the room.

I turned to regard my reflection in the mirror. My hair was pulled into a tight bun at the nape of my neck, making my sharp cheekbones more prominent. I'd done my makeup out of habit more than anything. My natural freckles were covered with layers of La Mer foundation. My signature wing lined my eyes, and a vibrant red, which almost matched my hair, was slathered on my lips.

Despite what many publications said, it was my natural color. It was a random thing to be so controversial, but I was well known for refusing to cut or dye my hair for a role. I'd lose weight. Gain it—though not many directors had asked for that. Apparently, "no one wants to see a fat woman on screen. If they do, they've got those Bridget Jones movies," a direct quote from one of the owners of the biggest studio in Hollywood. Yeah, men were assholes. But we knew that already.

This legend of my hair was tied to many reports of me being

"difficult" or a "diva"—the two D words that men loved to paint on women who didn't blindly take their orders. I had a few choice D words of my own for those men.

There were never any reports of the fact I'd happily worn wigs for various roles. Wigs that itched, made me break out in rashes and sweat profusely. Arguably much more uncomfortable than sitting in a hairdresser's chair for a few hours.

But people didn't want that story.

They wanted the bitch.

On the flip side, my hair was one of my signatures, the bright, thick waves something that had been replicated countless times over.

I hadn't kept it to start a trend or various rumors.

I kept it because that bright red hair was the only thing I had in common with my father. My one and only tie to him.

Not what I said in interviews, of course.

My hands—nails painted in that same bright red—smoothed down my cashmere turtleneck. I hadn't known the dress code for being spirited away to an unknown location so I wasn't murdered before testifying in open court, but I figured all black was a safe bet. My cigarette pants were close cut, elegant, and comfortable for traveling.

The six-inch pointed black heels with the red bottom were not comfortable for traveling but you wouldn't catch me in a flat shoe unless I was in a gym.

Most people would call that high maintenance, that I didn't leave the house unless I was in one-thousand-dollar shoes.

But I didn't care about the shoes themselves—okay, I cared a little, I was a woman.

I liked towering over the men who "directed" me. I was already tall and the extra six inches gave me an edge. Men didn't like their women like that—they liked them small and vulnerable —which was why my romantic interest in every movie was usually on a step and creative camera work made me seem a lot smaller than I was.

People always commented on my height whenever they saw me in person.

In addition to the extra height from the heels, I liked the pain. It was a reminder. Kept me grounded—pardon the pun—so I hurt just like everyone else. That my position gave me nothing but more money and more people who knew my name. It seemed like a stupid thing to a regular person. But fame did something to you. When you had enough people treating you like a goddess, you couldn't help but believe it, even a little. Sure, there were many celebrities with a core group of friends, family, and good values that managed to stay kind and humble. But those were few.

I didn't have friends or family.

I had heels by Christian Louboutin.

They clicked against my marble floors as I made my way into the foyer. I hated it. Large. Echoing. Cold. Expensive.

It looked great in photos for Vogue, though.

Duke was standing with his back to me, staring at the large painting on the wall. It was the one rebellion in this place. The one thing that my expensive decorator had not picked out.

It wasn't by a dead, famous artist. It wasn't worth millions. It was a print that I'd found online. I'd had my assistant track down the artist and pay them to create it in a large canvas.

It was a woman in the ocean, wearing nothing but panties and a tee pulled over her head so her boobs were almost showing. Her face was covered and she was flipping off the camera.

I didn't know why, but this woman hit me. She leapt off the canvas and commanded your attention. You couldn't see her face. She didn't *want* you to see that. She didn't want you to see anything she didn't. She was confident in herself. She was sexual without showing parts of herself that would've made this erotic.

I wanted to be this woman more than anything. And I'd never

wanted to be anyone else before. Of course I couldn't be this. But I could pay thousands for the art. I could look at her every day, reminding me what I was and what I'd never be.

It felt incredibly strange having a man like Duke stare at the painting so intensely. No, not a man *like* Duke. Just *Duke*.

The man who'd crept into my dreams every now and then.

The man who'd also appeared in my mind when it was late and I opened the top drawer of my nightstand to find some relief.

He turned around with the click of my heels. His eyes flickered over my body. There was no appreciation there, only a cold indifference that I pretended I didn't see, didn't feel all the way into my bones.

My eyes flickered over his body too. I did my best to mimic his expression—that's what I was paid the big bucks for, after all —but I feared I fell short.

Because there was nothing cold nor indifferent in what I felt about the man in the tight white tee and faded jeans, with piercing blue eyes, perfect blond hair, and the square jawline that every actor in the industry would be jealous of.

This was *man* pure and simple.

And my body reacted violently, even in the midst of the drama.

"You good?" he asked, voice clipped.

Good?

I was about to leave everything I knew, my lavish life, my full schedule, my trainers, stylists, assistants and ever-present paparazzi. I was about to put my life in the hands of a man who made no effort to hide his dislike of me.

"I'm ready to go, if that's what you mean," I said, making sure to make my voice sharp. Bitchy. That was the only way I'd survive this thing with Duke.

His jaw ticked. I shouldn't have noticed such subtleties in a man who was employed to protect me, but I did.

"Yeah, that's what I mean. Sorry if I don't lay out the red carpet." His tone was mild, but it still hit its mark.

I straightened my shoulders and only now noticed Andre watching the entire exchange with a wicked grin.

My glare settled on him, which of course, only made him smile wider. He was used to the glare, and definitely not scared or intimidated by it.

"I've drafted releases to everyone that you're scheduled to work with for the next three months," Andre said, tapping at his phone as he spoke. "I've already sent them over to the lawyers and Greenstone Security to make sure it won't infringe on anything going on with the case or the trial. I've also had all communication with said lawyers forwarded to Greenstone Security office as Keltan requested."

I didn't have time to be impressed at what Andre had done in the small amount of time allotted to him—that was Andre anyway—I was too busy focusing on the start of what he said.

"Three *months*?" I repeated.

Andre nodded. "To be safe. I'll readjust if it looks like things will take longer than that."

Longer?

Longer than three months? With Duke? The man I was already uneasy with after three goddamn minutes? Three months of that cold stare? Three months of trying to hide my attraction and borderline infatuation with the man?

I snapped my head to focus on blue, impatient eyes. "Surely this isn't going to take longer than three months?"

He just stared at me at first, his gaze unreadable. Maybe he was already regretting taking this job. I hoped so. There was still time for him to call any one of the other badasses to take his place. They most likely wouldn't feel any different about me, but what was important was me feeling differently about them.

"Can't say how long this takes, I'm just the guy employed to make sure you stay alive for however long you need to in order for this to be over," he said finally. The longest sentence I'd heard him utter.

"That's not good enough," I declared. "I'm not leaving until I can have some idea of how long my life is going to be turned upside down."

How long I'm going to be tortured with my want for you, was what I didn't say.

Obviously.

Another jaw twitch.

"We're leaving in two minutes," Duke replied. "You can either walk out on those stupid fuckin' heels or I can carry you over my shoulder."

* * *

Duke was pissed.

And not just because he was fuckin' disappointed he didn't get to carry Anastasia over his shoulder like the brat she was being. Fuck, he had to battle the urge to put the woman over his knee.

Especially wearing those fucking shoes. The shoes that made her legs go on for days, that put her on a level height with him. Even without them, she'd reach a space on his chest that not many women could match. He was tall, over six foot, and used to towering over women. Not that he used it to intimidate them, but there was something primal in him that liked it.

But Anastasia Edwards was not someone who could be towered over. Even if she wasn't tall, she wouldn't let herself be towered over. She was far too fucking stubborn and superior for that.

Duke didn't think he liked that. Tall women. But Anastasia

descending the stairs in that all black outfit, looking every bit the movie star...he liked that.

Well, he liked her legs, he liked her tits—though she was too fucking skinny—he loved her lips and that red hair.

He did not like the woman herself.

Did not like her spoiled, superior tone, or the fact that she could not seem to get it through her head that she was in a fucking serious position. She was too busy worrying about spending three months without her marble fucking floors, grandiose mansion, and army of assistants. Three months out of the spotlight.

With him.

Jesus, it was going to be torture.

Duke had never wanted to fuck a woman so badly in his life. He'd never disliked a woman as much either. As much as she had lorded her apparent superiority over him on the last job, she didn't do anything radical to justify him disliking her that much. Plenty of clients were rude, plenty more were insulting, but Anastasia hadn't called him names, sworn at him, or threatened him like one starlet had after he refused to fuck her.

She was nowhere near the worst of the lot, yet he disliked her with a power that shook his very bones.

Maybe he hated the effect she had over him, hated that he was attracted to such a haughty bitch.

Hated that she glared at him, tilted her head upward, and strutted out the door to his waiting vehicle. She left her bags by the door, obviously expecting him to carry them.

Her publicist was still grinning, and Duke didn't like that knowing glint in his eye. It was one Duke himself had worn watching the chaos his best friends had enjoyed throughout their courtships.

He gritted his teeth.

Andre picked up the bags. "You know, she's not everything

she seems, big guy," he said. "She's a great actress, and pretending she's not scared of what's ahead of her is her most challenging role." There was something moving in the man's eyes. A fear of his own? He seemed to care about this woman, even though she'd treated him like shit this entire night.

He turned and walked out the door.

"Fuck," Duke muttered under his breath.

His eyes zeroed in on the single bag left by the door. Had the publicist left it there as some kind of test? Taunt? He didn't really seem like the guy to pull that shit, in fact, Duke liked the guy. He had a quick wit and was calm under pressure. Seemed genuinely nice too—which begged the question as to what the fuck he was doing working with someone like Anastasia Edwards?

No, that wasn't even the question. Despite his years in this town, Duke sometimes forgot that everything here can be bought with money. Fame, friendship, love, hate. All of it was for sale.

Duke wasn't going to pick up the bag, and he sure as fuck wasn't going to listen to what Anastasia probably paid that man to say about her. Duke had worked with celebrities long enough to know that most of them were assholes. Entitled, spoiled, and considered themselves better than everyone.

Despite that, Duke had been raised not to judge a book by its cover or "a woman by another man's opinion of her, especially if that man used to sleep with her" (coming from his grandmother, of course). No, his opinion of Anastasia did not come from the multiple rumors swirling around the industry. It came from personal experience.

Heading out.

Duke sent the message to Keltan, who had already informed him that they'd been in contact with the State's Attorney. He, of course, wasn't happy, but didn't exactly have a leg to stand on considering they'd let two of their witnesses "disappear" while in protective custody—and there was a strong possibility someone in that office was on Kitsch's payroll. It still amazed Duke the sway that Keltan had over powerful people. Of course, now that they were established and had a reputation, it was because many of those powerful people were clients. They'd done a lot of things, fixed fuckups that could've ended campaigns, stepped in when it looked like villains weren't going to get locked up.

Good luck.

Duke scoffed at Keltan's response. Yeah, luck was not what he needed for this shit.

He picked up the bag on the way out the door.

* * *

The inside of the cab had been silent for almost two hours.

Duke drove a truck. Big surprise. One that I practically needed a ladder to get into. I bet Duke got immense satisfaction from seeing me scramble into the passenger's seat without an ounce of grace. He, of course, wasn't about to help me up. Which was good, since my skin had still been tingling after envisioning Duke throwing me over his shoulder.

The goodbye with Andre had not been emotional. We didn't do that kind of thing. I wouldn't have been able to handle it.

As it was, I still couldn't handle it, since I'd spent the last hour trying to hold my shit together and not let Duke see any weakness.

He'd seemed more than happy with the silence. Well, he hadn't seemed happy. At all. But he'd not been radiating menace like he had in my foyer, so that was something.

But I would not mute myself to quell his macho-man fury. I was not one to silence myself because a man was more comfortable with the quiet.

"Where are we going?" I demanded.

I should've asked this a little earlier, like before I got in the car, considering the answer.

"Montana," Duke said, eyes on the road, jaw hard.

When he'd worked for me before, he hadn't tried to pretend that he liked me. But he'd also held onto a thin veil of professionalism that I'd prodded at because I was darkly fascinated with him. Because I was obsessed with him. I'd wanted a response, hadn't I? And he was giving me one. Just not the one I wanted. Not the one I craved.

He was not here to give in to my fantasies. He was here to protect me. Nothing more. Nothing less.

"Montana?" I repeated.

He nodded once.

I quickly calculated the distance from LA to Montana. Granted, without the location of where in the state we were going, this wasn't going to give me an accurate number but the ballpark was bad enough.

"That's like twenty hours of driving."

Duke didn't look at me. He kept his gaze on the road as if he was taking a test on it. "Ah, the superstar can also calculate distances."

I glared at him. "Pull over, I'm not driving for twenty hours with you." Even though I put all my authority into the tone, he didn't look like he was going to obey.

This was not a man that obeyed.

"Not doin' that."

I sucked in a breath. Tried to calm my rapid heart rate. My past made it so that it was integral for me to be able to control almost every moment of my life. My present made that possible. That's what I'd wanted, the second I turned eighteen, the second I could escape. I hadn't wanted to be famous, be in movies. I'd wanted to be in control. And I knew enough about life to understand that poor people had no control. So my singular goal had always been to accumulate enough wealth to control everything.

I'd sacrificed so much to get that control, and it was stolen from me with that gunshot. I lost it even further when I got into this truck with a man who made it obvious he didn't care about my feelings and was prepared to drag me kicking and screaming to the state of his choice.

I was having a panic attack. The rapid heartbeat. The fact I was sure that doom was on my horizon, inescapable and fatal, my lungs unable to suck in enough air.

I was not about to hyperventilate in the cab. Cry. Pass out. Throw up. Though I did feel like doing all of those things. I wouldn't give that to this man who was certain I was nothing but a damsel in distress. But not one he wanted to save, one he was getting paid to keep alive. I got the impression that if he had a choice in the matter, he would leave me on the road and not lose a second of sleep over it.

"Well then, why aren't we flying?" I said, careful to keep the hitch from my voice.

He glanced toward me. A quick glance. It managed to scathe like it was intended to. "You fly, you go into all sorts of systems, caught on hundreds of CCTV cameras. Something that'll be picked up by the multiple men and women looking for you. Not only that, you're gonna get about a thousand star-struck assholes recording you, uploading to shit. Easiest way to get yourself killed."

Well shit. I hadn't exactly thought of that.

It was rare I forgot who I was. Forgot that there was no such thing as anonymous with me. I couldn't go to the fucking drugstore without a handful of cars trailing me, waiting to get a photo of me that might hint I'm pregnant, fat, or on drugs.

"Why are we going to Montana?" I asked, furious at myself. At this situation.

He didn't look at me this time. I was pissing him off with the questions, but his anger birthed some of my own. I welcomed it. It was easier to deal with than fear or panic.

"Because it's off grid. Fucker has a lot of power at his disposal. Can't scour the whole country."

I bit my lip. They had taken my phone from me, obviously so I couldn't contact people, or book flights to New Zealand once reality set in. And so I couldn't Google this man, who would apparently kill me once he found out I was testifying against him.

It should've filled me with panic, the loss of something almost permanently attached to my hand. But it was the one part of this whole scenario that didn't fill me with anxiety. It was almost peaceful being untethered from the constant stream of calls, messages, emails, and demands from people who wanted to suck me dry.

"Where in Montana are we going?"

He still didn't look at me.

"You'll find out when we get there."

I wanted to scream. I wanted to cuss at him. Worse, I wanted to cry. Sob and beg him to be kinder, to treat me with more care, pretend like I was a warm woman.

Instead, I stayed silent.

Silent like death.

* * *

"Can you tell me a little more about this safe house, at the very least the quality of the beds?" I asked Duke, trying to roll the kink from my neck.

It was the first time we'd spoken today apart from bathroom requests. And let me tell you, having to ask the hostile, tight-lipped man protecting you from murder to stop so you could pee at a filthy gas station was *not fun*.

Nor were the accommodations the night prior.

Now, I was well practiced at sleeping in squalor. Especially in those shitty, roadside motels that either charged by the hour or by the month. Half my childhood was spent in one or the other, where I'd never known Egyptian-cotton, new clothes—or clothes that fit—a clean bathroom, or full stomach.

When I turned eighteen, I vowed to myself that I would never stay in one of those places again. That I'd never try to wash myself in a shower that only made me feel a little less dirty. That I'd sleep in sheets made for royalty.

I'd managed it for over a decade.

And when Duke pulled into the motel outside of Utah, I knew my promise to myself would be broken. I couldn't exactly request the nearest Four Seasons. No, I would not cement his opinion of me.

So I sucked it up—the greasy food that I barely touched and he didn't comment on, the room I shared with him with scratchy sheets and a dirty bathroom. I didn't sleep a wink with the TV blaring and knowing he was *right there* in the other bed, quietly seething.

We spoke as little as possible. It made me uncomfortable, which I was sure was his goal, so I did my best not to let it show.

I didn't like talking to strangers, as a rule. I especially should not like talking to the man who was only little more than a stranger, was macho as fuck, and somehow fascinating to me, despite the fact that macho man was *so not my type*.

My type was groomed, rich and distant.

And dead, as it was.

Duke was definitely as silent as the dead since he ignored my question. This annoyed me. A lot. Sure, he didn't like me, he had good reason. I was a superior bitch to him when he'd worked for me, because I'd found him too attractive. It was my defense mechanism. I sensed that he could be dangerous if I let myself be nice to him, if I even opened up the possibility of him liking me. No, the worst thing would be trying to be myself with him—whoever the heck that was—and him rejecting me anyway. It was much safer for him to reject who I pretended to be rather than who I really was.

But he was also being paid by me. Handsomely. He took this job. This was his choice. No one was holding the proverbial gun to his head, he could've said no. He didn't. Therefore he might not have to like me, but he did have to answer my questions.

"You really need to stop acting like I'm you're captive," I snapped. "I did not force you to be here, I did not drag you away from your gym, from your infidels you have been no doubt beating into submission, or your no doubt soft, kind, and loving girlfriend." I ignored the pang I got thinking about some faceless woman I was instantly jealous of. "I get you don't like me. The feeling is mutual. But I witnessed a *murder*. My life is being ruined. I think I deserve to know where the fuck we're going."

I hadn't meant to say all of that. No, I had. Because I was angry. At Duke, sure. But at the world mostly. At this whole fucking situation. At me for deciding to stop by Salvador's house for a fucking orgasm instead of going straight home.

Having cameras follow you around constantly, people sending me hatred on social media, other people in "real life" being rude or condescending, I was well versed at keeping ahold of my temper. Keeping ahold of everything, in fact. I'd gotten an Oscar plus two Golden Globes for my work in movies, but I should've gotten them all for my acts in life.

Duke had stopped looking at the road. He was now staring at me. No more professional distaste on his face. He was irritated, but interested. He was likely considering whether he'd still have his job if he just dumped me on the side of the road.

I was fixated on him. His eyes. The connection between us that was annoyance and dislike. I was also ashamed at how deep it cut, his dislike. How much I longed to be the soft, strong and loveable woman like the one at the table who had stared me down. Like the one who he'd have waiting for him at the end of all this.

As quick as my anger had appeared, it fizzled out. I was too tired to fight this man, who was looking at me, daring me to say more. The air was thick with aggression, and something else. Something else I had to be imagining. Duke kept my gaze for a couple more beats then looked to the road again, professional distaste firmly in place.

"We're going to my family's ranch."

He was annoyed he had to tell me this.

I got over the fact that he seemed so put out at telling me where I was going to hide out from murderers because I was too focused on the specific.

"Your *family's ranch?*" I repeated.

He nodded once.

My stomach swirled with unease. "Why aren't we going to some rental in the middle of the mountains, or a motel?"

I'd been so sure I'd rather be anywhere than that shitty motel room with two beds and no clean bathroom, but the idea of going to his family's ranch was nauseating. That Duke's family had a ranch was interesting to me, in the middle of all the other feelings. I didn't peg him for a cowboy. I hated how much that image pleased me.

The whites of his knuckles were evidence of just how tight he was holding on to the steering wheel. Just how pissed off he was at me.

"Because all of that leaves a record," he bit out.

"Don't you have a designated safe house?" I asked, refusing to let him intimidate me into silence.

"Yeah," he said. "But it's in use right now. And I'm not risking shit by taking you somewhere I'm not familiar with. I know every inch of that ranch. Trust everyone there. I know what I'm doin'. You'll stay alive long enough to testify, put this fuck away, and this will all be a distant memory."

The way he said it cut through me. *He was already preparing to forget me.* And yet I knew this man would be a ghost, following me around for the rest of my life.

However long that was, remained to be seen.

* * *

We pulled up to the ranch.

For whatever reason, I'd been expecting something...shabby. Which made no sense at all, since Duke was nowhere near shabby. He was well groomed and well dressed in good quality clothes. Not showy, just good quality.

He had impeccable manners. I knew how to spot that, since I hadn't been raised well. Early, I was taught how to be a respectful person. Blurry lessons taught by an honorable man. One that I wondered if I imagined—just to keep myself sane—to comfort myself with the lie that someone in this world had loved me, had wanted to teach me how to be good, kind, and soft.

But lessons from future dirtbags erased anything valuable I'd learned. So I'd had to learn all those things, all of those *good* things when I was old enough to know how embarrassing it was not to know how to use a knife and fork correctly. How to speak properly. Basic manners.

So yes, you learned to spot things that came naturally to people when you were trying to mimic it.

And it was more than apparent that Duke was raised well. That he had money.

But still, I expected a crumbling shack in the middle of a yellowed farm, almost as an absurd punishment for how much he didn't like me.

That was not what I got. The entrance to the driveway itself was a large gate, two horses reared up on each pillar.

The driveway was dirt, but free of potholes.

There was green everywhere. Fields that seemed to stretch on for days, peaks of mountains bordering the unobstructed view. Very few signs of humanity marred the land. Some fences. Not much else, from what I could see.

"This is your ranch?" I asked, a whisper.

"My family's," Duke said, voice hard.

My eyes were glued to the rolling landscape—something I'd definitely seen before as I'd traveled all over the world—but this was different somehow. Maybe because I knew that this was Duke's.

"You grew up here?" I imagined a smaller, less jaded and less macho version of the man beside me growing up in the midst of this beauty.

I wondered what had happened to make Duke leave this place, swap the wide-open skies and mountain ranges for the smog-filled city full of assholes.

"Yeah, I did." There was a slight change in Duke's voice, something I might've tried to dissect had I not been creating a past for him.

Maybe it was a woman. A beautiful, fresh-faced Montana girl with long thick hair and warm eyes. Maybe she broke his heart and he'd never gotten over her. I instantly hated the girl I'd made up in my mind, coveted what she'd had that I'd never experienced.

The driveway was long and winding, showing off the beautiful ranch. I almost didn't want the ride to end, but the assault it
was giving my emotions needed to stop. It was distracting me
from being so goddamn nervous at the prospect of facing Duke's
family as an unwelcome stranger.

The homestead was nothing less than extraordinary.

I actually let out a gasp seeing it, immediately covering up my
mouth in embarrassment. I really hoped Duke didn't hear that, as
that would be more proof I was the vapid, dramatic movie star. I
didn't dare look at him. Plus, I was too busy taking in the house. It
was built for a large family. Maybe added on to over generations.
Everything about it called to parts of my soul that I didn't know
existed.

I was expecting a deep brown log cabin. Isn't that what they
specialized in here in Montana? But this wasn't that.

It was a grand, Victorian-style house with a wrap-around
porch. Pure white, stark against the landscape surrounding it. It
had two floors, and had been taken care of with generations of
love. Even from inside the cab of the truck, I could feel what
this was.

A home.

Flowers everywhere. Colorful. Healthy. Well-tended, like
the house itself. I had flowers around my house too, but I
employed a small army of landscapers to tend to them. I had a
feeling that the people who planted these in the soil were people
who lived here.

There were outbuildings scattered around the vast property.
Fields, mountains, animals, beauty, all stretching to the horizon.

I'd been all over the world. I'd seen many beautiful things. I
was virtually numb to them now. Nothing wowed me. But right
now, staring at this, it was safe to say I was wowed. For the
smallest of moments, everything else melted away. The very

reason I was here melted away, and I had a moment to just...marvel.

To covet this place, the life that must be lived here.

I wanted it more than anything. Right at this moment, I wished I'd done my whole life differently, that I'd chased other things, things that made me warm, easy and able to live a life in a place like this.

"One thing," Duke said when he stopped the car.

His voice, terse and bordering on cruel jerked me from my fantasy, which was a blessing really, considering how dangerous it was to linger in fantasies. I moved my attention from the view to him. He was staring at me in that way I hated. In that forced, distasteful, professional mask.

As someone who was not a stranger to distaste—heck the media loved to hate me, and just check out the comments section of my Instagram—it affected me in a way it shouldn't.

Duke's dislike of me was a weapon. Something biological. He let it out into the air and I breathed it in. It seeped into my pores and sickened me.

"We're together."

I blinked at the words. They made absolutely no sense, nor did the meaning behind them. My heart skipped a beat nonetheless and I hated myself for continuing such a juvenile, school girl reaction to this man.

He was annoyed by my silent confusion. Everything about me annoyed him. Duke nodded his head to the house. "I don't want my family caught up in this. I never see them. I sure as shit don't want them thinking that the first visit in two years is because of a *job*." He paused, still gripping the steering wheel. This pissed him off. Infuriated him. "So we're together. Here for a break from the spotlight for you. Vacation for me."

It took great effort to keep my expression even. "You want me to pretend I'm your girlfriend?" I clarified.

A muscle in his jaw ticked. He nodded violently. Only a man like him could *nod* violently. "Shouldn't be hard. You're an actress, aren't you?"

People came rushing out of the house as Duke left me sitting in the car with the bomb that I was not only having to stay with his family, but also pretend I was his fucking *girlfriend*.

He was right, I could act, and I was great at it. No matter what anyone said about me getting roles for my tits, ass, or the fact I slept my way to the top, my one talent in life was pretending to be anyone but who I was.

In my childhood, it was a survival tactic.

In my adulthood, it was my ticket to millions.

Right now, I was certain it spelled destruction.

But I didn't have any other choice but to get out of the car and pretend to be Duke's girlfriend.

So I got out of the car.

Duke was being let out of a hug with an older woman with long blond hair in loose braids, wearing faded jeans with a huge belt buckle, a rust shirt tucked in and turquoise necklaces slung around her neck.

The closer I was the more beautiful I found her. She wasn't wearing makeup. She had lines on her face, although not as many as she should for the age I guessed she was. She had an aura about her. I had always rolled my eyes at people spouting that shit in LA, but it was the only way I could describe it. There was an energy that surrounded her, that bounced off her fricking pores.

Her gaze was a weight on me. I carried it over the dirt driveway, onto the cobbled walkway toward the house. She was smiling. Easily. But there was something else in her eyes. Not recognition. That was something I easily saw in people. No, not that. It was something I didn't understand, because it wasn't shallow or hostile, the only things I had true experience in.

Duke was doing the whole, handshake-hug type thing with an older man that was about his height, slightly less muscled and leaner than him and a good few decades older.

"Mom, Dad, this is Anastasia," Duke said, extracting himself from the man hug and moving back toward me.

To my shock, horror, and secret pleasure, he moved to put his arm around me and kiss my forehead tenderly. Naturally. Like it was something we'd done about a thousand times. He smelled of simple, expensive, and classy cologne, slightly like the burger he'd eaten for lunch and something altogether uniquely him.

All of this was so jarring to me that I froze and stood there like a stumped, mute robot. This was the first time I'd ever frozen in front of people. From the second I decided I'd become an actress, any stage fright or shyness was impossible. That would hinder my goal. My goal was to get enough jobs to make money. My desperation was stronger than anything else. Maybe there was a natural talent to act in there somewhere, but it was mostly desperation. I'd always been confident. Articulate. I'd met some of the most famous and powerful people in the world, I'd been flawless in my interactions with them. But now, in front of Duke's parents, I was a mute idiot.

To their credit, both were polite enough to ignore this and moved forward to greet me.

His mother smiled warmly, her gaze on Duke and his arm. "It's so nice to meet you, Anastasia. I love you already since you brought my son home to me."

And somehow, as quickly as I had been in Duke's embrace, I was in his mother's. She smelled like Chanel and the outdoors. She was warm, and a hugger, and I hated it.

I was not a hugger. I did not know how to give casual, genuine human affection. Nor did I know how to receive it.

I could fake it all day long. I could portray intimacy and love so well I'd made a fortune off it. Won awards for it. But that's the only thing I could do—fake things. In LA, it served me well, because even when the cameras were turned off, no one wanted real.

This place, these people—even though they were strangers to me—were not fake. This was the furthest thing from it. It was impossible to be fake in the face of this kind of real.

So I stood awkwardly and stiffly in the hug until she let go. But she didn't let all the way go; she held on to my upper arms in a strong grip and regarded me. "Now I could pretend I don't know you from your movies, but I'm no bullshitter and I love them, so I'm not going to pretend. I am going to say, you are just as stunning in real life, if not more." She paused. "Then again, it could be that beautiful blush you seem to still have for my Duke. And I'll tell you, I like that too." She let me go then. "I'm Anna, by the way."

I gaped at the woman, unsure of what to say. The blush that she mentioned was not something I was putting on. Duke's touch, his nearness had triggered it. I smiled my *movie star* smile. I prepared to go with my *movie star* script for being introduced to people. But instead, I blurted, "I can't believe his name is really Duke. I thought he moved to LA, decided to go on the badass track and changed his name to something to suit his badass life."

My blush that I hadn't known I'd gotten from Duke turned into a full-face flush once I realized what I'd said, how I'd inadvertently insulted their choice of name for their son and potentially blown my cover for being Duke's girlfriend. Surely if I knew him well enough to travel to meet his parents across the country I'd know his fucking birth name.

Instead of looking insulted or disbelieving, his mother looked at me straight-faced for about a second then burst out laughing.

It was a nice sound. Throaty. Not delicate and feminine. Strong, but easy at the same time.

His father looked similarly amused, but he just shook his

head and let out a low chuckle. "My wife does like to think she had the powers to look into the future and see that her son would actually grow up to suit a name like Duke, but more accurately, it's due to the drugs coursing through her system after giving birth and me being the schmuck who let her choose the name of the second-born son since I got to name the first."

Duke had a brother? An *older* brother?

Interesting, since he definitely had an older brother vibe about him. If this was the youngest of the clan, I was interested to see just how macho his brother was. Could the world handle two men with that degree of machoness? His father surely had it, but it wasn't as prominent, the years not so much shaving it off him but subduing it. I had no doubt Duke's father was a badass in his day.

I didn't dare glance to my side to see what shade of pissed off Duke was at me for this outburst, so I focused on his parents. The attractive couple that laughed easily, and obviously loved their son and each other. There was an easy happiness to them, but a sadness too. I saw something in their eyes that told me that Duke was a source of this. He didn't come home often, that much was apparent. For what reason, I couldn't understand, seeing the surface, but everything was always so much more than surface. The more beautiful, usually the uglier it was below.

"I stand by my choice," Anna said, looking to her son fondly. "And my ability to see the future."

Her husband rolled his eyes in what seemed to be a practiced way. "I'm Andrew, by the way," he said with that same ease. There was no hesitancy in Duke bringing me here. They weren't bracing for me to be a bitch. They weren't expecting to disapprove of me. Weren't reserving judgement. They loved their son and the mere fact he brought me here seemed to show them that I was worth...something.

I smiled again. But this was not my movie star smile. It felt odd on my face, since it was not one I had much experience with. It was genuine.

I expected Duke's father to be the handshake type of guy. He looked every bit the rancher, down to the tanned skin from working in the sun to the slightly tattered flannel shirt, belt buckle and boots. He looked older, for sure, but not old enough to have a son Duke's age. It boded well for Duke, not that I'd be knowing him long enough to see that happen. Before I could stretch out my arm, he yanked me in for a hug.

Another hug.

He didn't smell like his son. It was a different cologne, but you could also smell the outdoors on him. Again, I was unused to such a gesture, the warmth of it.

Every man that tried to hug me in a friendly interaction was trying to cop a feel. It was a horrible thing to learn to get used to, that casual sexual assault, but it was more familiar than a genuine, welcoming hug from an older man.

Luckily, he let me go and I stepped back, right into Duke.

My body jolted and I tried to scuttle away but he grasped my hips firmly and yanked my back to his front. My body reacted violently to this, heat crawling up my cheeks. His body was hard, all muscle. But I molded into it perfectly. Like we were made to stand like this. But of course not. This was an act. Less than five minutes and I was already forgetting that.

He began playing with my hair. My nerve endings were about fried with so much human contact...and authenticity. It was like culture shock after being immersed in Hollywood for so long. I'd faked almost every single gesture of love and intimacy in the book, all with an audience of directors, producers, writers, cameramen, assistants and countless others. I'd engaged in cold, casual sex with strangers and not felt an ounce of embarrassment or shyness. And yet I was damn near falling apart with Duke *playing with my hair*.

"It's nice to meet you both," I said, recovering ever so slightly, despite gritting my teeth against my reaction to Duke's affection.

He's acting, I reminded myself.

"I can't believe you're dating a movie star and instead of flying us to Hollywood land and taking us to the Oscars, you bring her here," someone yelled from the porch.

The owner of the voice was a woman older than Anna, by my guess, her mother since the resemblance between the two was uncanny. Except where Anna's long hair was mostly blonde, her mother's was all gray and its wild curls were flying around her shoulders as she moved quickly down the porch steps.

Unlike her daughter, she wasn't wearing a kickass female rancher outfit. She was just wearing a plain kickass outfit—a Rolling Stones tee I suspected she wasn't wearing how the youth shopping at Forever 21 did. It had rhinestones on it and was tucked into ripped jeans. She was wearing bright red Chucks.

Her arms were stacked with bracelets and her lips were painted the same red as her sneakers.

She looked like the most interesting rock 'n' roll grandma I'd ever seen. I immediately wanted to be her when I grew up.

She stopped in front of us, grinning with youth and beauty. She pointed to Duke, brows furrowed. "I'm mad at you. Not mad enough to take you out of my will, but mad enough to refuse you a hug until I've had my first drink." She looked to me. "You drink?"

I laughed at the question, then I realized that could be construed as rude so I quickly composed myself. "Yeah, I drink."

"Great." She locked her arm with mine and all but yanked me toward the house. "I made margaritas." She turned her head. "Duke, you'll get the bags, won't you? And if there isn't an expensive jar of face cream in there somewhere I will be taking you out of my will." She grinned to me. "Welcome to the family, dollface."

4

"Here you go, sweetheart, this will straight-up change your darn life," Harriet, Duke's batshit crazy—read *fucking awesome*—grandmother said to me.

I looked down at the gigantic slice of pie, smothered in vanilla ice cream that was already melting lazily over the crust.

My mouth watered at the smell alone before my brain shut it down. I hadn't let myself crave food in years. It was just another thing about my life I'd accepted. Another thing I wouldn't have. Another sacrifice. It wasn't something that was difficult in my life. Not with my trainers and chefs I paid for. When I went to dinner parties, they were thrown by the Hollywood elite, who served food in miniscule portions and didn't expect anyone to finish them.

I'd never really inspected my relationship with food closely, because I knew it was fucked up—and because it was part of the circus that was my life. *Something always in my control.* Now, with all the trappings of fame gone, it seemed utterly ridiculous that a slice of pie could cause so much panic. *Be so confronting. Outside of my control.*

I glanced up, awkwardly. I didn't want to offend these people, these warm, funny, and genuine people. That feeling itself was foreign. Itchy under my skin. I'd never had to worry about such things. I hated it. I grasped the Anastasia Edwards I'd been for decades, who was somehow slipping away after a couple of hours on a ranch in Montana. "I'm fine, thank you."

Harriet blinked, once. Then looked to Duke, then back to me. I didn't dare look to Duke. I'd been studiously avoiding his gaze and any interactions with him since we sat down at the dinner table.

"You on a diet or something?" Harriet asked.

Or something. Does ten years of being constantly hungry but never able to eat what I enjoyed because the media scrutinized every pound I gained and directors didn't like me "chubby" count as a diet?

I was pretty sure that counted as an eating disorder everywhere but Hollywood.

"No, just not a dessert person." The lie was easier and a lot less shameful. I was meant to be a strong, modern woman—I played enough of them. I was not meant to conform to Hollywood's standard of beauty. Publicly, of course, I didn't. In every interview when asked, I talked about my naturally fast metabolism, and lied about eating whatever I wanted just so I didn't seem pathetic.

It wasn't a morally acceptable thing to do, since I knew thousands of young girls read or watched those interviews and devoured those lies. Then they'd starve themselves of everything else. I was perpetuating something I hated about the world and was too fucking weak to do anything about it.

"Trust me, you'll be a dessert person once you get some of that," Andrew interjected, his plate already half finished. He hadn't caught on to what the two other women in the room were understanding.

I had a feeling that Duke understood it too. He'd been in the industry long enough. He'd been around me, watched me pick at the salads—dressing on the side—I'd ordered on the way here. There was a very slight narrowing of his brows when he'd glanced at me, but no comment.

I felt uncomfortable with all the attention on me.

Duke's older brother, Tanner, was seated across from me— tall, leaner than Duke, more wrinkled, definitely more cowboy than macho man but no less handsome. Well mannered. I sensed tension between him and Duke.

Anna was eating her pie with slightly less gusto than her husband and looking at me with a touch of sympathy to her gaze.

Duke was looking at me because Duke had been looking at me for most of this evening. Nothing like in the conference room of the Greenstone Security that night that seemed like a hundred years ago.

He was far too good an actor for that hatred to seep in, not since he set foot at the ranch. He played the part of macho man in love very fucking well. Too fucking well.

What happened earlier hadn't helped.

I'd had two margaritas with Harriet, which meant I was slightly drunk as I'd barely eaten today...and because the woman had a strong pour. That meant I forgot that Duke was just acting and I let myself think it was real. Liquor loosened things up inside me in a dangerous way. My tongue in particular. So, when Harriet finally asked how we met, instead of fabricating some story, I told the truth. I did it smiling like an idiot at Duke. Not the movie star smile either. This strange, new, genuine smile that felt itchy on my face.

"Oh, so I needed security for an event and obviously we hired Greenstone because they're the best," I said. "I was getting my makeup done and ready for the event when they brought Duke in to introduce me. He didn't see me at first because he was talking to my publicist. Andre was likely spouting all sorts of rules and NDAs that he always does." I rolled my eyes, thinking of the man who went above and beyond to protect my privacy and his paycheck. I missed him already. This was the longest we'd gone without talking in the ten years we'd been together.

"There were a lot of people in that room. Whatever articles tell you, even articles quoting me," I paused, thinking of all the lies that rolled so easily off my tongue. "*Especially* articles quoting me," I corrected. "Don't believe a freaking word when I say that I'm low maintenance and do my makeup for events. That's just bullshit."

I looked around the room, remembered I was in Montana in front of a family of ranchers likely raised here under God. They most likely didn't like coarse women who swore like sailors. "Pardon my French," I added quickly. Andrew's eyes crinkled with amusement, Harriet grinned, and I carried on.

"So yeah, it takes a village to actually make me look like I do at those events. What I'm trying to say is there were a lot of people in that room, but I only really saw Duke. I know that sounds utterly cliché, and if I were hearing this story I'd think I was full of bullshit." I paused. "Fuck, pardon my French again. Anyway," I waved my hand in Duke's direction. "You made him, you know he's a handsome macho man in a way that no other men in Hollywood or real life are actually macho men." I glanced at Tanner. "Well, apparently they're like this in this family or just in Montana."

He grinned. "Just this family, darlin'."

I nodded. "Yes, well it makes sense, seeing the lineage. You're from a bloodline of stone-cold hotties. Anyway. It was something more than being attractive, because I'd been around many attractive men in my career and I wasn't impressed easily. Duke impressed me because..." I trailed off, lingering in my memory far too long, thinking of the way his gaze had hit me. "He seemed like the most real person I'd met maybe ever."

I paused again to take another sip of my margarita—because I was becoming too sober and this was getting too real—*and* I had to finish. The air beside me was weird, considering Duke was occupying that air and he'd gone still. I chose to ignore that. "Of course, this scared the sh—life out of me. I decided it was far too scary to be real so I proceeded to act like I do to anyone else." I paused again. "Cold. Professional. A little superior." I glanced around the room. "It's necessary in my business. I've been burned badly a couple of times when I let myself trust people and I've become jaded. I learned to protect myself by crafting a reputation of being...difficult."

Harriet laughed. "We women who are worth it are always difficult, my dear. Makes us more interesting."

I loved Harriet and decided I'd adopt her. Or kidnap her.

I smiled at her and used her encouragement to continue. "So I did to Duke what I do to everyone. I acted like Anastasia Edwards..."

I didn't have an end to this story. Because it did not end happy like a mythical love story. Duke had *not* had the same reaction to me. The world hadn't stopped spinning when he met my eyes. It hadn't been love at first sight. No fireworks. No love. Nothing beyond my cold treatment and his professional distaste.

Love at first sight was not the reason I was sitting here. Murder was.

That day, I'd swallowed my reaction to him and treated him worse than I treated others, if I was honest. I never got over the way I treated him. It had kept me up many nights, self-hatred burning all over my skin. I'd lapsed into fantasies of what might've happened had I been a normal, well-adjusted woman able to be warm and inviting.

Everyone was now looking at me expectantly. "Then what?" Harriet prompted.

I opened my mouth, struggling to find the lie. Where had they all gone? Underneath it all, I was nothing but a lie. But in this house, with these people, I was unable to find a single one.

"Then I saw through her bullshit," Duke said, pulling me into his side, kissing my head. "And I made sure she knew that she couldn't act her way out of everything."

So yeah, that had been a fucking disaster.

Because the drunk version of me had let myself sink into that feeling, until we were called to the dinner table, at least. I'd been shocked sober enough to move quickly and not make eye contact with Duke.

Dinner-table conversation had been easy, with Duke asking about the ranch, his father updating him on things I didn't quite understand. There was definitely tension between Duke and his brother. I was infinitely curious about that, until I reminded myself it was not my place to be curious about such things.

I managed to eat almost an entire plate full of delicious pot roast and mashed potatoes, and all because the tequila needed something to soak it up.

Then came dessert.

And the pie, staring at me, showing me just how fucked up I was, and how I could never sit at a table like this and fit in.

Most people would've just shut the hell up and eaten the piece of damn pie. It was the polite thing to do. But I was not most people. I *wanted* to shut the hell up and eat the damn pie. I couldn't. Physically couldn't. The pie represented the last shred of control I had over my life, my body.

And even my body wasn't mine now. It was Duke's. It was a roadmap of tenderness he'd managed to fake so well that it was seeping inside me.

My words weren't my own, since they were all lies about how much I loved Duke. How he was mine.

And while other men were looking to control my death, my life certainly wasn't mine. My survival was dictated by men.

So yeah, this pie meant a lot more than a break in a long-held diet.

But refusing it turned me into something in the eyes of these friendly, kind people. People who had accepted me into their family like it was easy, like I was someone normal.

Tears crawled from somewhere deep inside my soul to threaten the backs of my eyes. I never cried. Not in real life at least. It was a weak and clichéd form of emotion I'd trained myself against. One thing I could thank my foster parents for—making me determined enough not to give them the satisfaction of my tears.

Their cruelty had made it impossible for me to cry, yet here I was, confronted with naked kindness and it was enough to break me.

Just as the tears were about to fall, a large arm stretched in front of me.

"I'll take her share," Duke said easily. "Trust me, her avoidance of dessert almost made me rethink this whole relationship. But even that couldn't keep me from her."

The way he said it, that the man had just saved me from having to eat the pie—from giving up the last shred of control I had over my life—I almost believed he cared.

Almost.

* * *

I had the ability to feel absolutely full of things one moment and utterly empty the next—the product of an upbringing filled with chaos, pain and fear. I'd perfected the ability to drain myself of those things quickly for survival. For sanity.

Never had that ability been as essential as it was tonight, when I somehow lost myself in the magic that this family—this place— had. Lost myself in strong margaritas. Or maybe let tequila find parts of me that I didn't know I had, a person I didn't know I was.

I was not someone who drank margaritas. Nor was I someone who shared personal details—real personal details, not carefully created—with strangers. I was not a person who pretended to be in a relationship with a macho man to whom I was utterly attracted, and didn't like very much.

Or I liked him too much.

No, I wasn't that person.

But being shown to the room upstairs, beautifully decorated —complete with a four-poster bed, vanity, and en suite—and then kissed on the cheek by Anna, I wanted to be that person. *Desperately.*

But the door closed. Then it was just Duke and me in the room. And I deflated. I emptied. Because the cocktails had worn off, and the façade was no longer required.

He was just the man paid to keep me alive until my testimony.

And I was Anastasia Edwards. Superstar. Bitch.

So I settled into her, even as Duke looked at me the same way he had when I told the story of how we met. Something in his eyes that hadn't been there before. Fire. Interest.

It couldn't affect me.

"Are we staying here the entire time?" I asked, my voice cold, superior, my expression the same.

He furrowed his brows. Surprise first, then more of that distaste that I found comfort in. I couldn't stand him looking at me like he was trying to figure me out. Many men had tried.

Many news organizations, reporters, and fans had tried to do it too. A lot of those people were stupid, lazy, and lacked the right motivation to really figure me out.

Duke was none of those things.

I would take him hating who he thought I was instead of finding out who I really am.

"Yeah. It's not the Four Seasons, but it'll keep a bullet out of that pretty little forehead," he said, voice tight, dripping with disdain.

I didn't let it bounce off me, didn't try to deflect it. I had to let it sink in. I had to find a peace inside all this. This here, this look, this tone was what was real. Everything outside of the door was an act. "You don't like me." I made sure to make the words flat. Not curious. Not hopeful.

"No."

He didn't even pause in his response.

It shouldn't have hurt like it did. Plenty of people disliked me. None of them knew me, which was what I told myself. Duke didn't know me. He knew who I wanted him to know, and he disliked me because I wanted him to.

Regardless, it hurt.

I pursed my lips and folded my arms. "If this is going to be a sticking point, we can arrange for someone else to take your place." Even saying it was an effort. Sure, it would be easier to have a hot stranger who I didn't feel these things for. I wouldn't be battling this inner turmoil. But then I'd have to focus on the reality of the situation. Then I wouldn't have Duke.

His jaw hardened. "Coupla things. I'm fuckin' good at my job. To be fair, every single one at Greenstone is fuckin' good at their jobs. Which means, you'll stay alive if you stay smart." He paused, to be sure it was made known he didn't think I was smart. "I'm also a professional. I don't have to like you to keep you alive."

I bit my lip and his gaze flickered down. He noted that, like it was something more than the nervous gesture it was, his brows furrowing for a beat before he kept speaking.

"Second thing, most of my brothers have wives. Kids. Goes without saying this job comes with more risks than most. Also goes without saying each of those men are pretty fuckin' capable of mitigating risks and danger. But Kitsch is serious. We've gone up against serious. We got our scars from that. We got through. But this fuckin' guy will use anything and anyone to get to you. I don't have a wife or kids to be endangered. So, princess, I don't give a shit if you'd rather someone more *agreeable* to you, you've got me."

That shut me up. Not because he called me princess in a way that was meant to be insulting and patronizing.

No, because just by doing this job, I was putting him in serious danger. Putting the kids of those macho men in danger.

I swallowed lead. "Is there a way that Kitsch could connect their families to me?" I asked, voice small. "Will Greenstone protecting me put them in danger?"

If the answer to that was yes, I'd make my escape in the middle of the night. I'd climb out the fucking window and find my way to a pay phone, call Andre, and figure out another way. I might not like Duke, but I hated myself a lot more. And that self-hatred would become suffocating if a child came to harm, or if the man who murmured soft things to Rosie and looked like she invented oxygen was in danger of losing her.

I was a bitch. Sure. A narcissist. Definitely. But this? No fucking way.

I was so deep in my panic, I didn't realize that Duke hadn't answered and was staring at me again, brows furrowed like last time.

"Answer me," I clipped in my best bitch-tone, uncomfortable with this probing gaze. "Am I putting them in danger or not?"

He jerked, ever so slightly, his face turned cold once more. "No," he said.

I made sure to measure that single word, weigh it to find if I could see a lie. I couldn't. Although, I thought Duke would be someone who could get away with a lie. So I measured who I considered him to be. A good man. One who helped people for a living, but wasn't afraid to do some dark things. He loved his family, was good to his mother, respected his father, and adored his grandmother.

He wouldn't bring me here if there was even a sliver of risk to those in this house.

"Okay," I said.

Then I snatched up my bags and stomped into the bathroom, making sure to close and lock the door behind me.

It was nice, like the rest of the house. Expensive, but it didn't scream at you like my bathroom did. The tile was gleaming. Two sinks, complete with little glass jars of guest soaps and cotton pads. Huge, claw-footed tub situated in front of a window that looked out onto the whole freaking ranch.

Walking over to it, it seemed like it looked over the whole freaking world. They said Montana was Big Sky Country, and for once, *they* weren't full of cliché and bullshit.

I didn't stare at the sky for too long. At its beauty. I couldn't handle looking at that, at something so beautiful when I had ugliness simmering inside of me. So I took a shower in the large shower, used hundreds of dollars' worth of products, donned silk, and commenced my lengthy skincare routine.

It was rude with Duke out there waiting. He likely wanted the shower just as much as I did. He had more rights to it.

But I was done being polite and considerate. I'd done that for a whole night. I was out of practice—meaning I'd never done that in recorded memory. It was exhausting.

Yet it felt...right. Everything felt right amongst Duke's

family. The easy conversation, the laughter, the smiles, Duke's fucking hand on my thigh. Hence me having to wash that feeling off, and replace it with multifarious synthetic versions of me.

Once I felt enough like myself, I opened the door.

I didn't know what I was expecting, an empty room, maybe? Duke sneaking off to his old room—lying to his parents about some fight—or maybe I'd find him sleeping soundly in the bed, owning all the pillows, leaving me to sleep on the large armchair in the corner of the room.

I deserved all those things.

He was sitting in that large armchair.

Shirtless.

Now, I'd had my experience with shirtless men. Handsome shirtless men. Not-so handsome shirtless men. Downright disgusting shirtless men. Most of those experiences involved a paycheck. And if it involved my pleasure, it was unfortunately a mixture of all three.

I didn't always have the opportunity to pick men for pleasure.

But that was another story, one I had paid a lot of money to make sure no one knew.

Plus, Duke shirtless, in that chair, in this house was the *only* story.

Of course I'd known he was cut just by looking at him. And he was. He had a body that men in the business paid thousands for. A body that wasn't from lifting weights or for impressing women. One that was for use.

But it wasn't the body.

It was the marks on it.

The scars.

I usually sought perfection in men so I could pretend I was perfect too. People with scars and imperfections only reminded me of my own.

But Duke was beautiful. With all his pain. I liked that he wasn't perfect. It made him not so terrifying.

He stood when I emerged from the bathroom, and just like I didn't hide the fact I was checking him out, he didn't hide it either. His gaze was physical, painful, from my head to my toes. It lingered on my boobs, where I knew my nipples were peeking out from the silk.

And not because it was cold in here.

He cleared his throat, met my eyes. There was still cold there. But there was something else. Hunger.

A hunger of my own crawled up from the most primal of places. A hunger I knew how to act better than anyone, but one I didn't know how to feel.

We were attracted to each other. That much was obvious. That much, neither of us could hide. But you didn't have to like or respect someone in order to be attracted to them.

I wished I didn't like or respect this man.

Because then I'd have no qualms crossing the distance between us, pressing my expensive silk-clad body against his scarred skin and kissing him. The rest would sort itself out from there. He was a strong man, but he couldn't say no to me. Just like if he did the same thing, I wouldn't say no either. And I was an exceptionally strong woman.

But I did like and respect him, despite my best intentions. So anything that happened between us would be more than just sex. For me, at least.

For a long moment, that possibility danced between us. Crackled. So much so that my thighs clenched in anticipation.

"I'll take the floor," Duke said, breaking the moment, averting his eyes, and focusing on the area right above my head. He severed the moment brutally and quickly.

I glanced from the large, comfortable-looking bed to the wooden, definitely *not* comfortable-looking floor, then to the large, muscled and pissed-off man. I rolled my eyes. "I'm not a chaste Southern Belle, honey. As long as you don't snore or wet the bed, I'm perfectly able to share a bed with you."

I didn't wait for him to agree or argue, I just walked to the bed, threw back the covers and crawled in.

In my mansion in Beverly Hills, along with my vacation homes around the world, I paid small fortunes to have the finest quality bedding in the world. The bedding royalty slept in. Presidents.

These were not the finest linens money could buy. They weren't brand new. They were old. Not in a moth-eaten way, but in a different way. They smelled of laundry detergent and lavender. They were soft from all the times they'd been washed.

They were, quite simply, the finest sheets I'd ever felt.

I made a point not to look at Duke, hating that I didn't have my phone. It hadn't been so clear how much I'd used it as a shield, until I didn't have it. Nor did I have the foresight to snatch up a book from the shelves on the other side of the room.

It would ruin the moment I'd created if I got up to grab one now. So instead, I acted like I was totally okay with lying in a bed that smelled of lavender, on a ranch in Montana, with a man who didn't like me, pretending to his family I was his girlfriend, and not the witness to a high-profile murder he was trying to keep alive.

Duke stared at me a good long while. Maybe he was trying to see through the act, maybe trying to figure out whether the floor was a more sensible option.

I wasn't sure what I hoped for more. I'd never slept with a man. I'd fucked plenty. But sleep was something personal. Intimate. Vulnerable. Something I never shared with anyone.

Not even the man I'd been engaged to. He said he couldn't sleep with another person beside him, as it interrupted his dreams.

The floorboards creaked ever so slightly as Duke crossed the room. The bed depressed with his weight. It was a big bed, so there was a considerable space between us, but the Grand fucking Canyon wouldn't be wide enough.

I held my breath and waited.

For what, I didn't know.

For something.

But nothing came.

Only silence that only a place with a big sky could offer.

5

"GOOD MORNING, SUNSHINE."

I squinted at Harriet, and she had a grin on her face to match the one in her voice. She was wearing a different outfit today, no less fabulous. A long-sleeved leopard print shirt, complemented by the multiple gold necklaces slung around her neck. Both arms were adorned with thick bracelets. She was wearing high-waisted black jeans and heeled boots, for goodness sake. At six in the morning. Not to mention full makeup.

"Hey, sweetie," Anna said, moving from what I guessed was a butler's pantry, warm smile on her face. She also looked arguably as good as Harriet, though a little less glam. She was wearing a denim chambray shirt, big wide belt buckle, and faded jeans. No makeup. Where Harriet looked like a beautiful rock-chick badass, Anna was the beautiful cowgirl badass. Their clothes helped, but more than anything that beauty was inside them.

I envied it.

"Morning," I said, feeling more out of place than ever. I was an early riser. Something in me was always wide awake before dawn. Maybe it was because sleep didn't give me rest nor respite like it did with other people.

It was obvious why, because throughout my childhood I always went to sleep hungry, scared, and powerless.

Sure, I still went to bed hungry these days, but I'd been so sure that when I had all the control I thought money and fame would give me it would fill me up. It would give me what I needed to sleep through the night.

Turns out, it didn't work that way.

Especially when you slept next to a man like Duke.

"How'd you sleep?" Anna asked, handing me a cup of coffee.

I took the cup happily, inhaling long and deep. I could tell this was good coffee—I was somewhat of a coffee snob—plus, I recognized the fancy machine on the counter.

"Great," I said after my first sip.

It wasn't a lie either. I might've awoken at my regular time, but it was the first time since I'd closed my eyes the night before, which was not the norm for me. I was up multiple times in the night, mostly because I was convinced I heard a noise, that there was someone watching me sleep. The little poor, hungry girl in me had been in charge when buying my six-bedroom mansion. Bigger meant better. Bigger meant I'd made it and it could swallow up my entire past.

In reality, to a woman with an active imagination who was waiting for everything to be taken away from her, it was another beast. A huge tomb where my murderer could hide in the shadows.

It didn't matter that I paid for the best security system money could buy, and lived in a gated compound with a twenty-four-hour security attendant. Fear didn't respond to logic like that. So I'd get at best, a full three hours, the rest of the night was spent wandering around the house, looking for my demise. Then, I'd turn all the lights on, read, or write, or do anything to distract myself from how alone and afraid I was.

I'd never felt safer with Duke beside me. It turned out my sleeping self didn't have the reservations I had about the distance we needed behind closed doors. I'd woken up sprawled on his expansive chest, one leg cocked and thrown over the two of his, my forehead on his large pec, using it like it was a down fucking pillow.

And I was not a fucking cuddler, which obviously wasn't a surprise. No way did I want to find comfort in other people, when they were the ones to give me all my scars in the first place. You never got close enough to let someone cut you—physically or emotionally. I'd done both with Duke. I'd just been glad I'd been able to extricate myself from the situation without Duke waking up.

"The boy still asleep?" Harriet asked.

I nodded, thinking of the way he'd looked sleeping.

She eyed me, much too sharp a gaze for this time in the morning, for this time in my life. "Needs it," she said finally. "I don't imagine that boy's had a good night's sleep in years, not with all that running around war zones and cities filled with miscreants and misogynists."

I almost choked on my coffee with her words. Both because they were funny, right on the point, and filled with love and sadness.

"Yeah," I said, swallowing the coffee. "He needs it."

"Help yourself to some breakfast," Amy offered, gesturing to the breakfast bar.

It was spread with enough food to feed a small army. Or a large ranch, I guessed. Scrambled eggs. Toast. Bacon. Fresh fruit. Pastries. Fucking chia seed pudding. All artfully placed like I had my chef do for me for an at-home photoshoot I'd done a few years ago.

Not that I actually ate like that. I had a celery juice, a coffee, and a cigarette right up until I quit. Then it was just the juice and coffee. Egg whites and whole wheat toast after a grueling workout. No butter. No sugar. Nothing on this bar.

"And before you politely refuse or nibble on one spoon full of chia pudding...don't," Harriet said. "You need to eat like a human being today. You're gonna need your strength if you're gonna go out on the ranch."

My head snapped up and my gaze went between the women. "I'm going to go out on the ranch?" I couldn't keep the child-like excitement from my voice.

Something moved in both the women's faces. Surprise, maybe. They'd expected me to turn my nose up it, no doubt.

"We've got a spare horse, and we're always looking for a spare pair of hands," Amy said. "If you're up to it."

I snatched up a croissant. "Oh, I'm up to it."

* * *

Duke had slept in.

He never slept in. Being in a family of ranchers meant you woke with the sun every morning, some mornings before it. There were no lazy teenage years for him where he woke at noon and lounged in front of the TV for hours.

He'd never done that.

And he'd never resented his family nor his life. Firstly, because he didn't know any different. Secondly, because he loved his family, he loved the land, and he loved the horses. He loved the way the sky woke up, being able to witness that. He'd loved ranching because it was in his blood. But there was also an itch inside him, a hunger to experience different things, to live a different life to his father.

His father was happy. Even through the hard years, hard

years on the land, and other harder years in his marriage. His parents loved each other fiercely, and they'd taught him that. They also taught him that love took work, hence the reason he hadn't been all that eager to fall in love. He didn't need the work. Duke had plenty of work. Inside himself. Because to sate that hunger, scratch that itch, he'd left home with the idea he'd spend a few years serving his country, come back satisfied. Come back ready for the big sky, the stars, the simple life. Maybe for the complication of a woman.

But as his grandmother said: "When you make plans, God takes a look, and she laughs her fucking ass off."

Which was what happened. It turned out, he was good at things in a warzone on the other side of the world. Things he didn't want to be good at, but he was nonetheless. Then he was contracted to a part of the military that technically didn't exist, doing things that never happened.

It fucked him up, you could say. Fucked him up so bad that he knew he'd never be able to live simply. Never be able to wake up and marvel at those Montana sunrises. Never be able to look his mother in the eye and pretend to be the son she used to have.

Good thing he met the right people and Keltan gave him the job, one that satisfied him. Or at least distracted him from how fucked up he really was. How much he missed home.

He went for holidays, Christmas, birthdays, but never for long. There was always a time limit on his stays, when whispers would sneak into his dreams, reminding himself of what he'd done, who he was now. Work was a good excuse. He knew it hurt his mother, worried his father, amused his grandmother, and pissed off his brother. But it was what it was.

Fuck, he'd never even told them he'd almost died in a hospital after getting shot by Lexie's stalker. No way would he put that on their shoulders. He'd chosen this life and he wasn't going to subject his family to it.

He hadn't wanted to come here, to pretend once more, especially with a woman he didn't like, but it was for the greater good. He could control shit here. Even after all these years, he knew the land like the back of his hand.

He'd been dreading bringing Anastasia to his family, only to watch them pretend to like her and silently judge him thinking this was the woman he'd picked to bring home to his family.

But then she'd surprised him.

To say the fucking least.

Upon setting her thousand-dollar shoes in the dirt of his home, she'd turned from ice-queen bitch to...a total goof.

The change jarred him, amused him, and hit him right in his fucking dick. And he continued watching her with his grandmother, get drunk off two margaritas—but two of his grandmother's margaritas equaled about five anywhere else—and spout a story about how they met.

All of it was true, but seen through a different lens. A different woman. One that he would be fucking happy to bring home to his family, into his bed.

Then she'd changed, put on that mask again. She was *playing* the bitch. It was the best role of her life, but she was a goof underneath.

He liked that.

He liked that she snored quietly in her sleep, and had rolled over and clung to him like a barnacle after she drifted off.

Duke was not a cuddler. When girls stayed the night—when he'd had a girlfriend that stayed over—he'd wait for them to sleep before he gently extricated them. He couldn't sleep while being touched, barely handled a woman in the bed. Which was why his relationships never lasted long.

But for whatever reason—exhaustion surely—before he could think about getting Anastasia off him, he'd passed the fuck out.

And woke up in an empty bed.

Late.

He knew this because his internal clock told him so, as did the late morning light peeking through a crack in the curtains.

It amused and surprised him that Anastasia's side of the bed was neatly made up. It still smelled like her. Not that expensive perfume she wore. No, just her.

She was neat. That was a surprise. He'd clocked her as a spoiled bitch who was so used to having someone clean up after her she'd forgotten how.

But the bed was made.

Her suitcase was propped away, closed, no clothes strewn about.

Once he'd gotten up and gone to the bathroom, he saw her products neatly lined up. A fuck of a lot of expensive bottles. She'd lined his up too. Not that there were a lot of them. But they were expensive. LA had rubbed off on him.

Duke felt that in his dick too. Their things on the same counter, toothbrushes beside each other.

It was fucking insane.

He'd never felt the urge for domestic shit. Not once. And especially not with her.

Something to do with being home. Seeing his parents. Playing the part of a couple.

That must've been it.

He tried to convince himself of that.

"You're up," his grandmother exclaimed. "I was worried that you'd never come out."

She was already handing him coffee, steaming from the fresh pot she'd no doubt brewed because she somehow knew he was awake. The walls were thick here, the house was big so she hadn't heard him. He'd stopped trying to figure out his grandma and just appreciated all the things about her that no one could explain. Although, there wasn't much about her anyone could explain. Her kooky, weird personality was something her straight-laced Baptist parents had puzzled over for years, but hadn't ever tried to change her.

Neither had his grandfather, who'd adored his "Kooky." And when he'd died far too early, dimming a little light in her eyes, she never lost herself. That was his grandmother, the strongest person he knew. Duke had encountered many hard-asses in his life, brave, cruel, and scarred men who'd done things that most people would run from. But none of them were as strong as his eighty-year-old grandmother.

"Your woman is out riding with your brother and father. They've got some cattle to check on out at the edge of the ranch," she said.

He almost spit his coffee out upon that. Trying not to, he'd damn near choked on it and spent the next minute coughing.

His grandmother watched him with amusement. She'd no doubt timed that little piece of news for this precise reason.

"She's out *riding*?" Duke repeated, trying to envision that.

She nodded. "Surprised me too, for about a minute. But then I remembered that Western where she played some cowgirl criminal. Great flick by the way. Everyone said she'd used a double, but to my eyes, old as they are, I thought she could ride, had that natural way about her. And, as usual, I was right. She lit up like a Christmas tree when they offered it." She took another sip of her —most likely Irish—coffee. "Don't think either of them expected her to say yes, of course. They were just bein' polite. And I rather enjoyed them trying to swallow their tongues when she saddled her horse and didn't need help, certainly didn't ask for it. Nothing like she seems, that one."

"No, she isn't," Duke said, half to himself. He was pissed that he'd slept in and had missed out on seeing that.

He also hated the way his grandmother spoke. She accepted everyone for who they were—didn't have a nasty bone in her body—but her respect didn't come easy. Duke had dreaded the day when he'd bring a woman home to his family. His parents were kind, easygoing, and just ready for him to settle down. They'd accept damn near anyone as long as she wasn't wanted for murder or hated animals.

But his grandmother. He knew it would kill him if she didn't give her blessing. And that was with a *real* woman. *His* real woman. He sure as fuck had been dreading seeing his grandmother's reaction to bringing home the surly, rude movie star for whom he was using everything he had to pretend he could love.

But it didn't come. That expertly hid disappointment he'd been expecting, he'd been bracing for. His grandmother was wearing it, right on her face. She liked Anastasia. More importantly, she respected her.

It made him happy—then pissed him right off. Because Anastasia wasn't his. And he'd never be able to measure up to this, once he finally did bring someone home.

Something in his chest pricked at the thought of that, at another woman meeting his family, telling some story of how they met. It didn't feel right. No one would be able to replicate the night they'd had last night.

"Me and Anastasia," he said, looking up. "It's not..." he trailed off. He couldn't tell his grandmother, whom he'd never lied to in his life, that this was all a sham. Mostly because it would put her in danger, but also because he couldn't do that to her. "It's not all what it seems," he finished.

His grandmother grinned. "Of course not. I'd be disappointed if it was."

* * *

"Well, hello cowboy," I said, making sure to sound sarcastic and cruel. It took effort, considering he wore the *shit* out of that cowboy hat.

Most of the men at the ranch did.

Obviously, Duke's father and brother had the same macho-men genes, so they looked the part in theirs. And the ranch hands, the same. They only had a handful, which I understood was unusual for a ranch this size. But what the fuck did I know?

Mostly they were older, grisly, graying and handsome as all hell. There was one young boy, barely able to shave and unable to put his eyes back into his head at seeing me. That was, until Tanner smacked him over the head and murmured something in his ear. Then, the rest of the morning, the men studiously made sure not to stare too long or act like I was a famous actress.

Nor did Andrew or Anna. They didn't treat me like they were trying to impress me. Or get something from me. They treated me like I was Duke's woman. With respect. I did know they were somewhat surprised that I could ride, and could do it well. They were impressed.

I liked that, being able to keep up with real-life ranchers.

I was only able to do so because it was a real-life rancher that trained me how to ride. That was after various arguments with my agent, my director, and head of the studio, who did not want the liability of their lead actress falling off a horse and suing them.

As I was known to do, I threw a hissy fit and got my way.

Which I regretted after my first lesson with my rancher. He was an old man with a hell of a moustache and an attitude to match. He made it clear he was only there for the paycheck, and the added bonus of watching me fail. He trained me hard, without sympathy, and with a healthy dose of dislike.

It was the only way a woman like me could be trained, to prove a man wrong.

And I did—after breaking my wrist, dislocating my shoulder, and putting the movie behind by three months. The studio would've been pissed off, had the movie not done so freaking well, with the publicity of my fall only helping the movie earn top spot at the box office.

I still sent Kyle—my trainer—an email here and there. Sometimes he returned them, other times not.

That I'd earned the accolades for my horsemanship seemed like an important thing at the time. But this, out here under the country sky, breathing in the dirt, and herding cattle with men that were real men—that meant more.

A lot more.

I would've stayed out for much longer, despite the ache in my thighs and my protesting ass, but Tanner decided to bring me back.

"Before Duke skins me alive for stealing away his woman," he said with a grin.

I did my best to grin back and not tell him his brother would most likely thank him. Instead I asked him a question. "Why aren't you married?"

He looked sufficiently taken aback. And I should've stopped there. It wasn't my place to ask and I never usually wanted to know such details about people. I did small talk for appearances only. But I wanted to know this. The past of this man, the empty ring finger, the reason behind the hardness in his eyes when he looked at his brother.

"I mean, you're a nice guy," I continued, unable to stop myself. "Easy on the eyes. Got a good family. That counts for a lot most places, except Hollywood of course, where your family only matters if they own a studio or an island in the Caribbean," I said. "But here, in the country, I'm thinking there is a shortage of men, and women aren't stupid—if your mother and grandmother are anything to go by. Smart women usually find good men. Hold on to them."

My stomach lurched ever so slightly when I said that. I considered myself a smart woman. I'd found a good man, despite the way he spoke to me. I wanted to hold on to him. But there was no way for a woman like me to even find a grip.

Tanner chuckled, but the sound was forced, his eyes faraway. "Ah, good men are much easier to stay with, I think. Or they don't let good women get away. Either way, I don't think I'm a good man, since *I* let a good woman get away."

I waited for more, interested in the sadness and loss in his voice. We rode in silence for a few beats.

"You can't just leave me hanging like that," I snapped. "I'm an actress. I need an ending."

He glanced at me. "Ah, if there's an ending you want, I've got that. Although I don't think it's all as exciting as what you're used to. Wish it was, if I was honest. But life isn't all that exciting." He paused for a long moment, looking out ahead of him. We were coming up on the ranch and I wanted to slow down so we could continue talking. "She was my high school sweetheart, cliché I know, but when you know, you know." He shrugged. "I knew. And I'm not like my brother. I don't have that yearning for different places, for a different life."

I didn't miss the resentment, anger there.

"I'm happy to be born on this land, work it, and die on it," he continued. "It's in my blood. I don't want to know anything else. The plan was to move here, build on land our parents set aside and...I don't know, do the cliché thing—kids. Family. Life."

I pulled back the reins ever so slightly, and Tanner matched my stride. Even though there was pain in his voice, he seemed to want to continue as well.

"But it was hard for her to get pregnant," he said. "We had

problems. Went to all kinds of doctors, were told all kinds of shit. It took us two years to conceive, and less than two months to lose our first. Then just a month for the second. It killed me. Losing them, sure. But losing Maggie too, I didn't understand."

He scrubbed at the stubble on his chin. "Fuck, I'm just a rancher. Just a man. I don't know what it's like to go through that. I'm ashamed to say it all got too hard for me so I just...checked out. Didn't give her the support she deserved. Worked too much. Then one day, came home, she was gone. I wasn't surprised. The only thing that surprised me? That she didn't do it sooner."

There was pain in his voice. Real, visceral pain. It cut through even my shields. I thought I wasn't capable of true sympathy.

We'd ridden to the barn, and various fenced-in areas that were for cattle, and a circular area for training horses.

The main business of the ranch was cattle. And it was a big business. Tanner told me they also specialized in breaking in horses and selling them off at a huge profit, as well as growing their own feed, which meant they cultivated and harvested that too.

The morning itself was enough to show me how hard this life was. I was envious, though. Of the simplicity of it, working with nature. There was an honesty in the work that I didn't think could be replicated in many other places in the world. Especially not in my industry.

I had no idea what urged Duke away from this place, especially when he looked so damn good in the hat, leaning against the fences, watching us approach. I ached to know. To find out who he was. But that wasn't part of the deal here.

Hence the sarcastic greeting after we'd all dismounted. Andrew had ridden ahead of us to meet with a vet. He emerged from the barn just as we tied off our horses. Tanner and Duke's father had fallen in step with me as I approached Duke.

"I'm not a cowboy anymore," he said in response to my greeting. His voice was tight. Clipped. He took the hat off and placed it on a pole on the fence, making a point, no doubt.

Andrew stepped forward, a sad smile on his face, hand outstretched. "Ah, son, unfortunately it doesn't work that way. Some things we don't want to be, we can change. With work. With distance. Violence." His eyes flickered to me for a second. "Love."

My stomach dipped. Not in a good way. Like I was going to be sick all over my borrowed cowboy boots.

He looked back to his son. "But other things, you can't change no matter how much you want. Some things are in your blood. Sorry to tell you, son, but no matter how long you're away from the ranch, from a horse, from the dirt, it doesn't matter. You're always a cowboy." He didn't wait for Duke to take the hat. He put it right on Duke's head, clapped his cheek, and walked away with the saddest grin I'd ever seen.

6

THE REST of the day passed quickly, in a blur of horses, of food—most of which I even ate—and of aching arms from helping in all manner of ranch work.

It ruined my manicure.

My hair.

The makeup I'd carefully applied before coming down to breakfast.

And I loved it.

The thin coating of dirt covering my body. The slight pinkness to my cheeks thanks to the sunshine and exertion. The aches in parts of my body even the city's best trainer couldn't reach.

I loved every part about this day, as it was the best one in recorded memory.

I'd studiously avoided Duke the entire day after the hat incident, but he was always hovering someplace. Watching. I didn't know if he was expecting someone to come and try to murder me or he didn't trust me with his family. Maybe both. But I didn't look in his direction, especially because of the cowboy hat and the entire look. It really worked for him. That, and I didn't need the dislike in his gaze to ruin my perfect day.

To ruin my act.

I was playing his girlfriend, the one that his family welcomed quickly, joked with easily, and treated me with respect and kindness.

I learned that his father didn't speak much, but had a dry sense of humor and a kind heart. His brother was cheeky, but with sad eyes and a broken heart. His mother was a mix of soft and hard. She worked alongside the men, and she was kind to me but I had no doubt that if she thought I'd broken Duke's heart, she'd turn nasty for her son in an instant. I loved that about her.

And Harriet.

Well, she was one of the most interesting people I'd ever met, which was saying something. My career had sent me all over the world, working with some of the most brilliant, eccentric and unique people in the industry. Most of them were a nightmare to be around, of course.

Harriet was not a nightmare to be around. She was warm, insane, funny, and I decided I wanted to be her when I grew up.

I decided that I wanted this family, even after one day with them. I wanted this to be real. And of course, I'd wanted Duke since the first moment I'd seen him. My story hadn't been an act.

I could purchase anything money could buy, though I'd never be able to have this. Denial worked best, so I did my best not to let that voice scream at me from the depths of my soul.

Around Harriet, it was little more than a whisper.

I'd showered off the dirt of the day, as much as I wanted to let it sink into my bloodstream. I'd reapplied a fresh coat of makeup, because even the best day with the best people wouldn't change my need for the mask, nor change years of dysfunction.

I'd dressed in black slacks and a black tank. Maybe a little dressy for the family dinner that Anna wouldn't let me help with, but Harriet seemed to approve, since it seemed she didn't give a shit about the fact we were on a ranch and dressed like she was about to go out for dinner in New York.

Everyone else was out doing things so it was the two of us enjoying cocktail hour in the house's amazing living room. It was vast. High-ceilinged. Exposed wood. Tan leather sofas covered in amazing throws and pillows. A giant fireplace. Bookshelves reaching the ceiling. Photos everywhere. Huge windows facing the ranch.

Harriet and I sat in armchairs that faced the window, enjoying the view and the company. Well, that was me at least. Harriet was most likely used to the view, since she'd been born here. That this ranch had been in Duke's family for generations impressed the heck out of me. I ached to google the history of it, but my phone had been confiscated and Duke had warned me against any kind of Internet surfing.

I wondered if the case had entered the news-cycle yet. Duke said that the attorney's office was trying their best to keep me anonymous but I wasn't sure how long that would last. Even with the best security company in the city—and arguably the country—I didn't like my odds. If Kitsch was as bad as everyone was saying, I didn't think I'd stay anonymous for long. And despite my ignorance on the man, I figured that Duke wouldn't have taken the drastic measure of constructing this lie and deceiving his family if it weren't vital.

The lie sat heavily in the bottom of my stomach like a stone, despite being practiced at deceit. My career was founded on it. It was part and parcel of the job and the overall politics of Hollywood. You didn't get to where I was by being honest and good.

I'd been sure that nothing would bother me, would penetrate the exterior I'd worked so hard to create. Especially not in one single day. But it had. It wasn't even the day. It was one fricking minute of being in the company of these people.

"We need to get a photo for Instagram," Harriet said, tapping at her phone and jerking me out of my head. The case was bright pink with black text reading "Cute but Psycho."

She was anything but predictable.

"You have Instagram?" I asked, dumbfounded with the eighty-year-old woman even knowing what Instagram was.

But I shouldn't have been surprised. Not with Harriet.

She rolled her eyes. "Of course I have Instagram. I have twenty thousand followers." She looked up. "That doesn't mean much considering your millions. But I think it's pretty fucking fabulous."

I blinked rapidly, caught up in Harriet's entire energy. "It is fucking fabulous," I agreed.

She regarded herself in the viewfinder of the camera, pouting, turning her head this way and that, winking at the camera.

"All right, I look great, let's do this," she said.

Never in my life did I let people boss me around. Well, that was a lie. Early on in my life, I did it because I had no other choice. My foster parents had controlled my food, my shelter, my hygiene. So I trained myself to obey them, even if every part of me rebelled against it.

It was a valuable skill early on in my career. But the second I had enough power behind my name, all of that stopped.

Until I watched someone get murdered, of course. Then all my agency was taken from me.

Obviously I was used to the picture thing. Everyone who approached me didn't really want to talk to me. They wanted physical evidence of the interaction. They wanted bragging rights, they wanted likes for their social media. I wasn't a person to them, I was social currency.

With Harriet, it was different. I was a *person* to her. If she had found me somehow lacking, I'd know. She wasn't rude or cruel enough to treat me with disapproval, but I'd felt her respect, treasured it, and I wanted to preserve this moment in any way I could.

So I posed for the picture.

I even copied her gesture and flipped the bird to the camera.

She regarded the picture. "Yeah, that's a good one," she muttered.

I looked at the screen. She was right, it was a good one. I'd posed for millions of photos in my life. In almost every single one of them, I looked beautiful. Flawless. Empty. Something about me flipping the bird at the camera next to an eighty-year-old woman in a sequined crop top and red lipstick was different. I looked...alive. I was a person, not just an instrument for likes or social cache.

"What the fuck is going on?" a low boom demanded.

Both of us jerked with the aggression in the familiar voice.

Duke didn't give either of us time to respond but stormed across the room to snatch the phone from Harriet.

"Weren't you taught not to do that as a toddler?" Harriet demanded. "I should know, since I taught you to never snatch a thing from a woman, unless it's her heart and she's willing."

Duke, of course, didn't answer her. He was too busy fuming at Harriet's phone. He tapped at the screen then looked up to me.

"We're talking. Now."

Harriet scowled. "I don't remember my grandson resembling a Neanderthal the last time I saw him," she said. "And the fact you're fucking with my Instagram engagement is basically elder abuse."

Duke didn't even glance at his grandmother. "Anastasia, now."

Again, I shouldn't have listened. Should not have obeyed. It must've been something to do with this family. Something in their genes. Because instead of telling him to fuck off, like Harriet was doing with a well-practiced glare, I stood. I walked toward Duke and let him usher me out of the room.

The walk to the bedroom was silent—which was saying something considering the living area was in a whole other wing of this giant homestead.

I refused to say anything because I was so damn pissed off at myself, and Duke by proxy. I guessed that he didn't say anything because he was too busy simmering in his macho-man fury.

He was ready to say plenty the second we set foot into "our" room.

"What the fuck do you think you were doing?" he growled, advancing on me the second the door slammed shut.

I didn't retreat, though I wanted to, though every single fucking cell in my body told me to. There was a time when I retreated from men, submitted, bowed down. There were plenty of times I did that.

And I vowed I'd never do it again.

So I didn't.

But it was hard.

Especially since Duke made sure to get right up in my face, so I could taste the mint on his breath, smell his cologne, mixed with the scent of him pressed into my skin. His fury covered me like a sheen of sweat, almost sticky. Uncomfortable.

I jutted my chin up. "Your grandma wanted a photo."

His eyes flared, whether in fury of the response or the fact I wasn't cowering or submitting. "You do realize that fucking photo could get you dead?" he hissed. "Could put my entire fucking family in danger? I know you realize that because you're smart. But you just can't fucking help yourself."

It was all back in those words. The resentment, the hatred.

"I couldn't say no to Harriet," I protested, covering my hurt with some resentment of my own. "I want her to like me." I hadn't meant to say the last part, but it slipped out.

Duke's face changed ever so slightly. The anger slipped, almost fell right off his face, before he got hold of it. He leaned in even closer, so our faces almost touched, lips almost brushed. "She doesn't need to like you," he whispered. "None of them do. You're not here to make a good impression on my family. You're here to stay alive. You're here until the trial. Then you go. You're never going to see them again, so it doesn't matter who the fuck likes you."

He hovered close to me for a second longer, to make his point, to make sure his words hit the mark.

Satisfied, he stepped back and left me standing in the middle of the room. Alone with the words. With the truth. The pain.

* * *

The smart thing would've been to stay in the room.

Well, no.

The smartest thing would've been to pack my bag and fucking hitchhike off this damn ranch, even though there was a high chance a crime lord could locate me and murder me so I couldn't testify against him.

I was a survivor.

I liked my odds at figuring out a way to stay alive outside of this situation because it was quickly becoming more dangerous than being on the run.

It might've been my dramatic nature to think that.

Yes, it might've been dramatic, but it didn't feel that way. It felt like a noose tightening around my neck, having to act like I had a connection with Duke in front of his family, having to act like he was nothing more than a man employed to protect me.

Which was the lie?

I couldn't tell.

Hence me not staying in the room.

And not running either.

Well, not off the ranch at least.

But far enough so I could breathe.

I didn't run into anyone on my escape, thanks to the size of the house and the fact everyone was doing other things. It was a good thing too, since I feared I might break down in tears, or worse, tell the truth to whichever of Duke's family I encountered.

I veered away from the outbuildings, the barn, and what I now knew were the ranchers' quarters. I walked in the direction of the horizon, hoping it might somehow swallow me up, or at least suck away all of this pain.

I walked for a while until my already aching muscles protested. But I didn't stop.

The air smelled of dirt, of sunshine, of something I couldn't describe.

There was nothing, as far as the eye could see. Nothing but nature. Mountains. The ranch was a speck in the distance. It was a surprise that I hadn't encountered anyone on my escape. But not really, I guessed. People weren't milling around waiting to become a secondary character in my story. I wasn't the center of the world here.

I was like the ranch, a speck. Life went on. There were things to do. I hadn't been here long enough to understand the kind of life that Duke's family lived, but I knew it was hard, simple, which didn't make much room for drama.

Pretty much the opposite of my life.

It showed me how empty my life was, despite the fact that every second of my days used to be accounted for, scheduled. I "worked" as much as they did, but not in the same way.

I had no family.

No true friends, except Andre.

There would be millions who'd mourn if I died, candlelight vigils, countless social media posts, news stories.

But no one would grieve after the news cycle was done.

That was not the case with Duke's family.

The family that I had been weak enough to let myself think I was a part of. After one day. One fucking day and I'd let myself believe the act, let myself fall just a little for all of them. How could I handle the months this might turn into?

I hadn't noticed that I'd sunk down to my knees, but it made sense, since I was feeling so fucking temporary, I needed the permanence of the dirt. I needed to feel connected to the earth, to something more than me.

Which was no excuse for sinking so far into self-pity I didn't realize that it wasn't only career criminals that were trying to kill me. There were other things out here in the world that didn't care what I'd witnessed, only that I was trespassing on land I didn't know.

The movement out of the corner of my eye was what caught my attention, maybe some kind of internal warning that danger was near.

The snake was staring at me with interest.

I didn't really have the same interest, at all. And I had no idea how I was meant to act with a snake staring at me.

So I just stared back.

I remembered the movie where I'd played a heroine in a situation similar to this. Granted, it had been an apocalyptic movie where animals had taken over the earth and snakes had evolved to have venom that could kill humans instantly, but still. In the movie, the snake and I had a long and intense stare off. The director had wanted it to be me staring death in the face and having death measure me for my worthiness.

In the movie, of course, I was destined to save the human race, so the snake let me be.

This was not a movie.

I was not destined to save anyone. I didn't have enough worthiness to tip any scales, so the snake struck.

* * *

He had been too hard on her.

Duke knew that the second she'd recoiled from his words as if he'd struck her. Although, she'd recovered quickly. Managed to wear the mask that he now understood was her second skin. She had managed to pretend those words hadn't hit, hadn't drawn blood.

But too late. He'd seen what she didn't want him to, what she'd made sure was invisible to the world—her vulnerability.

It took everything he had not to go to her, not to take her in his fucking arms and comfort her.

He had practice being cruel, shutting off emotions. It was a survival tactic in a world that used emotions against you.

And fuck if he didn't feel emotions for her.

Before they'd set foot on this ranch, those emotions were nothing but dislike, varying degrees of it, and that niggling fucking need he had to claim her, one that only made him dislike her more.

But then she'd changed. She'd morphed into something else entirely. Her falsity melted off her face with an ease that Duke didn't think Anastasia even realized. It was so drastic that it shook Duke, right to the core. Something in the dirt here, something in the air, had melted everything cold from her skin and showed her for who she was.

His parents loved her. His grandmother adored her. And his brother was almost in love with her. Only because the rest of his love was reserved for the woman who left him.

Despite what it seemed like on the surface, this was not normal.

His family were good people, polite. But they didn't warm to people that easily, especially outsiders. Not like they'd done to Anastasia. They saw everything in her that Duke hadn't, but that was because she *showed* them. She seemed unable to hold on to the mask she'd worn in Hollywood.

And that was fucking dangerous.

Because Duke had already been attracted to her.

Even before all of this.

She was a fucking knockout.

He was only human.

But her personality had worked against that. She had been rude, snobby, and cold, not enough to soften his hard-on—she was that beautiful. Forget your morals, forget your *name* beautiful.

Duke had managed, of course. To hold on to the healthy dislike instead of grasp the attraction.

That was until she'd set foot on the ranch.

Yeah, she'd changed then.

And everything turned into a battle. As if he wasn't already fighting being back at this place.

Seeing how quickly she took to it was torture.

No, sleeping next to her with that fucking little slip of a nightgown, *that* was torture, and that was saying something, coming from a man who'd done the things he'd done, who'd survived the things he had. Even more so when she fell into unconsciousness and came to him in his sleep.

He waited for it.

He fucking craved it.

And he didn't gently push her away like he should've. Fuck no. He held on to her. He sniffed her fucking hair. And then he fought every instinct he had to stop himself from waking her up with his lips on her neck, with his lips on her panties.

So he was angry when he saw her taking that photo with his grandmother. It was stupid, yeah. But Duke had also spent his

entire life with his grandmother. He knew how convincing she
could be. Shit, when he was twelve, she'd managed to get him to
steal fireworks and let them off in the middle of the night as a
punishment to someone who'd dared offer her a senior discount
at the store. He'd obviously taken all of the blame for that.

So yeah, he knew that things could easily get out of hand
with her.

He wasn't angry about the photo, the fact that the simple
thing could've put Anastasia and his entire family in danger.

That made him pissed off, sure.

But what made him furious was seeing Anastasia with his
grandmother, his family. Seeing her ride side by side with his
brother and talk to him with an ease that was impossible for
Duke. Her warmth with them. It seeped from her. It was as easy
as breathing. He watched her fight it at the start, for about the
first ten minutes, but then she stopped. She gave them all of her.
The parts that no one had ever seen.

But not Duke.

The only time he got her was in her sleep.

That should've been enough. Fuck, that was too much.

But he was a greedy fuck.

He didn't just want that.

He wanted all of her.

To compensate for wanting that, he was cruel. Too cruel.

And he felt bad. Terrible.

But he also knew if he turned around to apologize, he'd do
that by fucking her. So he didn't turn around and apologize.

He stormed down the stairs, his intention to get on a horse
and ride away all these fucking feelings.

His grandmother had other ideas.

She was small in stature, but she managed to bar his way
pretty well. No one in his family faced off against his maternal
grandmother.

Duke was tempted, but he wasn't that angry or suicidal.

She folded her arms and raised a brow in that practiced way of hers. "That was interesting," she said mildly.

Duke knew he deserved more than that, a fuck of a lot more. A tongue lashing that he knew his grandmother was more than capable of giving. He was brought up to treat women right. The way he cursed at Anastasia, the way he spoke to her was not right. But it was his only option.

He inhaled. "You know how I said there was more to this than it seemed?"

His grandmother nodded.

"Well, this is part of the more," he continued. "And I need you to trust me when I say we can't have photos of her here. No one beyond the family can know she's here."

His grandmother regarded him in the way she looked at everyone. Never a mere glance. Never half interest. She was always dissecting you, always seeing beyond. She stepped forward and cupped his cheek. "My beautiful boy. I may not know many things about the man the world has turned you into, but he's still my blood. My grandson. And he's still a good man, even if he acts like an asshole. I trust you. I trust that this is just a little bit of trouble, because you've always known how to bring it home."

He couldn't help but chuckle at that, despite the situation being not funny at all.

She was right. Of all the things that had changed about him it was that he liked to chase trouble around. But this wasn't stealing his father's truck and crashing into the local liquor store.

"I'm all for trouble, honey," his grandmother continued. "But I'm also aware that there's more to that girl than meets the eye, which I know you see because you're not a stupid man. What you might not have seen is just how soft she is underneath all that. And us women, we like a hard man in many ways." She waggled her eyebrows. "But we need to make sure they know when to be soft. So my boy, don't disappoint me by bruising that woman."

She squeezed his chin ever so slightly, a mix between a caress and a warning before she stepped out of his way.

"Now go. Ride out all that testosterone so you can come back and be the man I know you are."

"I love you, Grandma," he said, surprising himself.

She grinned. "Join the club."

* * *

He was coming back from the ride when he saw her. Duke knew it was her the second the figure cut on the horizon, and the second the pit of his stomach found a new basement.

He instantly urged his horse faster. And as if she sensed the same thing Duke did, she obeyed.

The sun was setting, and he might've found it beautiful had fear not been yanking at his throat the closer he got. It became more and more apparent she was injured. It was a skill that Duke was forced to acquire—to note casualties from a distance.

Although they were oceans away from the war zone where he acquired this skill, there were still many threats in the Montana countryside. His first thought was that somehow Kitsch had found her already, but he quickly discarded it.

Beyond the fact that there was no way to connect her to the ranch and there was no way for a stranger to get on without someone noting it, there would be no way she would be walking, even stumbling if that were the case.

She'd be dead in the grass.

That thought was a punch in the gut.

Duke all but leapt off the horse the second he got close enough. It had been a while since he'd ridden, but considering he'd been riding since he could damn near walk, it wasn't something you forgot how to do.

Anastasia didn't collapse in his arms as he expected her to. No, she scowled at him.

"You couldn't have ridden up here on your white horse *before* the fucking snake bit me?"

* * *

"You don't need to carry me into the house," I snapped. "I can walk."

Duke didn't respond, but only part of it was because he was in full macho-man mode. The rest of it was because the door to the house opened and Anna rushed out. Her eyes took us in, widened, but then calmed. "What happened?"

"Snake bite," Duke clipped, rounding his mother and walking into the living room where he deposited me like I was the most precious thing in the world.

It was a little late to treat me like I was fragile after he'd spent time breaking me.

"I'll get the car started so we can take her to the hospital," Anna said in a calm tone that matched her expression. This was not a woman to crack or panic under pressure. I tried to mimic that.

"No hospital," Duke barked.

This gave Anna pause. She stared at her son as he laid me down on the sofa. I waited for her to ask more questions. I certainly would want to know why her son—who up until this point, had acted like an overprotective macho-asshole—wouldn't want to take his girlfriend to be treated by medical professionals after she was bitten by a goddamn snake.

I was almost wondering that myself. Granted, my knowledge of rattlesnakes was limited, but I was pretty damn sure they were poisonous. But I knew as much as the man might not like me, he would've assessed the risk factors in taking me to a hospital. If I were a nobody with a highly connected murderer after them, it might've been different. As it was, Anastasia Edwards being taken into a hospital in Montana with a snake bite would be news.

And Kitsch was obviously more dangerous than a rattlesnake.

Anna had her pause, long enough for me to think all of this—but she didn't question her son further. It said a lot about what she thought of him, how much she trusted him.

"How about I call David Hollows?" she said. "He retired this year and is discreet."

Duke's hands were probing the area around the two small puncture wounds in my upper calf. "Yeah, call him."

Anna nodded once then moved to squeeze my hand. "You're gonna be just fine, honey."

Then she left the room.

"Aren't you supposed to elevate it?" I asked Duke, trying my best to sound brave and badass.

It was hard. Fricking hard. I was scared. I didn't want to die or lose my leg. But I also knew that Duke would do everything in his power to make sure neither of those things happened. Surely it would hurt his paycheck.

His eyes flickered upward, locking on mine. "That's a myth," he said. "Dangerous one. Raising the area only helps any blood containing venom reach your heart easier."

I sucked in a breath. "Oh, that's just wonderful."

The granite in his eyes softened...just a tad. "Know this is much easier said than done, and you're already doin' a great job, but do your best to stay calm. Rapid heart rate increases blood flow too."

"And let me guess, speeds up venom getting to my heart?" I asked dryly. "Good thing it's cold and black then, isn't it?"

His eyes went hard again. He apparently wasn't happy with me joking at a time like this—when he was trying to show off all his badass macho-man skills. Well that was just too damn bad, since it was my body and all.

"Here you go, hon, thought you might need this," Harriet said, holding out a shot glass. I hadn't heard her come in since my mind was split between focusing on Duke and the possibly fatal snake bite. My mind should've been focused on the latter, but I was getting more and more aware that even the prospect of imminent death didn't dull the man's effect on me.

If anything, it intensified it.

"You can't give her booze," Duke snapped. "It'll thin her blood."

"And calm her nerves," Harriet retorted, shaking the glass at me.

I took it and drank it quickly, not putting it past Duke to snatch it from my hands. It burned going down, but did give me something else to focus on rather than the hot, tight pain in my leg.

Harriet grinned, doing her own shot. "I'll get more."

"Don't you—" Duke started to say, but the woman was already gone.

"Fuckin' hell," he muttered.

"How do you know about all of this?" I asked, trying to distract him and me both. "Were you a medic or something?"

I knew he was former Army. I couldn't remember how I knew it. Did someone tell me? Or did it just make absolute sense considering the way he handled himself, spoke, and worked for a security firm?

He glanced back to me. His hand was still on my leg. Not on the swelling, hot, painful part, but up higher. Like on my thigh. *That* burning had nothing to do with snake venom.

"A medic?" he repeated.

"In the Army," I clarified, forcing my attention away from the hand on my thigh.

He blinked a couple times. "No, I wasn't. We learned basic shit but what I know about rattlesnakes comes from life here."

Oh. Made sense.

"How are you feeling?" he asked.

Confused. Suffering from emotional whiplash. Scared. In pain. Slightly turned on. "I'm doing okay, but I need you to distract me until the doctor gets here," I said.

He tilted his head, regarding me. "Distract you?"

I nodded. "I'd do better thinking about something else." Like something that wasn't his hand on my thigh despite no one being in the room to witness the gesture.

"Did you love him?"

The question caught me off guard, which I guessed was the point. For a second, I couldn't figure out to whom he was referring. Surely not Kieran. I didn't peg Duke as a gossip hound. Then it clicked, he wanted to know about the man who I'd been sleeping with who'd I'd also watched die.

Yeah, that made a lot more sense. It also said a lot about me that I hadn't thought of him much at all since I'd been in Duke's presence.

"No," I said truthfully. But that was only after a pause. I considered lying. That would make me look better, wouldn't it? Not that it mattered. Duke had already made up his mind about me and he didn't strike me as a man who changed it easily. "We both knew what the score was. Neither of us were interested in anything more than...physical."

Duke regarded me, face unreadable. I didn't know if this answer made him like me more or less. Or maybe he was indifferent at this point.

His hand was still on my thigh.

"Have you loved anyone?"

The question hit me square in the chest. My breath caught in my throat. It was a confronting question, bordering on cruel. Because to ask that question, Duke would have to consider me inherently unlovable—or a total psychopath.

"All right, David will be here in five and I intercepted Harriet with the bottle of tequila," Anna said, entering the room and saving me from the question.

But it had already found its way to my heart, faster than venom.

* * *

Thankfully, Duke and I weren't left alone for the rest of the evening. Tanner and Andrew quickly arrived since the news had somehow spread. Everyone hovered, offered words of encouragement and expressed genuine worry.

I tried to let that bounce off me, the fact this family who barely knew me—and what they knew sure as hell wasn't the real me—had dropped everything to make sure I was okay.

Which I was, for now.

That's what the doctor said at least.

He arrived quickly, carrying a weathered leather bag, wearing Levi's, cowboy boots, and a hat. It shouldn't have surprised me, considering I had yet to see a man without those accessories since arriving.

He spoke with a gentle, confident cadence that set me at ease. He examined me, and after asking me questions injected some antivenom into my arm.

This was followed by a laundry list of possible side effects and warnings. He was planning to come back tomorrow to check on me.

I had to give the doctor credit, he didn't ask why I hadn't been taken to a hospital nor did he give off the impression that he recognized me. It wasn't outside the realm of possibility. Sure, I was arguably the most famous movie star of the moment, but maybe the man didn't like movies.

Or so I thought until he left.

"Loved you in *Angel Tears*, by the way," he said with a wink, then he left.

The rest of the night was full of Duke asking questions about how I was feeling or barking at me if it looked like I might move from my spot on the sofa.

Harriet did her best to slip me a shot or two but Duke was too observant for me to get more than that.

Instead of having dinner at the large family table in the equally large dining room, everyone founds spots on various sofas, perched their plates on their laps, and ate dinner with me.

It touched me in a way that I couldn't quite examine—enough to encourage me to eat almost all the pasta and salad given to me. Duke had watched me eat in that same intense way he'd observed the doctor treating me.

The meal was delicious, but I couldn't enjoy it with Duke's eyes on me. Something had changed, something big. The bite had triggered his macho-man protective instinct, made him forget about the fact he didn't like me.

That was dangerous. I had to figure out a way to make him remember.

After dinner was finished, everyone sat around chatting for a while, but I found myself falling asleep in my chair. It had been a long first day, full of about a month's worth of experiences, both emotional and physical.

I flat-out refused to let him carry me upstairs, when everyone started mentioning bed. Duke hadn't argued, of course. Just bundled me into his arms and left Harriet and Anna laughing at my weak struggles. I didn't speak to him on the walk back to the room, but I was impressed he didn't even breathe heavily carrying me up the stairs and to the other side of the house.

Luckily, he let me use the bathroom on my own. I managed to change into my nightgown on my own too.

I'd chosen it carefully. For revenge. Whether it was rational or not, I was furious with him for acting like this, like the concerned fucking boyfriend, since he'd made it so goddamn clear that's exactly what he wasn't earlier today.

Luckily Andre had packed all my best lingerie. Whether or not he thought I'd be getting some while hiding from a murderer or he thought I'd being lying around in my nightgown, it didn't matter.

This particular one was longer than the rest. A deep emerald, pure silk with slits that went all the way up to my hips. It clung to my body like a second skin, and was delicately edged with lace. The entire body was sheer lace. It was meant to tease, so the lace design was perfectly poised to barely cover my nipples. And if you looked hard enough—which Duke most likely would, he was a hot-blooded male and my tits were excellent—you'd see the faint outline of them.

I fluffed my hair in the mirror, pinched my cheeks to redden them, and slid on some clear lip balm that made my lips shine and taste like cherries. Not that Duke would be tasting them.

My leg hurt. A lot. David had given me some decent pain pills which, combined with the two shots of tequila, took the edge off. But it was a low throb, the area was noticeably hotter than the rest of my body, and the skin felt hot. It was also swollen, which meant it was great that my sexiest nightie also hid the evidence of my weakness, stupidity, and the events of the afternoon.

Duke was waiting at the door, waiting to escort me to bed.

"I can make it a couple of feet on my own," I snapped.

He didn't respond, though he didn't manage to hide his sharp intake of breath seeing my nightgown.

Score for me.

Then his face evened out to almost blank and he snatched my hip, half carrying me, half dragging me to bed. I should've been a lot more against him manhandling me, but I was tired. And I did hurt. So the bed was welcome.

Duke did not say a thing after I'd settled in bed, but the way he held himself told me he was affected. Men were like that. They could hate you as a person but they couldn't stop themselves from wanting to fuck you if there was attraction.

Which there was.

A lot of it.

This little theory of mine went both ways. I wasn't sure whether I liked Duke or not, but I was certain I wanted to have angry hate-sex with the man.

I snatched the book on the nightstand and did my best to make it look believable that I was reading it. What I was really doing was watching Duke undress. He didn't make use of the bathroom for changing. No. He just dropped his trousers right here. It was a strangely intimate thing to have someone do in front of you and it hit me in that tender spot in my chest he'd opened up with his question earlier.

It was now hard to swallow, so I forced my attention back to the words on the page. They were little more than a jumble, but I made sure to stare and turn pages like someone engrossed in a book might.

The bed depressed as he got in it and I held my breath, still pretending to read. He didn't grab any kind of prop, nor did he try to feign sleep. He just lay there, staring at the ceiling, shirtless, the covers barely covering his abs.

I waited for him to say something. Entertained the fantasies I'd been harboring about him grabbing me roughly, kissing me, devouring me and fucking me violently.

That was not something I should've been doing with the

shirtless man in question in the same bed as me. My grip on the book tightened as I forced myself to not act on the desire that was coursing through my veins.

"You can't do that shit again," Duke clipped after we'd been silent for a while. "You can't storm off in a fucking hissy fit. This isn't the life you're used to. This isn't the world you're used to. That could've been much worse if I hadn't found you and you'd been there all night. You could've fuckin' died."

"If you hadn't *found* me?" I repeated, voice shrill. I abandoned the farce of my book and sat up turning to glare at him, not missing the way his eyes flickered to my thinly covered chest area. I also didn't miss the way my traitorous body responded to the simple, fleeting and hungry look. But I had lines to deliver.

"If you hadn't *saved* me, that's what you mean," I continued. "Because that's your role, isn't it, Duke? You're the big man on his big horse with his big muscles that is here to save the bitchy, ungrateful and vapid movie star. The damsel is the only role I could possibly play so of course the hero is yours. But I've got some news for you, buddy. I'm not someone that collapses and gives up because of a fucking snake bite. I know that rattlesnake bites rarely kill people. I also know I'm strong enough to withstand a little venom in order to make it across a fucking field in order to save myself. I've done it plenty of times before."

After delivering that—perfectly, I might add—I moved from the bed, careful not to flinch with the pain of standing.

Duke moved too.

Quicker than me, which wasn't at all fair. I managed to get out of bed, but because it was rather ungraceful, Duke rounded the bed before I could move to my destination. He was standing in front of me—shirtless—and pissed off.

"Where do you think you're goin'?" he demanded, eyes hard.

"I'm going to sleep on the chair," I said, most of my bravado being lost with his closeness.

He tightened his jaw and leaned in even further, as if he knew he was torturing me. "You're not sleepin' in the fuckin' chair."

I tilted my chin upward in defiance. "You're not telling me where I can fucking sleep."

Of course, I expected to get another growled demand, because that was his way.

But instead of that, he lunged. Much like the snake did, but I'd been expecting the strike. This one? After today? Not so much.

That was why I didn't struggle. That was why it was laughably easy for him to get me from my standing position to lying down on the bed with him all but caging me in.

"You can't manhandle me onto a bed and expect me to sleep with you," I protested, trying to move—to no avail. "That's sexual assault."

His grip tightened. "I can do it and I just fuckin' did," he said in my ear. My body shivered with the brush of his lips. He would've noted it. I hated that. "And you and I both know that anything sexual between us is gonna be as consensual as fuck. Beyond that, if we're going to start talkin' about pinning someone to the bed and label it as sexual assault, how about we mention what you did to me last night."

I froze.

I thought that I'd managed to escape that situation because Duke was so deeply asleep this morning. But of course not. This was Duke, macho-man. He noted shit even in his goddamn sleep.

What was worse, was he was right. I'd done the same thing to him, without his permission.

"Just let me go, Duke," I requested tightly, deciding not to comment on his last statement.

"Just go to sleep, Anastasia," he murmured in my ear, softer this time, closer, but still pissed off.

I tried to move again, more for the statement it made than anything else. Because Duke was right—he wasn't doing something I didn't want. His arms around me, his lips at my ear, the heat of his body pressed against me—I wanted that. Too much. Which was the problem.

7

"Pack your bags."

Delivering that line, Harriet entered without knocking. I jerked slightly from my position sitting in the armchair in front of the window pretending to read. I'd been on the same page for the last hour trying to figure out what the heck was going on with Duke and me.

Last night, somehow, I'd gone to sleep, with the throbbing in my leg, the discomfort in my soul, and Duke's arms around me.

This morning was even more confusing.

I'd expected him to wait for me to go to sleep and then shove me over to my side of the bed. But no, I'd woken up in exactly the same position I'd been so sure I'd never fall asleep in. My back to Duke's front, his arms around me.

When I'd woken up, I'd done my best to feign sleep so I could linger in the moment a while longer. I'd never woken up in the arms of a man, not even the man I'd been so sure was the love of my life. We'd have sex—he wouldn't be overly concerned whether I'd climaxed or not—then I'd skulk out of his bed and find my own in the guest room. I told myself that it didn't hurt, that Kieran was brilliant and he had curated a certain kind of life, I couldn't expect him to change himself because of me. I was very good at lying to myself.

The men who came after that didn't sleep in the same bed as me. Sex and intimacy never mixed.

I'd never even kissed this man with his arms around me, yet I was more intimate with Duke than any man I'd fucked, than the man I'd thought I was going to spend the rest of my life with.

So yeah, I was weak, I wanted to soak up a little slice of it, pretend it was real, store it away for later.

Duke, of course, wasn't about to let that happen.

His arms tightened around me and didn't let me go. "Mornin', baby," he murmured, voice thick with sleep.

I froze.

Baby?

He didn't seem perturbed that I wasn't replying, nor did he let me go. He continued to squeeze, to hold me in this embrace even though there was no reason to now.

Last night, it was to keep me in bed due to a misplaced form of chivalry.

Today?

He moved lazily and didn't seem to remember that he was meant to strongly dislike me and this whole "couple" thing was just an act.

The covers moved from the both of us and I jerked with the movement, trying to hide myself—another uncharacteristic gesture. I was proud of my body. I damn near starved myself in order for it to look the way it did, killed myself with workouts, spent a small fortune on a personal trainer. Beyond that, the entire world had seen most of it. Darker corners of the Internet had seen all of it. There was no reason for any sort of false modesty.

But I felt it, nonetheless, with Duke's eyes running over my scantily clad body. Though his eyes weren't on my body, or the three-hundred-dollar silk slip I was wearing.

No, he was focused further south, on my leg, to be exact. The swollen one, I now realized was throbbing faintly and felt uncomfortably hot.

Only waking up with someone like Duke would make me forget that I was nursing a rattlesnake bite.

His large hand cradled my leg, gently, like he'd carried me in the house last night. I tried to jerk my leg away but then he grasped it—the uninjured part—not so gently.

"Doesn't look too bad," he said. "Think you're gonna heal up just fine." His eyes flickered up. "Lucky."

"Yeah, I'm real lucky," I scoffed.

His brows furrowed, but then he looked back to my leg. Then he did something utterly and totally insane, the thing that caused me to stare at the same page of a book for an entire hour later that day.

He leaned down and very purposefully and slowly laid his lips just above the swollen, hot area of my leg.

And I let him. Because not in my adult life, had anyone ever touched me so gently and kissed me like that.

Then he got up. And I got distracted with his body—for a long time. Especially since he showered with the door open and I wasn't noble enough not to perve.

Because I'd been caught up in all of that, I'd also been there when he'd left the shower wearing only a towel. He'd obviously been intending on walking toward his open suitcase to get dressed.

But he stopped.

In the middle of the room. Eyes on me.

His gaze went dark.

Hungry.

No, *ravenous*.

A man hadn't looked at me like that before either. Duke was giving me a morning of firsts without even realizing it, cutting up parts of me that I'd been so sure were calcified over. Much more dangerous than any snake bite. They didn't heal the same. Or at all.

My body responded to the look immediately, almost violently. My heart thundered through my ribcage. My nipples pressed against the silk fabric of my nightie. His sharp intake of breath told me he saw that.

"Fuck, baby," he growled, holding himself still. His eyes moved from my nipples to my eyes. "You need to stop lookin' at me like that or I'll forget you need to rest."

I didn't move. "What happens when you forget I need to rest?" I asked, stupidly.

His eyes gave me no respite. "I'll fuck you so hard you forget about that snake bite, you forget your fucking name, even though the whole world knows it."

The words were spoken in a rasp. They were injected with pure sex and they hit me in every nerve ending dedicated to pleasure. And pain. Yes, this man would give me pleasure, at a price.

And I'd take it. Whatever he had to give me.

I moved ever so slightly on the bed, positioning my body as an invitation. Sure, Duke might be changing a lot of things for me, but he wasn't going to turn me shy, nor make me timid.

I made sure that I tempted him, that he saw exactly what he was going to get from me. If there was anything I knew how to do, that was sell sex. I was great at it.

Then I got up.

Duke's entire body tensed and it totally pissed me off that his eyes flickered to my leg and the slight limp that I started off on. I corrected this quickly, of course. I was used to working through pain. This was pain.

Agony.

He was a man made of stone when I made it to him. The restraint was making him damn near shake.

It infuriated me, because I could see his resolve. I knew that there would be no seducing this man. Not when he saw me as his wounded damsel. His warped sense of morals stopped him from fucking me, but he had no problem treating me like shit the previous night.

"So you think you can just walk around wrapped in a towel, making those statements and pretending you give a fuck about me?" I asked, voice soft, sultry. I didn't let him speak. Instead I leaned farther into him, never breaking my gaze. "Maybe that alpha macho-asshole works on the other women, but I'm like no one else you've ever known. I'm Anastasia fucking Edwards. No one will make me forget that. Not even you, cowboy."

On that, I stepped back, grasped the towel around his waist, pulled it free. It took everything I had not to look down, instead to drink in the anger, surprise and want in his eyes.

Then, I walked to the bathroom, making sure to close the door behind me.

He had been gone when I'd gotten out of the shower, mostly because I took my time and was very vocal about what I was doing in there. No way was he going to think he was the only one that could satisfy me. So far, the only person truly capable of satisfying me was myself.

And I definitely had some pent-up frustration that needed to be released. The fact it pissed Duke off—the slam of the door about halfway through told me that—was a nice bonus.

I would've actively gone against his wishes of resting, but even I wasn't strong enough to go against both Harriet and Anna, who all but pushed me back into the bedroom after feeding me breakfast and "shooting the shit" as Harriet called it.

Nothing was mentioned about Duke and the photo yester-day. Then again, the drama of the snake bite took over it.

Duke was helping with some cattle and that was something I would've loved to see, but my leg really was throbbing. And I didn't want to be in his presence. I was pissed at him. I was also afraid, terrified, to be precise. I'd been here for two days and everything was changing. Shifting, like tectonic plates getting ready to destroy everything that had been there before.

So I had been up here, reading—pretending to—and thinking all about Duke and interestingly not at all about my life in LA or the trial or the murder I'd witnessed.

Which brought me to Harriet bursting into the room, demanding I pack my bags.

I obviously hadn't moved fast enough for her, since she'd thrust open the closet before I had time to close my book and get up.

"Okay, even though you knew you were coming to a ranch in Montana, I really dig this dress," she said, pulling out a custom McQueen.

Unpacking that had made me smile. For the most part, Andre had done pretty well with casual, durable—yet fabulous—things for the trip here. Well, the footwear wasn't great but it turned out Anna and I wore the same size and she had some kick-ass cowboy boots.

But he wouldn't be Andre if he didn't pack at least one jaw-dropping dress. Matching shoes too.

Which Harriet was already slipping her feet into.

"Damn you and your tiny movie-star feet," she muttered, flipping them off and stomping over to my suitcase. She didn't seem bothered at the invasion of privacy, and weirdly, neither was I.

I struggled up. My leg was hot and itching but it didn't seem any more swollen, which I was pretty sure meant I was going to survive and keep my leg. "Are you kicking me out already?" I asked, joking.

She rolled her eyes. "Yeah, right. You're the most fun I've had in...at least a month." She stopped packing to look at me. "And that is a total compliment, since I usually make it a point to have a roaring good time every day. The well has been dry. Then boom! You. And Duke. And the interesting dynamic that I'm not about to pry into but can't wait to figure out." She paused to continue packing.

I waited for an explanation. She gave one. "Are you going to help me or not?"

I did what any sane person would do. I helped her pack.

* * *

"What is this?" I asked the second we both got out of the car.

Harriet hadn't asked about the state of my health or fussed over me, for which I loved her even more. She was obviously from an era and generation of women who didn't expect females to be weak and ailing. They were strong and took every hit and made themselves stronger.

She turned to me as I was regarding the small log cabin. It was only about a ten-minute drive from the homestead, and I figured that walking across the field would make it around the same length of time by foot, but it seemed completely and totally isolated. It was on a slight incline, which meant that the wrap-around porch had a breathtaking view of the entire valley, and the mountains beyond. It wasn't big. Maybe two bedrooms, from what I could see. Well maintained. Flowers surrounding it. Wicker furniture on the porch. Someone had tended to this place, the same person that had tended to the homestead—likely Anna or Harriet.

In short, it was the dream house I didn't know I wanted.

Not some huge mansion full of empty spaces and expensive furniture. Not the desirable zip code. The palm trees. The sprawling pool I never swam in but paid thousands to have maintained.

No. More than anything, I wanted this enchanting log cabin in Montana.

And despite that I had the money to buy any kind of house I wanted, I'd never get this. I didn't have the currency to buy this.

"What, you didn't think we'd make the two of you sleep in the main house with all of us, did you?" Harriet asked, jerking me out of my trance. "Then you can't walk around naked cooking bacon at three in the morning." She paused. "But I wouldn't recommend cooking bacon nude. Oil splatters and all that." She waved her hand. "Anyway. You two need your own space. We've had this sitting here, for family, guests. Well, that's what we've said throughout the years. It was always for our Duke, for his family, if he ever decided to come home to us."

The bravado in her voice trailed off at the end so I could hear the naked emotion, her love for Duke.

I looked over to see the woman staring at the cabin, at the alternate futures it might've had. But with something else. Hope.

Hope that I might be the person to bring all those things into that cabin.

It choked me, sickened me. The desperate need I had to be that. To fill up that fucking cabin, when the truth was I didn't have enough inside me to fill up a fucking bathtub, let alone the cabin, the life that someone like Duke deserved.

"It's taken a couple of days to get it ready," she continued. "That's why you've been stuck in the main house. That, and we wanted to spend some time with the both of you. I needed some time to decide if I liked you or not."

I couldn't help myself. "Does this mean you've decided you like me?"

She turned to me, grinning. "Honey, I decided to *like* you the second you said yes to margaritas, and decided to *love* you once you told that story about meeting my grandson."

I opened my mouth then, ready to let the ugly truth come tumbling out. It was selfish. Duke had been keeping his family out of this for a reason. A good one, most likely, one that might keep me alive. But I couldn't stand to continue to watch them welcome me. Couldn't stand that I was starting to fall a little bit in love with all of them. Fall in love with this lie.

But of course, the man on the white horse came to save the day. Save me from the truth.

"Ah, there's the man of the hour," Harriet declared, smiling at where the horse was trotting toward us. "Just in time too, he can take the bags in while we drink wine."

My entire body was tense as Duke rode up. I should've been holding on to the act from this morning. That nasty confidence. But I didn't have the energy, not with this fucking cabin staring at me.

So I looked at anything but Duke, right up until he got off his horse, and his boots crunched across the dirt and settled right in front of me. A hand went to my chin and tilted my head toward him.

He was wearing his cowboy hat. It did things to me—along with the faded plaid shirt, large shiny belt buckle that drew my eyes too close to his crotch, and the distressed Levis. It did everything to me. When had I been so certain that I needed a man in a ten-thousand-dollar suit? That was bullshit. All I needed was Duke in cowboy boots.

His eyes were full of things. Worry. Intensity. Warmth. None of that fury and hatred that I expected.

"How you feeling, baby?"

Baby.

There it was again.

It hit me in the stomach.

I couldn't keep up with this. He couldn't keep doing this to me, shifting all my foundations, calling me by this endearment like it belonged on me. I had to stop this, had to put on my bitch face and get him to hate me again. As horrible as that was, it was safer.

But then I realized. Harriet was here. He had to keep up the act.

Yes, that was the reason for it. He really should try to get himself an agent when this was all over, he was better than any man I'd ever performed with.

"I'm fine," I said, coming off harsher than I intended.

Duke frowned, first at me, then down at my leg.

"I swear if you're even thinking of carrying me inside, I'll break your kneecaps," I snapped.

Interestingly, this didn't infuriate him into letting me go or hating me. Instead, his hand moved to the back of my neck and he chuckled before he leaned in to kiss my forehead.

Kiss. My. Forehead.

"Plus, you can't carry her in!" Harriet yelled. "You have bags to take, we have wine to drink. You two can canoodle later. Me and Anastasia are getting wine drunk."

Duke was still smiling when he moved his lips from my forehead. Still, he didn't let me go. He moved his hand to my hip, squeezing it in a way that hurt a little and held way too much promise.

"You go and get wine drunk with my grandmother. I'll take care of the bags."

I tried to move out of his grip. It only tightened.

"But not too drunk that you're not prepared for later."

I blinked rapidly and my stomach dipped. "Later?" I hated that my voice was all breathy.

"Yeah, your punishment for this morning," he said, pulling

me in, speaking low. "You didn't think I was really gonna let you get away with that shit, did you, sweetheart?"

His lips brushed mine softly. I let that happen.

"I see too much canoodling and not enough carrying," a voice called.

I was grateful to Harriet for many things already, but for this, I loved her fully.

* * *

As it was, Duke's muttered promise of "later" didn't come to pass.

I told myself repeatedly that this was a good thing, that this was the best thing, the only thing that would keep me sane in this place.

I didn't know how long I was going to be here for, but the only thing worse than acting like I was someone to Duke in front of his family was him acting like I was something to him when no one else was around.

Harriet was my lifesaver. My hero.

Not just because of the cabin.

And this brought me to tears. Actual tears. Ones I'd been sure I'd never be able to spill unless a camera was rolling somewhere.

"Of course, we have this cleaned on a weekly basis," Harriet said after she opened the door and ushered me inside. "Just in case..." she trailed off, her eyes darting to the window where Duke was visible unpacking the car. As macho and as scary as he was, even he wasn't about to try and argue with his grandmother.

She was strong, seemed so solid. So even. But I saw it with that glance out the window. The pain in her eyes. The love. There were wounds in this family. Gaps.

And they all seemed to be centered around Duke.

Harriet didn't give me much time to contemplate this because she recovered quickly, moving to fluff some pillows on the white-slip sofa.

"But there were some touches I wanted to make before you both came in."

She was already walking toward the kitchen.

The living room and kitchen was open plan. After walking through the small but beautifully decorated foyer, you faced a wall of windows, showing the beauty of the ranch.

The living room was similar to the one at the homestead, all earth-toned, slightly bohemian, warm, inviting, impeccably decorated in a way even a celebrity designer couldn't replicate. More photos in frames on every surface, including a few artfully arranged on the hammered white concrete coffee table. Another impressive, stone fireplace with photos on the mantel. A chandelier hanging from the ceiling looked like it was covered in multiple candles.

I ached to take my time, explore every inch of this home that was made for Duke—because even on first glance, it was him. Despite the fact I didn't even really know him, it was. It wasn't harsh, masculine, in grays and sharp angles. No, it was a side of him that no one would likely ever know—only a woman who was soft, kind, and knew how to coax all of that out of him. It wasn't me.

Harriet wasn't about to let me soak it all in.

"I had to stock the essentials," she called from the fridge, which, from where I could see, was fully stocked. When I came closer, there was an entire shelf filled with champagne.

A loud pop reverberated through the room as she opened one. "We've got to christen it," she said with a pause and a wicked grin. "Well, of course you and Duke can christen it properly later, but that's *after* the champagne."

She reached into a cupboard to retrieve flutes, pouring expertly before handing me one.

Still, she didn't stop, talking or walking, didn't give me a chance to catch up.

She ushered me out of the kitchen, down a wide hallway—more photos on the walls—and past some closed doors. "Boring stuff," she explained. "A study. Another bedroom. Laundry room...tick." She opened the door at the end of the hall. "But this, this is the best part of the place."

I would've choked on my champagne had I not swallowed before the door opened.

Walking in, there was another wall of windows, this one facing the mountain ranges. French doors opened onto a small patio area with wicker furniture and a fire pit. There were comfy-looking armchairs on either side of the doors, maybe designed to look at the view when it was too cold out. The four-poster bed faced the windows and was covered in luxurious throws, pillows and a beautiful comforter.

"There's a walk-in closet, of course," Harriet said. "Not huge, but doable. We can always get it extended...you know if things change." She waggled her eyebrows meaningfully.

My stomach dropped again, but not like it had with Duke's hands on my hips. This was like someone had cut it open, let all my insides spill out. Harriet was already planning on making changes in this place to accommodate me, after knowing me for only a couple days.

"The master bath is absolutely epic," she continued, luckily turning her back on me so I didn't have to perfect my mask.

That Harriet uttered the word 'epic' and somehow pulled it off didn't even get through to me.

I was too busy trying to breathe through that stone that had come up from the bottom of my stomach to my throat.

Harriet was still saying things about the shower pressure, the bathtub, the shower, most likely cheeky things full of double entendre. I couldn't enjoy them, though.

I was too busy standing in the middle of a beautiful bedroom that Duke's family had designed and preserved for their son, with the hope that he would come back to them. Not only that, the hope that he would come back with a woman, with a family. I wasn't blind to what those other rooms were...for Duke and a family. They had kept this because they had faith in their son.

Had hope.

And the happiness was pulsating through Harriet, through all of them, peppered with the sadness I was yet to understand. But it was because of me. Because I witnessed a murder and forced Duke back here. Forced him to create this lie that brought his family happiness and hope.

A lie that had an expiration date. One that would have Duke leaving once again, that would ensure that I would never come back to this place. Even though, inexplicably, I wanted it to be mine. I wanted to abandon everything in LA so I could live here —after *two fucking days*.

I was not an emotional person. That was hammered out of me quickly, cleanly and harshly in my childhood. But here I was, crying in the middle of a bedroom that would never be mine, for a man that already belonged to someone else—even if he hadn't met her yet.

Of course, this was the moment that Duke walked into the bedroom, carrying the bags, his muscles taunting me with the way they bulged from the weight, his presence immediately sticking to me, clinging to me and embedding itself underneath my skin.

I tried to recover, there was no way I wanted him to see me like this, for him to have this part of me. But it was too late, he was far too observant.

He dumped the bags on the floor carelessly—something that should've pissed me off, considering they were all I had on this ranch to tether me to my previous life—and was in front of me in two strides. His hands cupped my face in a gesture that was far too intimate for this moment. For this situation. For this life.

"What, baby?" he demanded, searching me as if he'd missed a bullet or stab wound.

There it was again.

Baby.

The word was meant to be soft and comforting, but it scraped against my skin, drawing blood.

I tried to struggle from his grip, but he wasn't about to let me.

"Stop calling me baby," I hissed, mindful of Harriet still arranging things in the bathroom.

Amusement danced with his concern. "Not on your life."

I scowled, angry that I couldn't escape, couldn't wipe away my tears.

"Tell me what's wrong?" he asked, gentle this time.

I almost told him, almost spilled my emotional guts on these beautiful hardwood floors, almost confessed all sorts of things that I'd never told another human, almost told him about my feelings for him.

Almost.

"Not on your life," I snapped, tilting my head up and thankfully escaping his grip.

"Duke, you've got champagne on the counter for when you finish with your task," Harriet said, walking back into the room. Something moved in her eyes as she took us in, but thankfully her gaze flickered over to the abandoned bags. "Boy, you were raised better than to treat vintage Louis Vuitton luggage like that. Rectify your mistake immediately while us girls get tipsy."

Yet again, Duke wasn't brave enough to argue with his grandmother, so he let me go, but not before giving me a meaningful *this isn't over* look.

Harriet took my arm and saved me from the man that I was dangerously close to falling in love with.

* * *

Harriet, as promised, had gotten us wine drunk. She hadn't mentioned a word about my little episode in the bedroom, and I didn't have to be alone with Duke for the rest of the afternoon and evening so he couldn't make good on the promises his eyes were making.

After our first bottle of champagne, Harriet and I had decided to have a fashion show with all the clothes in my suitcases. She had "liberated" some of the things that wouldn't be suitable on the ranch—meaning she stole all the designer clothes that were in her size.

Anna had entered at some point, with a glass of her own and an easy smile on her face.

"You suit it here," she said softly, when Harriet was in the closet changing into yet another outfit. She looked out the French doors, which we'd opened to let the breeze in. "You both do." She looked to me with Duke's eyes. "I know that a mother can't expect to have her entire family within a ten-minute drive. Especially not Duke, that boy has too much of his grandmother in him, a restless soul. I've accepted what he's needed to do with his life. I'm so proud of what he's become." She reached over to squeeze my hand. "I'm not asking or expecting anything from either of you. But I just want to thank you for giving me time with my son. Thank you for giving him that light in his eyes. I haven't seen that in a long time."

Her words filtered through the air and into my heart, curling around it, warming it and breaking it at the same time. I desperately wished I'd had a mother like this. Strong. Understanding. Loving. Accepting.

I desperately wished this was all real so I'd have Anna and Harriet in my life.

But wishes weren't for anything but teenage girls and genies.

As she had already done countless times that day, Harriet walked out of the closet and saved the day.

"I think I've got the legs to pull this off, don't you?" she asked, posing in the mirror.

I broke away from Anna's gaze to see Harriet in a leather skirt and silk blouse. "Definitely," I agreed.

Tanner and Andrew arrived some time later, with arms full of food that Anna turned into dinner. I was still banned from doing anything like helping, so I was banished to the sofa with wine and Harriet.

We ate at the long table this time, conversation still flowing easily. Everyone finished their dinner, cleaned up, and left early, Harriet murmuring something about "the christening."

I was lucky when Duke stepped outside with his father, and I managed an escape of my own.

I couldn't get far, with my leg still throbbing, and a decent amount of alcohol in my system. The food that I wasn't used to eating managed to soak up a great deal of it, so I was, unfortunately, painfully sober.

My arms rested on the wood of the fence and I leaned most of my weight onto it, giving my leg a break. If only there was something I could lean on to give my heart a break. No such thing existed.

It wasn't dark yet, we'd arrived in the Montana summer, where the nights were long. Plus, ranchers went to bed early, as I'd learned, since they were up before dawn.

The quiet rang in my ears. Not like that silence of death. No, this was a quiet that hummed with life. The birds, horses, cattle in faraway fields.

Still, that gunshot rippled through it all. The fear. I hadn't let myself think of that properly since it happened. It was going to fuck me up somehow, for sure. You couldn't watch someone be murdered and not feel anything. Even someone like me. I'd held it together because I had to. I couldn't let the trauma weaken me in the midst of all this. It could wait, I could mix it with my heartbreak after the trial.

"What are you doing?"

I didn't look back at Duke. I'd expected him to find me here, after everything that had happened today. It was insane that so much change could be packed into a measly twenty-four hours. Especially change in a man like Duke, who I would've thought changed about as easy as a mountain might.

But it seemed that his mind was changing about me. Despite how much I hated it, I already wished for his cold dislike, craved it. It was more manageable.

His scent wrapped me up when he got close. Leather and spice. It comforted me, so I held my breath trying to escape it. There was no reason for me to find comfort here. In him. It would be taken away from me soon enough. That was something to hold on to.

"We've got to get some shit done with the cattle," he said, not seeming annoyed at the fact I was ignoring him. "Which means I'm gonna be late and not gonna be able to make good on my promise." Some hair moved from the nape of my neck and he twirled it in his fingers.

My shiver had nothing to do with the slight bite in the air.

"Anastasia?" he said after more silence.

"This place," I said, looking out at the sprawling landscape, at the shadows of the mountains. "It makes me feel different." I turned my head back so I could take in this man.

Duke wasn't looking at the view that millions of dollars couldn't buy. Not even billions. This was a view you inherited, like brown eyes or mental illness. This was a view that couldn't be owned.

But nonetheless, he wasn't looking at the view that he held in his blood. He was looking at me. Like I was worth looking at. I hated that. I fucking hated that he wasn't avoiding me, detesting me. I hated whatever I'd done to make him look at me like that, like I was the view you couldn't buy.

"No," he said finally. "Doesn't make you different. It sheds everything you've been pretending to be." He sighed, finally giving me a respite from his gaze. "That's the beauty of the open skies of Montana. You can't stand under them wearing lies."

It was now that I turned to him, feeling more pissed off than brave. And fuck if he didn't cut a beautiful profile. Etched out of the land, with the week's worth of stubble quickly turning into a beard. With that fucking cowboy hat. He belonged here more than he belonged in that city of lies, protecting vapid movie stars like me.

"Why are you so sure I'm telling the truth now?" I demanded. "Why can't you consider that the me you were so sure you didn't like was the real me and I'm just acting now?"

Maddeningly, he paused again, either that fucking pensive or trying to rattle me. I'd bet on the latter.

But then he looked. He had the sunset and teasing in his gaze. "Because, baby, you're just not that good of an actress."

Then he turned on his boot and walked away, leaving me with a view I didn't earn, would never own.

8

ONE WEEK LATER

I HADN'T MEANT to stop.

I was on a mission to feed the horses. It was something I'd come to love to do and the ranch hands loved me for it, since it meant that they had less to do.

The work wasn't glamorous, that was for sure, not that I was overly attached to the idea of glamor. Since that was all it was. An idea. A veneer. A thin coating of shine on top of layers of ugly.

I couldn't remember a moment when I was truly happy, when my thoughts were quiet and my life seemed calm. Until I was feeding those horses. Doing something completely simple for another beautiful being.

So I'd been on my way to do that, find my quiet, my calm in the middle of all of this.

My leg had healed nicely, the doctor had cleared me for doing most things, though Duke was still hovering and overprotective. He'd tried to tell me I couldn't ride. Tried, being the operative word. He couldn't be around me constantly, and Harriet proved to be a great partner in crime.

He'd been pissed off when I got back from the ride with Tanner—at both of us. The tension between the brothers was getting thicker, with the novelty of Duke's presence wearing off. I hadn't asked Duke about it because I was on my mission to distance myself from him as much as possible, and avoid his sexual promises, despite what my libido craved. I'd actually managed it this entire week. In a beautiful turn of events, one of the ranch hands they'd been expecting to arrive back from college for his summer break had decided to flit off to Europe with his girlfriend. Another had an appendicitis and was currently recovering from surgery.

The ranch was down two men and they were very busy. That meant Duke was *very* busy—gone at dawn and not back until dinner. Every dinner we had at the homestead, mostly because I was avoiding Duke and also just because I liked it there.

If you'd told me this before I'd arrived, I would've laughed in your face. The thought of being alone in a stranger's house, having to make small talk, having to be polite would've turned my stomach. I couldn't keep up an act for that long. Even villains needed a moment or two to themselves to take off the mask, stretch the facial muscles.

But I didn't need that, didn't need the mask. Because they didn't feel like strangers. None of them. The first few mornings, I'd pretended to be asleep when Duke left. I wasn't sure if he realized or not, but he still held me tight, kissed my head, and brushed my hair from my face before leaving.

Then, once I was sure he was gone, I'd get up, get dressed, walk to the homestead for coffee or walk into the kitchen to see Harriet.

We'd sit and eat breakfast together, talk. One morning she'd decided I needed to know the basics of gardening, so we donned sunhats and gloves and spent the day in the soil.

That was where Duke had found us. By this point we'd taken a margarita break and forgotten about lunch. Anna had joined us and we had dirt on our hands and laughter in our hearts.

I'd sobered immediately when something started blocking the sun. Something large. Duke was staring down at us, cutting a harsh yet beautiful silhouette.

It was the look in his eyes that cut through any kind of buzz tequila could give me. Each day, it got more intense. Softer. Full of something that couldn't be real, again making it hard to know where the act ended and the truth began.

So I did the only sane thing, I drank more margaritas and got myself buzzed enough to the point I passed out the second we got home from dinner that evening.

I woke up the next morning in bed, with a faint headache, and not wearing a night gown. Instead, I was encased in Duke's scent, wearing a faded tee that he'd obviously worn before. It felt better than the finest silk.

"Figured you might need this."

Duke entered the room, fully dressed, and placed a steaming cup of coffee on the nightstand.

I moved up in the bed and made the mistake of making eye contact. His eyes were twinkling with a little amusement, warmth, and a whole lot of hunger. He leaned in to kiss my head. "Like you in my tee, babe," he murmured against my forehead. He pulled back just when I was going to forget all my promises I'd made to myself and pull him back into bed.

His expression told me he was feeling the same. "Don't look at me like that, baby," he rasped. "Gotta be out of here in less than a minute. And what I'm planning on doing to you is gonna take hours. Not gonna start somethin' I can't finish properly."

I clenched my thighs together, and my panties were already

soaked with need. I couldn't even find my tongue. Couldn't sling a retort back to him.

"Gotta say, Anastasia," he continued. "I like walkin' in here and seeing you've planted roots."

And on that note, he left.

The words followed me around for the rest of the day. Even with Harriet to distract me, I was troubled. I did my best to avoid Duke at dinner and feigned sleep while he was showering.

This wasn't an act I could continue. This week had been pure luck, with ranch tasks pulling Duke's attention away from me. But it was just a matter of time.

I was no closer to finding a way to build my shields back up, so feeding the horses was an essential part of the routine to keep me even.

But in order to feed the horses I had to walk past the arena— where Duke was training the newest horse.

It was running around him in circles, and he was guiding it. All of his focus was on that horse. Normally, he'd notice me watching. That was just who he was. Whatever he'd done in his past had made it so there was no such thing as calm for him. He was always alert, expecting the next threat. The more time I spent with him, the more I understood why he'd had to leave this place. Whatever he'd seen and done over there had changed him, changed his insides. He couldn't be in a place like this, a place of beauty. Love. A place where the ghost of his past self formerly walked.

I totally got it.

Even though my heart broke for him.

Broke for whoever he used to be. He would've had a good life here, a good woman, children.

But life didn't work that way.

So I tried to shake off my sorrow, my grief for him.

And I just watched.

Watching Duke longe this horse was weirdly erotic.

Well, it wasn't weird, as watching Duke do *anything* had become erotic.

It was weird how deeply he touched me, beyond the fact he was a hot guy in a cowboy hat, jeans that were made for him, training a horse. That was part of it, sure. But there was something else. Something inside me that was desperate to sink my nails into his skin, clutch his bones so I never had to lose him.

But I would.

Lose him, that was.

We all lost everyone eventually.

Both Duke and I were too focused that we didn't notice Tanner had climbed the fence until he was in the middle of the arena.

The horse stopped abruptly, as if it could sense the aggression in the air. I could taste it, and I wasn't even near them.

Tanner snatched the rope connected to the horse.

"This isn't your horse to train," he said.

Thankfully, I could hear him, since he was speaking loudly enough for the audience he was obviously too pissed off to realize he had. This was it. I had been waiting for their tension to come to a head. I knew the rest of the family had as well.

Duke's stance was casual, but I didn't miss the tightness in his body, so starkly different to the way it had been moments before with the horse.

"I wasn't aware that I was banned from touching horses," he replied.

Tanner leaned forward, the scowl not suiting his features. "You're not banned from shit. But we both know you're here for a fuckin' holiday with your woman. Show her some country, give her the opportunity to fall in love, and then you'll go back to your life in Hollywood. We won't see you for another five years. So no, I don't want you thinkin' you can get horses used to you."

Tanner wasn't yelling. He didn't need to. He was getting his fury across rather well.

"You think you know shit about my life, about Anastasia's life?" Duke asked quietly, but still loud enough to hear the danger in his voice.

Although it wasn't my place to interfere, my body worked on its own. I was climbing the wooden fence without consciously making the decision to do it.

Tanner was ready to explode. "I know enough to be certain you're gonna break Mom's heart all over again when you leave. And you're gonna break Anastasia's heart too, 'cause you ain't got it in you to treat anyone decent."

Oh fuck. Tanner was going to bat for me, which would've been sweet if things were real. On Duke's side at least. I was plenty prepared for my heart to be broken. I was also a big girl, able to fight my own battles and I sure as shit didn't need two brothers fighting over me.

"And what the fuck do you know about treating someone decent, Tanner?" Duke asked this even quieter, but since I was getting closer I could hear him. "I know you're well versed at breaking women's hearts."

Tanner stepped forward. "You watch yourself, brother."

Duke stepped forward too. "No, I don't think I should. You started this shit. How about you finish it? Be a man. For once."

"Hey," I said, trying to step forward in between them—right about the same time that Tanner tried to land a punch on Duke's face.

"Fuck!" Tanner yelled.

Or maybe Duke. I wasn't sure. Of course, at the best of times I would've been able to pick up Duke's voice immediately, but my ears were ringing, black spots danced in front of my vision, and the pain radiated all the way to my toes. *Because, yes, I'd walked right into Tanner's punch.*

"Anastasia," Duke said. Voice urgent but soft. A hand cupped my face. I blinked away the spots, or tried to. Tanner had not been holding back with that punch and those muscles were *not* for show. I had been punched before, but I'd forgotten just how much it *hurt*.

"Fuck, Sia, I'm so fucking sorry." Tanner, this time. He did sound sorry. In fact, he sounded like he was in a considerable amount of distress. Tanner was not a man to hit a woman, on purpose or not. He might've tried to comfort me somehow but I was jostled ever so slightly in Duke's arms, as he pulled me away.

"Don't you fucking *touch* her," Duke hissed with more fury injected into his words than I'd ever heard. "You're lucky that my main concern right now is my woman or your fucking teeth would be embedded in my knuckles."

A pause.

My hair moved.

I realized I'd been squeezing my eyes shut, which was why I'd only been able to hear what was going on. I blinked rapidly, trying to make the world come back into focus, so then I could tell Duke I was okay and that he should not be killing his brother, because he sure as hell sounded like he was going to. It hurt, blinking. But I was persistent and Duke's face came into view. Furious. Concerned.

"Baby, I'm gonna stand now," he said, gentle, almost a whisper.

I didn't say anything because I was too busy trying to get my bearings, think through the pain.

Duke's brows furrowed, more concerned now. "Anastasia, I need you to talk to me."

I swallowed, tried to move my thoughts past the pain and say something to stop Duke looking so fricking panicked. "You have good eyebrows."

Something moved in his face, maybe a glimmer of amuse-

ment. But it disappeared when he focused on my cheek, that
already felt like it had a pulse and the skin was stretching.

Duke's head snapped up toward where I guessed Tanner was
hovering. "You need to make yourself disappear." Not gentle
now. Deadly.

"But—"

"Now," Duke said.

My body turned cold with the malice in that single word.

Duke didn't wait for Tanner to heed his warning. He stood,
fluidly and rather gracefully for a man of his size. But that didn't
really help with the pain.

He winced with my sharp intake of breath and walked
quickly toward the house.

"Duke, you can't kill your brother," I said through the pain.
"It was an accident."

"When a man throws a punch, he knows where it's gonna
land," he clipped. "It lands on a woman, he's responsible for that.
In every fucking way."

I rolled my eyes. Or tried to. The gesture itself hurt. "And
when a woman tries to stop a fight between two macho-men, she
should factor in the fact she might get punched."

Duke's jaw stiffened even more. "You need to stop worryin'
bout that shit now, baby."

I tensed. "What's with all this *baby*?" I snapped. "I'm not
your baby."

He glanced down. "Oh yes, you are."

I didn't get time to argue with him, since we were at the
house, and he was explaining to his family why his brother
punched his girlfriend in the face.

* * *

"Outside. Now."

Everything went silent in the living room with Duke's words. I glanced up to see Tanner standing in the doorway. He was focused on my face. Well, what little he could see beyond the wall of Duke, who'd leapt up the second Tanner had entered the room.

His father stood now too, eyeing his two sons, the ones that were at odds because of me.

Well, to be fair, their animosity had been brewing for much longer than I'd been in the picture, but I didn't think it would be this dangerous had Tanner not punched me.

Anna, who was sitting beside me, grabbed my hand and squeezed. She looked between her boys with pain and concern in her eyes, but also with a weary acceptance. Harriet was in the corner, sipping her margarita, amused. Not just amused, though. She had some of Anna's pain dancing around in there too.

Despite this, both of the strong, outspoken women stayed silent. They didn't try to interrupt what I was guessing would be a brawl.

I stood, grabbed Duke's hand that was clenched into a fist. "Duke, no."

"Stay out of this, baby," he clipped, not looking at me.

I narrowed my eyes, throbbing head or not, he was totally not talking to me like that.

But I didn't get time to educate him on this, since Tanner had nodded once and was already walking out the door. Duke had shrugged off my hand and was following.

"Oh shit, I wish I'd made popcorn or something," Harriet muttered, leaping up and following them.

I did the same, though not as quickly as the dynamic matriarch.

The two men took off their hats, laid them on the gate into the property, and started to circle each other.

Both of them were already at blows by the time I'd made it

down the porch steps. I was ready to try and break them up, despite what had happened the first time. A hand on my wrist stopped me. Andrew was looking at his sons, then to me.

"They need this, honey."

He didn't seem glad about this. Resigned.

Anna slipped her hand into his, and he leaned into her.

Harriet outstretched her hand to offer me a sip of her drink. I took it, not taking my eyes off the two men.

"I didn't mean to hit her," Tanner said, fists up.

"I know," Duke replied. "But you did anyway. You want to work your shit out, do it now. Before, I might've held back, since I deserved a lot of it. Now, I won't."

Tanner nodded once.

Then there were no more words, only thuds of fists on flesh.

"Was that really the most civilized way to go about working out your shit?" I asked, pressing the ice to Duke's swollen cheek. The fight wasn't exactly even. I totally thought Tanner was holding back because he thought he deserved the beatdown. He held back for the first part of the fight, let Duke give him bruises to match mine. Then he started hitting back, because he also was looking for an opportunity to punch his brother. For whatever reason.

Duke grabbed the ice and pulled me down onto his naked chest.

We were in bed.

After the fight, each man went their separate ways. I shared a beer with Harriet on the porch—I had intended on going after Duke, but she informed me he needed time to "lick his wounds" and she needed someone to "talk about their form with."

So we did that, though she didn't tell me the origin of the

hostility between the two brothers, which I guessed she thought was Duke's story to tell.

By the time I finished my beer—the first one I'd had in ten years—and walked to the cabin, Duke was just getting out of the shower, hair still wet, body still taunting me with its scarred perfection. How I had managed to keep myself from pouncing on him this past week, I had no idea.

He winced when he saw me, moving across the room to cup my face. "I'm so sorry, baby," he murmured.

I hated how tender his touch was, especially when paired with the whole shirtless thing. It was an inconsiderate seductive spell that rendered even the fiercest feminists mute.

"I've had worse," I said, trying to make him feel better.

By the way his body tensed and his eyes darkened, *that* didn't help. "Say again?"

Shit.

I tried to move, but his other hand fastened on my hip. "Anastasia?"

I scowled at him. "You can't just manhandle me into telling you shit," I snapped. "Especially when I can't do the same."

"What have you had that's worse than this?" he asked, moving the hand at my chin up to lightly brush my already-bruising cheek.

I didn't miss the fury in his voice again. Mixed with that unexpected softness. Nor did I understand it. Where were all the emotions coming from? Sure, I knew he was the kind of man that would totally and utterly protest violence against women. I got that. But this was different. This was a complete 180. And in addition to the shiner, I was getting whiplash from this man.

I should've told him to mind his business. Should've jerked myself out of his touch, averted my eyes, and locked myself in the bathroom until he was safely in bed, but hopefully asleep.

I sighed, resigned to the fact he wasn't going to stop. If I was honest, I wanted to tell him. There was no one I could share my past with, my truths. That was supposed to be a good thing. But suddenly it all felt so heavy, I needed to share it with some strong shoulders. "I was young. Stupid. Thought that the bad boy was a great exciting boyfriend. Until he beat the shit out of me one night, while high on meth," I said.

Duke flinched, worse than he had when Tanner's fist connected with his cheekbone. He'd barely moved when that happened.

"Jesus, Anastasia," he whispered.

"It was a long time ago," I said, trying to gloss over the memory and the hurt in his voice. I hadn't dealt with what happened. Not really. I'd just stored it neatly in a box with all of my other traumas.

"I dumped him the next day," I continued. I didn't add that it was very late the next day since I couldn't walk for most of the morning. I hadn't checked into the hospital because I didn't have any insurance or money, so I was in agony for almost a month. But I healed. "Plus, it gave me good insight into domestic violence—and I was able to get an Oscar for that role. I should've thanked him in my acceptance speech."

Duke's other hand went to my face so he was cupping my cheeks. "Don't do that," he growled. "Don't try to act like your past is nothing but material. Like it doesn't matter."

His words hit me much like Tanner's fist on my cheekbone. I swallowed roughly and worked hard at trying to make it seem I was indifferent. "It doesn't," I said. "I'm not someone who lingers in the past, and I'm not going to pay a therapist thousands to dissect me like a teenager might a dead frog in science class. Shit happens."

Duke didn't like that response. It was in his face that I'd only known previously as carefully empty or with a thin veil of detachment over dislike. But he didn't argue.

Instead, he snatched the ice from my hand and in an impressive move, changed our positions so he was slightly on top of me pressing it to my cheek.

My sharp intake of breath had nothing to do with the cold against my bruised and swollen skin.

"You didn't answer me earlier," he said, voice soft and rough at the same time.

Fuck. I thought I'd gotten out of that.

"Answer what?" I asked, figuring playing dumb would be my best way out of it.

Duke raised his brow and gave me the impression that I wasn't fooling him. "You didn't love Salvador. Is there anyone you have loved?"

I bit my lip. There were many responses to a question like this coming from someone like Duke. Namely, I could tell him it was none of his damn business and that our relationship was strictly professional.

But that wouldn't really hold the same weight considering we were in the same bed together and his body was pressing into mine without rational argument from me.

I could lie, could try my best to settle us into our respective corners—macho security man and bitchy spoiled movie star. Tempting.

Lying was basically just acting with higher stakes. The two were almost interchangeable in my life, since most of it was a carefully constructed lie. I was great at it. An expert. Usually. I wasn't as good with Duke. My lies were thin, felt weak coming off my tongue. I didn't commit to them like I should, because I didn't want him to think less of me. Well, I didn't want him to think any less of me. I wanted to redeem myself. I was harboring some girlish fantasy that he'd discover that there was more to me, here underneath the Montana sky, and we'd live happily after.

But happily ever afters were just well packaged lies that sold a lot of movie tickets.

"There was someone," I said after a long pause. "Someone who I *thought* I loved, I should clarify." I averted my eyes because I was ashamed, and the weight of Duke's attention was far too heavy to shoulder in addition to the truth. "I don't know if it really counts if the person I loved was one big lie. I guess it does, since it was one I told myself. He made no illusions about the kind of man he was. I was the one that made excuses for the behavior, convinced myself that love wasn't like that candy cane bullshit that movies pumped out on the masses."

I thought of the times where I locked myself in the bathroom, sat at the bottom of the shower with a bottle of vodka, and let the shower wash away the tears.

"I told myself it was better because it was harder," I said. "Because it hurt more. Because every moment was agony. I told myself it was special. No one else could boast their love cut them into tiny pieces."

I shrugged. "I guess it was a cynical form of romanticism. Or denial. Or daddy issues. Whatever. I'm not going to lie. Somewhere packaged up in that toxic package of love was the satisfaction I got with the labels. I loved that the world was obsessed with us. I loved that it catapulted my career into spaces that I wouldn't have reached without a man at my side." I took a breath. "As much as I wish I could say feminism has eradicated that shit, it's just not true. If you really want to be famous, like everyone in the world knows your name kind of famous, then you have to abandon all of your morals and beliefs. You have to abandon the chance at love." I laughed. "So I guess that's my long way of saying I don't even know if I've loved anyone. And I'm very fucking aware of how screwed up that is."

The words had all tumbled out of my mouth before I could really take stock of what they were, how heavily injected with ugly truths they were. When it hit me, I wanted to escape. I wanted to unzip my own skin and crawl out of it to escape that moment. But short of challenging Duke to a straight-up fight, I didn't think I was going anywhere.

So I had to brace.

For fuck's sake, I'd watched someone I was sleeping with get murdered and handled it. I could stand the reaction of the guy I was possibly in love with when he worked out I was really a garbage person.

The brave, feisty feminist thing to do would've been to meet his eyes, to adopt a hardness to my gaze to communicate I wasn't ashamed, that I was totally comfortable with myself and my truth.

My eyes stayed on the ceiling.

Duke didn't speak immediately. He just let that naked truth sit there in the air, decaying in front of us.

Then he threw the ice over my body to land on the floor with a thud. His hand moved to my chin and he forced my face to his. I didn't have to move my gaze. I could focus on the space over the top of his head. But I didn't. I met those blue eyes.

"You haven't had anyone, all these years?" he asked. His voice was gentle. Sad, almost. I searched for the judgment or dislike that I'd come to expect behind his words. It was nowhere to be found. I missed it.

I laughed, covering my discomfort. "I've had plenty of people, Duke."

He flinched. I barely caught it, but he flinched. "You know what I mean."

I sighed. Yeah, I knew what he meant.

"Who do you tell your stories to?" he asked after I was silent for a minute. A full one. I'd counted.

I blinked at him, at his deep question. Not one I would expect to come from a macho-man/cowboy. Or maybe it was.

"No one," I answered honestly. "I don't tell my stories to anyone. I play out other people's stories for them. That's all I am. That's what I'm good for."

He frowned. Moved. I held my breath at the closeness. "That's bullshit," he murmured. "You're so much more than that."

* * *

Duke and I had said plenty of words last night, so the rest of the evening was spent with silence. Spent fucking *cuddling*. We drank wine and watched a movie. It was exceptionally strange doing such normal things together when things were so complicated.

I'd tensed at one point, maybe during the first glass of wine.

Duke sensed it immediately, of course. He grasped my chin in his hand—gently, because he'd made sure every touch was gentle tonight—and locked eyes with me.

"Hey," he murmured. "I see it, shit swirling, moving in that beautiful head of yours." He pushed the hair from my face. "I fuckin' love your hair, have I told you that?"

"No," I said on a whisper.

"Well, I do," he said. "Redheads are fiery. I can't believe I ever thought you were cold. You're warm. Hot. You're a fuckin' inferno, baby."

I stared at him. "I didn't think men actually talked like this in real life."

He chuckled. "Ah, I'm not sure this is real life or a dream yet. But I'll be damn sure we try to inspect it right now. How about we just have tonight?"

"Okay," I replied. I wasn't ready to let go of the dream either, and surely there was enough of a nightmare ahead of us.

So we watched the movie. Drank good wine. I fell asleep in his arms.

Today, well, today was different.

The dream had to end at some point, right?

We all sat outside enjoying dinner. It was warm, but not sticky. They had lit tiki torches so mosquitos weren't feasting. The food was good, and somehow, I was eating it and not thinking about the calories.

The fight from yesterday was only visible in the bruises on each of our faces. Mine had gotten the worst overnight because my skin was so pale and clear, there was no manly ruggedness to hide it behind like Tanner and Duke. Each family member had winced when they'd seen it today, none more so than Tanner. He wore his guilt etched into his body. He was torturing himself over it. That's what good men did. They didn't run from their mistakes, didn't try and brush them off, didn't try to lay the blame for them at the feet of a woman. They wore them. Suffered through them.

As much as I tried to convince Tanner that it wasn't his fault, that was the truth.

"I'm not going to let you make me feel better," he said when I'd tried to placate him with the knowledge that I was okay and that it was my fault in the first place. "I threw that punch. It landed on you. That responsibility lies with me. That sin is mine, accident or not." His hand lightly brushed my bruise. A whisper of a touch. "Duke should've fuckin' killed me, markin' you like that," he muttered. Then he turned and walked away.

I'd done my best to avoid Duke for most of the day, proud of myself that I'd managed to get up early and sneak to the main house for breakfast and coffee with Anna and Harriet.

He'd stalked into the kitchen, still shrugging off sleep. His eyes had found me, then the bruise on my face, and they'd turned murderous. He stalked across the room, whirled me around on the stool, cupped the uninjured part of my face, and kissed me. Hard. On the mouth. In front of his mother and grandmother.

I was so shocked that I not only let it happen, but I participated.

He took his lips from mine before I could participate too much more. Luckily. "You're takin' it easy today," he growled.

Growled.

That jerked me back. "You're under the impression that that's your call to make, how sweet," I replied, leaning back in my stool to grab my coffee. Both because I needed it and having something to replace the minty and fresh taste of Duke's mouth was absolutely fucking necessary.

Of course, he folded his arms across his far too expansive chest and turned his gaze to Anna, who was hiding her smile with her own coffee cup.

"Make sure she doesn't do anything else to hurt herself today," he ordered his mother.

"Excuse me," I cut in. "I'm a grown-ass woman, one that likes being healthy and having all of her limbs attached. I'm not going to do anything else to hurt myself. Stop with the macho-man crap and go and do whatever cowboy stuff you've got on the cards today."

Duke's eyes went from his mother, who was now not hiding her laugh, to me. "You have a rattlesnake bite still healing and were punched in the face." He snatched the coffee cup from my hands in a move that was far too smooth. And in another far-too-smooth move, he grasped the back of my head and pulled me in for yet another hard kiss.

"Be fuckin' careful," he murmured against my mouth.

Then he snatched a croissant, turned on his heel, and walked out.

"He took my coffee," I snapped, still slightly bewildered.

"Good thing that we've got more, because honey, you're

gonna need all your energy fighting with that grandson of mine," Harriet said, already pouring me more. "And you better fight with that little alpha male. He needs to be challenged."

She winked at me.

The teasing in that wink and the warmth in Anna's smile were spears through my heart. Along with Duke's kiss, that stayed with me through the rest of the day.

I was just lucky that Duke had thrown himself back into cowboy work, that it was a busy time of year, and they were short-handed, because I didn't see him until dinner. I'd designed it so that we were not alone in that cabin that scared the absolute shit out of me.

So now it was dinner, outside, three of us bruised, a slight amount of tension in the air. I had yet to get to the bottom of the reason for the anger between them. The plan was to ask Duke last night, but well, after spilling my emotional guts, I didn't have the energy to ask Duke to spill his.

Duke was beside me. His hand was on my thigh. He had to eat one-handed in order to achieve that feat, which meant he used his fork as a rudimentary knife. Normally, lack of table manners disgusted me, mostly because it reminded me too much of my past, but considering he was doing this in order to touch me, I didn't mind.

I should mind, of course. He didn't need to go this far to convince his family we were together. I was pretty sure they believed it, apart from Harriet, of course. Who knew what that crazy bitch believed? I loved it.

"So," Harriet said, clapping her hands and glancing in between Duke and me. "When are you two getting married? May I request a destination wedding? Tahiti? Or Peru? All-expenses-paid of course. And none of this coach crap. I'm expecting first class in the event that a private jet is not available."

I was sipping on my wine when Harriet started speaking so I choked when she asked that.

Duke absently patted my back as I coughed.

"Married?" I repeated, looking to Duke for help. He was still rubbing my back, even though I was no longer coughing. I glared at him, and he merely smiled back. He didn't look like he was at all bothered by the question of marriage to the woman he was only pretending to love.

Asshole.

I was very aware that all eyes were on me, and for once in my life, that made me very, very uncomfortable. Having all the eyes in the world on me at any given time, an audience was like second nature. Watching, adoring, secretly waiting for me to stumble, go down in flames. Of course, that's not what this audience was doing. They didn't want me to fail, for *us* to fail. They wanted us to soar and that was that much worse.

"We haven't talked about it," I said, words sounding flat and lame.

I was going to kill Duke, right here in his family home. Damn that asshole for not jumping in to save me from this. Wasn't that what he was all about? Saving struggling women?

But he seemed totally content in letting me flail.

"Of course you have," Harriet said. "Or at least, Duke has. He wouldn't bring you here unless he was dead serious about you." There was challenge in her eyes.

A dark, evil part of me really wanted to give them the truth, relieve myself of this act before it destroyed me. Before Salvador's murder, I wouldn't have hesitated to make an entire table of people uncomfortable to make myself feel better. I wouldn't have cared about who I hurt—on the surface at least.

But I couldn't bring myself to. Even with the fury I was feeling toward Duke, my need to punish him.

"I know he's incredibly *serious* about his feelings for me," I said, moving my eyes to the man in question, fake smile piercing. "Just like *I'm* incredibly serious about my feelings for him."

Instead of being riled with my words and the true meaning behind them, Duke merely moved his hand back to my thigh, squeezing just to the point of pain then moving it higher.

My brows narrowed at him while my body responded to the movement.

"What do your parents do, Anastasia?" Anna asked, obviously trying to change the subject. She glared at Harriet who didn't seem at all bothered.

The hand on my thigh was not necessary, but at this very moment, with this very question, it seemed as essential as breathing.

I took my time to chew. Swallow. Meet Anna's eyes. "They're dead," I said. No matter how hard I tried to make those words soft and light, they always came out heavy and barbed, cutting through all pleasant conversation.

Normally I didn't mind, because it put an end to small talk at whatever function or party I was at and I could make my escape to the bar or bathroom to take a couple Valium.

But tonight, I hated that everyone paused, that the air turned sour, and that all the easy smiles disappeared.

Duke's hand squeezed my thigh. Hard. I knew he'd turned his head to look at me, but I kept Anna's gaze. It was really difficult, considering her eyes held real pain, empathy, when most people I told had manufactured the emotions in order to curry favor with me.

"I'm so sorry," she said, words quiet, but hitting me square in the chest.

"It's okay," I said, my tone even, despite the lump in my throat. "It was a long time ago. I never knew my mother. She died giving birth to me. My father died when I was six. Hit and run." I shrugged. "I don't remember much about him, but he was a good man." I took a breath. "My foster parents were great, so I was lucky." The lie was practiced and I usually uttered it without thought or guilt, but it was rancid on my tongue.

Lying to these people felt entirely wrong, but it was necessary, considering everyone *was* truly sorry for my loss. Plus, I was pretending to be in love with their son. What was one more lie?

"Well it's a good thing you met our Duke then," Harriet intercepted. "We've always been too much family for just these two boys. We've got plenty left over for you."

I would've been able to handle the moment if Harriet hadn't spoken. Or even if she had and Duke's hand wasn't on my thigh. Or maybe if I hadn't actually liked every one of these people, if I didn't wish with everything I had that I could actually belong with them. That someone like Duke would actually want me.

But this was the perfect storm, for lack of a better metaphor, and it was their kindness and warmth that broke me down.

My knife and fork hit the plate with a clatter. I moved quickly, pushing my chair upward and losing Duke's touch. That was a good thing, I told myself.

"I'm so sorry, if you'll excuse me," I muttered, through tears and shame.

Then I bolted.

I actually ran from the table, like some dramatic heroine in any one of the movies I'd been in.

* * *

Duke followed me.

And I really didn't want him to. I definitely didn't expect him to. I knew that life was not like the movies, that the man didn't usually chase the girl who ran away. Real-life men weren't like that.

I was quickly realizing, however, that Duke was unlike any real-life man I'd ever encountered.

I wasn't crying. I wasn't *that* cliché of course.

I was pacing.

Treading tracks in the carpet of the room that I still considered "ours" in this house.

Duke didn't stop me, didn't say anything. He just quietly closed the door and watched me pace.

At first, I tried to ignore it. I figured he might leave if I kept ignoring him. But it didn't really work that way.

He was trying to play a game of emotional chicken with me, just standing there staring. Usually, I'd be able to win at such a game since I held this part of myself as close to my chest as someone like me could.

Of course, the media had dug up details about my background. But as soon as I got enough money to do so, I hired a professional "fixer" to bury parts I wanted buried and alter parts I didn't need in the public eye.

Such a thing worked.

You couldn't erase history. But if you had enough money, you could change it.

So the media knew some of my past—the carefully cultivated version.

That I'd been orphaned at a very young age, been lucky to be adopted by a young couple who couldn't conceive naturally. They had given me a happy, healthy childhood. They'd tragically died just before I made it big—convenient so they couldn't give any interviews or pose for photos with their daughter.

The real ones, the ones who were unfortunately still alive and well weren't really ones to follow Hollywood starlets. And even if they did, I had a new name, new nose, and sufficient cosmetic alternations to my face and body that they'd never recognize me. Even if I didn't do all of that, they'd never looked hard enough at me as a child to pinpoint me as an adult.

No one knew the truth beyond the people I paid to make it go away and the people that were involved.

I'd planned on it staying that way until the day I died.

But here was Duke. Staring at me.

I stopped pacing, stared back. I wanted to glare but I didn't have it in me.

"I don't remember my father," I said. "Not what he looked like, at least. Not from memory. I can recall the photos I've seen of him. I can tell you what a one-dimensional version of him is like. Dark hair. Extraordinary mustache. Smile on his face and in his eyes. But I can't say what he looks like in motion. How tall he was. None of that. I can't even really remember him at all. Sometimes I get snatches, like how he used to do my hair."

I squinted into the past, tried to call up one of the precious few images I had of the man.

The harder I tried to remember, the blurrier and grainier the memory became.

"He'd spend so long brushing it, getting it just perfect," I said. "I don't know if it was because he liked doing it, or he didn't want it to be so obvious I was a girl without a mother." I shrugged. "I guess it doesn't matter, since I quickly became a girl without a father too." I paused.

Yet the night the police came to the door, and the teenager babysitting me broke down in tears—that was in stark detail.

"An orphan, and I didn't have any extended family. My mother had no one and my father's parents had died young," I continued. "They put me into foster care. I got a home quickly. They were good actors, my foster parents, maybe they're where I got my skill from. Because they looked nice, kind. Loving. They played their part perfectly, to everyone but me. I don't know if they were just evil or if I wasn't what they expected."

I didn't look up at Duke, as I wasn't brave enough for that. So I looked down instead.

"Whatever it was, they made it clear their love was only for show and the paycheck. They never hit me or anything. They just liked to lock me away for hours, not buy me clothes—not that they had much money anyway—so I'd always go to school wearing things too small. Kids teased me, of course. It didn't bother me. Or at least I acted like I didn't care. I got so good that I fooled myself. They wouldn't feed me much either. So it was a good thing I didn't grow much so my clothes weren't comical on me. And it prepared me for a lifetime of hunger."

I laughed. "I've always thought it's ironic, that I thought freedom and riches meant a full stomach, as no one controlled what I ate. But the riches came, and since then, I've never known a truly full stomach. Not that it matters. I'm sure it sounds ridiculous. The movie star complaining. I *could* eat, if I really wanted to. But I will say, I'm no longer quite as good at convincing myself I don't care what people think of me."

Only after all the words came out, the look on Duke's face penetrated, did I realize just how much I'd spilled. Everything. My whole fucking soul on a platter for him to devour. To own.

"What I'm trying to say is, you're lucky," I said, trying to recover, trying to put a chill in my voice. "I know how annoying it is for people to point that out when you're feeling pissed off. But it's true. Your parents adore you, Duke. And I know that you don't think they know the real you, the one that changed into a macho-man, but they see it. Because they're your family. And, because you're not that great of an actor." I'd meant to end that last bit on a joke. A tease. Something light to distract from how unintentionally heavy I'd gotten.

From the look on Duke's face, it hadn't worked.

Fuck.

I'd been so sure that I'd do anything to get that blank dislike from his gaze, to be something more to him. Be careful what you wished for, because I didn't like this. I hated how much I loved Duke looking at me like I was...somebody.

I tried to move. "I—"

No sooner than I had tried to make my escape, his hands were stopping me, yanking me, smashing my mouth to his. I was so shocked I didn't do much at first. I let him control the kiss, mostly because he wasn't letting me do anything but follow his lead. But then I gained coherence. Then hunger crawled up my throat. Then I kissed him back, gained control of my own.

The kiss was like nothing I'd ever experienced. I knew I'd acted to make a kiss look like this before, for the farce that romance and passion really existed. To sell a movie. But never, ever had I felt as if my entire body was on fire and my clothes were weights that needed to be lifted from my body immediately.

A throat cleared.

Loudly.

In a way that made me suspect the throat clearer had already tried to do this quietly previously, but we'd both been too lost in making out to even notice.

Not that this was making out.

I didn't know what this was.

Sex.

This was sex without penetration, without being horizontal. Which made sense, as Duke was a walking sexy macho-man, he kissed like a fucking macho-man. And I'd thought that was all bullshit.

I tried to extract myself from the kiss knowing the audience, since I could suck face with some asshole in a movie with a whole crew watching, but this was nothing like acting. This was nothing like anything, and I didn't need nor want an audience.

Or maybe I needed to show womankind this in order to make sure they didn't settle for assholes and knew it existed. Or maybe it was just Duke. He was an anomaly and it was my duty to hold on to him.

"Babe?"

I blinked.

Then I looked to see Duke was looking at me, mouth quirked in amusement, but eyes still on fire with the kiss and the promise it gave.

His brother was full-on smiling, arms across his chest, not looking at all embarrassed or sorry for interrupting.

My face flamed. "I was just conducting research to see if the perfect kiss existed and now that I know it does, I'll return the information back to womankind, so they can all dump their deadbeats who don't know how to kiss."

The words tumbled right out of my brain and into the air. My face flamed. I tried to withdraw so I could escape and hide under some rock to die of shame.

Duke's embrace tightened. His grin widened.

His brother chuckled. "Well, I'd appreciate it if you kept it under wraps, since I don't need all the women in this town gunning for my brother." He raised his brow. "I'm a pretty good kisser too."

"I don't doubt it," I replied without thinking.

Duke's grip tightened and his smile wavered slightly. This reaction was welcome, since I knew how to deal with the crazy jealous alpha.

I rolled my eyes. "Oh chill out, macho-man," I told Duke. "I was merely pointing out that such a thing as good kissing runs in the family, like handsomeness. I bet your dad's great at it too. But it's not like I'm going to set out to find out firsthand."

Fuck.

I thought I'd lapse back into sounding sane and bitchy, but I just sounded like a loon who wanted to make out with their dad.

The smile returned.

Another chuckle from his brother.

"As much as I'd love to continue being a part of this conversation, and trust me, I would," Tanner said. "I'm gonna have to break you two up. We got some shit going on with the cattle in field twelve and we need all hands on deck."

Duke's jaw tightened. He glanced back down at me.

I smiled sweetly. Now that I had some time to recover from the best kiss of my life—and from spilling my guts about my past—I recalled being mad at Duke for the whole wedding thing. And then I remembered that Duke wasn't supposed to be kissing me in the first place. Not behind closed doors, at least.

Tanner had saved the day. Yet another hero in the family.

"This isn't over," Duke said, grasping the back of my neck.

I didn't lower my eyes. "Oh yes, it is."

9

LATER NEVER CAME.

Duke didn't arrive until after I'd gone to sleep, real sleep. I'd been planning to feign it when he got back. The kiss had shaken me to my core. If I'd let him in last night, I would've been doomed. I was nothing but a raw nerve after spilling all of that, giving Duke that.

I'd woken up before Duke yet again. I was getting good at sneaking out while he was still asleep. He was getting better at storming into the family kitchen with a scowl on his face, Frenching me in front of his grandmother and mumbling all sorts of things.

He'd whispered promises in my ear before storming out for the day.

Harriet and I had become fast friends.

Anna and me too, but she was more active with the day-to-day activities on the ranch. She might've been in her fifties, but she worked harder than I ever had.

I helped out where I could, but there was a limit to my skills, and I also knew that Duke didn't want any visitors to the ranch catching a glimpse of me and fucking it all up. As it was, the ranch hands were all briefed on how important my "privacy" was and Duke was policing my interactions with them, which was totally fucking annoying, because they seemed extremely cool. Like real-life cowboys. They weren't impressed with me, and I loved that.

So when Duke was out with his father or doing any of the million things that there were to get done in the day, I usually snuck off to tag along on rides or to watch them do cowboy shit.

They didn't mind. In fact, they definitely enjoyed it. They loved the audience.

But today, Harriet and I were enjoying a cheeseboard on the porch of the cabin. She'd brought everything over and insisted that she organize it.

I'd let her, because I knew little about organizing a cheese board, considering I'd never really eaten one in my life.

And when she set it down on the small wicker table, I totally got what she meant. It was on a rustic wooden cutting board, filled to the brim. Grapes. Apple slices. Chutneys, various cheeses. Sliced bread. Crackers.

"This is all meant to be for us?" I asked.

She grinned at me while lifting her phone up to take a photo of the board from above. "No, I'm very aware of your eating habits, and though I'm happy to see they've gotten better in your time here, I don't think we've changed what I'm guessing is years of habits in a week." She tapped at her phone, no doubt adding filters and working her magic.

Harriet was, in fact, the bomb at Instagram. Her feed was full of earth-toned aesthetic shots of the ranch, of food, of her hands holding various drinks. Even some sneaky ones of the men in her family standing with their backs to the camera, the sun setting on the ranch.

I blinked at her response, at how astute she was and how little judgment there was in her tone. After the first night, no one had tried to push baked goods onto me and let me serve myself. Harriet was right, things had changed. Drastically, considering now I ate three meals a day when before I was lucky if I had one. I'd helped Anna cook most of them—well, tried to. After she saw the extent of how bad I was at cooking, she had decided we'd have weekly cooking lessons.

Duke hadn't mentioned it either, and I knew that he'd noted it. He noted everything. It seemed such a fucking stupid thing to be obsessing about in the midst of all of this, but it was a big part of my life before. It was attached to my image, my worth, not something I could easily just shake.

I was proud of myself for smearing the bread with chutney then topping it with cheese.

Harriet grinned in approval.

"You make a good board, Harriet," I said after swallowing.

She lifted her glass to clink with mine—another thing I loved about her, and the entire family in general, their healthy drinking habits. "I do, don't I?"

We fell into silence for a beat, staring out at the view I'd never be able to get used to, and all things going well, I wouldn't have time to get used to it.

One thing I had gotten used to was the fact that Harriet was rarely ever content in silence.

"Now, I am very interested about what your girlfriends think of Duke and how many you had to bitch-slap from stealing your man," Harriet said. "And I know it sounds incredibly biased to think my grandson is sufficiently good-looking to have your friends try to steal him from you, but I also have eyes. And they show me he is a handsome man and no doubt in demand."

I sipped my drink. "No doubt," I agreed, thinking of all the woman in LA most likely waiting for his call. Or the girlfriend that I'd created in my mind. She was petite. Much shorter than him, even in heels. But she didn't wear heels much. She went hiking. She was a kindergarten teacher, was close with her family, volunteered at soup kitchens, had plenty of girlfriends she could have book clubs or movie nights with or pretty much whatever women did when they hung out with each other.

"Am I wrong?" Harriet asked in response to my brooding silence.

I glanced up to her. "No, I don't think you're wrong. If I had girlfriends, single or married, with half a brain and a functioning libido, they'd be going to war with me for Duke."

Harriet raised her brow. "If? You don't have girlfriends back home? But I've seen you with all sorts of people on Instagram. You were at a Kardashian's party not long ago."

I smiled. You couldn't help but do so around Harriet, especially when it became clear the eighty-year-old was addicted to social media and was more well-informed on popular culture than your average millennial.

"Of course I go to parties," I replied. "I pose for photos. I play the game." I paused, looking out for a beat before meeting her eyes. I could totally lie, could say that I was tight with all the Jenners and Kardashians alike. But not under this Montana sky, not under her sharp gaze. "But the only true friend I have is my publicist and the only reason he wouldn't scratch my face off for his chance at Duke would be because it would make his life that much harder having to deal with the fallout of doing such a thing." A strong pang went through my gut thinking of Andre. It was a strange feeling. Unfamiliar. I missed him.

I hadn't realized that he was the first person I spoke to in the morning and usually the last person I spoke to in the evening too. It had only been two weeks here, but it was the longest in a decade that I'd gone without speaking to him.

"Yeah, he's the only friend I have," I said, clearing my throat. "I've never really had girlfriends. When I turned eighteen, I wasn't in college making bad decisions at frat parties. I was auditioning, going for every shitty job I could, along with hundreds of other girls who looked like me. Obviously, I didn't make friends then, because we were all hungry, desperate, and willing to stab each other in the back if it meant we looked better." I paused. "It hasn't changed that much, even though I'm now surrounded by women who have found the necessary success to not sell pimple cream. But we're all still hungry." I glanced down to the cheese plate. "In more ways than one."

Harriet was shocked, maybe. It didn't make sense if she was. Anyone who spent even a little time with me, worked with me, could totally understand why I didn't have friends.

Then again, I wasn't that person at the ranch. I hadn't been since the second I'd climbed out of the truck. I'd spent time trying to find that woman I'd been these past years, trying to put on my mask, protect myself.

But Duke—the asshole—was totally right. I couldn't lie in this place.

"I'm a good person," I whispered surprising myself. "I've been pretending to be a bad one for so long because it's easier. And now I'm not sure I know how to be good. I think I've been pretending for so long that I actually am bad."

She reached across the table to squeeze my hand. "This world is far too preoccupied with creating two columns of people. Good or bad. It's dangerous, because we've all got a little of both in us. But for the sake of this conversation, I'm gonna go binary." She sipped her wine leisurely. "I consider myself a good judge of character. I haven't seen much of the world, so I'm not versed on many luxuries and such. But I know people. And honey, you're not bad person. You're a good person who's lost your way." She squeezed again. "You're findin' your way back now though."

I blinked through tears. "I'm not really Duke's girl," I admitted.

She smiled. "Oh, I knew when you walked in here that you weren't. You're a good actress, my dear, but my grandson has never had a good poker face. You might not have been his girl when you walked in here, but you sure as heck are now."

* * *

I was eating breakfast at the breakfast bar. The sun was only just starting to rise above the mountains. The French doors were open, letting in the slightly frigid morning breeze. The lilies planted right outside mixed with the unique perfume of the outdoors.

I didn't have the television on. No music. I'd never had a morning with such stillness, such quiet. It wasn't at all remarkable. But it was the best morning I'd had in my life.

Especially since it started with me waking up in Duke's arms.

This time, when I'd stayed awake to revel in his embrace, he didn't wake up. It was our norm now, pretending we were a couple to his family. And when we were sleeping. It was creeping into the waking hours now too. Him brushing my hair from my face when there was no one else around. Forehead kisses. Oh, and the dirty talk about how he was going to fuck me.

My stomach dipped with the mere memory.

My stomach dipped even further when the man in question walked through the door to the kitchen.

Shirtless.

I made sure to sip my coffee so he didn't see me all but drooling over him. How long had it been since I'd seen him like this for the first time? Why hadn't the effect worn off yet? Then again, I had the feeling if I had a hundred years, Duke wouldn't wear off on me. But I didn't have a hundred years. Every single day was numbered. I wasn't even sure if I had tomorrow. When had that stopped being a good thing and started being the beginning of a nightmare?

Duke's eyes drank me in with that same look that had been glued to his face since...that morning, that very first one—maybe before. Hunger. Something else. Something softer.

His gaze flickered down to my plate, then his eyes widened in surprise. "You're eating a bagel."

Of all the things I'd expect him to say with that look on his face, that didn't even factor into the top ten.

I looked down at the half-eaten slice of bagel, slathered in cream cheese—because it was absolutely criminal to eat a bagel without it. "Yeah, I am."

No response when I looked up.

"Harriet has them flown in from New York," I continued.

He nodded, leaning on a doorjamb in a way that should be criminal. No man should be able to make such a simple thing so damn sexy.

"She does. She lived there for a year or so in her twenties. When she met my grandpa. She calls it her 'rumspringa' from the ranch." He chuckled.

I smiled too, only imagining the crazy things a twenty something Harriet might've got up to back then.

It was now he pushed off the doorjamb, walking over to me, slowly. Purposefully. I didn't move as he settled in behind me, lifting my hair from the back of my neck and laying his lips there. My entire body shivered. My thighs clenched with the way the simple gesture turned me on. "Another thing," he said, lips now at my ear. "You don't leave the bed while I'm sleepin'. You wake me up so I can make sure we both start our day right." His voice was pure sex.

I didn't even care about the orders he was so used to speaking in. I didn't care about the reasons why not.

"Well, there's still time for us to do that," I said, my voice thick.

Who the heck knew why I said that. Maybe it was the magic in the morning. Maybe it was the cabin. Or maybe it was because I was totally and utterly sexually frustrated and was sick of fighting this anymore.

Duke's eyes flared. He was surprised, I knew. He'd expected a fight from me because that's all that I'd given him thus far.

His surprise didn't last for long, after all, he was a macho-man and macho-men were all about action.

My chair whirled around quickly, my robe was opened only seconds after that. Duke's gaze turned midnight when it landed on my nipples poking through the delicate fabric.

He leaned forward and laid his mouth over the silk, sucking at my already hard nipples. I thrust my hand into his hair, pulling at it with the force the act was affecting me. I was somewhat of an expert on sex and orgasms. I'd had enough of both, but they were definitely not mutually exclusive. And the vast majority of intense orgasms I'd had in my life came from a really good vibrator. Sure, there were some men who had been taught about a woman's body and weren't selfish enough to ignore the idea that a woman deserves pleasure too, but those men were only slightly less rare than unicorns.

Having had experience with bad, mediocre, passable and great sex, I knew that the act of having a man suck on your nipples was not enough to make you come. Sure, if done right, it might get you excited, not for the feeling but for the fact a man who takes the time to worship your body in that way is usually going to pay better attention to things south of the nipple.

I'd never been fond of it, if I was honest. It was either sloppy, too rough, or too weak.

But like Goldilocks, I'd found a nipple sucking that was just right.

My thighs clenched, my stomach tightened, and I let out a small noise from between my pursed lips.

Duke returned this with a deep and feral growl from the back of his throat. One hand was on my neck, the other pushing up the fabric of my nightgown.

He didn't stay at my nipple for long, which I was glad about. He was good with his mouth and I was greedy, horny, and really ready for an orgasm.

Duke didn't waste any time with kissing his way down my stomach, didn't even look up at me. He was too focused on his task. There was a desperation to him that turned me on even more. Popular culture liked to paint men as liking the act of going down on women, but in reality, they were lazy and happy to receive oral, certainly not give it.

Duke's lips over the top of my panties told me he was a giver.

Big time.

My hands yanked at his hair, not even caring if I pulled it out from the roots. I wanted to hurt him for showing me this kind of pleasure—knowing it was only temporary—that I'd carry around the memory that this existed and not even my vibrator would be able to live up to it.

Such thoughts were violently silenced the second Duke pushed my panties aside and laid his lips right there.

Then he worked the fingers too.

The fact he was doing this without so much as kissing me first was that much more intense and erotic. He was devouring me with an intensity I'd only entertained in my fantasies—with the cynical knowledge such hunger to please couldn't exist in men.

My climax came quick, intense, and never ending.

Duke didn't relent during my cries, during the spots that danced in front of my vision. He was ruthless, and I almost pleaded at him to stop, unsure if my body could handle another orgasm.

As it was, it hit me before I could regain control over my motor functions.

I must've blacked out or something, since the next thing I heard was banging. Knocking.

Duke was no longer in between my legs. My panties were back in their previous position, my robe covered my body. That happened without my help. Duke was quick and efficient, even so far as to readjust things in his pants so the erection was not bulging out as it had been previously.

As if we'd choreographed it, Harriet appeared in the doorway at the exact moment we became decent...ish. I figured the flush on my face and my general expression would give me away, especially to Harriet's eagle eyes.

She looked between us and grinned wide. "Oh good, I'm interrupting something."

* * *

Duke loved his grandmother.

A lot.

She was one of his all-time favorite people. But this morning, he had to fight off the urge to remove her body from the cabin. He finally got to taste Anastasia, to hear what she sounded like when she came.

And fuck, was it good.

Not to mention the fact she was a natural redhead.

He considered himself relatively robust in the bedroom, but it had been a fucking battle not to come in his pants like a goddamn thirteen-year-old. He'd managed only knowing he was about to plunge into her.

Then his *grandmother*.

His well-meaning grandmother, to be sure, but the ultimate cockblock.

He'd taken the day to try and lock himself down, to stop himself from tearing Anastasia away from both his grandmother and mother, throw her over his shoulder like a caveman, and fuck her senseless. He had a pretty good idea she'd fuck him senseless too.

With a somewhat clearer head, he'd realized that senseless fucking would send the complete wrong message. It was too cheap for her. As much as raw, carnal fucking had its place—and it would have a very good place with Anastasia—Duke didn't want it for their first time.

Especially with Anastasia still recovering from a fucking rattlesnake bike. David Hollows had checked in on her, as promised, and she was recovering quickly without any of the more severe side effects. Still, Duke watched her closely. The worst-case scenario hung over his head, taunting him with how easily he could have lost her. Before he'd even fucking had her.

She was his.

It was a Neanderthal thing to even think and no way was he stupid enough to say it out loud to the feisty, independent woman who was still pretending she didn't feel for him the way he did for her.

Her shields had all fallen away this morning—with her submission. The fucking *memory* made his cock twitch.

He had to stop thinking about it before he drove himself crazy. So instead, he focused on something else that was driving him crazy. Not just crazy, it was something that sent murder coursing through his veins.

That was better to focus on at this juncture, especially since Anastasia was out with his father and brother, the only two other men he'd consider her safe with.

"You good?" Keltan said, on alert.

Duke knew why, he was meant to keep contact at a minimum, as a precaution. They had excellent safeguards against anyone tapping into their shit, but they weren't stupid enough to risk it.

Duke felt comfortable risking it for this. "Anastasia had foster parents," he said by response. "Didn't treat her good. Want you to get in contact with whoever you need to, make sure they can never take in a child or collect a paycheck for doin' so again. If they've got any kids with them right now, get them out."

A small pause on the other end of the phone. A small pause filled with fury. Keltan had kids. He had fuckin' morals. He had certain ideas about what to do with people who treated kids and women badly. As did Duke. "Got it," he replied easily.

"Appreciate it."

"Do I owe Rosie a thousand bucks?" Keltan asked, tone less tinged with fury.

"Come again?" Duke asked, watching Anastasia walk from the stables with his father. Her hair was piled into a ponytail, most of it jostled loose from her ride. She laughed at something her father said. The sound carried with the wind and it was fucking sweet.

Because it was real. Watching Anastasia here was like watching that fucking ponytail. It was ordered, perfected at the start, controlled. But slowly, this life, his family, maybe even him, had together jostled it loose. Jostled her. So she fell out of that fucking act. That image. Watching her become herself was something to marvel at.

"We've had a pool going," Keltan said in his ear. "It's about half and half. Between who thinks you're gonna come back with her, drop her off, and never work again. Or come back with her as yours. Rosie, interestingly is more romantic about it all. As is Heath, also interestingly. Luke disagrees, maybe 'cause of the cop in him or maybe 'cause he just likes disagreeing with his wife. I would've pegged George as a realist, but he's with the romantics on this one. Not that I'm not romantic. Every man worth his salt is, and if you repeat that, I'll beat the shit out of you." Keltan paused. "But I also know that people are sometimes exactly as they seem. Am I wrong?"

Duke shouldn't have been surprised at all this shit. The office was like a bunch of fucking high schoolers, especially since he was the only one not married. Well, apart from the new hire, Knox. But no one knew fucking shit about him. He did his job, spoke as if words were rationed, and didn't offer anything about his personal life. Rosie had considered it her personal mission to find out more about him, using interpersonal skills instead of hacking into his background—only because she'd tried to hack into his shit and there was nothing to hack. An interesting first for Rosie.

So no, Duke wasn't surprised that they were taking fucking bets on this shit. He should've been more pissed off than he was. But he was too busy listening to the sound of Anastasia's laugh and watching her legs move in those jeans.

"Yes, brother," he said, as she walked toward him, still smiling. "You're totally fuckin' wrong. She's everything *but* what she seems."

* * *

Duke had had a weird look in his eye since I got back from herding cattle with his father and brother.

No, that was a lie.

He'd had a look in his eye ever since he ate me out at the breakfast bar, and then after Harriet had interrupted before things could go further. Although I wasn't sure I would've survived much further, so maybe the interruption was a good thing. At the time, I didn't think so, of course. At the time, I would've been willing to let the life drain out of me in order to continue...whatever that was with Duke.

He had looked pissed off at his grandmother, the one he'd shown nothing but respect and love to since I got here. But he masked it quickly. He masked it all quickly. It was impressive the way he could wipe that entire moment from his face, as if it had never happened, as if it weren't as pivotal and important as I had thought it was.

Which had me second-guessing the moment the entire day.

Had me overthinking every moment I'd spent here.

I didn't have experience in men wanting me. Sure, they wanted my tits, my ass, the bragging rights to say they'd fucked a movie star. If they wanted more than sex, it was also for the same reasons, plus money, status, whatever they could suck from me like a leech.

I had been kidding myself thinking Duke wanted more. There was no evidence in my entire life that I was worth wanting, that I was worth anything.

Maybe Duke wanted to make the act that much easier if we fucked. Maybe he was just horny and there weren't any other options.

"Baby?"

I jerked myself from my self-pity. I'd been unsaddling the horse I'd taken out riding today.

Duke took the saddle as I heaved it off. I glared at him. Of course I couldn't do the heavy lifting.

I was pissed off at him. I decided that was easier. If he really wanted to do the dirty work for me, he could be my guest.

"Anastasia! Jesus," he yelled at my back while I walked out of the stables.

I ignored this. Unfortunately, Duke had longer legs and the macho-man purpose stride, so he caught up with me easily.

"You runnin' away from me now?" he asked as I walked in the direction of the house. Harriet was bound to be there.

"I'm not someone who runs from anything," I replied, though that was not completely true.

"You sure seem to be walking fast," he shot back, sounding far too amused.

I stopped abruptly, put my hand on my hip, narrowed my eyes—the patented female battle stance.

Duke's eyes twinkled but he knew better than to grin.

"I'm not running, Duke," I said, voice quiet this time. "Why don't you tell me what's going on between you and your brother?"

That took the twinkle out of his eyes. "It's complicated."

I raised my brow. "You think everything else is simple?"

He shook his head. "Touché." He sighed, looked out on to the ranch, to the home in front of us. There was regret, loss in his expression. I hated to see it. I wished that I was a woman who could take all of that away.

"It's not just one thing," Duke said after a long pause. "Not a huge event that split us apart. Guess nothin' in life is truly that dramatic." He looked to me. "I left. Things got fucked from there. I lost the ability to be a good brother, a good son, a good man."

I stepped forward, grasping his stubbled chin in my hand and jerked his face to meet mine. "You need to stop," I snapped. "I've had the displeasure to encounter many men in my life. Many terrible men. Selfish. Cruel. Violent. Everything in between. Up until I witnessed a murder, I wasn't sure that good men existed. Now, you sure can be an asshole when you want to be." I grinned at him. "But you can still be a good man and an asshole at the same time. You do it beautifully. I'm not an expert on how to be good, but I can see you're not bad, just human. Unfortunately, even macho-men bleed." I placed my hand in the area where I'd seen his two most prominent scars.

His eyes never left mine. There was no amusement now, no anger, no coldness. There was something else entirely.

Duke didn't speak. Instead, he lowered his mouth and kissed the ever-loving crap out of me.

The crunch of boots against gravel and a throat clearing made us stop, which was good, because I was ready to tear off his clothes and mount him right here in the dirt.

We both looked to our left, and Anna was standing there, watching us with a smile on her face.

I stepped back. Or tried to. Duke didn't let me go far, as he intertwined my fingers with his.

"Are you two okay with lasagna for dinner?" Anna asked, looking between us. "Anastasia, we can work on that being your first go-to dish. It's easy and a crowd-pleaser."

She meant it in the kindest way possible, of course. Anna was selfless, giving, patient. I was coming to look forward to the evenings in the kitchen with her and the conversations we had.

But the last sentence caught me.

Crowd-pleaser.

I was well acquainted with crowds. In fact, I felt more welcome in them than at the dinner table with this boisterous and loving family. The fact I was familiar with large groups of people had nothing to do with the number of friends I had. Whatever dinner parties I had were full of alternative motives, whereas carbs, gluten, and cheese were never present.

After this was all over, I wouldn't have anyone to cook lasagna for.

That wouldn't make me refuse her offer, of course, but it would sour it slightly.

"As painful as it is for me to refuse your lasagna, we have other plans," Duke said to his mother before I could reply. His arm was light on my hip, but heavy with promise.

"Other plans?" I repeated, tilting my chin to look at his profile. And damn, if it was a good one.

"That's okay, we'll do lasagna another night," Anna said

quickly. Dragging my gaze from her son, I saw a warm and slightly sad smile on her face.

Duke didn't wait for me to say anything else. "See you tomorrow, Mom."

Then he directed us away from the house, toward the field leading to our cabin. *Directing us* meaning I would've had to fight him in front of his mother in order to stay in place. Granted, I wasn't opposed to fighting him in front of his mother if he wanted to manhandle me—she was apt to support me—but I didn't want to fight him.

It was sad, really. We hadn't been at the ranch that long. I should've held out. Should've held on to sense.

Duke's hand was strong and dry intertwined with mine on the walk back to the cabin. It was a routine we'd fallen into, morning and evening. Sure, driving would be quicker, but it wasn't about quicker around here. It was about hearing the birds in the morning and crickets in the evening. It was about sunrise, sunset, and the midnight stars. It was about the breeze that smelled of grass and sunshine.

Duke and I had not held hands on any of the previous walks.

Granted, up until this morning, he hadn't used his mouth to give me two of the most intense orgasms of my life.

I hated people that held hands. No one really liked it. Someone's palms were always sweaty, the other gripped too hard or not hard enough. No one's strides were exactly the same, so someone had to walk awkwardly in order to make it work.

It was just assholes who wanted to scream at the world "we're in love."

But here I was, holding hands with Duke. Our strides matched each other, both palms were dry, and our grips equally firm.

I should've let go.

"What are our plans?" I asked about halfway home.

Duke glanced at me but I didn't dare make eye contact. Walking while holding hands was one thing; holding hands, walking, *and* staring into each other's eyes was quite another.

"Figured that the way we've done things is pretty jacked to say the least," he said. "To be fair, I don't think either of us had expected it to go this way."

Yeah, I definitely didn't expect any of this. Hoped for it, in some dark recesses of my mind, but expectation was emotional trauma wanting to happen. I tried to avoid it.

"Not sayin' I'm not fucking pleased with the turn of events," Duke continued, squeezing my hand. "I really am. But figured since everything else around us is jacked, I'm gonna try and do at least one thing right."

"What?"

He grinned at me and fuck if that grin didn't make me want to do the melty girl thing.

"You'll just have to wait and see."

* * *

Dean Martin was playing when we walked into the cabin.

I loved Dean Martin.

This was not something I'd told Duke.

It was something, however, I'd told Harriet.

The lights were on low, and there were a few candles scattered on various surfaces, candles that Duke would not have been able to light since he'd been out all day and at the homestead when I'd ridden in earlier. He had been freshly showered, though, I'd noted that with hunger and slight disappointment. I liked the dirt of the day clinging to him. It seemed natural.

I, however, hadn't showered. And though the day hadn't involved a lot of dirt, riding was hard work, and I was more than aware of the dirt and sweat dried on my skin.

Not to mention the low throb in my calf. I'd been surprised how quickly I'd recovered. It was nothing more than a bad bee sting. This was lucky, I knew, just another part of the magic of the Hammond ranch.

Duke, of course, asked about it intermittently throughout the days since the bite. He'd been gruff and aggressive when he thought I was doing too much. This was followed by me getting aggressive back, much to the entertainment of whatever family member was watching at the time.

Duke's lips at my neck put my attention right in this moment, although I wasn't sure how I'd let it shift in the first place.

"You go have a bath, baby. I'll take care of dinner," he murmured.

"A bath? Dinner? Are you trying to woo me, Mr. Hammond?"

A grin. Lips on mine. "You bet your beautiful ass I am, Ms. Edwards." He swatted my butt. "Bath."

Now, I wasn't inclined to take orders from Duke, but it had already been established that I'd lost much of my resolve this morning. Plus, I needed the bath. I had coveted it since we first moved in here but had always thought it was too much—soaking naked in the bath if Duke was on the other side of the door.

Showering was bad enough.

Thoughts of what this night was meant to be trailed along behind me as I made my way toward the master bedroom. How much had changed since this morning? Surely Duke was a guy able to separate sex from emotions. In fact, it didn't take an evolved man to do that. It just took any man. Duke was not any man. He was exceptionally smart and aware. Sure, I saw the wild passion in his eyes this morning. It had been damn near feral. But he was also not a man who I thought would lose control easily, especially in a situation like this, where our relationship was meant to be strictly professional.

He knew what he was doing.

I had no fucking clue.

But right now, I was taking a bath. One step at a time.

I undressed in the bedroom, throwing my clothes in a hamper that was magically emptied at some point during the day. My clothes—underwear included—were always neatly folded and put away. For someone used to having almost everything done for me, that felt uncomfortable here. I should be able to do my own laundry. Did Duke have it done because he thought I was a pampered princess who would throw a fit if she had to do her own laundry?

No, if Duke thought that, he'd make sure I was the only one that did the laundry.

A mystery. A small, seemingly insignificant one at that, but one that bothered me nonetheless.

I wrapped myself in my robe, snatched a book, and went into the bathroom. I gasped softly with what I found. More candles. A shit of a lot more. Every surface was piled high with them, enough to illuminate the full bath, bubbles and all. I stuck my hand in the water.

Warm.

Bordering on hot.

Freshly filled.

Harriet. Yet again.

I should've found it weird that the grandmother of the man I was...whatever I was, had drawn a bubble bath for me, lit candles and prepared a romantic night where her grandson was going to get lucky.

It was weird.

It was totally Harriet, and I loved it.

I also loved that Duke had not only thought of doing something like this, but enlisted the help of his insane grandmother.

Sinking into the water, I tried to shake off my reservations, wipe at them with a loofa as if they would glide off me. It was kind to call them reservations. The more accurate description would be fears.

I was terrified at how happy a fucking bath and some candles made me, how the gesture and the people involved were snaking under my skin in a way I knew would mark me forever.

They'd eventually be nothing more than marks...scars. Because this was a good, clean family. Even Duke, who I was sure had marks on his soul—had done some bad shit—was clean too.

But the dirt was more than just under my nails. The shine, the fame, the money, it was all smoke and mirrors so no one saw how filthy and broken I really was.

Self-deprecating thoughts were cut short when another person entered the bathroom. I jumped, swishing the water over the edge.

"It's me," Duke said, calmly, apologetic.

Of course it was him. No way would macho-man Duke let anyone come skulking into this place.

Even though bubbles were covering most of my body and Duke's lips had been on my pussy this morning, I felt shy.

Shy.

Me.

Considering my history, I would've thought such a thing was impossible.

But my stomach dropped ever so slightly and my cheeks warmed with a blush that makeup artists had only ever applied.

The candles were the only light in the bathroom, but Duke was clearly visible for me to see he wasn't averting his eyes. No protecting of my modesty. No apologizing for the intrusion. He walked in here like it was totally natural.

It was another intensely intimate moment, the likes of which I hadn't experienced.

He placed a large glass of wine on the small side table beside the bath, right where my book was resting. Seemed my mind had been too chaotic to even think of picking it up.

"Thought this might help you relax a little," Duke said.

He was towering over me in a way that should've made me feel small, vulnerable. But the thickness of Duke's voice, the tight way he held his body, showed me I had an effect on him. I had power over him, lying here naked with him above me, fully clothed.

I had a hard time thinking of anything else but yanking him into the bath with me, finishing what we started this morning.

"Don't," he growled.

I blinked. Could he read minds now?

"Don't what?"

"Don't fuckin' look at me like that."

I hid my grin. "Like what?"

His fingers grasped my chin as he bent down to put his face inches from mine. "You play a lot of things well, baby, but innocent isn't one of them. Don't you look at me in a way that makes me want to drag you out of the bath and fuck you on the floor."

I really wanted him to do that.

Really. Fucking. Wanted. Him.

He leaned back just as I was about to push my body forward and lay my lips on his.

"But I've got a plan for tonight. I want to feed you. Then I'll feast on you again."

And then he left.

He fricking walked out on that line.

The bastard.

* * *

"First off, did you have some kind of radioactive spider or mosquito bite at some point in your life to give you way too many skills?" I asked. "Either that, or God was not making mountains or constructing sunsets when she made you. No, she was focused. Because this..." I looked at my plate. I made a kiss with my mouth and put my finger to it. Never had I made that gesture before in my life and it was awkward and embarrassing and totally fueled by my second glass of wine.

Time to recover before Duke could say anything. "Secondly, why are you in LA?" I asked after finishing my third bite of the ravioli Duke had cooked.

I hadn't been able to speak for the first two bites because he'd cooked it.

From scratch.

Yes, this macho-man cowboy could make pasta from scratch. I'd already grilled him, tried to get him to admit that his mother had prepared it for him, but he promised it was all him. And Duke was a man who didn't make a promise if he didn't mean it.

I'd emerged from the bath clean and frustrated. The wine glass was empty, I'd drunk it trying to even myself out.

It almost worked, until I saw Duke at the stove, the table set for two, bottle of wine in the middle of the table.

He was so into his task he didn't see me at first. Good thing too, since my reaction to this scene was visceral and terrifying.

After composing myself, I'd walked in, refilled both of our glasses, and listened to Duke's order telling me to sit and watch.

It wasn't exactly a tall order, watching a hot guy who I totally didn't deserve cook me a romantic dinner.

Although I had experienced almost every sex act that could be experienced, I had never had a man cook for me. Not after my father, of course. I had blurry memories of pink plates, of smiles under moustaches, of the man feeding me.

That must've been the reason for my strong reaction to this whole scene.

"First question, I haven't been bitten by anything radioactive that I know of," Duke said, waiting until he'd finished chewing. "Also I don't think God had anything to do with much. Just been raised by two strong women." His eyes never left mine. "Second, my job's in LA."

"You know that's not what I asked," I said, trying to decide whether I really wanted more of the wonderful dinner or to consume as many pieces of information about Duke as I could. "This place, it is...magic, compared to the bullshit of LA. Your family is here. You suit it here. What made you want to make a living babysitting spoiled celebrities?"

He put his fork down, the teasing left his eyes. "I'll say that babysitting spoiled celebrities has paid off big time." A pause. I took another bite, because my famous self-control was failing me. Duke sipped his wine. "Also, that's just a small part of what we do. Good for the image. Rakes in a lot of money. But the rest of it utilizes things I'm good at."

He didn't have to elaborate for me to understand what he meant. Dark shit. Messy shit. I didn't know how messy or dark. Remembering the team, they'd all looked clean-cut, impressively attractive, and the offices were expensively appointed. Greenstone Security was one of the most reputable firms in the country.

But did I believe each of the men and women I'd sat at that table with were capable of illegal shit?

Totally.

"You're good at being a cowboy," I countered.

"Yeah," he said. "Good at it 'cause it's what I was born for, but life turned me into something different."

"Why did you leave?" That was the big question. Plenty of boys left farms because of poverty, because of shitty parents, but this ranch had neither of those things.

Duke shrugged. "Would like to give you a valid reason, one that makes sense. But don't have one, other than I was a stupid kid. Angry when I had no right to be. Bored. Thought I was meant for something more than this. Then September 11 happened. I felt it my duty, thought fighting for my country would be my calling." Another pause. "War isn't anything like they show you in the movies. People know that, because it's the fucking cliché. But they don't prepare you for how fucking boring it can be. Long stretches of nothing and short bursts of horror. It put everyone on edge, that kind of atmosphere, turned everyone into something different. Turned me into something different. Something useful for Uncle Sam. Then war did look like the movies, in all the worst ways."

Duke still held my eyes in his gaze, forcing me to see just how haunted he was. "Came back different. Like they all do. Didn't even try to come home. Knew that shit wouldn't work for me. Couldn't act like I was the son or brother they'd had. I made peace with it. My family accepted it because...well, you've met them. Because they accept just about anything from people they love. I came home for holidays, for as long as I could handle. Then helped Keltan build Greenstone." He took another sip of wine. "I came here because I didn't think I had any other choice. I came here thinking it would be torture. Not because of you, but because every time I've set foot in my home since I got back, it's been like that. But not this time. This time it feels...different."

I would've choked on my last bite of ravioli had it not been frozen on the fork halfway to my mouth.

Duke was saying things from my fantasy. Well, he wasn't saying it outright, but the fucking meaning was there. Things I thought I wanted to hear.

My fork hit my plate with a clatter. I stood abruptly, gathering my plate and his too.

"I'll do the dishes," I said quickly, averting my eyes.

I didn't give him time to answer, since I escaped to the kitchen. It was a shitty, selfish thing to do, something befitting of Anastasia Edwards. I should've been kind in the face of his brutal honesty. He was sharing all those pieces that I'd been craving, and I'd eaten it all, flesh and bones. But I didn't know how to be kind. Didn't know how to take the responsibility for this feeling.

I expected Duke to follow me. I wanted him to be pissed off at me—for not showing the emotional intelligence that a woman who deserved him would have.

But he didn't.

He sat at the table, drinking his wine, and looked out the window at that view he owned, despite what his past was trying to tell him.

* * *

I took my time with the dishes, made the process as slow as I possibly could. But there was only so long dishes could take. The second the sink was empty, Duke was there. He'd been sitting at the table, drinking wine, watching me silently.

He wasn't sitting now.

"It's time," he said, advancing toward me. There was purpose in his step, desire in his eyes, and sex in his words.

I retreated, quickly and clumsily.

He didn't stop, not until he made me back into a wall and he caged me in with his hands on either side of my face.

My lungs struggled to get air with his closeness, with him pressing into increasingly sensitive parts of me.

"Duke," I warned. It was meant to come out as a warning, at least. But I was thrown, by the change in his demeanor, by the aggression in which he'd backed me into the wall.

I'd known he wanted me. Of course. I'd stopped trying to convince myself it was all part of the act for his family. I was an attractive woman. He was stuck out here for however long. I didn't doubt he had a healthy sex life before all of this. From what I'd seen, there weren't any badass and sexy female ranchers in the immediate vicinity. It made sense that he was looking past his dislike of me and taking what he had in front of him.

That's what all of the other things had been. Him pulling me into his arms in bed. The touches, gentle. The way he had looked at me. He was buttering me up.

"You're not fighting this, Anastasia," he growled, lips on my neck.

My knees quivered and threatened to give out on me with just that. The memory of our kiss assaulted me, and I needed his lips on mine like I needed oxygen. But I stayed on course.

"Yes, I am, Duke," I snapped, hands at his chest trying to push him away.

He stopped kissing my neck, but he didn't move from the wall.

There was still a butt-load of desire in his gaze, but there was irritation peppered through it. Irritation I could handle. It was familiar. I just needed to tease some more out of him.

"We're not doing this," I said.

"We've been doing this since the second you told that fuckin' story to my family after two margaritas," he growled.

That gave me pause. Since the first night? No, that would mean that this was something more than him being horny. And I couldn't deal with that.

"Stop," I said. "Stop with all this shit! You're trying to mess with me just so you can fuck me."

He reared back. Not completely, but enough to show just how offended he was by my statement. "Come again?"

I swallowed my unease at seeing the dangerous version of Duke come out so easily, so close to me, caging me in—with no one else around. Not that he would hurt me. I knew what *those* men looked like. How they spoke. How they touched women. Too gentle when they were trying to woo them and much too rough when they thought they could get away with it.

Duke wasn't that.

But he was dangerous nonetheless. He was trying to intimidate me, and it might've worked if my self-preservation wasn't as
solid as it was. "Don't gaslight me, Duke. You're trying to make it
seem like you actually give a fuck about me so you can get sex out
of the job you've made it very clear that you don't want to do."

That didn't help.

Not at all.

Duke leaned in. His eyes captured mine. His fury coated my
body. "You're so fucking full of shit," he murmured against
my lips.

That was not the response I'd been expecting, at all.

I'd been expecting him to be offended, to throw some nasty
words, to yell, then to storm out and we'd be safely back in our
corners.

But no.

"What?" It was little more than a whisper and I hated myself
for how small I sounded.

"You are full of shit," he repeated, face hovering inches from
mine. "You starve yourself in every facet of your life that means
something. Sure, you live in a ten-million-dollar mansion, own
bags that cost more than people's first cars. All that shit is in
excess, but the stuff that really means anything...you won't pay
the price for."

His hand moved to brush along the fading bruise on my
cheekbone. "I get it, baby. Some of it, because I only know some
of your past. And even some of it is enough to understand why
you've lived how you have, why you've fucking starved yourself. I
get it, but I'm sure as shit not accepting it. It's time you feasted
and I'm gonna be the one to fucking serve you."

Serve. Me.

My panties were obviously drenched at this point.

I was only human.

I knew he was smart. I knew he was strong. But I didn't know he could see that deeply, string such substantial stuff together. Put me on a fricking hook and reel me in.

I was squirming now, desperate to get away to preserve the pathetic life I'd led prior to him.

"I used to do porn," I blurted.

That got him. His face turned blank. Carefully blank. But he didn't immediately let me go in revulsion as I'd expected. "Excuse me?"

I swallowed. It was easier now, since I didn't have a single lie left inside me. Well, maybe one and it was a big one, but it was nothing to do with my past and everything to do with the man in front of me.

"When I first moved out of my foster parents' house, I was poor—ten dollars to my name kind of poor. I had couches to crash on, but welcomes quickly wore out and I was on my way to becoming homeless."

The past surged forward, the memory of that fear clutching me. I never knew where my next meal would come from, my next shower, where I'd sleep. And that had been better than my entire childhood. At least I was in control then.

"But I was beautiful," I continued. Even before the cosmetic procedures, I had been pretty. Something my foster mother had hated. She'd been a cheerleader who'd married an asshole and pissed away her future. My beauty had been just another reason for her to treat me like shit. But it was somewhat of a currency in the real world.

"Young, beautiful, and desperate," I whispered. "The trifecta for the sharks circling the waters for such opportunities. He was nice, the first guy. It was through some crappy audition I didn't get. He said he liked me, gave me a card, said I'd get a job, good money. By this point, I was close to living on the streets. There was no backup, no one to bail me out. I would've done anything."

I paused, squinting my eyes as if that would help blind me to those memories I'd been so blind to in the past.

I straightened my shoulders, forced my chin up in defiance, dared Duke to look down on me. "So I did anything," I continued. "It was horrible, as you'd expect. But not *that* horrible. I was good, by then, at disconnecting myself from things happening in the present, in putting myself away in different compartments. And then there was the money. It seemed like a fortune to me then, even though they were taking advantage of my desperation and naiveté." I didn't look at Duke. "Though I didn't stay naive for long. I was determined, smart. I didn't spend a dime of what I made on anything but the essentials. Got out as quick as I could. Got my first real job on a fluke. I used every dime of that for the best plastic surgeon in the business. He didn't do anything drastic. It was in the subtleties. I changed my hair, my name, everything. That's why no one's ever connected it before—in case you were wondering. I guess it'll come out eventually, but I'm not ashamed of it anymore."

He didn't say anything.

Not for a long time.

I blinked at him, at the blankness on his face, and not even that polite, judgmental blankness that people wore until they could safely leave your presence and never see you again.

No, true blankness like I'd told him I wasn't a fan of mushrooms. Like he'd just received information that wasn't shocking or obscure.

"What?" he asked, reading my face, as he was getting better and better at doing.

I fidgeted with my rings. "Well...that's it?"

He tilted his head ever so slightly. "What do you mean?"

"I just told you I used to have sex on camera for money and it's just this reaction." I waved my hand in front of his face.

He shrugged. "You needed to do it? To survive?"

I nodded.

"It's a decision that got you standing right here, in front of me." He moved forward to grasp my hips. "So yeah, that's it."

I continued blinking at him. "It doesn't make you think...less of me?" My voice was small, vulnerable. "Like I'm...unclean?" I hated how small I sounded, like I needed his approval.

His eyes darkened.

"Baby, I plan on fucking you dirty. So it doesn't matter how fucking clean you are before that."

10

My ENTIRE BODY WAS NUMB. No, not numb, just spent. Every single muscle I had was used up, drained with the force it took to give me an orgasm like that. Three orgasms like that. The thing that I'd been absolutely certain was impossible without a vibrator.

There was no way I was going to be able to move from this spot for...the rest of my life. But that was okay, because this was the most perfect moment I'd ever had.

"Where did you learn to fuck like that?" I demanded. Or tried to demand. My voice was breathy and the words dragged out with the energy it took to speak them.

A pause. Duke's arms tightened ever so slightly around me before he moved us so our eyes met. His were dark, hooded with lazy satisfaction.

"You really want to know where I learned to fuck like that?" he asked, teasing in his voice. It was slow, like mine though. Even the big man seemed to be spent, which made sense, since he'd exerted a lot of energy.

I smiled. That was easy to do. "Yes, I do need to know

because then we're going to open a fucking academy so you can teach the masses your skills."

He grinned and his arms tightened around me. "I'm not teaching the masses about how I fuck my woman."

My heart skipped with the *my woman* address, something he'd referred to me as before, of course, as part of the act. But never with the two of us. As much as the title should've pissed me off, it fit better than any of my custom gowns. Mostly because they'd always been made a size too small, forcing me to constrict myself in order to slip into them.

"Yes, we are," I argued, swallowing my emotion. "We'll make millions."

The grin went wider this time. Arms tightened even further so that my ribs started to protest. It was harder to breathe with him holding me this tight, but it was easy to...exist.

"You already have millions," he pointed out.

I rolled my eyes. "Yes, I wouldn't keep the money we make, would I? It's technically yours, since we're basing a lot of the curriculum on what you've just demonstrated. But I get a cut since I'm going to be the main investor, and going to be building this academy."

Duke nodded seriously. "Naturally."

"Whatever profit comes after the investment will obviously be donated to various charities. But womankind need you to spread this talent. And I'm not going to allow you to do it the conventional way, so this is the next logical step."

Duke's face was blank but his eyes danced with amusement. "Of course."

I frowned at him. "This is serious, you know. Countless men don't know how to do what you just did. There are millions of women suffering right now, millions sneaking off to bathrooms to satisfy themselves while their husbands snore in the bed. It's my duty to help these women."

"Baby, it's nothing to do with the man's skills and everything to do with the man himself," Duke said. "A man who doesn't make an effort to satisfy his woman so thoroughly she has trouble forming sentences—until she gets a crazy idea about a sex academy—is not a man at all."

My stomach dipped yet again. First with the "baby," then the rest.

The. Fucking. Rest.

"Contrary to every porno and movie ever made, there are very few women who are unable to use their limbs after sex, or women who orgasm three times before the man has ever done so once." I made sure to put the sex into my voice.

If the look in Duke's eyes was anything to go by, it translated well.

"Well, baby, there are very few true men out there in the world," he said, voice rough. "Count yourself lucky you're in bed with one right now."

I smiled. I couldn't help it. "He's humble to boot."

He shrugged. "Confident."

"Well, I think I'm going to have to do some more research on this academy," I continued, trailing my finger down his bare pec. "You know, just in case."

I'd no sooner finished my sentence than I was flipped onto my back, Duke's lips at my neck.

He didn't say anything else.

But I sure did conduct a decent amount of research.

* * *

"What are these from?" I asked, trailing my fingers over two puckered scars on Duke's stomach. They marred his otherwise perfect abs. He had other scars, not as deep and violent-looking as these, though.

My head was resting on his chest and it was my first chance to inspect him up close. And to slow down my thundering heart. It was only now getting down to a resting rate, and we'd been lying here like this, silent, for at least half an hour.

I had no idea what time it was, or, fuck, what day it was.

All I knew was that Duke's arms felt nice around me and made me feel as safe and sated as I'd been...ever.

"Knife wounds," Duke said, answering my question. "Friend of mine had a fuckin' piece of shit stalker after her. Somehow got through security, took me by surprise."

He was angry about that, it vibrated through his voice. Not even at the man who did the stabbing, but at himself.

But I wasn't in the right frame of mind to inspect that. I was too busy focusing on the fact that the two scars I was touching were from someone fucking stabbing him.

"You were stabbed? Was it serious?"

A totally stupid question, I was aware, since two knives slicing into your stomach deep enough to cause a scar like that were most obviously serious.

Duke paused. "Was in a coma for a few days. Hospital for longer. Rehab was a bitch. I'm here to talk about it, but the fucker who did it is in the ground."

The only reason I was able to jump up from the bed was because Duke was not expecting it. I wasn't even really planning on getting up either until I started pacing the room. "You were in a coma? That's serious, Duke," I snapped, still pacing, trying to work out the images of this strong man lying in a hospital bed.

Duke sat up in bed. "I know it was, I was there," he said sounding mildly amused. "But I'm also here. So you can come back to bed."

I ignored this. "What does your family think about you classifying a stabbing that put you in a coma like you got a fucking graze on your knee or something?"

A pause. A heavy one. "They don't know."

I stopped pacing at this point to gape at him. "They don't know? How the heck do your parents not know that you were stabbed and put in the hospital? Weren't they your emergency contacts?"

I had no idea why I was getting this hysterical over something so far in the past it was nothing but scar tissue, but I was. The idea that Duke's family had been here going about their daily life while their obviously beloved son was in the hospital baffled and upset me.

"Because I had Greenstone Security on that list so as not to worry my parents over shit," he replied. "It's part of the job, and I certainly don't want them worried about shit they don't need to be."

"They need to worry about their son being stabbed and lingering on death's door," I snapped. "They'd want to know that. They'd want to sit at your bedside and fucking feed you ice chips when you woke up. But they weren't there. Who fed you ice chips, Duke?"

Duke got out of bed and I had a moment of sheer appreciation at his naked body outlined in the moonlight. It was a full moon. Of course it was, that's why I was acting like such a crazy person. It had nothing to do with my intense feelings for Duke.

His hands landed on my hips and yanked my body close to his. I reacted to that too, even though I wasn't sure if my body would survive another round of sex.

"First off, baby. I was not at death's door," he said, still sounding too amused.

"I was using dramatic license," I bit out. "And I think it's safe to assume when a badass man casually mentions he's in a coma that things are a lot more serious than aforementioned man was letting on."

The corner of Duke's mouth moved and if it turned into a

full-blown smile, he was in a buttload of trouble.

"Secondly," he said, ignoring that little outburst. "I had the entire team there, and nurses are employed to do things like get ice chips."

"It's not the same," I muttered, looking downward.

"I promise, next time I get stabbed, I'll let you feed me ice chips," he said.

My eyes snapped up. "No, you need to promise not to get stabbed." The thought of Duke bleeding, Duke in a hospital bed, Duke not existing on this earth...it chilled my bones.

There was a long pause. He was most likely calculating his odds of getting stabbed in the future before agreeing to the promise. He wouldn't make it if he didn't think he could keep it.

"I promise, baby." He laid his lips on mine, sealing the promise. "Now come back to fuckin' bed."

I frowned at him. "I'm going, but be sure to remember that me obeying an order from you is not the norm."

He chuckled. "Oh, I know that, babe." His hand trailed down the column of my neck and slipped under the silk of my nightie, caressing my breast. "But I'll make it worth your while."

And he did.

He totally fucking did.

* * *

I found Harriet in the kitchen sipping coffee. She grinned at me knowingly. "You're late this morning."

I couldn't help but smile back. Usually I had more control over such expressions—since a woman knew a misplaced smile could send the wrong message to the wrong man and at best, end in unwanted attention and at worst, an everlasting trauma.

But this morning was different. I woke up with Duke's mouth on my neck, his hands working between my legs. I was barely awake before my first orgasm tore through me. I was definitely more aware with the second.

We lingered in bed, which meant Duke had to go straight out to the barn to get his horse and help with his ranch duties.

Before he'd left, he'd landed a hot and soul-shattering kiss on my already swollen lips, so I'd wandered to the homestead in a trance. Everything looked different, smelled different. It was like I hadn't been seeing colors before. Now everything was bright, vibrant.

Hence the smile.

I took the coffee Harriet offered.

"I'm guessing I have you to thank for last night," I said.

She sipped her coffee. "Oh, no. That smile on your face is all thanks to my grandson."

I rolled my eyes, still smiling. "Thank you." The two words were filled with so much else. Of course she didn't know that we weren't together before this. She didn't realize what last night really was. Or maybe she did. There was a glint to her eyes, a knowing that made me think Harriet saw a lot more than she let on.

"What I've learned in my years is that men aren't good at romance," she said. "Not because they don't want to be, but because they're men. What I learned in almost forty years of marriage to a man I loved is that men really are wired differently than us. Now, I'm a feminist, always have been. I didn't want to admit that bullshit. I was convinced men were just lazy, entitled. Marriage teaches you differently." She looked out the window, sadness edged her gaze. I'd known that Duke's grandfather had passed. Anna had mentioned it cooking one night, in passing, glossing over the wound that so obviously hadn't healed right.

Harriet wore multiple gold rings on her fingers—they switched out daily because that woman liked to accessorize—but there was a simple diamond on her left hand that never moved.

"We had a love that lasted," Harriet continued. "Not because it was special or different to anyone else's, but because we worked at it, because I understood that my husband loved me but he didn't always know how to show it. It might be that Montana men are bred to be tough so being soft is a little harder. But I think it's men in general. My Duke's a romantic at heart underneath all of his macho, tough-guy crap. Just needed a little push in the right direction." She winked at me.

"How did he die? Your husband?" I asked the question before I understood how invasive and rude it was.

Harriet didn't look to be offended, thankfully. "Ah, I'd like to say my Hugo—yes, Harriet and Hugo—went out guns blazing in a manner befitting the man he was, but life doesn't work out that way. Death is rarely spectacular or the crescendo we expect it to be. He had a heart attack." Harriet went back to looking out the window. There was a strength and resignation in her voice; it had been years, after all. But the look in her eyes told me she was looking at it like it was yesterday. Or today.

"He was out in the fields repairing fences. Fell down, didn't get back up. I'm not gonna say he would've wanted to go that way because he wouldn't have wanted to go at all. He still had many years ahead of him. We had a whole life to live." She shrugged, looking back to me. "Things didn't work out the way I wanted, they rarely do. Well, the big things at least. That's why I make sure I'm in control of all the little stuff, like helping my grandson woo his woman."

* * *

I carried Harriet's words with me. Carried them around until they grew bigger, louder, and I couldn't sleep with them inside me. Not even wrapped up in Duke's arms.

"What are you doin' out here?" he demanded, his voice a low

growl. "It's fuckin' freezing and you're wearin' nothing but that nightie." His hands fastened around my middle and he pulled my back to his front.

He wasn't wearing a shirt, so he wasn't one to talk. Then again, his skin was like a furnace against my own cold.

"In sayin' that," he said against my neck, "I fuckin' love the nightie, babe."

My shiver had nothing to do with the cold.

"Well, I have plenty more where this came from," I replied.

He squeezed me. "Lookin' forward to seeing every one of them."

I stilled. At his words. Because of that statement. That statement that reached into the future, beyond this moment.

"But," he said, interrupting those thoughts. "When I see them, they'll be worn in temperatures where you're not likely to catch hypothermia. I highly doubt you'll be wearing them for very long." He rubbed my arms. "So, back to my original question. What the fuck are you doin' out here in the cold?"

I smiled at him, at all his macho. It should've pissed the feminist in me off. It should've felt more uncomfortable than the bite in the air against my bare skin. No one had ever been mad at me because I was standing out in the cold. No one had ever wanted me to be warm, safe...not without wanting a slew of other things.

I told myself that's how I liked it.

I didn't know how good I was at lying until now.

Instead of answering, I looked up. "The stars," I whispered. "I'm out here because of the stars. I've never seen them like this before, seen the sky so open, been in a world so quiet I can actually hear the stars. Experience their...resonance." Slowly, I moved my gaze to Duke. "Thank you for taking me somewhere I can hear the stars."

* * *

"Wait, why didn't you tell me there was a gym here?" I demanded with my hands on my hips.

Talking with Duke last night, I'd told him how much I'd missed my workout sessions. Then he'd raised his brows, moved his fingers down my belly right to the place between my legs that was still recovering from the way he'd fucked me.

"I thought I've been working you out pretty good," he murmured. "But if you want more..."

He made good on his promise and my body and mind forgot all about gyms and workouts.

We'd gotten up earlier than usual to drive to the homestead where he parked and took me to a side door leading down to a basement gym.

A kick-ass basement gym.

This was almost as nice as the one I'd had installed at my house in LA—a *house* I couldn't even call a home after staying here.

Duke's arms went around my waist with my accusation. I was totally pissed off that he'd hid it from me this long. It was true I was getting thoroughly worked out by Duke, not to mention the work I'd been doing on the ranch, but there was something I craved about a workout.

Music blaring. Muscles screaming. I didn't do yoga or any of that crap. I didn't want something soft, gentle, peaceful. That didn't work for me.

Plus, I loved feeling strong. Loved lifting weights.

I'd seen barely any change in my body these past weeks eating whatever I wanted—my version at least—and doing all the outside work. If anything, my muscles were more sculpted and I looked less like the stick-thin movie star I'd thought I'd needed to be.

Before this, I'd danced on the edge of a sword when it came to how I looked. I had to be thin to be appealing to the world, but strong enough to carry that same world on my shoulders. I was starting to get why Hollywood and the fashion industry wanted to promote that sickly thin aesthetic. Because they wanted to convince women that looking weak, looking vulnerable, looking like the damsel that needed to be saved by the muscled hero was the only role for us.

The world was scared of strong women.

And as strong as I'd considered myself, I'd played into it.

It was strange what a huge change that had been made in my lifestyle and how little I cared about it—about the cameras following me everywhere, about the staff at my beck and call, the fucking celery juices, the massages, the bullshit. I'd been sure it was everything I'd ever dreamed of but in reality, dreams didn't do anything.

"Are you kidding me?" Duke said in my ear. "No fuckin' way was I showin' you this place and having to torture myself watching you work out in those little shorts and not fuck you against that wall."

My body flushed with need as I looked at the wall he was talking about, the mirrored wall. I got a flash of having Duke inside me and watching him fuck me from all angles. Once I entertained that thought, I found it really hard to think of anything else.

"How did you know I'd be wearing little shorts?" I breathed. "Did you go through my stuff?" It was meant as a joke but Duke's pause helped me shelve the thought of him fucking me against that mirror.

I stepped out of his grasp and he let me, which was a bad sign. "Duke, did you go through my stuff?"

He didn't even have the decency to look sheepish. He eyed me carefully, likely gauging the way my irritation was rapidly turning into fury.

"I had to make sure you hadn't snuck in a phone or computer

or somethin' like that," he said.

"And you didn't think you could ask me instead of invading my privacy?" I asked him quietly—a special kind of quiet, the restrained quiet that every man should take as a warning and immediately agree, apologize, or go shopping for gifts.

Duke did none of those things. He crossed his arms over his chest. Whether he was doing that out of stubbornness or to distract me, it didn't matter.

Although, it was distracting. I'd thought his arms were nice before, but they were one hundred times nicer now that I knew what they felt like wrapped around me. Now that I knew how he could use them to hold me up while he fucked me in the shower.

"Baby, you know I couldn't be sure you were telling the truth then."

"Don't you baby me," I yelled. "I need you to get out of here and leave me alone."

Duke stepped forward. "That's never gonna happen."

There was a strange weight to his words that suggested he didn't just mean right now.

The door to the gym opened, and I was totally expecting Tanner, or maybe one of the younger ranch hands. But to my surprise—though I didn't know why I should be surprised now—Harriet walked through the door wearing leopard print leggings and a tank that said "Radical Feminist."

She grinned between the two of us. "Oh goodie, I'm interrupting something."

"You're not interrupting anything," I told her. "I've made up my mind to be mad at Duke, and there's nothing he can do about it."

He looked like he was going to have something to say about this, but of course Harriet had other ideas.

"Why don't you fight him?" Harriet suggested.

I looked at her to gauge her seriousness but then followed her gaze to the open area in the corner, which had a punching bag and a small sparring space.

I immediately grinned and Duke stiffened. "No fuckin' way."

"Why?" I asked. "Afraid you're going to lose?"

The corner of his mouth twitched. "No, I'm just not willing to hurt you and I don't hold back."

Whether or not he knew what that statement was going to do, I didn't know, but instead of answering him, I stomped over to the corner and began putting on gloves.

"Wait! You can't start until I get us an audience and a betting pool," Harriet called, tapping on her phone.

* * *

"Sure about this?" Duke asked, standing in front of me.

"Gonna back out now that you've got an audience to see you get your ass kicked by a woman?" I snapped back. I was still sufficiently pissed off at him, even more so as he hadn't yet apologized.

"So I've got fifty on the movie star, who wants to bet against me?" Harriet called from the side.

No one spoke. And Andrew, Anna, and Tanner were all in the audience. Apparently even a busy ranch can put its morning on pause to watch their son and his girlfriend spar in an underground gym.

I wasn't sure whether they were being polite or scared of offending me, but no one was willing to put their money on Duke.

This made me happy.

"I punch like a girl, just to let you know," I told Duke as I began to circle him. "Meaning I do it smart, clean, and in the places that will do the most damage. I'm not striking out to show off, I'm doing it to beat you."

There was a whoop from the sidelines that most likely would've come from Harriet.

Duke's eyes flared with amusement and a dark heat. I recognized the latter since it was the gaze he'd worn the entire night last night.

My thighs clenched with the memory.

He struck, and I managed to dodge...sloppily.

I glared at him and the smirk on his face. The asshole was trying to distract me with his sexy look...in front of his family no less.

We continued to circle each other, and I made sure not to let his tactics get to me. I was the first to land a punch. It was clean. Effective. Enough to make him go back on a foot. He was as surprised as I was at that.

He recovered with a grin. Impressed. I shouldn't let it get to me, but it did—and he kicked my feet out from under me so I landed hard on the mat.

Although the wind was knocked out of me, I managed to roll up quickly, smiling. "Good, you're not holding back."

He raised his fists. "Baby, I'm not gonna hold back with you ever."

* * *

The fight was declared a tie, much to Harriet's dismay.

Duke hadn't held back, but he'd fought so he didn't land punches anywhere on my face. He was more focused on getting me on the mat. On testing me. He reminded me of my trainer. Tough but not cruel.

It was interesting to me that a man like Duke would even agree to this. I would've thought his alpha maleness would've stopped him from potentially "harming" a woman. Of course, such a thought was rooted in a belief that women were inherently weaker.

It impressed me that Duke had been willing to fight me. That surprised me.

I was falling more and more in like with him.

The rest of the family had given their praise then scattered off to commence their tasks for the day. Except Harriet, of course. She was on the elliptical with Beats on her ears watching an episode of Buffy on the screen mounted on the wall.

Duke and I were sitting on the mats. I was stretching out, pretending not to want to lick the sweat off Duke's bicep.

Yeah, it was gross, but it was an urge that came from my growing obsession with him.

"Where did you learn to fight like that?" Duke asked.

I shrugged, uncomfortable with the power behind his gaze. I'd been sure I'd seen every expression on Duke's face by now. But here he was giving me something else. Something that seemed deep. Like...reverence. But surely I was just imagining it or he was trying to trick me with those smoldering baby blues into forgetting I was mad at him.

"I had a role where I was a female boxer," I replied.

Duke wasn't willing to leave it at that. "Yeah, plenty of actresses have roles like that and don't fight like you do."

I swallowed my water. "I don't believe in playing a part unless I've one hundred percent dedicated myself to the character. Just like I learned how to ride like a cowboy, I learned to fight like a boxer. Same way I learned Russian for my movie set amongst the Cold War. I don't believe in doing things halfway."

He blinked. "You speak Russian?"

I tilted my head. Was he faking the impressed tone to butter me up? "Surely you would've already known that. I would've thought your office did their research before taking me on as a client."

"We didn't need to research you deeply for basic security work," he said. "And things became urgent before we could do the deep dive." He stepped forward, grasping my hips and pulling me into his sweaty body. I couldn't help but inhale his natural scent. "And, baby, even Wire, who I consider to be one of the greatest hackers of our generation, couldn't find the extent of your ability, all of your depths, everything I'm learning." He moved some hair from my face. "It's like you have no bottom," he murmured. "You're never-ending. You're everlasting."

ONE WEEK LATER

It was easy.

Happiness.

Life with Duke.

Maybe because I knew it wasn't real—because it was temporary—so I was living like I was dying. I knew this relationship was terminal so I was sucking all I could from it while I had it.

Of course, it was not at all the healthiest way to approach this situation, and the me from a month ago would've been disgusted at my actions.

It felt insane that I had only been here a month, that so much had changed. And it was even more insane that the fact I was testifying against a brutal and powerful murderer was barely even on my mind.

Part of the success of these past weeks of happiness was being careful not to inspect too much, not to think too much. To not try so fucking hard at being Anastasia Edwards and find out who I was—who I really was.

I was a woman with an eating disorder that she was slowly managing, thanks to Anna's amazing cooking and the fact I worked so hard every day I needed the energy that food gave me.

I was a woman who could now successfully cook a lasagna for

a family of people and not poison a single one.

I was a woman who laughed easily and had her *own* horse called Spearmint.

I was a woman who slept in a cabin designed for a man and his eventual family.

I was a woman totally and terminally in love with Duke.

Even though I was a practiced liar, I was finding it impossible to lie to myself, to distinguish where the act of our relationship and the truth behind it started, and ended. I hadn't said those three big words to Duke, of course. I wasn't stupid. Falling in love with him was outside of my control, but I could control whether he ever knew it or not.

Sometimes, like when I was falling asleep and I felt his lips gently touch my forehead, or when I caught him staring at me while I was reading a book, I liked to fool myself that he felt it too.

He was fond of me, to be sure. Duke was a man who didn't hide his feelings, didn't shy away from affection. But that was because he was a macho-man. He was an alpha male. It was part and parcel of it all.

So he was fond of me. Loving me was a whole different story all together.

I didn't dwell, though.

I lived. I experienced.

Although I couldn't help the way my heart skipped when I saw him walking toward me. We'd only been apart a couple hours, but I'd missed him. Craved him.

"Hey," I said, breathless from the ride, from happiness that filled every part of me, right to my fingertips. "I helped your brother lasso a fucking cow. Lasso. Like I didn't know they really did that shit anymore. I thought it was stupid Hollywood shit. But it's real. And I did it!" I was practically shouting now.

Tanner chuckled beside me, clapping me on the shoulder in a casual, brotherly gesture that filled me up further. "She did fuckin' good, bro. I swear she's more suited to being a rancher than anyone else is. Taken to it like a fish to water." He eyed me. "Sure you don't want to give up making millions in movies and come help us run the ranch?" His eyes twinkled.

Not for the first time, I tried to think of a way to help him get his wife back. "Don't tempt me," I said seriously, too caught up in this little moment in my life to remember that that would never happen.

As it was, moments of happiness were only moments, fleeting. I knew that with the look on Duke's face, one that I hadn't noticed until now because I was too busy being happy, believing in things I knew were only in the movies.

Tanner noticed it about the same time as I did, since his smile disappeared and his body stilled.

"Duke?"

The man in question didn't answer his brother. Didn't even look at him. His eyes were on me. "Baby, I need you to brace," he murmured in a voice I didn't recognize, one that sucked all that happiness from me. Dread filled me up, right up into my fingertips.

"What's going on?" I demanded.

He stepped forward, like he was going to touch me, like he was going to catch me, like he expected me to fall.

I stepped back, my feet steady. No one needed to catch me, not even Duke. Especially not Duke. I didn't fall, because I'd never had anyone to catch me and I still didn't, no matter what lies happiness told me.

He didn't like me stepping back. Not at all. But he stopped moving forward because he knew I'd run the length of this whole fucking state, until my feet bled and my muscles failed, before I'd let him catch me. Save me from whatever blow he was about to land.

"Ana," he said. Voice soft. Careful. Non-threatening. I'd

heard it before. That day, with the horse. The wild one. The one he'd tried to break.

"Just say it, Duke," I hissed. No matter how gentle, how rough he was, I wasn't going to break, no matter what this news was.

He didn't abandon my gaze. "Andre is dead."

Three words. I knew as an actress the power of words was in their delivery, in the meaning behind them. It was only talent that made words heavy, sharp, soft or light—in the movies at least. All it took was disaster to make words that damaging. And for me, disaster seemed to be all I had.

I swallowed the words. They scraped my mouth, my throat. All I tasted was copper.

"How?" It was only because I was an excellent actress that I managed the word to sound strong. Even.

Duke was struggling with the space between us. It wasn't in his nature to stand there and watch me bleed, as hard as I was trying to seem untouched. That's what I was. Bleeding. Wounded. Because I already knew the answer to my question.

Duke didn't speak because I knew he didn't want to hurt me more.

"It was Kitsch, wasn't it?" I demanded.

Still, he didn't speak. So this time, I stepped forward. Pushed myself into his face so he couldn't avoid it. "It was my fault, wasn't it? Because they thought he'd know where I was."

Duke's face turned stormy. "It was not your fucking fault. You need to get that shit out of your head. Now."

He was wrong.

It was my fault.

Of course it was my fucking fault. Andre was dead because I made a choice. He was dead because I was a witness. He was dead because he was close to me. That wasn't delusion. They were cold, hard facts.

11

I was pretending to sleep.

It just seemed easier, because it was the only escape from Duke. From his kindness. From his strong presence. His watchful eye. The fact he was worried about me.

That made it worse. If I allowed that to penetrate, it would become far too easy to use him as a crutch, to get used to him. Andre's murder was a wound that would never heal, and Duke would eventually be gone from my life. If I let him in, if I let myself fall for him even further, there was no way I'd be able to stay upright when this was over.

So as soon as we rode back to the house, Duke suggested I shower. I did it because I'd been riding all day and I needed it. I needed the comfort of the shower stall to break down in—the water to wash away the salt from my tears—the only tears I'd ever shed.

Duke didn't come and check on me, although I would bet he wanted to. He wanted to take care of me—in his own macho-man way to be sure—he wanted to save me. But there was no saving to be done.

He also knew me too well. So he didn't come into the bathroom.

I took my time with my skincare routine, paying specific attention to every single step, filling my mind with it so I didn't have room to think of anything else.

Duke was sitting on the bed, waiting for me. Of course he was.

He stood when I opened the door. He was holding two glasses, whisky by the looks of it.

I took mine without comment and downed it in one swallow.

He then switched glasses with me, giving me his, still not speaking. I did the same thing, letting the liquid burn my throat, hoping it would burn away this wretched sickness coming from my very soul.

It didn't work.

Duke set both glasses down on the nightstand, then he looked at me. Carefully. He was dissecting me. He was deciding whether or not I was going to break down.

Maybe that's what I was doing too, standing in the middle of the room, hair still dripping wet, damp body wrapped in a towel.

After a beat, Duke moved. He did it slowly, as if I were a horse, as if I hadn't been broken yet and he was trying to talk with his body, let me know I didn't need to be afraid.

I didn't move, just let him settle in front of me, let him pull my towel off me. It pooled to the ground. He sucked in a harsh breath and it did something to me. It still did something to me, through these horrible feelings. My need for him cut through the deepest grief I'd known in my adult life. I didn't know what that meant. I didn't want to know what that meant.

So instead, I pulled him by the neck so his lips pressed into mine. I let him break me.

* * *

It was raining. Pouring.

I should've loved this, that the weather matched my mood, that it was a reasonable excuse not to go and ride or help out with any of the jobs on the ranch.

I fucking hated it.

I wanted it to be like every other day. I wanted something to be the same so I could pretend that yesterday didn't happen, so I could pretend that Andre was still somewhere in LA.

But life didn't work that way. So instead I sat in front of the French doors in the bedroom drinking whisky and staring at the rain.

Duke hadn't wanted to leave me. I was hurting. I was threatened. I was angry. Andre hadn't known where I was...yet Kitsch had still fucking killed him. *Why didn't he just kill me the same night he ended Salvador's life?* So, yeah, I was seething. *Guilty.* But I'd urged him to talk to his family, help with whatever tasks needed help with. I knew life on the ranch didn't stop because of rain. The only thing that changed was that you got wet.

He'd left with a kiss on my forehead and a promise he'd come back.

He must've said something to his family about coming over here since I'd been alone since he'd left. Just how I wanted it. I hated that Duke knew me well enough to know that's what I wanted. Most people, especially overprotective alpha males, would make sure that the grieving woman wasn't alone, was getting taken care of, clucked over. But without me having to say anything, Duke knew that was the last thing I needed.

I'd wandered around the cabin looking at photos, exploring in a way I hadn't been able to do since we'd moved in here. I made sure to collect the images, burn them into my memory so I could revisit this place in my dreams. Thoughts of Andre were carefully shoved to the side. When it became too hard to avoid them, I'd started with the whisky.

I didn't know how long ago that was. Not long. I wasn't drunk, even though I'd had a lot on an empty stomach. Life wasn't kind that way. I wished for oblivion, for a blurring of the edges. But everything was in stark detail. The images in my mind were too realistic. How had he killed him? A basic bullet to the forehead, his brains splaying out all over the floor? Or had Kitsch tortured him trying to get information he didn't have?

I had a hard time distinguishing the fact that this was real. I hadn't spoken with him in weeks. And I wasn't speaking to him now. He could be alive now. They could've made a mistake.

But no. Duke would never have me hurt in this way unless he was certain. He would never make a mistake like this.

"Baby?"

I blinked.

The man in question was standing in front of me, and the way he spoke my name suggested he'd been standing here the entire time.

He was holding something. A plate of food.

"You need to eat something."

I could've argued with him. It would've been something in character for me. Stubborn. Surly. Didn't like being told what to do.

That person seemed so far away.

I reached out and took the plate and the silverware.

Duke sat down across from me. He was watching me. I didn't take much notice, didn't taste the food that I was putting in my body to simply placate him. It could've been delicious. It most likely was. But all I tasted was ash.

I was surprised when the plate was empty, when Duke took it to set on the small table between the chairs.

He'd refilled my whisky and poured one for himself. I was thankful for that.

He didn't say anything, didn't ask me if I was "okay" or

anything vapid like that. Didn't touch me either. I was thankful for it. I didn't want hands on me, didn't even want to be inside my own skin, but there was no choice in that.

We were silent for a while, the sound of the rain on the roof both a roar and a whisper.

"I didn't think about it," I said after a while.

Duke looked toward me, I could see that in my peripheral. I kept staring at the rain, at the darkness it was welcoming in. Was it night? Or did the day just welcome darkness once in a while?

"At Greenstone, I thought about it," I said. "About the murder, about what it meant for me, of course. I didn't give much thought to Salvador. Isn't that horrible? I was sleeping with him, I watched him be murdered and I didn't shed a single tear. That's something off. Something wrong. You saw it from the start."

"Baby—"

I held up my hand. "No. It's okay. I'm a big girl. You didn't like me because you had no reason to. I wasn't likeable. The only person that liked me, not the characters I played, not what I could do for them, not who they thought of me, was Andre. He knew who I was and he liked me anyway." I thought back to that night in the parking lot. "He saved my life," I said quietly. "He didn't even ask me where I wanted to go after I gave my statement. He drove me straight to Greenstone." I looked at Duke's eyes now. "To you. He was the reason for this. And then we got here and I forgot it all, the why of it all. I was just here and I let myself linger in that. Now Andre's dead and I'll never not think about it."

"Anastasia," Duke said, his voice harsher now.

"What did you tell your brother?" I asked. "He heard all of it. He's smart enough to come to conclusions close enough to the truth."

Something moved in Duke's face. Surprise, maybe. He was likely expecting the breakdown now, the tears. But maybe not.

"He already knew," he said after a pause. A long one.

I stared at him in shock. "He already knew?" I repeated.

Duke nodded. "Both he and my father knew."

"From the start?" I clarified. "They both knew from the start that this wasn't real? That I was a job for you?"

Duke flinched, and I knew he'd try to cage me in, to grab me. For once, I was quicker than him. Even in my grief, even with the whisky in me, I was quicker.

I put the chair between us and made it very clear I didn't want him near me.

He glowered at the chair. Then at me.

"You were never a mission for me, and you know that," he said slowly. "This has been real since the second you set foot on Hammond dirt."

I tilted my head, trying to weigh that statement for truth and lies, but I didn't know the difference between them anymore.

"Why did you make me pretend then?" I yelled. "Did you guys all have a good laugh over beers, knowing the truth?"

"That's bullshit and you know it," he clipped. "I told them because I needed them to be aware, to protect you when I wasn't around. They're the only people I trust with you."

"No," I said, quiet now. "No, that's not it. You couldn't lie to them about something like this. Maybe you could lie to your mother and grandmother because you had some warped idea that you were protecting them, even though your grandmother knew something was up from the beginning. But you weren't doing it to have them protect me. You were doing it because you couldn't lie to them. You were doing that because you hated me at the start of this, and you didn't want your father to be ashamed of you thinking I was the woman you picked to bring home."

"I didn't hate you," Duke said after another long fricking pause.

He didn't say anything else. He didn't even attempt to try to tell me I was wrong about the rest—because I wasn't.

It seemed totally pointless to be having this argument in the midst of what I'd lost, but at the same time the anger was something more tangible to hold on to. A lifeboat in the middle of stormy seas.

It did make my emotions more powerful. That and the whisky.

Which was what had me darting to the French doors and sprinting out into the rain, barefoot.

Duke cursed behind me, and he was no doubt chasing me. He might've caught me any other time, with longer strides, more power behind them. But grief, heartbreak, and anger were a unique fuel, so I managed to run a long way before I stopped. Before Duke's hand grasped my arm and yanked me to face him.

The rain had soaked us both, plastering his shirt to his body, rendering the white shirt I was wearing see-through.

"What the fuck, Anastasia?" he roared, yanking me into his chest.

He tried to, at least. I fought him this time. I fought him like a banshee, as if I was fighting for my life.

"Let me go!" I screamed, the wind and the rain stealing my voice away.

He didn't let me go.

"Damn you!" he yelled.

"Damn you," I yelled back. "Damn you for bringing me here. Why did you need to take this fucking job? Why did you have to bring me here? Why did you force me into a lie that I would eventually believe? Why would you make me fall in love with you? Is this a sick game for you? Punishment for being a bitch to you as I did my best to hide my reactions to you? I fell in love with you the first moment I saw you, Duke Hammond, and it's been torture every moment since. So, congratulations."

He was still now. He was holding me, his grip still viselike.

But he was staring at me with something other than the frustration of before.

His chest was falling and rising rapidly, much like my own. The rain continued to pelt us, so we were both drenched. I barely noticed it under the heaviness of Duke's gaze.

I waited for more fight from him. He gave me none. Instead, he let my arm go only so he could violently grab hold of my neck and kiss me.

I should've fought it. I should've known this was my absolute last point of escape. Anything after this would be forever and impossible to recover from.

But I didn't stop.

I kissed him back with all my anger, all my fear, all my grief.

All my love.

* * *

We had just gotten out of the shower.

I barely remembered how we got there in the first place. I did know we damn near had sex in the middle of that field in the rain, in the mud. I'd wanted to. The urge to do it in the dirt, under that moody, angry sky was almost primal.

Duke had wanted to as well. But it seemed the alpha macho-man had more control over the animal inside him than I did, since he carried me all the way back to the house.

Well, not all the way.

First, we made it to the verandah.

The wicker furniture left welts on my thighs.

Duke left scars on my soul.

The transition from wild, violent, and urgent fucking to silence, stillness in the bed, was jarring and uncomfortable.

Too many things had happened in this day. Too much hurt. It

had spilled over my happiness like acid, dissolving it, melting it, disfiguring it, ensuring it would never be the same again.

* * *

The next morning, I woke to an empty bed.

It seemed Duke had forgotten our rule as to the way we woke each other up. Then again, he probably thought sleep was a gift to me right now.

As it was more often than not, he was right.

Waking up without him was jarring, confusing, and exactly what I needed. I needed to breathe in his scent, be comforted by it, but also learn how to be on my own. Learn how to breathe around the pain.

It wasn't easy.

I'd never let myself feel loss before.

My father had died before I could really remember him. There was no point in crying about a stranger, was there? Plenty of people lost parents. Plenty of people entered the foster system, got fucked up by it. Plenty of women had to use their bodies to survive—but not many of them managed to claw themselves out of that life.

I was luckier than most, so it seemed in poor taste to feel sorry for myself.

However, last night changed everything, forced me to feel it all, even when I really didn't want to.

Life happened whether you wanted it to or not.

Voices trickled in from behind the closed door, along with the smell of coffee. As much as I wanted to sink into these sheets that smelled of Duke and denial, I wanted to drink coffee with the man himself, with whatever member of his family was out there. I wanted to look at the mountains and live in this present moment. Who knew how much longer I'd have it for?

Duke had said a lot of things last night, however three important words were missing. He was not a man to say them out of a sense of duty or politeness. If he felt them, he would've said them. It was that simple. And it hurt. It really hurt, no matter how selfish that was in the midst of grieving my only friend. But it wasn't going to force me back into my shell, as my first instincts urged me to.

I was going to lean in. More than that, I was going to jump in. I wasn't going to hold back, wasn't going to pretend that I didn't feel the way I did just to protect myself from hurt. I was already hurting. It wasn't going to change, so I'd hold on to this for as long as it was in my grasp.

After brushing my teeth, performing my skincare routine, and throwing on a robe over my nightie—as liberal as Duke's parents were, I didn't think they'd appreciate seeing my nipples while drinking coffee—I tentatively walked down the hallway to the kitchen.

Harriet sat at the breakfast bar, leaning on her elbows and talking to Duke as he manned the stove.

This gave me pause.

Even in my zombie, grief-ridden state, it hit me—*that man* at the stove.

I'd never really thought of cooking as something that could be sexy. Duke showed me that it definitely could be. He was already dressed, wearing jeans and a long Henley. It was tight enough so I could see his muscles move fluidly under the fabric.

My mouth watered, and it had nothing to do with the bacon he was frying.

Harriet saw me first, a knowing grin on her face. "They say a woman should be barefoot and pregnant in the kitchen," she said. "But I think it should be the other way around. Although, if men had the ability to get pregnant, get periods, the human race would've died out long ago." Her voice was easy. Warm. It wasn't practiced, wasn't hesitant, trying to probe around my grief. She was acting like it was any other morning.

I loved her for that—and the fact she made me smile. I hadn't thought such a thing would be possible this close to yesterday's events.

As always, Harriet proved me wrong.

Duke turned with his grandmother's words, eyes finding me immediately. He fiddled with the stove, put down his spatula, and moved.

His hands rested on my hips and he landed a gentle but purposeful kiss on my lips. My body melted into him ever so slightly.

He lifted his hand to stroke my jaw, eyes glittering with a thousand things that were impossible to decipher without coffee.

"Mornin', baby," he murmured, lips close to mine.

"Good morning."

"Hungry?"

"Ravenous."

His eyes flared with my response and the hand that was still at my hip tightened. Then he caught himself, most likely remembering his grandmother was at the breakfast bar, shamelessly watching the exchange. He stepped back and pointed to the seat beside Harriet.

"Sit," he ordered.

Any other morning, I would've stayed exactly where I was and shot something sarcastic to him for ordering me around.

This was not any other morning.

So I sat.

Harriet's hand landed on my thigh and squeezed for a second, then it was gone. A show of support. Comfort, but not pity.

My eyes watered as they met hers.

"Coffee."

Duke held out the mug, and I was so thankful for the caffeine and the interruption. The last thing I needed to do was sob all over this moment.

I took the mug and my fingers brushed Duke's. Sparks spread from my hand all the way to my toes. It was insane to still have this reaction to a man I knew so intimately. Or maybe it wasn't.

Conversation flowed easily throughout breakfast, and no one mentioned the elephant in the room. We weren't ignoring it, per se, just maneuvering carefully.

"Are you sure you don't want me to stay?" Duke asked after the food was finished. His hands were at my neck and eyes searched mine. He was probing for weakness, for the sign that I was apt to break down and do something crazy like run off into the wild and get eaten by a bear or something.

"I'm sure," I said, hopefully with no crazy in my eyes.

He frowned, inspecting me. It was as if he didn't want to leave, not just because of the obvious, but because of last night. Maybe it was as life-shattering for him as it was for me.

But those three words lingered between us. Mine said, his unsaid.

Duke leaned down to press his lips to mine. "I'll have my phone. Harriet or Mom can call me if you need anything, if you need me to come back—"

"I'm not going to need you to come back," I said. "As sweet as the gesture is, I need to...just deal."

Duke lingered close for a moment—too close for me to breathe—and close enough for me to grasp his shirt and beg him not to leave, beg him to love me.

But he stepped back, saving both of us.

He glanced to Harriet. "Take care of her."

"She's capable of taking care of herself, but I'll hang out anyway," she replied in true Harriet fashion. Duke shook his head and grinned. He kissed my forehead, then hers, and he left.

"Okay, if any day calls for a Twilight movie marathon, it's this day," Harriet declared once the front door to the cabin closed. "Well, any given day is a great day for a Twilight movie marathon, but I think today is most important."

I raised my brow. "A Twilight movie marathon?"

"What? Do you not think that watching a move about vampires, werewolves, and the struggle between wanting to screw someone and suck them dry isn't the perfect thing? I'll make margaritas, of course, because you're allowed to drink them at eight in the morning when you're going through something like this. You're a grown-ass woman, so you're allowed to drink them whenever. You get my point."

I smiled. It was weak and shaky, but it was a smile. My eyes watered with the thought that Andre would totally approve of such a way to grieve. He was a Twihard from way back.

A single tear trailed down my cheek.

Harriet stepped forward and wiped it from my face. She cupped my face.

"Grief is a funny thing, sweet girl," she said. "It's about the worst thing a human can feel but it springs from the very best thing we feel. Love."

Her eyes searched mine.

"I would like to say I have some wisdom about death," she said. "I'm surely old enough to know it well, to feel it creeping up on me. But no matter how old you are, no matter how many times you brush it, meet it, stare at it in the damn face, you're never familiar with it. No amount of pretty words can soften its blow, no amount of bullshit can salve the wounds it leaves. You've just gotta experience it, weather it best way you know how. I'll tell you this, though. You always come out the other side. A little different than before, sure. But you will come out."

12

ONE MONTH LATER

"WE'LL BE BACK in a few hours," Duke said.

"Okay, I'll try not to set myself on fire or anything in the interim," I replied.

He furrowed his brows in annoyance.

I rolled my eyes in response. "Oh, come on, Duke. I'm a big girl. I'm going to be totally fine on my own for a few hours. I know you're playing into the idea that I can't function without you, or that I can't stay alive, but you're giving yourself too much credit there, baby."

His eyes darkened—in that good way—in the way that made my stomach dip like I was a fucking virgin.

He moved forward and grasped my hips, yanking me forward so my body pressed to his. Yeah, another stomach dip, deeper, more violent, desperate. Despite the fact he'd given me many orgasms this very morning, I wanted more. I was greedy for him, because I knew this wasn't going to last. So instead of doing the smart thing and distancing myself, I had binged this past month.

Soon enough, I'd be back in my big house, in LA, starving.

I'd grown in every way I'd thought possible, including physically. Instead of going into a spiral like I might've before, I shared a bottle of wine with Harriet and Anna and we spent a small fortune online shopping—using Duke's credit card, of course, since mine could've been compromised.

Duke had very much appreciated what his money had bought and he made sure to let me know this by ripping off my new clothes almost as soon as I put them on. He also worshipped the changes in my body. "Will take you any way I can get you, baby, as long as you're happy. Healthy. Although, you weren't that before." He'd run his hand across the new curve to my hip. "This, though. It's a sign that you are."

Cue melty moment and then hot sex.

So, yeah, I had indulged this past month, filled myself up, despite the empty place Andre's death left inside me.

It hit me sometimes, at odd moments, when I was playing poker with the ranch hands—which had made Duke furious until he realized that I'd cleaned them all out. Then he'd joined the game and I'd cleaned him out too.

He'd asked me who taught me and the hitch to my voice and the glassiness to my eyes told him everything he needed to know.

Other times I didn't even need a reminder. I could be feeding the horses and the pain would bring me to my knees. I'd sob quietly and heavily with no one but the horses to watch. Crying without an audience was not something I was used to, but it was cleansing, like I wasn't crying for anyone, wasn't structuring my feelings to appear a certain way. I was just feeling.

It hurt.

It killed.

But it felt right, just like everything had this past month: Duke teaching me how to make raviolis, getting covered in flour and having sex on the kitchen counter; Anna teaching me how to make Chicken-Fried steak, Harriet teaching me how to hot wire Duke's truck; Tanner taking me fishing in his favorite spot, sharing beers and conversation and company. Duke hadn't completely forgiven his brother, but things seemed to have improved between them. I liked that. I liked watching Duke find his family again, find himself again.

I wasn't just finding myself here. I was creating a version of myself that was completely and utterly mine, not designed by my agent, by directors, my trainers, the trolls on the Internet. Not even by Duke. Just me.

The trial hung over my head like a noose, waiting to strangle this life out of me. But I only thought of that in the hours after midnight, when I'd sneak out of bed and sit outside, staring at the stars.

Sometimes Duke would wake and find me. Other times I'd sit there alone.

"Need I remind you of the snake bite?" Duke asked, jerking me back to the present with his lips against mine.

I returned the kiss, of course. It was as natural as breathing these days. When we'd first got here, I'd thought the way he'd touched me was perfect for the act of us being together. But now we were really together, it was different. It was torture. Beautiful torture.

"Need I remind you that I didn't die from that?" I replied, pulling back ever so slightly. It shouldn't have been as hard as it was. It shouldn't have been like removing my oxygen mask underwater, but it was.

His lips touched mine. Maybe he was intending it to start out as a simple kiss, but nothing was ever simple with us.

"Hey! You can suck each other's faces later. We've got cattle to move."

Both of us detached to find a grinning Tanner staring at us.

I grinned back.

Duke did not. "Fuck off."

Tanner winked at me before sauntering out the door. His smile seemed almost genuine these days, but the ghost of what he'd let go would always haunt him. It shook me, since I'd be a version of that in the not-so-distant future.

Duke's jaw got hard and his eyes got tight whenever I tried to ask him for updates. He'd give me as little information as possible. It should've offended me. I should've been given all the information about when I could expect to get my life back—after I testified against a killer of course. But I was relieved. It wouldn't be my life I was getting back. My life was here. I'd be slipping into a stranger's skin, back into the spotlight as a stranger to myself. *But completely on my own. No Andre. No one to provide the compass for the full and insincere life of Anastasia Edwards.*

Duke grasped my chin so I was looking at him again. "I'm serious, Anastasia. I've got plans for you later."

My stomach dipped in the exact way it had since the first time. My hunger for him was never sated. He matched me with his needs. I moved my hand down his abs and toyed with the buckle of his belt. "I've got plans for you too. So how about you make sure you don't fall off that horse."

He kissed me again, hard and quick. "Honey, I fall off that horse, it's 'cause I'm dead. Nothing else."

I frowned with the thought of it. A sharp stab in my chest reminded me of Andre, of how easy it was to lose people when you cared about them.

"Hey," Duke said, voice soft. "I'm comin' back to you."

The words shook me to my core. They were simple but the meaning behind them wasn't. The way Duke looked at me wasn't.

It was the look in his eyes that had stilled my heart in rare moments this past month. It was fleeting. At first, it was quick enough for me to dismiss as something constructed from hope.

But it was becoming more frequent lately, this look. One that said three words, the ones I hadn't repeated since that night, the ones he still hadn't said.

But he stepped back giving my hips one last squeeze. "You call on the landline if anything happens."

I rolled my eyes, not just because they still had a landline. "Yes, but as I said, I doubt anything will happen in the two hours I'm alone."

I was totally freaking wrong about that.

* * *

The knock at the door surprised me, scared me a little too, if I was honest. But I guessed if anyone was coming here to murder me, they wouldn't knock.

Harriet was due back from her hair appointment soon, the only reason I was alone in the house in the first place. I wanted to go on the herding trip with them, but there were others from a neighboring ranch involved and Duke didn't want to risk one of them recognizing me.

Duke would be pissed at me for opening the door, but I didn't realize what a bad idea it was until I opened it and a very pregnant woman gaped at me in surprise and then recognition.

"You're Anastasia Edwards," she said.

Shit.

I *was* Anastasia Edwards. Despite what I'd said to Duke on that night a thousand years ago, I had forgotten. I'd forgotten I was the movie star. People had treated me differently for years. They'd treated me with respect—whether it was fake or not. They never let me forget that I was someone famous, that I was a celebrity.

And at some point, that turned me into something less than human. I'd let it convince me that I was nothing more than that.

But this ranch. Duke. His family.

They'd turned me into something more than the celebrity. They'd turned me into something human.

So yeah, I forgot who I was right up until I saw the recognition on this beautiful woman's face.

I was a movie star and a murder witness.

So I really hoped this woman wasn't a gossip.

"Um, yeah, I am," I said with the least amount of confidence I'd had admitting that.

"Are you with Duke?" she asked, cradling her stomach and frowning slightly.

Oh shit.

Was this woman, the soft woman I'd been so sure he had? She certainly looked like someone deserving of Duke—long dark hair, caramel eyes, skin that was the same. Native American, if I had to guess. And beautiful with very little makeup. She was small—apart from the belly, of course—wearing a tight black dress and cowboy boots, and perfectly kind eyes.

She belonged here, in this place, with this family. Something told me that.

"Am I with Duke?" I repeated.

She smiled. It was easy, but had pain behind it. "Yeah, I heard he was back from LA."

I frowned. "No one was meant to know that." He'd be very pissed off about his commando skills.

She smiled wider. "No one does. Tanner mentioned it. He's left me messages."

It clicked then. This woman. Her pain. The fact that she seemed to belong here. This was *her*. Of course it was. She was perfect for Tanner.

My eyes went back down to the pregnant belly—the very large pregnant belly.

She followed my gaze. "He doesn't know," she said quickly, as if she was reading my face. "Tanner." She paused. Frowned again. "Things didn't end well. When I found out, I didn't want to get my hopes up." She rubbed it again. "And now, well, I think it's time he knows."

I let out a laugh, a real, happy one. "Yeah, I think it's definitely time he knows."

Her gaze turned worried. "Do you think he's going to be mad?"

I stepped back from the door, to welcome her in. "No, honey. I think you're going to make him the happiest man in the world."

* * *

Leaving her felt wrong.

In his fucking bones wrong.

Not that he thought there was any way Kitsch could find her. No, they had all their resources and the Sons of Templar's resident hacker on the case. Duke had been assured he'd get a warning if someone was closing in.

But that wasn't why he was filled with unease.

He knew she'd be safe.

He also knew that the State was wrapping up their investigation and was almost ready to go to trial. That meant that they were ready for Anastasia. That meant leaving here, his family, putting her in danger.

Once she testified, she'd be safe, since Kitsch would have no reason to kill her, and he'd likely be locked away for the rest of his life.

But, then what? Duke knew what he wanted. He wanted her. He wanted this life. But he also knew that neither of them could have it.

She had a fucking mansion to get back to. Movies. The spotlight.

He might've been a bit of a romantic, but he was a realist. He knew that shit got tangled in situations like this. He also knew with Anastasia's past, she was going to be looking for a reason to run, for a reason to convince herself she didn't deserve this.

He didn't deserve her.

But he didn't know how to earn her.

So, yeah, all that shit had been eating him up on the ride. He'd barely acknowledged people he hadn't seen in years. They probably thought he was an asshole now. They weren't wrong.

Didn't matter, since it'd likely be another handful of years before he saw them again.

The ringing of Tanner's phone jerked him back into focus.

"Anastasia?"

Duke's stomach dropped when Tanner got the call, when his face turned white and he all but screamed, "I'll meet you at the hospital."

Then he'd torn away. Hadn't offered them any explanation, just galloped off, leaving a bunch of cattle that Duke needed to focus on, especially now he was a man down. He tried calling the house. No answer.

Anastasia would know to answer. She was stubborn, she was infuriating, but she'd never pull a stunt like this.

His dad could sense his tension, his simmering fury and worry.

But there was no room for anything else but work right now. It was how it went. Things on the ranch didn't stop or change because of tragedies going on in the family. Nothing stopped, no respite. They'd all learned to work through all the shit on the back of a horse.

Duke hadn't had a problem before—even when he was a teenager with too much anger—and especially not when the war turned him into a man. He could shut shit off and get a job done.

Here at the ranch, it was their family's livelihood. In war, it was his brothers' lives. Deaths.

So yeah, Duke considered himself focused on the task at hand no matter what was simmering underneath it all.

But finishing with the cattle with Anastasia on his mind, that was the hardest shit he'd ever have to do.

As soon as it was done, his father shouted orders at ranch hands and they both rode hard back to the house.

Duke forgot what it was like to have his father at his side, at his back through shit.

He would've noted how it felt if there wasn't pure fucking fear curdling in his belly.

Both his mom and Harriet were there when they made it to the homestead. Both were slightly pale. Both piled into the car and Dad drove them to the hospital.

It was the only time in recorded memory that his grandmother was dead silent.

And that scared the shit out of him.

* * *

Tanner came in first. He sprinted in, with wild eyes and a purpose. They found me quickly, and he was on me in two long strides, clutching my shoulders.

"Where is she?"

I pointed to the doors that they hadn't let me through. Tanner didn't say anything else, but tore through those doors and I pitied anyone who tried to stop that man.

Maggie's water had broken right as I was serving us both sweet tea.

I was proud of myself for how quickly I got my shit together, got her in the car, *and* to the hospital via navigation system. I knew that I wasn't meant to leave the ranch, but I also knew I couldn't deliver a baby, and no way in fuck was I risking this child. No. Tanner and Maggie deserved this, a healthy baby. I wasn't letting my shit fuck it up.

Nor was I leaving until I got the news that the baby was okay.

Hence why I was pacing the hospital waiting room. It seemed to be a small regional hospital's slow day. No one else was in the waiting room and the passing nurses and orderlies hadn't seemed to notice me.

Granted, I doubted they were expecting to see a movie star here.

It didn't take long for Duke to come storming through the same doors his brother had, wearing a similar expression.

He was on me in two strides also, and he grabbed me too—hard enough to have me let out a little yelp of pain and surprise—which he ignored.

"What the fuck is going on?" he demanded. His eyes flickered over my body, as if checking for injuries, even though I was standing in the waiting room and not in a bed as a patient.

I glanced behind him to see the rest of his family entering, all worried. I'd called Tanner on the way to the hospital using Maggie's phone, and he hadn't let me say much more than the fact that I was at the hospital with his estranged wife before he'd hung up.

Then I'd been too preoccupied getting her here to call anyone else.

"Maggie's pregnant," I said to Duke and the rest of the family. "And she's having the baby right now."

Anna and Andrew smiled through their worried expressions. I was sure they'd been through the same grief their son had. Harriet beamed.

Duke did not.

"What are you doing here?" he demanded.

I stared at him. "Her water broke on my boots." I paused. "Well, your boots, Anna, I hope you don't mind."

"Not at all," she said through tears.

Duke squeezed me harder, demanding my attention. "You should've called."

I stared at him. "Really? I was too busy with your pregnant sister-in-law going into labor. I wasn't about to wait for you to ride in on your white horse and save the day."

Duke glowered. I tried to hide my smile but it didn't work very well. "Come on, babe," I said. "I know it's hard, but shrug off the macho-man protective bullshit. Even someone like you can't change the past. How about you just enjoy the fact that you're going to be an uncle, that your brother is finally going to be a father, and worry about the rest later?"

Duke regarded me. He was doing it intently, like always. But now, after that day in the rain, that horrible, beautiful and life-changing day, he looked at me differently. He looked at me like he was committing me to memory every time our eyes locked, like I was...precious. And despite how many women thought they wanted to be looked at like that, you don't. The reality of it was too heavy, too blinding.

"Later," he said, but he didn't say it in agreement. It was a promise.

One I felt in every nerve ending in my body.

* * *

"To our grandchild," Andrew said, and lifted his glass.

"To your great grandchild," Anna added, smirking at Harriet.

"Honey, I'm comfortable enough with my age," she retorted. "I just went from a plain old GILF to a GGILF." She lifted her own glass with a smirk.

We all clinked our glasses, they echoed through the room, the happiness underpinning it all was silent but palpable.

Despite the drama of the birth, Maggie had given birth to a very healthy baby girl.

Obviously, they were still at the hospital and Tanner had refused to leave their side.

"That boy has got a lot of making up to do," Harriet said once we'd all toasted.

Anna smiled. "I think he's up for the challenge, don't you?"

It became clear then, at that instant, with those smiles, with the smells, the clang of dishes, glasses, forks against plates, the food in my stomach and the warmth in my heart.

It became clear how special all of this was. How rare.

Duke's hand moved from the beer he was holding to gently, but not too gently, squeeze my thigh under the table.

I glanced at him. His brows narrowed. "You good, babe?" he asked, on a low murmur so no one else at the table heard.

I wanted to cry then, scream, get down on one knee and ask him to marry me. I wanted to reach out, grab hold of this moment, and greedily stuff it somewhere inside me so I could have it forever.

So I could have Duke forever.

But I couldn't. I couldn't have Duke forever. Nor could I have this family, this life. I was a visitor, an unwelcome one. My life, my past, my present and future would mesh together to create an atomic bomb and blow this all to pieces.

I'd have to leave, quietly and masterfully, like someone disarming a bomb. Quietly and masterfully was not right now, obviously.

I smiled at Duke, real and true and full of the love I felt for him. "Of course, I'm great," I said.

His brow remained furrowed for a second before he squeezed harder, smiled, and kissed my neck.

I should've gotten an Oscar for that one too.

* * *

I waited until Duke was asleep. Then I waited an hour more. I had to make sure he was deep in his dreams to not notice that I was extricating myself from his arms. It only worked because he was dead tired. It had been a long day, and not only that, he'd more than exhausted himself fucking me earlier.

But it hadn't been that, had it?

It hadn't been fucking.

As much as I wanted to throat-punch myself for even thinking it, he had made love to me tonight. Twice.

He'd fucked me earlier, after we'd got back from the hospital. Hard, desperate, violent against the front door of the cabin.

But later, after the family dinner, after all the celebrations, the love and happiness so dense it sank into our very pores, he'd done it first outside on the daybed under the stars.

Then he'd carried me inside the cabin and done it on the bed.

We hadn't spoken a word, because what he was doing said it all. The stars said it all.

Which, of course, was why I was leaving.

Not just because there was a chance I'd put Duke's entire family in danger by going to that hospital. That was a part of it. But it was mostly because he had made love to me under the stars.

I dressed quietly, watched him for longer than I should've. It was taking too much of a risk. He could wake up and this wouldn't work. He'd chain me to the bed before he let me pull this shit.

But still, I stayed a beat longer, wished for a different life, a different name.

Then, I grabbed his phone off the nightstand and walked out

the door.

The night was quiet.

Which was all too fucking loud for my liking. The crunch of my boots against the gravel taunted me, because it was the sound of me walking away from the only good thing I'd ever have in my life. At the same time, walking away was probably the only truly good and selfless thing I'd done in my life.

I was on the crest of the hill, could see the faint outline of the main house as they always left their porch light on. If I looked back, I'd see the cabin. But I didn't look back.

I looked down and tapped at the phone.

I didn't know the members of Greenstone Security well. That night that had begun all of this was the first and only time I'd seen the entire team in one room, and I'd been understandably distracted. This decision was an important one, one I'd thought on for hours while I'd been smiling, talking, laughing with Duke's family—while I'd been silently saying goodbye.

I needed someone with loose morals, someone deadly. The latter was the entirety of the team. And the former was another large chunk. So, even with my limited knowledge, I had a good chance of finding someone with the skills I needed for what I was planning. But there was a small chance I'd choose wrong, that this person would have ethics or whatever to do anything but contact Duke, who would likely yell at me a lot and then lock me in a room or chain me to a bed.

So yeah, my future was in the balance of the person I had decided to call.

"Duke, dude. I swear the only acceptable reason you have for waking me up is to tell me you've got some action for me—non-sex related, of course. I'm married now, remember?"

"Rosie?" I asked.

"Who is this?"

"This is Anastasia Edwards, and I need your help."

13

I HAD no idea how she got to me so quickly, considering I called her late last night and it was the early morning. The sun had only been up for an hour and I was prepared to wait a lot longer. As much as I thought I was a strong woman, with the resolve I had last night, the utter aloneness of these past hours had been terrifying. Duke's absence was a physical thing. But I couldn't let that show, especially not to a badass like Rosie who pulled up to the shitty motel an hour away from the ranch I'd been hiding in these past hours.

She'd given me detailed instructions the moment what I was doing became apparent. There were no warnings, no hesitation, no straight-up refusal—which I'd been expecting. This woman didn't like me. She had no reason to like me, and definitely had no reason to drop everything in her life and travel across the country because I was having a crisis.

The one and only person who would've done that for me was dead, buried, maybe, or cremated. Who knew? I didn't get to go to his funeral.

But I didn't think about that.

I focused on Rosie's instructions, which included stealing a car that wasn't Duke's as "he'll have some kind of tracking software in there, the shifty asshole."

I definitely felt terrible about stealing Anna's SUV, but I'd already committed to this and I'd either have it returned or get her a new one. It was a small price to pay to make sure they weren't in danger.

Rosie had walked me through, in great detail, how I could hot-wire a car. It didn't surprise me in the least that she had this knowledge. As it was, I didn't have to, since this was a ranch in Montana, in a town where people seemed to still be mostly good —or at least pretended to be. So the keys were in the freaking car. Then again, from what I'd come to gather, Duke's family was powerful, known and respected around these parts. It would take someone with brass balls to fuck with them.

Or brass ovaries.

Once I'd told her I'd made it off the ranch without incident, she directed me where to go and hung up. No goodbyes, no asking if I was okay. I liked that.

The fact that she'd managed to organize a room in a moderately shitty hotel in the middle of nowhere in the middle of the night was nothing short of magic.

There weren't even any witnesses because to add to it all, the key was in the door of the room she'd texted me the number of.

The room was exactly as I'd expected: small, smelled like cheap cleaning products and damp. Ghosts of my past lurked in every corner, and not just those of my foster parents. No, that first night with Duke, when things had been so drastically different, when I'd been so sure I couldn't survive him.

But here I was, now making sure he would survive me.

I hadn't slept, of course.

I'd paced, I'd panicked, I'd considered getting back in the car so I could drive to the ranch and crawl back into bed with Duke.

Almost.

My resolve was too iron clad for that, my heart far too fragile. I knew for a fact if I'd stayed a day longer on that ranch it would ruin me, absolutely fucking level me. There would be no coming back, no rising from the ashes.

Not only that, I didn't *want* to testify. I didn't want to fucking sit in a room and watch a judge hand over a sentence, didn't want to stare this man in the face and watch him try to wriggle out of it. Duke hadn't spoken of it much, another way he'd tried to protect me most likely. Didn't want me to think that all of this was for nothing, that the man might figure out a way to get out of this. He had powerful friends. Rich men with powerful friends made deadly enemies.

If that happened, I knew Duke would take things into his own hands, because that was the steadfast and deadly man Duke was.

But I didn't want a man—even Duke—to take my problems, to solve them for me.

I wanted to handle this deadly one myself.

This man had taken my only friend, stolen a vibrant, driven and extraordinary person for no other reason than he didn't want to face the consequences of his actions. He wanted to be invincible.

He'd taken away my cold, empty life. Forced me into one that was full, warm, and one that would haunt me for the rest of my days, along with the guilt of Andre's death.

It was all his fault that I'd been on the ranch with Duke, that I'd attached myself to him and his family—another casualty.

So I didn't go back to Duke.

I stayed in my room and prepared myself for what was to come.

A future without him.

* * *

"Now, I'm all for abandoning my family in the middle of the night to pick up a movie star who happens to be the key witness in bringing down one of the biggest assholes around, but you gonna clue me in to what we're actually doing here?" Rosie asked, Aviators on me.

She'd arrived early morning, coffees for both of us in hand. Somehow, she'd known how I took it. That was just another mystery to the woman who'd made the twenty-hour trip in less than eight. I did figure out that she'd "borrowed a friend's jet." I wasn't a stranger to flying in private jets, but I also knew it was hard to procure one in the middle of the night with a moment's notice. I also knew that if anyone could manage to do something like that, it was Rosie.

She sure as shit didn't look like someone who'd been torn from her bed and traveled across the country. She was wearing high-waisted leather pants, a black silk shirt tucked in, spike-heeled Valentinos, and her hair was piled into an artfully messy bun. Her cat eye was sharp and her blood-red lips lined to perfection.

She'd also handed me a change of clothes, almost as badass as her own. And she'd known all my sizes, right down to the La Perla bra she'd provided. I was back in designer armor—a Balmain blazer for Chrissakes.

Staring at the clothes on the floor of the motel room was like staring at the corpse of who I'd become at that ranch.

I was careful not to stare too long.

With makeup—again, that Rosie had supplied—applied and clothes still on the floor, we left the motel room and got into a black Range Rover.

It was only then she'd wanted to know what she was doing here.

I sucked in a breath. "This man killed my best friend," I said in response.

Her face stayed blank. She'd known this of course. But something moved in her eyes, something that wasn't the open dislike she'd worn the last time we saw each other. She was still wary of me, to be sure. I was wary of me.

"Andre had two brothers," I continued, looking out the window. "Macho-men in their own right. They run a gym. One of them is a UFC fighter. They're alpha all the way, and they adored their very openly gay and fabulous brother. They would've died for him, same for his parents."

I'd met Andre's family of course. They didn't really like me since I had made sure not to be warm or kind. But I liked them. I liked how accepting and supportive they were of Andre, even though they didn't understand him. They were staunch Catholics, had emigrated here from Mexico, been through poverty to give their sons a life, and did not hesitate to accept their son.

I was fiercely jealous of the strong family unit he came from, though I'd never admitted such a thing out loud.

I sipped my coffee. "They have a hole in their family because of me," I said, my voice shaking only slightly. It wouldn't do to crack right now, to crumble. Not in the car with this woman. Not on the way to do what I was going to do. I'd break down once it was done. I'd entomb myself in my mansion, drink vodka in the bath, not talk to anyone for a month and come out of my chrysalis the cold, unfeeling butterfly I had been before.

Rosie didn't try to argue with me for taking the blame for Andre's death like Duke had. She didn't try to convince me that this wasn't my fault. This was not a chick to pull punches, and it seemed to me she was someone who understood all the harsh truths of the world. She was definitely not the kind of woman to comfort someone with soft lies.

"I could wait it out at the ranch, for however long," I continued, still looking out the window, letting the Montana landscape seep further into me. "I could continue to get in deeper with Duke, with his family, keep up the lie, tangle it up so tightly that there would be no way to remove myself without hurting more people."

I paused, taking a breath and then turned my gaze from the window to the woman driving. "I'm not going to do that. I won't do that. So I want to figure out a way for this to end. Not with me on the witness stand. Not with him in prison, for however long. If he's as dangerous as everyone says he is, then he's either going to be powerful inside of prison, or he won't stay there for long. So I want this to end."

I waited. I wasn't waiting for Rosie to get it. She was smart. That much was clear. She knew exactly what I meant.

I was waiting for her to digest it, figure out whether she was going to be a part of doing something like this for a complete stranger she didn't even like.

It didn't take long for a response. And not at all one I expected. She grinned. *Beamed.* Full-on ear-to-ear.

"You know, I'm pretty good at reading people," she began. "A result of how I grew up around all kinds of people, people that looked really fucking bad on the outside, but were mostly good on the inside. And I've learned the hard way that most of the people that look good, safe, straight off the bat, they're gonna be the complete opposite. It's my job to read people, to know them, figure out what column they fit into. I'll say straight up, you fit into the 'bitch' column quickly—and not a good bitch." Her eyes flickered over me. "I was pretty darn confident in my assumptions, but it seems I was wrong. And, honey, never in my life have I been happier to have been wrong."

She started the car and screeched out of the empty parking lot.

We were speeding and back on the interstate before she spoke again.

She eyed me, speculative, curious, surprisingly not angry. "You know this is a bad idea, right?"

"Yes," I replied.

"Just checking," she said before returning her focus to the road.

I waited for more, because everything down to Rosie's shoes told me that she was a *more* type of woman.

Nothing.

"If you also know this is a bad idea, then why did you come?" I asked finally.

She grinned. "Because I love bad ideas, especially when they come with the promise of some action. Don't get me wrong, I love being a wife and a mother, blah, blah, blah. But sometimes I really feel like killing sex traffickers in Venezuela, and this is the next best thing. Know what I mean?"

I didn't know what she meant. But I smiled and said, "Totally." After a pause, I asked, "Where are we going?"

Another grin from Rosie with mischief in her eyes. "We're going to Amber, California, baby."

The drive to California was very different than the one from there. Rosie had obviously decided that escaping my safe house and wanting to enact retribution for my best friend meant that I was cool in her books.

As much as I told myself that I didn't need validation from another woman to confirm my decisions, I couldn't help but sit straighter. Someone like Rosie approved of me. It was much like Harriet's respect, something tough to earn, something to be treasured.

My heart pulsed with pain at the thought of the crazy old woman I'd never get to see again, never get to drink with, eat cheese with, watch fucking *Twilight* with. The grandmother I'd never had. Shit, the grandmother *no one* else had.

But just like Duke, just like that ranch in Montana, she was never mine.

Rosie cranked music louder than I'd ever heard a car stereo get up to. Not hard rock, like I expected someone like Rosie to listen to. Alanis Morissette and the fucking Spice Girls. She stopped for snacks, shared her lip gloss with me, smiled, pretty much acted like we were on a girls' trip across the country and had been friends for years. Not that I was some celebrity that had gotten her and her company—which I gathered was a family— embroiled in murder, corruption, and danger.

Maybe that's how people like Rosie knew you were solid.

Somewhere after we crossed the state line into Utah a call came through her Bluetooth.

"Here we go," she said, grinning, turning down the music.

My entire body froze at the screen. *"Duke calling."*

Despite the fact I'd stolen his phone, Rosie had somehow either known he was going to call from another number or was in fact, a very powerful witch.

"What's up, cowboy?" Rosie answered, winking to me.

"Where is she?" Duke clipped, his fury carrying through the phone and the miles between us.

Rosie put her finger to her lips. "Who?" she asked innocently.

"Cut the shit, Rosie," Duke snapped. "Anastasia's gone. I know she hasn't been taken because I would've found her fuckin' corpse within the vicinity, which I just *finished lookin' for.*"

My stomach lurched like I'd been punched in the gut with the pain and haunting in Duke's voice. He'd woken up and looked around his family ranch for my corpse.

I was *such* a bitch.

Rosie was not as affected, or not affected at all. She rolled her eyes. "Oh, come on, dude. You don't give me or our resident hacker much credit. If Kitsch was rolling up on you, we'd be giving you like at least an hour warning. She's likely fine."

Rosie was a good liar. Better than me, and that was saying something.

"She is, because I know she's sitting right beside you."

Rosie frowned, taking her eyes off the road for a disturbing amount of time checking random spots in the car for what I guessed was a hidden camera. "You couldn't possibly know that," she snapped. "I have this car swept for bugs weekly."

"I don't need a bug to know that my woman got the fucking wild idea that she'd be saving us by running away and getting out of danger. I also don't need a bug to know my woman is smart, so she likely went into my phone, found the number of the one person fucking stupid and reckless enough to drive across the country and take her fuck knows where for revenge."

Rosie blew out an impressed breath. "Dude, no offense, but that sounds like you think a lot of a movie star who doesn't know a thing about danger and just the right amount about me, who does. But I'm a *mother* and *wife* now. I wouldn't dream of doing something so stupid."

"I called Luke first," Duke shot back, without even a pause. "Said he woke up to a note that said, and I quote, 'gone to do some vigilantism. Be back later.'"

Rosie scowled, pressed the end call button and muttered "that fucking traitor."

She tapped at the screen, only paying vague attention to driving as she swerved through traffic. Arguably, I should've feared for my life, but I felt as safe with this woman as I did with Duke. That, and I was fascinated to see what she was doing next.

"Calling Husband/Traitor" lit up the car screen.

There was barely a ring before a voice answered.

"You're in deep fuckin' shit," a voice growled. The voice was attractive, like caramel, smooth, manly, all-over alpha.

It belonged to the man who had been sitting next to Rosie that night a million years ago. He was the only one who'd never been on my mental list. Something about him just seemed too...good. He wouldn't participate in something like this. And he definitely didn't sound like he wanted his wife to be doing it either.

"Right back at you, honey," Rosie said in a sickly sweet and deadly voice. "You really think you're going to get away with ratting on me?"

"It's not fuckin' ratting when I wake up to my wife gone and figure out that she's involved herself with one of the deadliest organized criminals currently operating in the country."

Rosie scowled. "It's like you don't even know me. *I'm* the deadliest criminal currently operating in the country. Just because I married a former cop, and popped out some kids, people think I've gone soft. Well, I haven't. So you stay home and be dad; I'm going to go out and kick some ass."

On that, she hung up the phone.

* * *

The drive with Rosie didn't suck.

In fact, I would go so far as to say I had fun.

Had fun driving away from the one and only man I'd ever loved, the one family I'd ever known, and into a quite possibly deadly situation that I was nowhere near equipped for.

That was Rosie.

She didn't seem like she was driving me to violence or death. It was like we were on our way to fucking Coachella.

We took turns driving since we couldn't exactly stop, not with Duke on our tail.

"I consider myself smarter than all those men put together, but that only gives us a day's head start. If that," she said. "And when a man loses the woman that he's gone batshit over—thanks for that, by the way, it won me a thousand bucks—that time frame is even more unpredictable."

I winced at that, trying my best not to think about what I'd done to Duke and his family right after they celebrated Tanner's child.

He was going to hate me.

They were all going to hate me, probably think that the movie star couldn't handle the spotlight being on someone else so she ran off dramatically in the middle of the night to find more attention.

That was the plan, at least.

He hadn't called again. I wasn't sure if that was because Rosie had blocked his number or if he knew he wouldn't get anything out of the woman.

She was active enough, calling people almost constantly including someone called Gwen to make sure she had plenty of alcohol ready for our arrival.

She called another woman named Amy, and ordered her to collect a boss-ass outfit for a woman with all my measurements.

Another call was to a woman called Evie to tell her to prepare for a "small war," and with an order not to tell any of those "alpha assholes in leather."

She'd looked to me after she said that. "We're going to surprise them all with this shit."

* * *

Amber was impressive.

I'd heard of it since it was where Lexie Descare lived most of her life these days. Somehow, there wasn't that much information on it, which was unheard of in today's media. I'd figured it had something to do with Greenstone Security and the motorcycle gang her husband was involved with.

The town itself was quaint, beautiful, and welcoming.

Again, something unheard of today. It was on the coast in California.

It should've been bastardized by corporations and tourists by now, yet it hadn't been.

The main street was busy, but not crowded, not a Starbucks to be seen. Every store seemed to be mom-and-pop. The street itself was lined with flower boxes. Each business looked to be lovingly taken care of. It was a snapshot into a fantasy that was only supposed to exist in the movies—I should know.

Rosie double-parked outside a classy-looking boutique called Phoenix. The name was written in a classy script, the store itself was impeccable, and the girl in me was definitely excited at seeing something like this. I was on the run from the man I was in love with and planned to confront the asshole that murdered my best friend, yet I still found a small, superficial part of me that wanted to *shop*.

Rosie somehow looked fresh and ready for anything after the drive where we only stopped to use the restroom and took turns sleeping. She hopped out of the car without a word for me, and I had no choice but to follow.

"Rosie, what are we doing here?" I asked as she made it clear she was going into the clothing store.

She raised her perfectly shaped brow at me. "You really think we're going into a takedown of this magnitude without some fresh outfits? Come on, don't disappoint me now."

Then she opened the door, holding it for me like an invitation.

The woman had a point.

"Attagirl," she muttered when I walked in.

The store was larger than it looked outside, and way more impressive, which was saying something. I felt transported back to LA, but somehow without the snootiness. There was exposed brick all down one side of the store, carefully arranged jewelry displays, expensive candles burning, placed so they weren't over-powering, but welcoming.

"Rosie!" a woman screamed, running through the store on six-inch heels.

The two women hugged like old friends, sisters.

It was only when they let each other go that I got a good look at the woman. She was an absolute knockout. Again, I'd become accustomed to beautiful people living in LA, but there was some-thing different about this woman, similar to the aura that Rosie carried around, maybe without the air of danger—with something softer.

Her long chocolate-brown hair fell down her back in soft curls, emerald-green eyes glowed with happiness. I thought she might've been around my age, but I couldn't really tell. Her skin was flawless, and eyes free of the typical jadedness that came around your thirtieth birthday.

She was dressed exactly like the store: expensive, classic, approachable, with a long white maxi-dress, belted at her tiny waist. Strings of gold and diamonds were slung around her neck, bracelets the same. There were only two rings on her hands, though, a massive diamond and wedding band on her ring finger.

Her green eyes widened as she took me in. "You're Anastasia Edwards! Oh my gosh, I fucking love you. My daughter does too."

She had an accent that I thought was either New Zealand or Australian, peppered with a slight American twang that told me she'd lived here for a while.

I smiled warmly at her, because that was what the woman invited. There was no way I'd be able to hold on to my cold mask if everyone in this place was like her. "I hope I get to meet her then," I said that with honesty, the first time I was actually curious and looking forward to meeting a child. I didn't really like them, as a rule, maybe because I never got to be one. Maybe because I knew I'd never have one.

"I'm Gwen," she said, moving forward and hugging me. "I'm Rosie's sister-in-law."

That made sense.

Gwen let me go and narrowed her eyes at Rosie. "Is Cade going to be totally pissed off that you're here?"

Rosie smiled. "I couldn't imagine why."

Gwen clapped her hands. "Epic!" She looked us up and down. "Now I'm guessing you stopped here because you're about to cause some trouble and you need outfits to go with it?"

"You know me far too well, sister," Rosie said, moving toward the clothing racks. "Think, mafia takedown combined with an Olivia Pope in *Scandal* vibe."

Gwen's heels clicked as she walked to the front door, flipped the sign to "closed," then locked it. She clapped her hands together and smiled. "I've got you."

And she did.

They both did.

Which was a good thing, since I definitely didn't feel like I "had" myself.

No, the only person who truly had me, I'd left behind on a ranch in Montana.

14

Rosie and I spent just over an hour with Gwen. I could've spent all day with her, as she had something about her that I wanted to soak up. There was a comfort in her presence, a kindness.

It was almost like, for that hour, I was a woman with two kick-ass, beautiful friends and we were just out shopping. No furious cowboys chasing after us, no broken hearts, no dead friends, no crime boss looking to kill me so I couldn't testify against him.

But then, as it tended to do, reality rushed back in.

We left the store with two bags...each. I didn't know how long this takedown was meant to go on for, but I doubted it would be long enough for all those outfits. It was only when Gwen was bagging everything up that I realized I didn't have my wallet with me. Duke had confiscated it on the first day, because he probably thought I'd try to escape his protection and be stupid enough to use my credit cards. Rosie had paid for everything on the trip, I'd noted that, but I'd been in too much of a haze to understand the fact I had no money, no identification, no phone, nothing. I was relying totally on Rosie.

"Okay, so due to the current situation, I find myself without a way to pay for this," I began to say to Gwen.

Rosie interrupted by holding up a black credit card with my name on it. She passed it to Gwen. Gwen frowned at her, but didn't take it. "I'm here as a supplier of bad-ass outfits, I take no currency. This is the most fun I've had in a while."

"Take the fucking card, Gwen," Rosie snapped.

I didn't even ask Rosie how she got it, because it didn't surprise me that she'd have the ability to either find and steal my credit cards or get a whole new one.

"Isn't using that like some kind of flashing sign to Kitsch that I'm here?" I asked.

Rosie smiled. "Yes, it is exactly that—which is why my sister needs to run the fucking card."

Gwen looked between the two of us, shook her head but took the card. "Luke is going to be pissed at you," she said.

Rosie smiled. "Who?"

Rosie had not said anything about what was about to go down, or even where we were going. She was too busy trying to decide which outfit she'd wear.

She'd taken the keys to Gwen's house from her and drove us out to a beautiful home right in front of the ocean, letting herself in, and showing me to where I'd be staying.

The house itself was decorated in boho glam, whites everywhere, signs of children too—which Gwen mentioned were hanging out with someone called Mia's children, who were possibly teaching them how to make homemade bombs. She'd sounded disturbingly serious too, though not at all worried.

She hadn't seemed concerned that I was staying at her home, even though she didn't know me and I had a powerful murderer after me.

I should've fought it more, especially with the many signs that children were here. But I didn't. I let Rosie show me to the guest room, order me to shower and change into one of the new outfits, and be "ready for battle in an hour."

Then she disappeared, presumably to do the same.

I looked around the beautiful room. The welcoming bed with the plush bedspread called to me. The urge to sink into it and close my eyes until this was all over was strong. The urge to sink to my knees and sob was even stronger.

But I did neither of those things.

Instead, I showered. I reapplied my makeup.

I put on a pair of leather pants, a soft pink camisole, and spiked heels. And I readied myself for battle.

Rosie was knocking on the door exactly an hour later. She was impressed with my outfit and I was with hers.

Although, impressed was too light a word.

She was wearing lace-front short shorts, thigh-high metallic boots, and a plain white cropped top.

Her hair was plaited into intricate braids and she looked like a fucking Viking queen.

"Good, you're ready. No rest for the wicked." She winked. "Now get in the car, bitch. We're going crime lord hunting."

After starting the events that would eventually lead Kitsch to Amber, we drove to the outskirts of the town to a more industrial and decidedly less picturesque area.

There was a sizable fenced-off area at the end of the street, barbed wire topped the tall fences, and cameras were perched on each side of the gate. The gate opened the second Rosie pulled up.

She drove forward into a garage area that was owned by the Sons of Templar MC.

I'd heard of them. Everyone had heard of them, not just

because of their connection to Lexie Descare. They were infamous as one of the largest motorcycle gangs in the country.

I didn't know how Rosie connected with bad-ass bikers, but it seemed to make sense. "You know the Sons of Templar?" I asked.

She turned to me as she stopped the car. "Know them? Honey, I'm the heart, soul, and everything else of this place. If they let women wear the cut, it would be me wearing the president patch, not my brother. Good thing for him, I prefer variety in my wardrobe."

I followed her lead as she walked across the concrete toward the bays with cars propped up and various men in coveralls working on them. Well, they had been working on them. Everything stopped with Rosie's entrance.

No sooner than our heels had started clicking on the concrete did a man appear, a man that scared the ever-loving Christ out of me.

He was tall.

Dark.

Deadly.

Handsome, as he got closer. Yes. One of the most handsome men I'd ever seen—in a totally intimidating and terrifying way. His gray eyes were furious and narrowed on Rosie. If they were focused on me, I would've liked to think I was brave enough not to run away or at the very least cower, but I couldn't be sure.

He was wearing a Sons of Templar Cut with "President" scrawled on the front.

"What the fuck, Rosie?" he growled the second he stopped in front of her. His voice was low, manly, and full of that same fury his eyes held.

"Hello to you too, Cade," she said.

"*You're* Cade?" I blurted, unable to stop myself.

His eyes found mine. They didn't flare in recognition, as they were still pissed off, but not the same as when they were directed at his sister. It totally made sense they were related.

"Gwen's Cade?" I clarified.

The corner of his mouth twitched in what I suspected was his version of a smile. "She'd be more than happy to hear me being referred that way instead of the other way around."

"Holy crap," I muttered.

At first, I couldn't compute the glamorous, beautiful, kind woman from the boutique with this gruff and terrifying biker. But I saw it with that mouth twitch, with the way something moved in his eyes with the mention of his wife.

Oh yeah. I got that.

Every woman in the world would give up their soul to have a man make that expression when their names were mentioned. I know I would.

"We don't have long to execute a plan, so I'm going to need you to save whatever lecture I know you have prepared for me and just call church so I can explain this all once and we can get cracking," Rosie said. "Wire, of course, is already briefed. Again, save whatever tongue-lashing you have for that little nerd until later. We have a crime organization to topple and not much time." Rosie said all of this with the confidence and casual demeanor that one might have ordering a fucking burger at a drive-thru. She didn't even wait for Cade's response; she just grasped my hand and dragged me across the parking lot toward a structure off the garage, which I guessed was the clubhouse.

"I already texted Amy," she said, nodding to a cherry-red convertible in between the Harleys. "Since Gwen had the fashion part of our mission under control, she's got margaritas waiting for us. Trust me, we're going to need them."

The weight of what I was doing hit me the second we set foot in the biker clubhouse. I hadn't let myself think how shitty this was. But no, it wasn't shitty. It was on-brand for me.

I don't know what I expected an MC clubhouse would look like, but this was the furthest from my expectations. Then again, looking to Rosie—who I knew was the sister to the President of the MC, a big deal—and Gwen, who was married to said president, and the fact they were swathed in designer clothing, I guessed they wouldn't really put up with bikers who had used condoms and heroin needles littering the floor.

Not even a few half-naked women and men passed out on various surfaces.

It smelled like Gwen's store, the same expensive candles burning.

The décor wasn't exactly elegant but it was classy for a biker compound—enormous sofa in front of a giant TV, man-sized coffee table with a neat stack of books and candles in the middle.

There were a handful of armchairs scattered around, free of stains. Various Harley art hung on the walls and what looked like a framed collection of mugshots.

It was a massive house, much more impressive than it looked from the outside, but my perusal was cut short when yet another beautiful woman came rushing toward us on six-inch Manolos.

Her fire-red hair was falling in excellent curls around her face. Two margaritas were in her hands, in glasses, salt rim and all.

"You're here," she said, smiling wide and handing us the drinks.

I took the glass more out of habit than anything. Plus, I'd been through so much these past thirty hours or so, tequila was medically necessary.

Up close the woman was even more beautiful. Her makeup was expertly applied but a dusting of freckles showed through. Her eyes were wild and warm, her smile the same.

She was wearing a white Balmain blazer and white slacks. She looked like she should be sitting at the head of a conference table, not in a biker compound. But somehow, like Gwen, she fit.

"I'm Amy," she said, the same warmth in her voice that was in her smile. "I could go through the farce of pretending I don't know who you are, but I'm not going to. You're Anastasia Edwards, and you witnessed a murder by a really bad dude. Until a couple of days ago, you were in Greenstone Security witness protection on Duke's ranch in Montana, which sounds like a total nightmare to me but you did the alpha male, badass bitch dance and you got together. But of course, there had to be some badass bitch behavior that landed you here."

I blinked. I was used to people knowing details about my life. It was part of the game, but all those details were meant to be top secret, not to mention the personal shit.

I looked between the two women. "Okay, I need to know it right now. Did you two make a deal with the devil or something, to give you badass skills, style and overall glam?"

Rosie grinned.

As did Amy. "Honey, the devil wishes he was as badass as us."

I could've seen this conversation going a lot further had two men not entered the room.

Two fricking hot men.

The majority of beauty found in LA was carefully constructed and curated by plastic surgeons, facialists, and makeup artists. There was a slight sheen to it. Everyone looked the same, fake.

Yet every single person I'd encountered in Amber thus far was as attractive as all hell, naturally. And beyond that, they were all unique.

The two men were no different.

Both were large in stature and in presence. They both wore Sons of Templar cuts. The one on the left was taller, leaner, and muscled to be sure. His blond hair effortlessly fell around his face in a way that most talented hairstylists in LA couldn't replicate. His tanned arms were covered in tattoos, and his eyes lit with a smile focused on Amy, beyond focused, zeroing in, like she was his center of gravity.

The one beside him was shorter, but not by much. He was bald, about the same amount of tattoos, but an air of menace about him.

"Sparky, you're here. The kids are with a sitter—until further notice—and you're giving out margaritas. How worried should I be?" the blond guy asked, yanking Amy to his side.

She beamed up at him. "Oh, I'd say about a five."

His smile dimmed ever so slightly. "Fuck," he muttered.

The large, bald, scary-looking—but totally sexy—Hispanic man gaped at me. "Ohmigod, you're Anastasia Edwards. I *love* your movies." He said this all in a rush, his cheeks flushing with what seemed like embarrassment. I'd had this reaction before—from teenage girls—but not from big burly men like this one.

It was wholesome and somehow sweet.

"Dude, way to geek out," the hot blond, but still scary-looking surfer said with a chuckle.

Bald guy glared, and there was nothing at all wholesome about that glare. "She's the Meryl Streep of our generation. Fuck off." He then focused on me and extended a tattooed hand, expression changing from the deadly menace he'd shown surfer guy to a soft adoring smile. "I'm Lucky. I'm not going to say I'm your biggest fan, because I'm sure you've got people that go through your trash and send you ears and shit. But I'm definitely up there." He paused. "Not in a creepy way. I'm totally and utterly dedicated to my wife. I'm a feminist. I don't see you as a sex object. I admire your artistic talent and what you've done for movies and women in acting."

I blinked rapidly at the man, the man who had been totally intimidating...until he started speaking.

Usually I was practiced at handling fans like this, praise like this.

But I was no longer Anastasia Edwards, movie star. I was just...Anastasia Edwards. I tried to grasp the former as best I could. That's all I would be after this was over.

"Thank you, Lucky. That really means a lot," I said, smiling. "And I haven't had any fans that sent me an ear. I have gotten toenail clippings though."

"Are you fucking serious?" Amy demanded.

I nodded. "Yeah, and that's not even the worst."

Her eyes brightened with a spark that I guessed was dangerous. "Oh, we're going to have to talk about that over cocktails."

"Church. Now," a voice boomed from behind us. I jumped, but naturally, the other women didn't. I guessed they were used to scary alpha males yelling at them.

Cade had entered the room at some point during the interaction with Lucky and he didn't look happy. He had the whole murderous glower thing down to a T, but no one seemed to blanch in fear, so it seemed I was safe.

And that's how I felt.

Safe.

Safe around these beautiful strangers, in a fucking biker clubhouse. miles away from the one person my entire body craved like a drug, the person who I could guess was either tearing apart the country to find me or on his way here. Duke was a smart guy. He would've made the Rosie, Sons of Templar connection, especially if he even suspected what I might've been wanting to do.

That was my mistake.

I should've thought this through more, should've taken my time to distance myself from him, start adopting my old coldness and bitchiness.

Then it would've made it seem like I'd left for different reasons, made him less inclined to find me.

Maybe.

It hadn't even been three days and I missed him like a limb, missed his touch, his smell, fucking everything.

But this was for the best.

Cade pointed two fingers at Rosie and me. "Both of you, in there."

Rosie smiled bitchily at her brother, the facial version of a middle finger. Something I made note of—that was a perfect expression to replicate in movies. I did that, collected gestures and expressions of interesting people. There was a total wealth of material here, but it remained to be seen whether I'd be able to put it to good use after all this was done.

"We're finishing our drinks," Rosie said when Cade continued to stare at his sister.

His jaw twitched ever so slightly, everything else on his face remained blank, empty, which made the jaw twitch all the more terrifying.

Rosie put her hand on her hip and narrowed her eyes, then took a slow drink of her margarita. It was a power move I recognized, and I'd done such a thing in boardrooms with executives who thought I was their toy. It was simple but effective.

"You can glare at me all you want, Cade. I'm still going to finish my drink, catch up with my girl, and we'll come in in our own good time. Five minutes isn't going to kill anyone."

"It just might," Lucky muttered.

I grinned then sipped my drink to hide it.

Cade gave Rosie one more measured stare, as if he was figuring out if he could win this. In my eyes, this man would win most things, if not by the air of danger about him then by the straight-up hotness.

But even the badass hot president of a motorcycle club was

no match for Rosie. "Longer than five minutes, I'm fuckin' drag-
gin' you in there," he grumbled.

"You can try," Rosie offered.

Cade turned on his motorcycle boot and made his way into
the room labeled "Church." I knew what that was thanks to *Sons
of Anarchy*. I also knew that civilians sitting at the table was not
something that was done. Biker church was a sacred thing, where
they discussed gun-running, murder, and how to perfect smoldering glares.

The surfer guy laid a hot kiss on Amy without any concern
that such a kiss was usually reserved for a time when there wasn't
an audience.

My heart clenched with a memory of a certain macho-man
who engaged in similar PDA, someone who I wasn't supposed to
be thinking about.

"Stay here. No running after murderers. You're a mother
now, remember?"

Amy frowned at her husband. "Who says I can't run after
murderers just because I'm a mother? I can have it all."

"Amen, sista," Rosie muttered.

The man sighed and looked to Lucky, who held his hands up
in surrender. "Don't look at me, bro. I've got a pregnant wife who
I'm still not stupid enough to say that shit to."

Brock glared at the man and then kissed his wife again. "Just
stay here, Sparky," he growled then walked off.

Lucky gave me a wink and followed him.

I watched men trickle into the room, each of them wearing
the Sons of Templar cuts. A couple of younger looking men wore
"Prospect" on the bottom without the patch. Most of them were
covered in tattoos. Not all of them looked like they could grace
the covers of GQ, as there were some more stereotypical older
bikers with beer guts, but very few.

"Rethinking your choice?" Rosie asked with a glint in her eye.

"My choice?"

"Duke," she said. "Sure, he's a hot piece of ass in an All-American, polished type of way—which I totally get—but the bad-boy thing is hard to turn away."

"Try impossible," Amy offered.

"It wasn't a choice," I said without thinking. "Duke. He wasn't a choice. And even if he was, it'd still be him. Always."

Both women stared at me, something serious moving in their eyes. Not for long, of course. They both grinned after a beat.

"Oh shit," Amy said, draining her drink. "I'm going to have to make more margaritas for this." She turned on her heel to walk toward what looked like a fully equipped wet bar.

"And shots," Rosie called after her. She drained her drink too. "Ready for this?"

"Not at all," I told her honestly.

She grinned wider, not perturbed. "Perfect."

✳ ✳ ✳

"Okay, as you can see, we've got somewhat of a situation," Cade addressed the table.

We had finished our drinks, did a tequila shot each, and only then did we walk into "church."

The table was full by then, and I had to admit, it was damn intimidating. Well, that was until Lucky caught my eye with a grin, pointing to the empty chair beside him hopefully.

Yeah, that helped.

Rosie exchanged greetings with most of the men at the table, which showed the admiration and respect these men had for her.

Cade watched her do this with that same blank gaze. He no longer had the pissed-jaw twitch. I figured he was resigned to such behavior from his sister and she was definitely not a woman who would ever change.

"As you can see, we have a guest." Cade nodded toward me and I held my breath as every eye at the table focused on me.

Lucky fucking applauded.

Then everyone looked to him. He gaped at his brothers. "Come on, guys, this is a three-time Oscar winner."

Cade ignored this. "For those of you who don't know, Anastasia is the key witness in the case against Coleson Kitsch. He's a fucking piece of shit that has been thus far untouchable." Cade paused for effect, and it totally worked. I was following every move, mostly because of his charisma, and also because I had no fucking clue what the plan was here.

"Untouchable until now. He's been looking for Anastasia, obviously to make sure she doesn't testify. Because her main goal would be putting him behind bars." Cade looked at me and I did my best to keep my stare even. "I understand that goal has changed."

I nodded once. "It's changed."

He looked back to the table. "Now I know that a lot of you have been happy with the direction the club's taken, especially after what happened with Fernandez." Cade paused again. This time was not for effect. There was something heavy about this pause.

"If you don't want to be involved in this, you can get up, walk out. No questions asked. No repercussions." Cade waited.

So did I.

Even if these men looked like they bench pressed Volvos for fun, this was a stranger—unless they'd seen my movies—asking them to go up against one of the most powerful and dangerous men in the country. I would've been surprised if anyone wanted to help me with this. A number of the men wore wedding rings. There was Gwen, with her easy smile, with her children, and Lucky's pregnant wife.

No one got up from the table.

Cade nodded his head once. "Okay, let's take this fucker down."

* * *

"You go ahead, I've got to talk to my brother and Wire," Rosie said, nodding her head toward Cade and the skinniest guy here, who was holding an energy drink. I was using the term "skinniest" very loosely since the man still had impressive muscles.

"Good, you can answer all my questions about *Angel Tears*. I can't say it's a favorite because playing favorites with your movies would be criminal. We'll just start there," Lucky jumped in, guiding me out of the room and toward the sofa.

"Did you really die in the end or did you just go to an alternate plane of existence?" he asked, then looked toward the mess of leather-wearing men dispersing. "A Prospect better get me a fucking beer and Anastasia a drink or they'll be target practice as warm-up," he yelled.

A younger man with impressive tattoos ran to do just that and returned quickly with a beer for Lucky and a fresh cocktail for me.

I smiled. "Thank you."

He blushed and all but ran off. The tall, tattooed man *blushed* at me. Now I'd seen it all.

I turned to Lucky. "So, I know that the director is pretending it's up for interpretation, but I know for a fact that he..."

I then proceeded to inform him of the most closely guarded secret about one of my biggest films. It was only fair, since the man seemed to be risking his life for me.

Normally, I worked on autopilot talking to fans about my movies. They mostly asked all the same questions and very few actually cared about the answers. They just wanted the bragging rights to say they spoke to Anastasia Edwards. And as social media got bigger, people cared more about the fucking selfie than they did a conversation.

Many times I'd wanted to snatch the phone shoved in my face and crush it with my designer shoes. But of course, I couldn't do that. Imagine the publicity, the names that would be hurled around in the media, talking about how the "crazy" female star had snapped at a loving fan. It didn't matter that the fan in question stalked me coming out of a fucking gyno appointment when I was walking with discomfort and just wanted to get out without speaking to anyone.

I became jaded and slightly hateful toward the hoards.

But Lucky was a breath of fresh air. He really was a true fan, and a bit of a geek. An intelligent one at that. A couple of the other men had joined the conversation, surprising me with the fact they were huge fans of the movie where I played a woman who exacted revenge on any man that wronged her.

It seemed that most of these gruff, alpha bikers were feminists. The wedding rings on their fingers helped tell me that they'd either changed for the right woman, or the right woman hadn't been willing to put up with any patriarchal bullshit.

"I'm back," Rosie declared, interrupting the conversation. She glanced around at the men. "Don't you have infidels to beat into submission?" she questioned. "It's girl time. And you"—she pointed to Lucky—"call your wife and tell her to meet us at Gwen's place."

Lucky's eyes darkened ever so slightly. "I'll tell her that you suggested that, but no way am I ordering her to do shit. She's growing a human inside of her. My *child*. Where she takes herself is totally up to her."

Rosie rolled her eyes. "Whatever. I'll text her." She got her phone out. "Pussy," she muttered under her breath.

The men quickly got up, offering me goodbyes.

Rosie took Lucky's place beside me and grabbed my drink from my hand, draining the last sip.

"Okay, so tonight is kind of a write-off regarding the whole revenge thing," Rosie said. "So I was thinking we have a girls' night."

"Girls' night?" I queried.

"We'll get dressed up so everyone's husbands grumble about the outfits, because their wives are just that fucking hot. We'll go to our favorite, get one tier down from blackout drunk—those of us not preggos of course—and talk about men. You'll have to share your story about you and Duke because, honey, we've been waiting for it. He might not be in the Sons of Templar universe, but he's the kind of guy who *transcends* universe, if you know what I mean. He's been around for a while and we've all been waiting to see what version of shit his woman puts him through. I'll say so far...I approve." She winked. "We'll go to Gwen's place, I'll kiss my niece and nephew. We'll pregame, torture Cade a little. Then go out. I've got word that every old lady is gonna be there and it's been a hot minute since I've seen all those bitches. It's gonna be fun. You down?"

This was a lot to process. I'd just had a sit down with the Sons of Templar. That was after driving across the country in twenty hours. That was after sneaking out of the bed of a man I love, leaving behind the only home and family I'd ever truly known without even saying goodbye, because I wanted to inflict vengeance on the man who had my only friend killed.

"Yeah," I said. "I'm down."

15

We went to Gwen's house to "get ready" and pregame—two things I'd never done in high school. I was too busy trying to survive when all the other girls were putting on their prom dresses and planning on letting the football captain take their virginity.

My virginity was long gone by prom. If I'd stayed at one school long enough, I was sure I'd get the reputation of the school slut. As it was, I was never somewhere long enough for a label or to even make girlfriends. I didn't need a therapist to tell me my sexual exploits at such a young age were connected to losing my father and never really being loved since then.

Yeah, of course they were fucking connected.

Whatever.

The point was, I didn't have the experience of the blaring music, the clink of glasses and popping of corks—because everyone getting together was cause for celebration, even if they were planning on murdering a crime boss—and just the general atmosphere.

I'd gotten to meet Gwen and Cade's two children, a girl and a boy, both of whom got all of the best qualities from their parents —and there were a lot to choose from. Looking into Isabella's beautiful wide eyes and watching Kingston squeal and run away from his aunt Rosie made my womb clench suddenly and unexpectedly.

My thoughts crept away from the beautiful beach house in California to a ranch in Montana. I remembered the family gathered at the hospital, Tanner coming out with wet eyes and a smile that seeped from his very soul.

I thought about a baby with blond curls, with Duke's eyes, in his arms.

"You with us, honey?"

I jerked out of my thoughts to focus on Gwen. Her hair was tumbling around her face in messy curls, an expertly applied green smoky eye turning her already piercing gaze electric. She was wearing a black bustier and a black leather skirt.

In short, she looked hot, damn hot.

"What?"

She smiled with an empathy that told me she was suspecting what I was thinking about. "Now that the children have been passed on to their grandparents, we're actually going to have a peaceful afternoon outside, a calm before the storm." She paused. "But if you're not feeling up to it, we can call this whole thing off, put on sweats, eat terrible things, watch equally terrible movies. None of yours of course, as they're all good."

I smiled. "No, Rosie is totally set on this girls' night. I don't think I'd fare well being the reason for it ending."

"I can handle Rosie," Gwen said, a hard edge to her tone that told me Gwen was yet another badass woman in this town.

"I don't doubt it," I said truthfully. "But it's okay. This will be good for me. As long as I'm not...intruding?" I couldn't hide my unease.

It was starkly clear how much all these people meant to each other, what a family they were—bonds of blood and something else entirely. It was intimidating to say the least. I felt like some imposter, forcing myself somewhere I would never belong.

Gwen squeezed my hand. "You stop thinking that shit right now," she said. "Our group is big. It's complicated. It's crazy. But there is one thing always constant about it, newcomers are always welcome. Especially newcomers in the midst of a romance with an alpha male while dealing with emotional trauma and or murderous crime lords." She paused. "You're not alone, Anastasia. You belong here. We'll take care of you."

All of this could've sounded patronizing and cheesy very easily. But it didn't. It sounded genuine.

Which was why a tear trickled down my cheek. Then another. I quickly wiped them away, mortified I was crying in front of this relative stranger—someone who had said some of the nicest things to me I'd ever heard.

Gwen reached to grasp my hand. "You're allowed to cry, you know. This is some shit. Whoever said that big girls don't cry was either Fergie or a man. We need to let it out or else we drown. It takes a strong woman to handle this kind of stuff. It takes an even stronger one to feel it." She wiped my face. "You'll survive this. I promise."

Even though all evidence was pointing to the fact something like my survival couldn't be promised, I believed her.

* * *

Arriving at the bar was a circus, to say the least.

Not for any reasons concerning me, for once in my life. No reporters, paparazzi, or even fans asking to stop for a photo. It could've just been because I was lost in the crowd of beautiful, impeccably dressed women who I'd arrived at the bar with. We'd needed four cars.

I was introduced to many women, each as beautiful as the last. Each was completely freaking different. And as Gwen had promised, each of them was welcoming in their own way. There was none of that irritating female hesitation and judgment that was almost bred into us. There was something inside of us trained to be dubious of new women, especially if those women had qualities we lacked and coveted. Now, each of these women had qualities I coveted. Each of them was extraordinary, that was just on first impression.

So I had that urge to hate them, to keep my distance, to act cold.

What was that urge? Did it somehow come from men realizing that women who united were more dangerous?

And all of these women were dangerous, in their own way. Each of them survived things many men—most men—wouldn't have gotten through.

I was impressed. And happy after being served our first drink by a bartender who was yet another beautiful woman. She had more of a country glam going on though, with hair as big as I'd seen in a while, face covered expertly with makeup. She was wearing a fringed leather jacket and matching pants, and somehow made it look classic and timeless instead of the tacky way it might've looked on anyone else.

She gave me a drink and a warm smile. "I think you're gonna need this, honey," she said, a soft twang to her voice.

I learned that her name was Laura Maye, the owner of the bar, the maker of some strong drinks and who the women at the table regarded as their own personal Yoda.

The urge to give in to my baser instincts went away. I sunk into the conversation and the rhythm of the women easily. I appreciated that they didn't focus all the attention on me. Even being used to it, I wouldn't have been able to handle it with these women. They didn't ignore me either.

"I thought Lizzie was coming," Gwen said.

Each of the women's smiles died from Mia's earlier story about her sons who seemed absolutely insane.

"I thought she was too," Amy replied. "But she texted me just before we got here to cancel."

Rosie's brows furrowed and sadness crept into her eyes, anger too. "Fuck," she muttered. "You've seen her lately?" she asked Gwen.

Gwen bit her lip. "Yeah, I take the kids over to her place. They play. We drink coffee or wine depending on the time, depending on the day, studiously avoid the obvious topic. She seems...okay. As okay as anyone could be." Pain leeched into the woman's words.

"She needs an intervention," Rosie decided.

"She lost her husband," Lily—a beautiful quiet woman interjected. "She needs time."

I didn't even know this woman, but the pain for her permeated the air. She was loved. That much was clear. She was hurting in a way that even these extraordinary women couldn't help.

It hung over the conversation for a while—that sadness, that helplessness.

Until attention was finally focused on me. I had a feeling they were waiting for me to become acclimated with them, and to suck down a couple of drinks—which were strong.

And they were right.

"You gotta spill," Amy demanded. "The Duke thing. The murder thing. Come on, girl, tell us your story. We've all been there. One way or another at least."

She grinned at the group.

It felt pivotal, this moment. I didn't know why. It likely could've been the strong drinks, or the situation, or my mind trying to preserve its sanity by attaching something to these women so I wouldn't fall to pieces when Duke was taken away from me—even if I was the one to push him away in the first place.

Whatever it was, I told our story.

* * *

I'd initially expected the story to be short, to provide the rundown of what had happened without emotion—without sounding like a total lovesick fool.

But...the drinks.

My broken heart.

My willing and empathetic audience.

So it was long.

Two drinks long.

Especially when there were breaks in the story for each woman to ask a question.

"You got bitten by a rattlesnake and walked yourself back to the house?" Mia asked.

"Not all the way. Duke arrived about three quarters into my journey."

Mia leaned back in her chair. "You need to claim that shit. It's like in that movie where the snake didn't bite you because you were the savior of the generation, except this time you got bitten, survived, showed that snake and Duke who was boss."

I decided that Mia was one of the funniest people I'd ever met. Even though I didn't agree entirely with what she said, I'd never argue.

I just continued the story.

"And now I'm here," I finished.

Everyone blinked at me. This was the longest silence we'd had at this table since we sat down.

"Girl, I thought your movies were good," Mia spoke first.

"But it turns out your real life is so much better." Her face paled slightly. "Of course, I don't mean that you witnessing the man you're sleeping with die and losing your friend is good. *Fuuuudge.*"

I smiled. "I know what you mean. It is fucking crazy, hearing it all out loud."

Rosie winked at me. "Thank God. A crazy story is a requirement for membership into the girl gang."

I let each of them discuss getting jackets or tattoos to signify membership into this gang. My bladder was definitely letting it be known just how much liquid I'd consumed in a small amount of time.

If I'd announced I was going to the restroom, I was sure I'd get a bunch of women accompanying me. Women traveled in packs, after all, and then there was the whole fact that I was the target of a murderous crime boss.

But I figured that said murderous crime boss wasn't about to kill me in the bar, especially since he didn't even know I was here yet. The "plan" would apparently commence tomorrow.

They'd somehow leak I was here, they'd lure Kitsch somewhere and then...you know. I definitely should've known the exact details since I was an accomplice to murder, but whatever.

All of these thoughts happened in the bathroom, of course, where tipsy women have long since realized just how drunk they were at the same time as having all sorts of deep thoughts.

So I spent a hot minute crying in the stall over Duke. Crying over a man while drunk in a bathroom was a rite of passage I'd never experienced. I figured it was about time.

But I only gave myself a minute. Since I still didn't have a phone, I counted very carefully. When my minute was up, I wiped my eyes, exited the stall and washed my hands, taking great care so that was all I was thinking of. I fixed my makeup. Then I walked out of the bathroom.

And, to be totally freaking cliché, it all went black.

* * *

I'd expected to be dead.

That's what generally happened when you were kidnapped by the goons of the man you were about to put away for murder and had just plotted to kill with a motorcycle club.

I knew that movies got almost everything wrong, especially these parts where the heroine is kidnapped but somehow kept alive long enough for the muscled man to come and save her.

In reality, criminals intent on murdering someone didn't fuck around unless they were into torture. I really hoped that was not the case here. I'd survived a lot in my time but I didn't think I'd be able to withstand torture.

I was tied to a chair. My mouth was dry and my wrists ached with the tightness of the handcuffs. I tried to move and that only served to break open my skin with the metal of the cuffs. My blood was warm.

"Fuck," I muttered.

My feet were bound too, and I was not going to MacGyver out of this. Instead, I took in my surroundings. Surprisingly, I was in a very nice-looking living room, really fucking nice. I was facing floor-to-ceiling windows that boasted views of the ocean. Everything in the room was in neutral tones—white sofa, tan vintage rug, bookcases covering the wall to my left, seriously expensive artwork arranged tastefully on the walls.

Murdering people in luxury seemed to be this guy's style.

I tried to think how long it had been since he'd taken me. It was still light outside. Barely, the sun was just beginning to set on the horizon, but that gave me hope. Unless I'd been out for a full twenty-four hours, it was the same night, which meant I couldn't have been gone for longer than an hour. Was that good?

Surely one of the women would've raised the alarm within a few minutes of me not coming back.

I'd heard the CliffsNotes version of each of their stories and had I not met them all and trusted them, I would've said they were full of shit. It didn't sound real. The kidnappings, the bombings, the drive-by shootings.

But it was.

They wore the scars in their eyes.

I fucking hated that these women who smiled easily and laughed even easier had that. But the second a cloth settled over my mouth and I was roughly yanked back into a stranger's body, I was hopeful that their past might help me ensure I had a future.

A door opened and closed, and I stiffened.

I didn't crane my head to see who it was, though everything inside me ached to do that. Maybe I wouldn't see them at all. Maybe I'd feel cold steel at the back of my head and then I'd feel nothing else.

But I couldn't change that by looking death in the face, and it felt oddly weak to try to crane around to see whoever had entered the room. If they wanted to make eye contact with me, they were doing all the work.

I saw his shoes first. Gucci. Snakeskin. The tacky style that rich guys thought made them look rich but just made them even slimier than they were.

The suit was slightly better. Charcoal. Custom. Tailored to perfection, crisp shirt underneath, no collar. Neck was smooth, tanned, attractive. Then there was the face. What I'd been avoiding. I was trying to prolong this, my survival.

His eyes were cold, familiar, full of interest, the same interest a spider might have over a fly caught in its web.

"Ms. Edwards. You've proven yourself difficult to locate," Kitsch said. His voice was pleasant, the same as it had been that night at the charity function. There was a calmness to him that scared the shit out of me.

He was a psychopath. It shouldn't be surprising, really, with all that data saying that a good percentage of successful men were psychopaths.

Most of them weren't driven to murder. They just ruined people's lives without thought of what might happen beyond them adding to a fortune.

"Well, you've got me now, haven't you?" I replied, forcing myself to stay calm. "I will say, you're meant to be smart but kidnapping one of the world's most famous actresses right before she's going to testify against you isn't really going to clear your name."

He smiled, moving over to a bar cart tucked in the corner of the room. He leisurely grabbed two glasses and poured from a whisky decanter.

"I'll apologize for not giving you use of your hands," he said, glancing up to someone behind me.

A large figure moved to grab the glass from Kitsch and move in front of me.

The man was well over six feet tall, all muscle, close cropped hair, no neck, and wearing all black.

Private security was being paid far too much to feel anything about the fact he was attempting to feed whisky to a woman chained to a chair.

As much as the hot burn of whisky would be welcome right now, I wouldn't let some goon fucking feed it to me. I wouldn't let the last thing to pass my lips be something forced on me.

The cold glass stayed pressed against my lips until Kitsch made some kind of signal. Goon stepped back to put the whisky on the coffee table. But he stayed right in front of me.

"I wish you'd accept my hospitality," Kitsch said, nodding to the glass. "It's a great bottle, very rare. Makes everything that much...softer." He sipped from his own tumbler.

I wasn't about to play along with this. He probably had a vision in his mind of how this would go. He was going to get to play the gentlemanly villain who shows his victim hospitality before he kills her. At best. I didn't miss the way his eyes lingered on my thighs, with my skirt riding up almost to my waist.

"He here to do your dirty work?" I asked, nodding to the goon, trying to banish thoughts of getting raped before he murdered me. "You want to kill me. Need to kill me if you want your freedom. But you also want to make whatever fucking speech you've built up in your mind because the only way a woman would really listen to you is if you kidnapped her and tied her to a chair?" I snapped.

Something moved in Kitsch's eyes, he clenched his hands around the tumbler. I'd got to him. Men who thought they were smart, powerful were usually the easiest to unravel.

"Mommy didn't love you, huh?" I continued. "So you decide that you'll hate women for the rest of your life, punish them when you can? Newsflash, buddy. In my eyes, you're always gonna be the pathetic, scared little boy who only wants his mother to love him."

A muscled twitched in Kitsch's jaw.

The satisfaction didn't last for long, since he nodded once to his goon, who then stepped forward and punched me square in the face.

The pain was immediate and blinding. The goon had put all of his weight behind it. My cheekbone screamed, the entire half of my face felt shattered.

My stomach lurched and vomit worked its way up my throat.

With effort, I tilted my chin upward in defiance, making eye contact with Kitsch.

"You really think you're going to be that cliché?" I asked.

"You think that having your steroid-freak beat the shit out of me while I'm tied to a chair is going to make you seem scarier? Make you tougher?" I laughed. "You are really just doing what generations of weak, scared men have done before you. You're not original, strong, or powerful, and you don't scare me."

It was now that Kitsch grinned. The gesture chilled me right to the bone. "Ah, but I will."

No one punched me again. I was waiting for it. I didn't know whether it was my words stopping him from doing it or his plan all along.

He did have his goon use the knife strapped to his belt cut through all of my clothes until I was sitting in tatters in my bra and panties.

Yeah, *that* scared me.

It all scared me. The prospect of more violence, more pain, of death. I was terrified of it all. All of my words and bravado were nothing but lies—good ones, excellently delivered, to be sure.

A little bit of stubbornness helped them along. I refused to let them see the fear, refused to give them that mental power over me. Kitsch was trying to demean me further, not just by beating me, but by brutally bringing the prospect of rape to the forefront of my mind.

In truth, that prospect never left a woman's mind. It was a ghost that followed her as she walked to her car late at night, stalked her when she was out with friends and a stranger offered her a drink, and taunted her as she broke up with a violent or unpredictable boyfriend.

There was never a moment when a woman forgot the tool men used to fool themselves they had the power.

Kitsch was watching me, waiting for the tears, the pleading. He was experienced in it, after all.

I refused to give anything to a man who thought he had the right and ability to take it by force.

So I didn't lower my gaze. Nor did I speak. I didn't trust myself to. I only had strength in silence, because I feared if I opened my mouth, I'd beg. I'd turn myself into a weak woman. I couldn't die like that.

He smiled after a few beats. "Ah, you're not the pampered princess I pegged you for. That's interesting. Impressive." He stepped forward to brush the back of his hand over my jaw. It took everything I had not to flinch. That caress was more disturbing than the punch to the face delivered minutes ago.

"It's a shame, really," he said with a sigh, stepping back. "I would've liked to keep you. But you've got yourself some impressive friends. Which is ironic, because without them, you might've lived a long life—with me."

I narrowed my brows. "As horrifying as that prospect is, I'd much prefer death."

Kitsch smiled. "Well, I'll be able to oblige you on that." He glanced to the goon, who took his gun out of the shoulder holster. Then back to me. "Goodbye, Ms. Edwards." Despair crawled up my throat as Harriet's words echoed through my brain.

"Grief is a funny thing, sweet girl," she said. "It is about the worst thing a human can feel but it springs from the very best thing we feel...love."

I thought about what I was leaving behind, which was ironically so much more than it ever could've been had I not witnessed the murder in the first place.

Life worked in mysterious ways, apparently.

Death, on the other hand, didn't. Death was simple. And it was staring me in the face. I stared at the barrel of the gun and my last thoughts were of Duke.

* * *

Duke's very blood felt like acid, coursing through his body, melting, cell by cell.

He'd arrived at the Sons of Templar compound around the same time as the rest of the team, right about the time that most of the bikers had just set out on a rescue mission.

A fucking *rescue mission*.

For Anastasia.

Duke had been driving for almost an entire day. He hadn't slept, had barely eaten. He'd sped through the fucking interstate and somehow managed not to run into a cop. He'd wasted too much time when he'd woken up to the empty bed, hadn't trusted the pit in the bottom of his stomach, the fear. He'd convinced himself that Anastasia had crept out to make coffee, maybe to have breakfast with his mother and grandmother. He told himself not to panic, even when his phone was missing from the nightstand.

He'd damn near sprinted to the homestead.

His mother's SUV was not parked out front.

The pit of Duke's stomach dropped further. And he knew it then, that Anastasia was gone. It took him too fuckin' long to look all over the ranch, even with his father, brother and mother there. They didn't ask questions, likely because of Duke's demeanor. He knew he scared his mother, but he couldn't help it. He had to turn everything off, had to prepare himself for finding the woman he loved dead.

There was no relief when they didn't find her, especially when he realized what she'd done, who she'd done it with.

Rosie was the only one brave enough and stupid enough to pull this shit off. Duke had offered his family little to no explanation, banned his father and brother from coming with him.

Or he thought he had.

Until, after he pulled out from the ranch, a truck came up behind him, kept pace with him for the entire drive.

He'd planned on slashing their tires at the first gas station. But his father had approached him first. "Anastasia is family, son," he said, putting a hand on his shoulder. "You're my son. And I'll be damned if I let you do this alone. We're getting our girl back. No arguments."

"Tanner needs to be with Maggie, his kid," he said to his father.

"I need my kid to have an aunt and uncle," Tanner said from behind him. "I'm not lettin' you fight this battle alone, brother."

Fighting wasted time. So instead he got in the truck. His father and Tanner did the same.

Neither of them said a word when they arrived at the Sons' compound. They just followed his lead.

Killian was the first one they'd seen. Duke was surprised that the man was not out on the mission, but seeing Lexie on the sofa with a child bouncing on her knee, he figured he understood why.

That didn't dampen his fury.

Killian glanced to his wife and then jerked his chin toward church.

Duke only went out of respect for Lexie, their friendship. She gave him a kind look he couldn't return right now, which said something about his state of mind. She was one of his closest friends, and generally one of the best people he knew.

He could find kindness for that woman on the darkest of days.

But this wasn't dark. This was something fucking deeper than that.

No sooner had the door closed, he advanced on the man he considered a brother.

Duke felt his father and brother at his back, either readying themselves to jump in, or pull him off Killian.

Killian didn't move, because Killian was a hard fucker and it would take nothing short of a nuclear blast to send him into retreat.

"Where is she?" Duke demanded.

Killian's gaze was blank as it always was. Duke had known him for years, known that he'd had that blank, deadly look since the moment they'd met. It was unnerving, even for someone like Duke, to see that on someone so young. It wasn't a farce either. The fucker was deadly.

To everyone but his wife, children, and people he considered family.

Despite that, Duke wanted to wipe that fucking look off his face with his fists.

"We got word on the location," Killian said. "Boys rode out less than ten minutes ago. She was taken from a bathroom of the bar downtown. Rosie raised the alarm immediately. She'd slipped a tracker into a pair of shoes Anastasia was wearing. Sons rode out within twenty to thirty minutes after she was taken. Kitsch has had her less than an hour."

None of this did shit for Duke, not a fucking thing. Acid still ate away at his tissue, his bone. He wouldn't be able to move right, wouldn't be able to breathe right if he found Anastasia in the state they'd found Polly, in the state Lance had found Caroline, nor if he was like fucking Keltan, who'd had Lucy bleed out in his arms. Same with Killian. He'd fucking watched his woman be shot and heard doctors tell him she wouldn't make it.

They'd all defied the odds and gotten their women back. Whatever was controlling this world was looking out for it. But they were well overdue for their luck to run out, for Duke to find a corpse of the woman he'd been too much of a fucking asshole to tell her he loved.

"We both know you need less than a fuckin' minute to kill someone, Killian," Duke bit out.

Killian didn't respond, because he knew that all too well. He'd never technically ever been with Greenstone, but he'd been protecting Lexie ever since she'd been targeted by a murderous stalker. He was part of the Sons of Templar but his wife came first. He was with her every moment she was on tour, because he knew that all he needed was a second of absence to lose her.

Something clicked in Duke's mind. "Rosie put a tracker in her shoe?"

And then he saw it. Killian had been waiting for Duke to ask that.

Fuck.

"She knew that they were going to take her?" Duke's mind went still. Dead. He met Killian's eyes. "Give me the fucking location. Now."

16

THERE WAS A GUNSHOT.

It was deafening and vibrated my very bones.

What it didn't do, was kill me.

I hadn't realized that my eyes were closed until I blinked them open. The goon was lying dead at my feet. A pool of blood was slowly creeping toward my feet. I watched it with disinterest.

Rosie was standing in front of Coleson, a gun in her hand, pointed at his head. His arms were up in surrender and he looked scared. I found comfort in that.

Rosie glanced to me. "I know you might think you want to do this, but trust me, honey, you don't want this on your soul."

"Please—" Coleson started but was cut off with another gunshot. This one wasn't as deafening thanks to the silencer on the end of Rosie's gun.

He hit the floor with a thud.

Rosie pushed his body to the side with her foot and turned to me. Nothing in her face looked like she'd just killed a man. There was a hardness, a menace in her eyes that was quickly retreating, one that scared the crap out of me and reminded me never to get on her bad side.

"Sorry we took so long," she said. "I really thought he was enough of a narcissist to drag the evil villain speech out a little longer."

I blinked at Rosie as a click resounded behind me. My arms fell like the deadweights that they were. It was a struggle to move them into my lap and inspect the damage.

It could've been worse, much worse. They were still attached, so there was that. But it had felt worse than it was. There were raised red welts around my wrists, some cuts and dried blood, but nothing that wouldn't heal.

Someone kneeled down in front of me. Someone who still had the scary thing going on, but there was concern in his eyes.

Cade.

His gray eyes flickered over me. "You good?"

I swallowed roughly, doing an internal assessment as if I could've missed the fact that I'd somehow been shot or stabbed in the chaos.

My cheek ached like hell. My wrists burned. My heart was either in my throat or at my feet, I couldn't be sure. I'd just watched two men be killed, bringing the total of people I'd seen die in the past two months to three. My head pounded with the reminder. I was also slightly hungover.

I wanted to throw up the contents of my stomach right over Cade's expensive and bad ass biker boots.

I wanted to burst into tears.

"I'm good," I said.

Cade regarded me still, as if he were weighing my words, trying to figure out if I was going to do the girl thing and go into shock due to the kidnapping thing and with the dead body in front of me.

To be fair, I was trying to figure that out too.

Cade nodded once and stood, obviously giving me the badass seal of approval.

Although I felt the need to stay seated for a second longer, just to make sure I didn't vomit in front of the bikers slowly filling the room, I got up. I didn't want the goon's blood staining my shoes.

Rosie hugged me when I stood. She leaned back to inspect my cheek. She winced. "Fuck. I didn't think he'd have time to hit you. I'm sorry, babe."

"It's okay," I said, almost as a reflex. Then her words sunk in. "Wait, you used me as bait?" I clarified.

Rosie gaped at me. "Duh, how the fuck else were we going to get that asshole here?" She paused. "You got a problem with that?"

I thought about the man Rosie used me as bait to catch. *Ruthless, cold-blooded killer.* About the point-blank murder of the lover I hadn't mourned. *A memory.* And then I considered the man who was killed due to his loyalty to me. *True, devastating loss.* My wounds will heal. A malevolent monster was dead. "No, I don't have a problem with that."

"Dude, you know that you could totally sell the movie rights to this whole thing and you'd like, win the Oscars," Rosie said, waving her hand around the room.

I grinned. "I don't doubt it. But then I'd be implicating myself in murder and all of the stuff that goes with it."

Rosie furrowed her brows. "Bummer."

We didn't get to discuss this further, since the energy of the entire room changed with a new arrival.

I didn't need to turn to know who it was. Of course he'd come for me. He'd be pissed he didn't get to be the knight in shining armor; passing that task off to a bunch of bikers surely was a blow to his ego.

He'd also be pissed I'd slipped out in the middle of the night.

I was too afraid to even turn and look at him. I'd managed to meet the eyes of a man who'd murdered the man I'd been sleeping with and had been planning to murder me, but I couldn't meet the gaze of the man I loved.

"I wish I'd brought tequila," Rosie muttered, eyeing the area above my head.

I smelled him first. Then he was in front of me, taking up all of my senses. My body relaxed entirely, despite the fury rippling off him.

Duke's hand was rough on my chin, jerking it upward so he could get a better look at what I guessed was yet another bruise blossoming quite nicely. He was careful not to touch the cut on my lip.

Still holding me, but not looking at me, he focused on Rosie. "You let him fuckin' touch her?"

He didn't yell. It was the quietest I'd ever heard him speak. In fact, I'd never heard this tone in his voice. It wasn't Duke. I'd seen glimpses of a darker side in him, the side that killed, that did things he'd never speak about. But this was something else entirely. Goosebumps erupted on my arms with the chill this stranger brought to the room.

Rosie wasn't ruffled, of course. The woman was covered in blood and didn't seem to be worried at all. "I had to get him close enough to let his guard down," she said.

Duke moved in a flash.

One second he was holding my chin in that brutal grip, the next his was right up in Rosie's face. Even Luke, who I expected had fucking good reflexes didn't have time to move to protect his wife.

Not that she needed protection.

"You let him touch her!" This time it wasn't a whisper. It was a roar, right in Rosie's face.

Luke moved quickly then, with a danger of his own—one that wasn't the same as Duke's, but it was still scary.

"You back away from my wife now," he said. Words of steel, full of threats.

Rosie rolled her eyes at both of them.

"You." She looked at her husband. "You've known me for how long now? So what makes you think I've somehow changed drastically in the last few hours that you can go around fighting my battles for me, making threats for me? I fight my own battles, follow through on my own threats." She didn't wait for Luke to respond. Her eyes went to Duke. "And you. I get you've got the whole 'alpha male in love' thing going on. I get that you're one of the last in our group to get it. You're overexcited. Whatever. But you are not stupid. Nor are you anywhere near as misogynistic as you're acting right now. You know that your woman has and can take a punch just as well, if not better than a man can take it. You also know that justice is a dirty business. Revenge is even dirtier. Despite what all the movies tell us—even her movies—it's not a business that leaves anyone unscathed. Anastasia is a grown woman. She's a smart one at that. Smart mostly because she called me. And because she knew exactly what she was getting herself into and what could come of it. She was prepared for that. She handled it. Her face will heal. So get over yourself."

Rosie delivered the speech the same casual way she had delivered everything these past couple of days. She was probably one of the most impressive people I'd ever met.

Despite this, there was a tense moment, one that even the most badass of females couldn't break.

Then Duke stepped back.

I exhaled.

Luke glowered.

Rosie grinned.

Duke didn't say anything else, just snatched my arm and dragged us out of there.

* * *

I had been shocked to see Tanner and Andrew in the next room, both of them holding handguns and harsh glares.

They were still wearing their fucking boots and cowboy hats, milling with bikers.

Both of their gazes turned to stone when they saw me, more specifically saw what I was guessing was the already large bruise on my cheek.

Duke seemed to struggle to let me go when they both approached, but had no choice when I was engulfed in two different cowboy, macho-men hugs.

Andrew cupped my face when he finally let me go. He did it in the gentlest way a man could touch a woman, like a father might. That and the shimmer in his eyes hit me square in the stomach.

"You scared the crap out of me, darlin'," he said, a rasp in his voice.

"You came all the way here?" I asked, stupidly. Obviously they were here.

He smiled, but there was sadness and love in it. "You're family."

It was that. That sentence right there, delivered from the patriarch that got me. That shattered me. I had planned on saving my breakdown for the privacy of my own mansion. But it started here, in front of all the bikers, Tanner, and Duke.

My sobs racked my body, and Andrew held on to me the entire time.

At some point, I got a hold of myself. The well ran dry.

Andrew let me go, kissed my forehead, and stepped back.

He looked behind me.

I knew who was behind me, who hadn't touched me or said a word during all of this.

"You good, son?"

"Good." Duke uttered the single word with a deadness to his tone. "We've got somewhere for the both of you to stay, but I need to get Anastasia sorted."

Andrew nodded. "You go, take care of our girl. I think we can handle ourselves here." He looked around. "I need to buy some of these guys a beer."

I wanted to smile at that, wanted to stay and watch Andrew and Tanner drink beers and shoot the shit with the bikers.

But Duke wasn't having that. He snatched my hand again and all but dragged me outside. There were no words, no caresses, just his grip on my wrist.

I'd done it.

I'd gotten what I wanted. I'd pushed Duke away. I was going to get my life back.

And it killed me.

He hadn't looked at me since he'd got here. Not since the first moment he'd run his eyes over my body, assessing the injuries. He'd done that for practical reasons, obviously. But since then, nothing. He'd asked me if I needed painkillers, if I wanted anything to eat. I'd said no to both of those things.

He'd done all the things to ensure my comfort and health, like any good security expert or body guard would do. There was a chill to his voice that cut through layers of skin, muscle and bone, right to the core of me. It struck me harder than any blow had today.

I'd expected this, hadn't I? I'd wanted this?

Had a little part of me hoped he'd rush in, kiss me, hug me, declare his undying love for me like countless men had done on countless sets throughout my career?

Yeah.

A tiny, naive part of me that he'd brought to life had hoped for that. My inner cynic chastised her for that toxic hope.

It didn't work that way.

I'd gotten the best possible result from this. The bad guy was dead. Justice was served. I could safely go back to my life in LA like none of this had ever happened.

The mere thought filled me with dread.

I'd been so deep in my self-pity, I hadn't realized we'd stopped. We weren't at a gas station on our way back to LA, not on the interstate. Somehow, we were still in Amber and I hadn't noticed.

We were parked in front of a beautiful B&B that I recognized from an article somewhere. It was right in front of the ocean, the sunset reflecting off it with a beauty that happened regardless of the ugliness in the world, inside of this car.

"What are we doing?" I asked.

Still, Duke didn't look at me. "I had a long drive getting here, haven't slept. Don't suppose you have either. It's late. We're not drivin' through the night, nor are we stayin' at some shitty motel on the side of the road. I know this place, know that the food is out of this world, rooms are nice, and the staff discreet."

He delivered that while looking straight ahead. In that same tone that bruised every part of me left unscathed throughout all of this.

Duke didn't wait for me to respond to anything he had said. He just got out of the car, leaving me in there with the toxic air of his indifference.

I got out, despite the fact I didn't want to.

We'd come full circle. The hotel room was nicer. The view

was better. My face had more bruises. My heart had more scars. But we were here.

We walked into the room in silence, like we were strangers. Strangers would have been better. I would've welcomed it. There was nothing worse in this world than someone you loved, someone who knew the deepest parts of you treating you like a stranger.

The room was indeed "nice." That was somewhat of an understatement. And that was coming from me, who'd traveled all over the world, stayed at the most lavish and expensive hotel rooms.

This wouldn't be considered the most lavish, nor expensive. Yet it was the most beautiful room I'd ever walked into.

There was a sitting area as you walked in, slip-covered sofa, white with a plethora of ocean-themed cushions, a coffee table with a pile of what looked like local art books, same with the art on the walls. None of that generic hotel room bullshit. No, everything was unique. One landscape in particular was breathtaking, so much so that I forgot about my heartbreak for a second and leaned in to read the artist.

Lauren Mathers.

I made a mental note to find her as soon as I got home and purchase every piece of art she had available. I'd cover the walls of my lavish home with it, to torture me, to remind me.

The rest of the room was decorated in that same style. Whites. Blues. Beach tones. A huge California King faced the balcony doors, which offered a final view of the sunset over the waves.

It was the perfect room for lovers, for romance.

It was a worst nightmare for...whatever Duke and I were.

He put my bag—given and packed by Gwen so I had faith that it was full of everything I might need—on the sofa.

It was then, he looked at me. Not in the eyes, but at my body, the long tee that Cade had put on me to cover my nearly naked body. I'd forgotten I was even wearing that.

"You need to tell me," Duke's voice was careful, slow and controlled.

"Tell you what?" My voice was not careful, slow or controlled.

"Saw your clothes...just tatters on the floor," Duke said. "You're wearin' another man's tee." He sucked in a harsh breath. "Did they touch you?"

"No," I said quickly. He wanted to know if I'd been raped. "No. They wanted to scare me. But they didn't do that. Rosie and the club got there in time."

Duke's hands were fisted at his sides. Fury was radiating off him. I waited for more. Surely there was more. Even if there weren't any hearts and flowers, which I pretended I didn't want, surely there was anger. Surely he was going to scream at me like he did Rosie.

"I'm gonna grab a shower."

Still, he didn't look at me, didn't offer any remote hint that he might have once held me in his sleep, that he'd kissed me in the rain, or watched me as I'd cried.

I nodded once because I didn't trust myself to speak, but he already had his back turned and was closing the door to the bathroom.

When I heard the lock click, I sank down to the floor. No, I didn't sink. That required grace. My legs simply gave out under the weight of my pain.

The floor was soft when I wished it was hard. I didn't need comfort of soft things right now. I needed hard, more pain.

My sobs were quiet, but my entire body shook with the force of them. The shower turned on in the background and I jerked myself up.

I suddenly couldn't be in this beautiful room, not with Duke locking a door, separating us, not with that horrible chill to his voice.

I had to escape.

* * *

The hot water did nothing to loosen the tightness in his muscles, but he had to try, had to lock himself the fuck down.

Anastasia was holding on because she was strong, because she was a fucking warrior. He had come to understand that woman—the one he'd once thought would crumble after chipping a fucking nail—could get through anything. But it didn't matter if she *could* get through anything, and he wasn't about to test that. She'd been through enough.

So he'd locked himself up. Tight. He'd called up the version of himself that he'd forced himself to be in the desert—in war— the cold killer that didn't feel a thing.

He had to. The second he'd screamed in his friend's face and was willing to come to blows with her husband, he knew he had to.

Seeing Anastasia marked had done something to him. Seeing her standing in a pool of blood, her fucking clothes shredded on the ground, had almost killed him. The thought of them violating her, doing that to her ripped through his insides.

The fact that they hadn't, didn't make him feel better. Not in the slightest. He was marked down to his bones, his core. Which was saying something, considering not seeing her at all and having only his imagination was what he'd thought was the worst form of hell.

He'd been through plenty in his life. Fuck, he'd almost died. He'd seen friends take their last breath, forced many enemies to take their last also.

But shit, waking up and realizing what Anastasia had done, that had sent him into a spiral, fierce and unyielding.

He knew Rosie had her shit together, knew that she was as deadly and capable as each of them—more so, if anything. But he also knew she was reckless, that she was willing to go further than even a fucker like Lance would go.

And the most precious thing he'd ever touched was in her care. Rosie was not cruel. She had a soft heart, underneath the brutal façade, but she also adopted her own battle persona, where she was willing to let things get ugly in order to win.

Which might've been why she'd come up against some of the most dangerous people in the world and managed to come out on top.

Even the most ruthless of men in Greenstone Security and the Sons of Templar respectively had codes, hard limits. And that included any violence against women.

Rosie didn't have that same code, because she was a woman— and maybe because she didn't have that toxic masculinity that was impossible to eradicate in men. She wasn't full of preconceived notions about women being weaker. She didn't doubt the fairer sex's ability to weather the storms.

She was willing to let a woman bleed so a monster would die.

He appreciated that within her, respected that—with anyone that wasn't his woman. And Anastasia was his.

He'd known this, of course, since the beginning. He hadn't understood it. The visceral part of him had discovered that. Fuck, Duke had winced for each of his friends as they'd experienced their own courtships. It wasn't just the unexplainable connection that the men felt with the women, it was that each of the women encountered hurt, pain and situations that left scars. He saw them every day. Even though that shit was behind each of them, even though they slept with their women every night, had families, Duke saw that shit. How it had marked them.

And yeah, the payoff was arguably worth it, but Duke hadn't felt eager to get into that impossible shit. He'd been perfectly content with the lifestyle he'd been living.

Until Anastasia.

Then the switch went off and the choice was taken from him. It sounded fucking pathetic and unrealistic, that instant connection, that knowing. But it didn't fucking matter what it sounded like. It was just what it was.

He knew that it would be hard with her. She'd be stubborn, guarded. Fuck, he didn't blame her. Every new detail he found out about her past, her life, it cobbled together the image she worked so hard to portray. The one she'd perfected so well that it had even fooled Duke.

Until the ranch.

He hadn't been lying to her that day with the sun setting over the fields, with her looking so fucking beautiful it had hurt his heart—you couldn't lie under Montana skies.

So he'd braced, prepared himself for the shit his friends went through. Technically, they were already in the middle of shit, but he had faith in the Greenstone Security team and himself to keep her safe. With the updates he'd been getting, Kitsch had been nowhere near getting info on her.

That was after they'd all fucked up with the assistant. Watching the pain etch into her very bones would be something he carried around forever.

None of them thought that Kitsch would be as bold or stupid to go that far. Mistakes in their business were rare, because when you made a mistake, someone could end up dead. They weren't going to make that one again.

Or so they'd thought.

Duke had let the rhythm of the ranch, the breeze of Montana, and the company of his family lull him into a false sense of security. He forgot everything he'd learned watching all the other

Greenstone courtships. It wasn't always the outside forces that invited the most danger.

It was the women intent on fighting their own battles, or escaping relationships that scared them.

He wasn't angry with Anastasia. He was furious at himself, and okay, slightly pissed at her.

Duke was planning on fucking her to get rid of the worst of it, then fucking her sweet later. Then a mix of the two for the rest of their lives—which would be long.

But he'd made another mistake. He realized that when he got out of the bathroom and was presented with an empty room.

***

I didn't get far.

Because this time I didn't steal Duke's phone to call yet another queen-wearing designer to come and save me.

They'd done their part.

All of them.

They'd given me my life back. It was my responsibility to figure out what the heck to do with it now.

Apparently, what I did was run from B&B rooms without a key, a phone, a wallet or anything that would actually help me. It wasn't smart. But I was too busy trying to hold a broken heart together, and it turned out movies were right about people who did that—they ended up doing stupid things.

The beach called to me because it was almost empty and there was a storm on the horizon. Barely any light was left from the sunset now, and I liked that. I didn't want the beauty of it.

Salty air stained my skin as I sank down to my knees, staring at the waves. What was my plan now?

After Duke dropped me off at the house I owned, I'd be reunited with my phone. Most likely it would be full of emails, voicemails, alerts from news outlets wondering where the fuck I was. Not messages from Andre, though.

Pain hurtled through my body.

I'd have to go back to everything I knew that was missing—the only thing that mattered. For the sake of sanity, I skipped over that. I'd grieve with a bottle of vodka and some Valium later.

There would be interviews. I'd have to explain my absence one way or another, and then the police. Rosie had already assured me that nothing would trace back to me, and I trusted her. I figured someone like her, along with a notorious motorcycle gang would know how to cover up a murder.

Then I'd have to get back on the movie I'd been filming before this had all happened—if they were even waiting for me. It was still in production, so they'd have to reshoot with another actress or abandon the film all together. Normally I'd never pull anything that damaged the livelihood of the hundreds of people working on a film, but this one hadn't exactly been in my control.

There was also the case of the ten or so extra pounds I was carrying around with me. Most directors would make comments. There would be pressure to starve myself again so I could be the familiar Anastasia Edwards everyone knew. But I wouldn't be her, no matter how much weight I lost.

I'd be busy when I got back. That would be good. There wouldn't be much time to think about how fucking empty my life would be.

"What the fuck are you doing?"

I jumped from my spot in the sand. It was fully dark now, and I could only see the shadow of the man standing in front of me.

"I'm..." I trailed off. What was I doing? Then I remembered how he wouldn't look at me, the way his voice had sounded. I straightened my shoulders and tilted my chin upward, even though he probably couldn't see that.

"What the fuck am *I* doing?" I snapped. "I'm doing *whatever the fuck I want*, Duke! If you didn't realize, I was kidnapped by a total asshole earlier tonight. I believed that same asshole was going to kill me. Maybe rape me. I think I have the authority to take a walk on the goddamn beach to process this. So how about you drop the macho asshole act for one fucking second." I was yelling, screaming. I hadn't realized how angry I was until just now. It was easier to be angry than anything else. "In fact, how about you stop acting all together? You don't have to *pretend* to give a shit about me. You don't have to drive me anywhere. You don't have to take me to some picturesque B&B by the ocean. I can drive. I'm rich. I have plenty of people at my disposal to get my life back in order. I don't need you anymore."

That last part was a lie. A lie came easy off an angry tongue, one that was forked, and wanted its words to wound.

Duke hadn't spoken or moved as I'd screamed at him. He'd just stood there and took it, stood there staring, but finally looking at me.

The sounds of the waves snatched away whatever words I'd hurled into the air. They didn't make their mark. Didn't wound Duke...because he didn't care now.

I wasn't strong enough to walk away. I wasn't strong enough to yell anymore. And I had a shred of dignity left that stopped me from falling to my knees and begging him to love me.

Duke didn't speak for a long time.

"Well I need you," he said finally. Quietly. The waves almost stole those words away too before I snatched them up.

He stepped forward now, all the way forward. His hands went to my neck, pulling our foreheads together. "I will dedicate my life to giving you what you need. Giving you beauty. Giving you a family. Fucking making up for the fact that I let you go, let you stare death in the face and I wasn't fucking there." His lips pressed into my head. "I love you, Anastasia. I know I should've said it the second you uttered those words. But I thought I was being fucking smart. Being fucking gallant. I didn't want your memory of me telling you my truth to be tied to the pain of your night. I didn't want it tangled up in all this shit. I didn't want to give you any reason to question. I wanted to wait until this shit wasn't hanging over us, for you to be safe, so I could take you out to fuckin' dinner, so you could get out of the prison that asshole put you in." He leaned back to lightly brush his hands over my bruise.

"I don't deal with fear well," he murmured. "Mostly because I didn't think I could really feel it after all that shit I went through. Thought I was broken somehow. But, baby, I've never even known fear until I woke up to that empty bed. I'm fuckin' pissed at you for pullin' that shit, but the punishment will happen later, and you'll like it. But I understand why you did it. I understand it, but you scared me in ways that I didn't think were possible. I imagined you fuckin' dying, Anastasia." He paused brutally, and his entire body shuddered. "You dying thinking that I didn't love you. You dying at all. Going through my fucking life with the memory of how close I'd been to having everything."

He kissed me, gently, right on my bruised cheek. His lips were like a feather. It was the most reverent and loving way a man had ever touched me.

Duke pulled back ever so slightly. "When I saw you, I didn't feel relieved. I couldn't lock it down. So I turned cold. I'm going to warn you, baby. That's gonna happen with us in the future. I'm going to work on it, gonna work fuckin' hard. But it's going to take time to shake that shit out of me. But I figure we've both got some shit to learn about each other. Then again, we've got the rest of our lives to do it, so I think we'll be okay."

Tears were streaming down my face at this point, at everything that Duke was throwing at me. All the feelings piled up on my skin. All of those hopes coming true. I flinched at first. It couldn't be true.

But there was emotion in Duke's voice, a naked pain that grated against my heart. That couldn't be faked, couldn't be denied.

"The rest of our lives?" I repeated. "Are you proposing right now?"

The grip on my neck tightened. "No, baby. Not because I don't plan on marrying you—if you're into it, that is—but because my mother and grandmother would straight-up kill me if I did it in a moment like this. They raised me better than that."

"Yeah," I whispered. "They did."

Duke didn't kiss me, not yet. I was aching for it, for his skin on mine, for his taste. "So, that's a yes to marriage?"

I smiled. "You're just gonna have to wait until you propose to get that answer," I said.

He shook his head. "I'll wait forever for you, baby."

Then, he kissed me.

EPILOGUE

"ARE you sure you're ready for this?" I asked Duke as the car slowed down.

He lifted our intertwined hands and kissed mine. "Baby, I'm ready for anything as long as I'm with you."

Cue stomach-melty thing that still happened when he said shit like that. The diamond he'd slid on my finger a couple months ago glinted in the light.

I hadn't decided what kind of wedding I wanted yet. Both Amy and Gwen were calling me daily with ideas. Then there were multiple texts with dress designs, table settings, and threats of bodily dismemberment if they weren't bridesmaids—well, that one was from Rosie actually.

It had shocked me that the women had kept in contact throughout all these months. They'd even come to stay in LA for two nights. One of those was spent drinking a lot of margaritas and getting fucked very well by my now fiancé when he figured out just how drunk I was.

They were my *friends*. It was something I'd only just realized, something warm and uncomfortable at the same time. I had people to call if I needed fashion advice, if I was going through an emotional crisis, or if I needed to murder a guy.

Moreover, they actually knew me for me.

And then there was Harriet.

She also made the trek to LA when she heard that Duke and I were looking to buy a new house, when it became apparent that we were going to live together. I couldn't imagine spending a night away from him and it seemed he felt the same, so both of our houses were unacceptable. His was nice, clean, impressive. But it did not have enough closet space and I was weirdly jealous thinking about all the women who'd been in that bed before me.

My place was obviously vetoed. I couldn't stand it there. Before the moving in together thing had become real, I'd already been looking for somewhere else. Somewhere that suited me more now that I knew who the heck I was.

Harriet had been the one to find our place. Of course.

It was in Malibu, because we'd wanted to get away from the mansions in Beverly Hills.

It was actually not too far away from the Unquiet Mind's beach house. We'd spent a lot of time with them already since Duke was tight with them.

There were no marble floors, no infinity pools. There was just the ocean. There was enough closet space for both of us. It was large, impeccable, of course. But it felt like home. Then again, it was most likely because Harriet and Duke had been standing inside it.

The rest of his family had made promises to visit us, something that they'd never done before and that I was happy they were doing now.

But the news I found out just this morning was giving me second thoughts about calling a beach house in Malibu home, no matter the views.

"You're ready for anything?" I repeated as the car stopped.

I quickly checked my makeup in my compact before slipping it in my clutch. I fussed with the custom-made gown—a dress made to hug the extra curves I'd gained in the past months, curves that Duke worshipped. I wasn't going to lie and say it was easy to get back to a borderline normal relationship with food. It was tied to all kinds of things. I was seeing a therapist to help me with that, and the trauma of being kidnapped, beaten, and then watching two men die. Well, I didn't tell her about the murder part of it, but I had seen Salvador die so she was helping with that. Then there was the army of women who called daily, allowing me a safe place to talk, vent...whatever.

And there was Duke, sitting in the car next to me, wearing his tux, holding my hand, and looking at me in that way that melted my heart.

"Anything," Duke promised.

I waited for the prime moment. It was cruel and dramatic of me, but I couldn't help it. "Well, I hope that's true, since you've got eight months to get ready to be a father."

The door opened the second I finished the sentence. Cameras flashed and a hand extended to help me out of the car. The fact that I shocked Duke enough for him to let another man help me out of a car said something.

Although I will say, he recovered quickly.

He was out of the car and kissing me in seconds. Obviously, he didn't care about the camera flashes, or that we were on the red carpet of one of the biggest award shows of the year, or that this was our first red carpet together.

Turned out I didn't either, since I kissed him back.

He stopped the kiss but didn't release me. His face was inches from mine. I knew that there were people yelling things, chaos going on all around us, but it was nothing but a dull roar.

Duke's eyes were full of that intensity I'd come to relish, full of love. They shimmered with tears. "You're having my baby?" he asked against my lips.

"I sure am."

Then he kissed me again.

That photo was on the front page of every newspaper, blog, and magazine for the next week.

I won the Oscar too.

* * *

EIGHT MONTHS LATER

The sun was setting over the mountains. The air was crisp as winter rolled in. Soon, there would be snow, which was why my husband was late tonight. There were many things to do on the ranch as winter approached.

I tried to help with as many things as I could, but the second I lifted something heavier than a coffee cup—decaf, of course—there was at least one person shouting at me and asking what they could do for me.

That person was more than often Duke. Despite all the cowboy-type things he was doing, it seemed he had an inbuilt macho-man sensor telling him his pregnant wife was trying to reach for a bag of sugar on the kitchen shelf.

We'd had many fights over the months about him turning into an insane, protective alpha male with every passing day.

"You're my entire world and you're growing another one inside your body," he'd growled. "If I wasn't doin' everything in my goddamn power to protect you both, I wouldn't deserve you. So forewarning you now, baby, that's something that's gonna happen for the rest of our lives, no matter how much you yell at me."

I'd stopped yelling then, naturally.

My pregnancy was an easy one, which surprised me. I was either growing a mini alpha male or a little diva inside me, and I'd figured they'd give me a lot of crap. But no, I'd had barely any morning sickness, tiredness, or swollen feet.

Pregnancy suited me, it seemed. Duke made sure to make that known every moment he could. If he was near me, he was touching me, touching my belly, kissing me, whispering in my ear how beautiful I was, growling at me for picking up whatever he deemed too heavy.

The press had picked up the story...somehow. Not all of it, of course. If that were the case I'd be paying a defense attorney a small fortune to keep me out of prison. No, the Sons of Templar and their resident hacker were far too careful to let anything about what happened in Amber leak.

With everything going on, I hadn't even worried about the possibility that I'd be connected to Kitsch's death. Not that he'd died, publicly, just "disappeared." I'd trusted the Sons of Templar and Rosie—trusted them with my life—despite barely knowing them.

Duke trusted them too, since he didn't seem too worried about me getting hauled in for interviews. The FBI and detectives had been in touch when I appeared back in time for the trial —which was announced days after the ordeal in Amber. I'd attended, of course. Kitsch was a no-show. They'd tried to get me to go into protective custody. I'd argued that I now had private security. Keltan had made phone calls.

At some point, someone talked. Someone told the media that I was the key witness in the case. Not just that, but that I was pregnant.

And there had been many attempts to get interviews. Millions of dollars for the first photos of the baby. Greenstone Security handled everything to do with our privacy and somehow, not one reporter had discovered the location of the ranch.

In this day and age, in this industry, such a thing was almost impossible.

Almost.

When you had a team of badass macho-men looking to protect their buddy and pregnant wife...anything was possible.

Wife—another title that was new to me, just like mother.

Both scared the absolute crap out of me, but I'd never had a free second to properly inspect them.

Since the second I'd told Duke...things had changed. Starting with him all but dragging me off the red carpet at one of the most important award shows of the year and fucking me in a bathroom. That was a very macho-man way of telling me he was happy about the pregnancy.

Neither of us really had the conversation about moving but it went without saying that we were going to the ranch. We were going home.

Duke was, of course, still working for the Greenstone Security team. As much as his family would've loved him to come back home and be a full-time cowboy, it didn't work that way. You can go home again but you have to realize that home might not have changed—but you certainly had.

Duke's family realized this now, as much as they could, and they accepted that. Whatever their son had to give, they took. Supported.

And the news of my pregnancy was welcome.

The news that we were moving up the wedding was not.

Well, it was welcomed to everyone but, you guessed it, Harriet.

"What are you having a shotgun wedding for?" she'd demanded. "We all know that neither of you are virgins and bastards are created inside of wedlock just the same as outside. I already ordered an entire new wardrobe for Tahiti. It's island chic."

"We never said we were going to have the wedding in Tahiti," I said with a smile. Duke was grinning too, since he knew his grandmother and had already predicted a response like this.

"You were going to have the wedding in Tahiti because it would've been my dying wish."

I froze. "You're dying?"

Duke stopped grinning now.

I knew that Harriet was old. I knew that grandparents died, it was the cycle of life or whatever. But since all my grandparents had already died before I was born, I'd thought of it with the same detachment I'd adopted until I met Duke.

But Harriet was different.

Harriet had more energy than most twenty-year-olds. She was healthy. She wasn't old, and she wasn't going to die.

It was selfish, me wanting her alive because I hadn't had enough time with her. But I also saw what a light she was to Duke's family. She was the spine of them all.

"Everybody's dying," Harriet said. "I could die tomorrow. We never know. So you should get rid of all this nonsense and fly us to Tahiti."

"You're not allowed to emotionally blackmail me into thinking you're dying just so you can get a free trip to Tahiti," I snapped and Duke had relaxed.

Well, kind of. Since the pregnancy news, he'd been hyper-aware of everything that may spike my moods. He'd taken away my fucking cheese and coffee, sushi too. Women were having babies in caves when humanity began. Surely I could have a fucking California Roll and a latte.

Duke didn't agree.

And usually I'd argue with Duke tooth and nail, but I couldn't exactly win this one since it was about the health of our unborn child.

"I am eighty-one years old, honey," Harriet said. "I am entitled to use any kind of blackmail, emotional and otherwise, to get what I want."

I smiled again. I was already going through a roller coaster of fucking emotions with this pregnancy, but naturally, Harriet had to add to it.

"How about this? I'll fly us all to Tahiti for your eighty-sixth birthday?" I offered.

A pause. "Now you're blackmailing me to stay alive."

"Of course I am. I'm pregnant, I'm allowed to do such things."

So it was decided. We had the small wedding on the ranch.

Well.

It was *meant* to be small.

Then Rosie heard about it. She, of course, called Gwen. Who, of course, called the rest of the motorcycle babes. I was still wrapping on a movie. Duke was still following me around as if he thought Kitsch might come back from the dead. Well, that and the fact the media attention had not yet died down since the story had broken. Whatever the reason, both of us were delayed and didn't end up making it to the ranch until the day before we'd planned the wedding.

And I'd been blown away. The entire place was transformed. There were people everywhere. The car hadn't even come to a complete stop before Rosie all but yanked me out—earning a growl from Duke to which she responded, "Dude, Viking women were giving birth on the battlefield. She'll survive this." She then dragged me off to our cabin.

Which Duke was banned from.

Again, there was some growling, scowling, and a macho-man mini tantrum, which might've worked if there was just me here. As it was, it did nothing but amuse Rosie, Gwen, Amy, Mia, Lexie, Lauren, Lily, and Bex. Harriet was front and center, blending in with the beautiful, stylish women effortlessly.

Duke was a man who knew when the battle was lost, so he threatened death and dismemberment if anything happened to me, kissed me hard and long enough to gather catcalls from the women, told me he loved me, and walked off.

I sighed and watched him leave, thinking about how nice his ass looked in those jeans.

"Okay, as nice of an ass that he has, we've got too many things to do to have you leering at your man," Amy declared, dragging me inside.

So commenced the night of pampering, with face masks and cheese boards—although I was banned from soft cheese. Most of the women were drinking Harriet's margaritas, and I surmised that they were powerful witches since every single one of them was still standing by the end of the night.

The women I didn't know well, I got to know.

Mia was crazy. Like batshit crazy. And funny, hilarious. Her daughter, Lexie, also known as the lead singer to one of the most famous bands on the planet, was sweet. We'd met at various Hollywood gatherings and played the game. But it was so much better to do it without the mask. And me. And I actually knew who I was now.

Bex swore like a trucker—though most of the women did and I fucking loved it. She had sadness in her eyes, a hardness to her that was a mask for the soft, and a pregnant belly only slightly larger than mine.

Lily was soft-spoken, shy, drop-dead gorgeous, and had a beautiful calming presence.

Lauren, as it turned out, was the artist of the painting from the infamous night at the B&B in Amber. I'd pulled her aside to tell her how much her paintings meant to me and how I'd tried to buy as many as I could, but it turned out even a movie star had to wait.

Then, she'd informed me with a smile that there was a

surprise for me, which was when she unveiled the painting. But it was more than a painting. There were no words to describe what was on the canvas. It was the ranch, at night time, under a thousand stars. It made no sense, but looking at that painting, I could hear them. Those stars. I could feel Duke's arms around me on that cold night when I realized I'd fallen in love with him.

Duke had had the painting commissioned—the fucking night of the stars—before he'd known what was going to happen with us, before the job was over.

"I've got to go," I said, wiping my eyes after I'd hugged Lauren.

Each woman looked at me with understanding.

"But come back," Mia demanded. "I've got so many questions about what movie stars are real assholes behind the scenes."

I grinned at her. "Honey, I'm the real asshole."

Then I ran.

To him.

He had plenty of things to say about me running. But I shut him up with a kiss.

The next day, underneath a wedding arch that Tanner had made for us, we kissed again. This one was supposed to be more official, but who was I kidding? I was his from the moment I got in that car.

* * *

Arms went around my ever-growing midsection. Duke's palms settled right below my belly button, where they mostly landed since I told him about the baby.

"It's too cold for you to be standin' out here, babe," he murmured against my neck.

I rolled my eyes. "Are you ever going to stop being over-the-top protective?"

His hands tightened ever so slightly on my stomach. "No, baby. I'm not. Got the whole world in my hands right now. No such thing as overprotecting that."

Well. I couldn't argue with the man.

"What are you doin' out here, anyway?" Duke asked after a beat.

"Listening to the stars," I replied.

He kissed my neck again.

"I'm just taking one last moment to get used to the silence," I said, stepping out of his embrace and turning around. The movement hurt—a lot. But I managed to hide my wince. "I think we've only got about thirty minutes, if that, before my screaming starts."

Duke went still. "You better not be saying what I think you're saying."

I smiled. "Oh, relax. My water only broke like ten minutes ago. I knew you were on your way back since you texted me, and I also knew that telling you wouldn't make you go any faster since you already break land speed records making it home to me. I'm not about to make this dramatic. We've had enough drama, don't you think?"

* * *

It turned out we had not had enough drama.

"Pull over," I gritted out. My hair was sticking to the thick sheen of sweat covering my forehead.

I was wrong. The screaming started much earlier than I thought, like as soon as we all got into the car.

Harriet had just happened to stop by.

I was certain that woman was psychic. She never "popped by" in the evenings without giving us a "thirty-minute warning to finish up and get your clothes on." But this particular night, she'd apparently been walking under the light of the full moon and thought it was time for a visit.

"I can't pull over," Duke said calmly. "We're in the middle of nowhere and we've still got ten minutes until we're in town."

Right then, I hated Duke. I hated his calm fucking tone. I hated him for being a man and not ever having to feel this. I hated him for breathing easily. I especially hated him for putting this demon inside me.

"This isn't like a full fucking bladder, I can't just *hold it*," I said, just as calmly. Well, I thought my tone had a slight hint of mania to it, but that was understandable since a tiny human was currently trying to claw its way out of my uterus. "Pull. Over."

There was a second when I thought he wasn't going to listen to me, when I thought I might very well have to reach forward and strangle my husband while simultaneously delivering his child.

But he pulled over. Lucky for us all.

"I'll call for a medivac, a helicopter, something so you're not delivering a baby on the side of a fucking road," he hissed as the car came to a stop.

"Oh stop with the hysteria," Harriet chastised, glaring at her grandchild before looking to me. For once, there was no chaos in the woman's eyes, only calm. She grabbed my hand. "You got this, girl. Womankind have been delivering babies in all sorts of situations all over the world for thousands of years. I'm not gonna lie to you, the fact you don't get the drugs is a big old bugger because it hurts like hell. But I also have faith in you. You're strong enough." She squeezed my hand.

"Now, Duke, deliver my great-grandchild," she requested.

Sariah Harriet Hammond was born on the side of the road under the Montana stars. She screamed loud and true, drowning out even the loudest of those stars.

She came into this world in a hurry, for she had things to do. She had a family to meet.

She had a beautiful life to live.

She had stars to listen to.

PLAYLIST

Broken Glass - **Kygo & Kim Petras**
Dancing On My Own - **Robyn**
Fallingwater - **Maggie Rogers**
Say You'll Be There - **Campsite Dream**
Bette Davis Eyes - **AZTX**
I'm a Mess - **Ed Sheeran**
Cmb (Catch My Breath) - **Carl Wockner**
This is the Place - **Tom Grennan**
Freedom - **Kygo & Zak Abel**
Give It All Away - **Sydnee Carter**
Denver - **Lauren Cook**
Waking Up - **Parachute**
exile (feat. Bon Iver) - **Taylor Swift**
Simple Things - **Alexander Cardinale**

ACKNOWLEDGMENTS

I know a lot of you have been waiting for Duke's story for a long time. I have too.

Let me tell you a secret. The beginning of this book had been sitting on my computer for over a year. I knew what I wanted from the story, but these characters had other ideas. They made me wait. They needed time.

I'm so glad I gave them that.

This story is a little bit of light in the darkness. It has the vibe of my older stories with my new style mixed in.

Thank you all so much for following me on this journey. Loving my characters, my family.

To the moon.

I'm so very thankful to have people in my life who nature my chaotic, creative soul.

Taylor. My partner, my best friend, my soulmate. You endure my moods, my ups and downs, my demons. Thank you for keeping me safe. For making me laugh. For letting me cry. For ordering me pizza and wine.

Dad. You can't read this. Or maybe you can, if heaven has Amazon Prime. But nonetheless, you are the reason I'm here. Because you taught me how to be a badass, how to believe in myself, how to leave my manners on the side of the court when I was playing netball. To be kind. And you're the reason I have such expensive taste.

Mum. You are my hero. My best friend. I am always so surprised when everyone doesn't list their mother as one of their best friends. Because not everyone is lucky like me. Thank you for taking my calls, for never judging me for buying shoes that I don't need, for urging me to get the matching bag. I know what a strong woman looks like because of you.

Polly, Emma, Harriet. My girls. You're still over on the other side of the world, but you're always there if I need an opinion on a selfie, or to have some form of breakdown.

Jessica Gadziala. My #sisterqueen. You are the reason I get through many of my writing blocks and general anxieties. You are a selfless friend, a kickass author and an all around queen.

Amo Jones. My ride or die. You tell me when I'm being crazy, you support me no matter what.

Michelle Clay. I am so lucky that you came into my life. You are such a special human. You're so precious to me. In short, you're family.

Annette Brignac. I'm so glad my books brought us together. I honestly don't know where I'd be without you. My books would not be the same. My life would not be the same. Thank you for being you.

Ginny. You are so important to my books. To my life. You know my characters almost as well as you know me. You know when I need a kick up the butt or some kind words. Thank you for being there for me always.

You. The reader. I would not be typing this without you. Without your support. You are the reason I get to live my dream. Why I get to write stories and call it a job. Thank you for making my dreams come true.

ABOUT THE AUTHOR

ANNE MALCOM has been an avid reader since before she can remember, her mother responsible for her love of reading. It started with magical journeys into the world of Hogwarts and Middle Earth, then as she grew up her reading tastes grew with her. Her love of reading doesn't discriminate, she reads across many genres, although classics like Little Women and Gone with the Wind will hold special places in her heart. She also can't get enough romance, especially when some possessive alpha males throw their weight around.

One day, in a reading slump, Cade and Gwen's story came to her and started taking up space in her head until she put their story into words. Now that she has started, it doesn't look like she's going to stop anytime soon, with many more characters demanding their story be told as well.

Raised in small town New Zealand, Anne had a truly special childhood, growing up in one of the most beautiful countries in the world. She has backpacked across Europe, ridden camels in the Sahara and eaten her way through Italy, loving every moment. She has settled down with her fiancé, their dogs and happy to be in one place...for a while at least.

Want to get in touch with Anne? She loves to hear from her readers.

You can email her: annemalcomauthor@hotmail.com
Or join her reader group on Facebook.

ALSO BY ANNE MALCOM

THE SONS OF TEMPLAR SERIES

Making the Cut

Firestorm

Outside the Lines

Out of the Ashes

Beyond the Horizon

Dauntless

Battles of the Broken

Hollow Hearts

Deadline to Damnation

THE UNQUIET MIND SERIES

Echoes of Silence

Skeletons of Us

Broken Shelves

Mistake's Melody

Censored Soul

GREENSTONE SECURITY

Still Waters

Shield

The Problem With Peace

THE VEIN CHRONICLES

Fatal Harmony

Deathless

Faults in Fate

Eternity's Awakening

Buried Destiny

STANDALONES

Birds of Paradise

Doyenne

Made in the USA
Monee, IL
21 November 2024